REVOLT

REVOLT

BENJAMIN VOGT

To my parents
Who have loved and supported me throughout this entire process.

"This is the strangest life I've ever known."

JIM MORRISON

CHAPTER ONE

Death is a funny thing . . . it really is. You feel little of anything; it's like you're floating away from your body as it's happening. See, I *cheated* death, just like everyone else here, watching me fight to stay alive inside this caged ring.

Sweat stings my eyes, my heart threatens to explode from inside my chest, and my teeth are hurting from all the grit. It's getting harder to breathe with all the tension in the air, the adrenaline soaring through my veins, and the blood pouring from my bottom lip.

It's overwhelming.

Marcus hurls his knife at me, loathing rage swirling through his wide eyes, "I'm going to decorate this *entire* place in your blood!"

Out of reflex, I leap backward, doing my best to concentrate and push out the unending jeers, chants, and cheers roaring from the enormous crowd flocked around the caged ring.

I aim my knife toward Marcus' throat and thrust, missing as he leaps out of the way. I try to regroup, but a sudden, sharp, forceful impact to my hip stops me.

I feel my eyes go broad, my mouth parting.

Sometimes I keep myself up at night recalling how I got into this bloody mess, and every single time, it's a different person's fault. I mean, how could I go from being a senior in high school to a killer who's looking for revenge?

Marcus rips his knife from out of my hip and thrusts it back in.

I ask myself the same question over and over again, *how did I get here?*

The answer is entirely scrambled as usual, because truth be told, there are multiple reasons. I just can't pinpoint what they are, which frustrates me.

Regardless, and as crazy as I know it sounds, I actually *want* to be here. I *want* to be getting my face pounded in because it'll make becoming a member more satisfying.

No, I'm not anybody special. I don't have god-like powers and abilities that can bring anyone to their knees. I'm not some chosen one who's been sent to save the world from its untimely demise. And I'm not some legendary prodigy who's capable of the impossible. I'm just some senior in high school who wants revenge.

And I *will* get it.

CHAPTER TWO

HOW I GOT INTO THIS MESS. . .

"Haven't I mentioned like five times before that we're a mess?" my best friend, Simon, asks. "You, of all people, know that she and I have our rough days, but lately it's just been-crappy."

I stride to his side, my breath transforming into an explosion of mist as it comes into contact with the bitter cold February air, "You need her, dude. You know that, right?"

He sputters with laughter, the setting sun forcing him to squint, "Do you know how *frustrating* it is to argue with her, man?"

"Not to your extent. What are you two even fighting about?"

"Dude, don't even get me started."

"Just tell me."

He sighs, pausing for a moment, "Well, for instance, she says we hardly communicate, and because of that, she doesn't feel like I trust her - but in reality, she grills me constantly about the whole thing with my dad and you *know* I hate talking about it."

"You're telling me she feels distrusted because you won't talk about being abused?"

"It's so *stupid*. I mean, she keeps prying for more, and more and it just, it hurts, man."

"I could always talk to her about it," I suggest, stuffing my freezing hands into my pockets. "Tell her how it makes you feel, and stuff like that. Your choice, though."

He shakes his head, "No, I gotta be the one to do it. I just need to work up to it, you know? You'd think after being together for four years, I could tell her how it is without getting all jittery."

I pat him on the back, our neighborhood's checkpoint partially coming into view, "Just tell her when you're ready, and, I don't know, make sure she feels loved and crap. I know it sounds stupid, but I'm sure, in her mind, Julie just wants to share more intimate feelings with you. You know it makes chicks happy when you let them into your mind."

We both stop in front of our checkpoint, fishing our wallets out of our back pockets and then retrieving our student identification cards.

Every subdivision, city entrance, and state border have a checkpoint. It's basically where two, or more armed soldiers from our country's military, known as Saints, confirm your identity and watch over their assigned area. Most Saints are vicious, bloodthirsty, money craving puppets who tend to maim or kill anyone who disobeys them or the law, but there are a few who are different.

"What's up, boys?" Thomas Price is one of the good ones. Tommy greets, "School any good?"

"Eh," I say, handing him my identification card. "it was school."

I watch him pretend to examine my card before handing it right back, "Come on, show some enthusiasm. High School isn't that bad, just a few more months and you're out."

Grey camo and black tactical gear topped with a black ski mask belay the fact that Tommy is usually kind-hearted and funny. He's had our backs since we were kids.

Simon hands him his card, "Dude, the stress is real."

"Oh, I know," Tommy chuckles while *examining* his ID. "I'm just trying to say that it's nothing compared to being a soldier and having to work with that guy," he quickly glances over at his partner, Logan Ellis, who's manning the security booth a few feet behind him. He leans in closer to the both of us. "Is it bad that I kinda hope he trips and shoots himself?"

The three of us share a little laugh, and after a moment, Tommy turns back and gives Logan a thumbs up. He messes with a few buttons inside the booth before the red and white security gate raises into the air.

"Remember you two," he starts, bringing his attention back to us. "if you ever need *anything*, you know where to find me."

We nod before each giving him a fist bump. We then pass him and enter our subdivision, Brookhaven Estates.

"Okay, so to recap," Simon says, sticking his hands inside his pockets. "we have two math evaluations tomorrow. Not to mention an hour-long prep-list in science for Monday's test. Guess we better get home and study for it all so we don't fail, right?"

I look down at the sidewalk, "Right."

The two of us exchange looks and laugh, eventually both sounding like fifty-year-old pot smokers who're being asphyxiated.

"Okay, okay, but for real," Simon says, calming himself down. "Whatcha wanna do?"

I shrug, "Kinda in a movie mood. My house or yours?"

Simon looks behind his shoulder before whispering, "Neither. I was thinking we might head down to The Manor."

I shake my head. The Manor is an old vacant mansion a little way from here. It's usually occupied past curfew by teens who love drug and alcohol abuse. On an occasion, though, it's used for parties. Simon and I have been there once, and within about the first hour, I witnessed two kids from my school getting into an argument, and it ended with one stabbing the other. I haven't returned since.

"I'll pass," I tell him in a dry tone. "Don't know about you, but I like *not* being assaulted and having more than five pints of blood in my body."

Simon rolls his eyes, "Dude, you're such a party-pooper."

"Whatever, man. There's a big difference between being a party-pooper and making a smart decision."

"*Ooooh*, look at me, my name's Jason Pinder, and I'm *too* smart to go out and have some fun," he mocks. "Dude, that's literally how you sound to me, right now."

I elbow him in the shoulder, "Piss off."

"Come on, man. Can't we just go? There's something special going down tonight."

"You know what? Fine. But if I get stabbed like Toby did last year, I will haunt the crap out of you, you know that?"

"Okay, sure."

I sigh and roll my eyes, exasperation evident in my tone, "When are we leaving?"

"Later tonight, genius."

I shake my head, "Can't. It's a school night, there's no way you *or* I, for that matter, can convince my parents of anything believable. Face it, it's not going to happen."

"You over-complicate things *way* too much," Simon cracks off a half smile. "We'll just tell them you're spending the night at my house."

"You know they won't buy it," I argue. "As I said, we have school tomorrow, and we've pulled this stunt before."

"Well, yeah. That's why we say it's for studying." Simon says, nudging me in the side.

I swear under my breath, "You're exhausting."

He glances over at me, an apologetic expression on his face, "I'm sorry, man, but I promise, you won't want to miss tonight."

"What is it?"

"Not saying. You'll find out later."

"If this isn't good, I swear . . ."

"I promise, you won't be disappointed. Also, you need to quit being such a whiny little pansy all the time. It isn't good for the soul."

"The soul?" I question.

"Yes, the soul, you idiot," he replies, rolling his eyes. "Now, do you want to watch a movie at your place while we wait for your parents to get home? Or would you like to keep bitching about the whole thing?"

I raise my hand up to his face and flip him the bird, "I get to pick the movie."

SIMON PLOPS DOWN ON THE OLD GREEN SOFA IN MY living room with a soda in his right hand. I take a seat on the floor and rest my back up against the same couch.

"Dude," I start, taking a sip out of the water bottle I snatched from the fridge. "Think Mrs. Feck will take it easy on us tomorrow?"

"Probably not," he says. "I mean, did you see her today?"

"Yeah, she was a mess."

"Bet you'd be too if your dad got diagnosed with terminal leukemia."

"I think anyone would."

"Except me."

"Well, you're an exception."

I grab the tv remote and turn the television on. Images flash onto the screen revealing two men on their knees outside of a supermarket. Two Saints stand behind them, guns trained on their heads.

"Wait, isn't that where James Becker works?" Simon asks.

"Shhh, listen," I interject.

The screen splits, and one half shows a reporter, while the other shows the chaotic scene at hand.

"After a twenty-minute stand-off with the Saints, two suspects have been detained," the reporter intones. "Eyewitness reports say that the criminals entered this downtown Deli-mart, armed with assault rifles. Soon after, the Saints responded and began an intense and life-threatening firefight. Thankfully, it has ended with no civilian or military casualties. If everything follows a standard protocol, we can assume that the Saints have been ordered to execute the criminals on the spot."

I watch as the camera zooms in on the Saints as they pronounce the last words to the men, "May God have mercy on your soul."

I quickly press the power button on the remote, resulting in the screen going blank.

"Dude," Simon says, groaning. "I was watching that."

I bring the bottle of water to my lips and feel the liquid flood my mouth before waterfalling down my throat, "We shouldn't be watching that crap. What's the point in seeing two guys get their brains blown out?"

"Oh, I dunno," he replies, rolling his eyes. "Maybe to keep up with current events?"

"Current events? We see executions all the time."

"Yeah, but still."

A loud knock at the door interrupts my train of thought.

Simon looks down at his watch, an eyebrow raised, "Your parents don't get home for another few hours."

I shrug while getting to my feet, "Definitely not my parents. Hold on."

I head over to the front door, pausing long enough to peer through the peep-hole. It's Julie; she looks worried. There are tears in her foggy blue eyes and a partial scowl plastered across her face.

Here we go.

I open the door, mouth opening, but before I can even get a word out, she beats me to the greeting.

"Hey, loser," she gets up on her tippy-toes and wraps her arms around me. "I've been trying to get a hold of Simon for the past hour, but he won't answer his phone."

"He's actually been with me; has been since school got out."

She sighs, her expression turning tranquil, "He has?"

I nod, "Yeah. Sorry he didn't answer his phone, we came from that new pizza place that opened up from across the school. Kinda loud in there."

"It's fine. Would it be okay if I came in?"

"Of course."

Julie flashes me a smile before sliding in past me. She takes her shoes off, heads over to the living room, and instantly the two bicker.

I roll my eyes before taking a swig of water. Their relationship is seriously screwed if they don't get over this fighting phase that's been going on for the past few months.

I walk back into the living room, leaning up against a wall as the two *love birds* argue with each other.

"I get so worried when you don't answer my calls. I can't help thinking something bad has happened to you," Julie says, her mascara running.

Simon, who's obviously caught off guard by his girlfriend's sudden appearance, covers the upper half of his face with his free palm, "I'm sorry, I didn't even feel my phone vibrate. You don't have to get all worked up about it though. I mean, why even be worried?"

"Because you could've gotten hurt or something. I don't know."

"Just because I'm not constantly on my phone like you doesn't mean I've been hurt."

"I *know* that, Simon," she snaps. "I get worried about you because I *love* you."

Simon's expression calms as he takes a deep breath, "I know, I know, you're right. I'm sorry I made you worried, I was busy with Jay, and I didn't hear it. Forgive me?"

She gives him a skeptical look at first, but then sighs, "C'mere."

Simon stands from the sofa, and the two of them a hug.

I step away from the wall, "Well, now that that's over, you should probably get up to date on tonight's mysterious adventure."

She looks over at me, "What's going on?"

"He's convinced me to go to The Manor with him for some sort of surprise. You wanna tag along?" I invite, flashing her a little smile.

"Wait, didn't some kid get *stabbed* the last time we went there?"

"That's exactly what I told him."

"Look, tonight will be different," Simon assures. "I can almost say with certainty that no one will be getting stabbed this time. Well, not in front of us, at least."

"Thanks, but no thanks," she rejects. "For one, you both know my dad's a Saint, so sneaking out isn't exactly possible. Second of all, that place isn't for me; drugs are more of your thing, babe."

Simon gawks, "Are not. The closest thing to drugs I've *ever* done was snort candy dust that one New Year's Eve, and you two did it with me."

I chuckle.

Simon glances over at me with a grin on his face, "I know you had a good time."

Julie brings us back on topic, "Look, even if I wanted to go, which I don't, what happens if we get caught out past eight-thirty?"

"Broken bones, mutilated limbs, the essentials," Simon jokes.

"Not funny," Julie says, punching him in the arm. "I want you to be safe and *not* in a body bag."

"There's something going down tonight that I *need* to take Jason to. I promise we won't get hurt. Trust me, it's important."

"What is it?"

He leans in closer and whispers something into her ear. She pulls away and stares at him like he belongs inside an insane asylum.

"You're taking him to *what*?"

"*Shh!*"

I stare at the two of them, my eyes narrowing, "Can't you just tell me?"

"Wait, dude. It'll be worth it."

"You always say that."

"But this time I *mean* it."

I switch my gaze to Julie, "Is he telling the truth?"

She shrugs, "Depends if you like mosh-pits, drugs, girls, and booze."

A smile creeps across my face, her words are the big reveal, "We're going to Nacht-fest?"

Simons sighs, now glaring over at Julie "Yeah . . . Way to ruin it, Jules."

Simon quickly shushes me before I can ask a bazillion questions.

"No questions. *Somebody* already ruined the initial surprise, and I will not let the rest be spoiled. You'll find out everything later."

"Fine, but can you at least tell me who's hosting it?"

"Zip it. You ain't gettin' nothin'."

"Piss-wad."

He ignores my insult, speaking to Julie, "So, you're not coming?"

She shakes her head, "Sorry."

"No worries. You will have your phone on you tonight though, right?"

"Yeah, why wouldn't I?"

"Just keep your ringer on. We might need you later, okay?"

"What for?"

He wears a patient smile, "Just keep your ringer on."

"Don't worry, I will."

She gives him a hug, explaining how she has to get going since her dad's having a work dinner that she can't be late for. She gives him a kiss; they say they love each other, and then she leaves after giving me a hug goodbye.

Once she's gone, Simon looks over at me with an annoyed face, "I still can't believe she told you."

I raise a finger, "Well, actually, she didn't. She just gave me a hint."

"A hint?" he scoffs, appearing dramatic. "She basically spelled it out for you."

I plop down onto the sofa, taking a final swig from my water bottle, "Don't get your panties in such a twist, dude," I grab the tv remote. "Now sit down, you're about to witness the greatest movie of all time."

"You say that anytime we watch a movie together."

"Just sit down."

CHAPTER THREE

Around two hours later, I hear clattering keys and a lock turning. Instinctively, I look over and see my father, Michael, entering the house with a restless vibe emitting from his posture.

"Hey, you two."

Simon sits up, looks over at my dad, and gives him a slight wave, "Hey. How was work?"

"Same as always," he looks at me, his tone now changing. "Jason, can we talk?"

I grab the remote up off the arm-rest and pause the movie we started, "Yeah, what's up?"

My dad looks behind his shoulder to make sure it's clear to speak, "Your mom is in an *extremely* pissy mood. So, do me a favor and be patient with her. *No* arguing."

"What happened this time?" I ask, sighing. "Another fight?"

My dad checks behind his shoulder once more, "Oh yeah, big time."

"Karron Caulfield?"

"Yep."

"So, in other words . . ." I start, "having patience is an understatement?"

My dad's about to speak, but my mother, Stacey, storms in through the doorway before he can even form the words with his mouth. She drops her purse on the floor, swearing.

"Hey, Mrs. Pinder," Simon flashes my mom a warm smile. "how are you?"

My mom takes one look at Simon, and she immediately relaxes, "I've been better. How was school?"

My dad and I exchange looks. My mom has a soft spot for Simon, and she definitely treats him like a son. Just by smiling at her, he can change her mood. It's a gift.

"It was great," Simon replies. "I heard work was crappy."

My mom fixes her long brunette hair so it's out of her electric blue eyes, "Just another stupid fight, but I'll live."

Simon nudges me softly, queuing me to ask my mom if I could *spend* the night.

I clear my throat, "Hey, so, we have some serious testing tomorrow, and I was just wondering if it would be all right if I could stay over at Simon's tonight to study for it all?"

My mom ignores my gaze and looks at my dad, "I'm okay with it, you?"

He thinks for a moment before shrugging, "I'm fine with it as long as they're actually studying."

She glares at the two of us, "Just make sure you make it to school on time."

<hr>

"BOO-YAH," SIMON SAYS AS WE WALK DOWN THE concrete steps leading from my patio. "Told you this plan would work."

"Yep," I mumble, the moonlight illuminating my driveway. "You told me."

I ended up wearing a baggy white hoodie, dark blue jeans, and my generic white sneakers. Simon, who has his own wardrobe in my house because he *practically* lives there, went with a skin-tight black tank top, loose-fitting blue jeans, white sneakers, and the black beanie he *always* wears after school.

As our shoes slap down my driveway, I ask, "Are we taking the shortcut?"

"Duh, how else would we get there on time? Plus, we can't risk getting caught by those stupid cameras on the lampposts."

"Fair point. So, what are all the details? Time to spill everything, man."

"Okay, well, for one, Mae Bernhard's hosting it."

My heart speeds up a bit at the sound of her name, "Wait, for real?"

We turn at the bottom of my driveway, sticking to the shadows so we don't show up on any security footage. If we're caught out, we're absolutely screwed.

"Yes, for real. She's the one who invited me."

"She invited you, but not me?"

"Well, she came up to me, and after telling me I could come, she asked me where she could find you, but since I wanted this to be a surprise, I told her I would pass along the message."

"Smart."

"I know."

The two of us take a left halfway down Brookhaven and head through the damp grass of the side-yard belonging to a newly built house. There's a gaping hole in the back fence of the property, and that's our entry into the backwoods.

"I hear someone's moving in soon," I mention as we enter the shadowy yard.

"I did too," Simon says while approaching the hole at the bottom of the wooden fence, "Let's just hope they don't repair this puppy."

He gets down on all fours and crawls through the gap.

Once through, he stands up and whispers, "Your turn. Remember, don't snag your clothes like last time."

I get down on my stomach and feel the moist grass from today's rain seep into my clothes, "I hate this- gets me all itchy."

"Stop being such a baby and crawl through."

I mutter under my condensed breath before edging my way through. I get up and brush myself off, a strand of stubborn grass sticking to the front of my jeans.

"See that?" Simon asks while pointing over the waving mass of trees below us.

The Manor. It's on top of a large hill beyond the forest. We have to go through a deep ravine to get there. It's massive, and the outside is all lit up with purple and blue stringed lights. If the Saints weren't paid off, as they always are when parties are thrown, then everyone over there would either be in the back of a patrol car, or in the back of a medical van heading down to the morgue right about now.

If a Saint doesn't beat you like a wild animal when you've broken the law, then he's one of the good ones. I say *he* because our President, or ruler, forbade women from joining the military. He says they don't fit the physical and mental demands the occupation requires. Many people are against this, but don't speak out in fear of being executed. I avoid being political and don't plan on ever being involved, so I don't associate with all the anti-government groups that are vocal about their hatred for President Mills. Those people are found and killed on live tv- they're shot in the face and denied an open casket, or any casket. Their bodies aren't seen again.

"Well," I start, eyeing my surroundings. "There's two ways we can go about doing this . . ."

"Slide down the slope like men or carefully find another way down like pansies?" Simon questions, already seeming to have his mind made up.

"Yep."

There's a steep slope that leads down to the forest below, and to get to The Manor, we have to make it down there. I'm not much for heights, but this isn't *too* bad.

"Well, I'm just going to do what we did last time," Simon says. "See ya down there."

I'm about to tell him to hold on, but he's already on his butt and sliding down before the words can even escape my mouth.

Do you ever just slow down, Si? I wonder before carefully getting down on the ground.

If I don't slide down, he'll give me crap the rest of the night. I'm not scared to go down the slope or anything, I don't want to get all wet and muddy, *especially* if Mae will be there.

I inch forward.

Please don't hit a tree.

My legs hang off the edge, and with one last little skootch, my entire body streams down the slope. I feel a euphoric rush in my veins as my speed picks up with intensity.

A chill wind blasts my face, causing me to let out a yelp of joy.

The grove appears closer and closer at an alarming rate.

"*Crap, crap, crap!*" my voice sounds lost in the wind as my speed picks up even faster.

Quickly, I slam my heels down into the dirt, and I feel inertia take over, forcing a cuss from my lips as my body flies head over heels. I somersault down the slope while my peripheral vision goes a blur from all the surroundings passing me at such a speed. I also feel vomit rising in my throat.

After what feels like milliseconds, I abruptly come to a stop after crashing into a bush at the bottom of the slope. I lie there, too pained to move

"*Ah,*" I groan as my eyes open to a dazed wonderland of darkness.

Screw me. . .

As my mind focuses normally, I realize something's not right. I lift my left hand up to my face and feel for my glasses, but nothing's there.

"Jason," Simon shouts in my general direction. "Dude, are you okay?"

I hastily feel around the ground for my glasses, anxiety flowing through me.

Nothing.

"Jason?" I hear Simon call out once more. "Where are you?"

"Over here," I'm still in a daze.

Footsteps rapidly approach my location, and in a tone of relief, Simon says, "What happened, dude?"

"What are you talking about?" a grin appears on my face, "Didn't I stick my landing?"

"You're such an idiot," Simon chuckles before holding something out for me. "Here, you might want these. I almost stepped on them trying to find you." Relief sweeps through my chest as Simon holds out my glasses.

I grab them, graciously putting them on, "You're a lifesaver."

"Wait, hold on," Simon says, his eyes wide with excitement. "Do you hear that?"

After a second or two, I can make out the bass line from some song off in the distance. It's coming from The Manor, undoubtedly.

"Music?" I ask while holding my hand out for Simon to grab.

"Uh-huh," he pulls me to my feet. "Let's go."

"Lead the way."

CHAPTER FOUR

———

Blaring music, strobe lights, and drunk high schoolers. These are all the key elements of Nacht-Fest. I've been here for about ten minutes, and I already can't wait to leave.

I thought it would be a lot more exciting; instead, everything appears generic and stereotypical. I'm honestly disappointed.

"Isn't this awesome?" Simon yells over the ear-shattering chaos.

I shrug my reply.

He pats me on the back, "Hold on, I'm going to go get a drink."

I watch him walk off, and suddenly the music cuts, and in its place is silence. Everyone looks over at the archway that connects the main area to the large and spacious kitchen. Mae is standing beneath it, holding a microphone up to her mouth.

"Hey, everyone," she greets, her voice pouring through the loud speakers set up all around the mansion's interior. "I hope you're all having a *great* time."

Everyone in The Manor erupts, making my head reverberate, and I can't help rolling my eyes. This all seems straight out of a movie. *Generic.*

"I wanted to give a special thanks to Jeremy Dorth- without him, none of this would've been possible. Jeremy, get over here."

I watch a tall and slender guy with super shaggy brown hair approach Mae, and as soon as he's by her side, she asks the crowd for a round of applause. The noise hits the roof, and Mae gives the guy a little kiss on the cheek.

My heart sinks a little.

The music resumes, and I quickly walk off and over to the grand staircase. I head up to the second level, feeling more hurt than expected over a dumb little kiss.

Yay. . . I'm so happy I get to waste my night stuck on this whole thing.

Truth is, and I'm sure it's obvious, but I've had a big crush on Mae since my freshman year. She broke up with her steady boyfriend sometime last year and has been single ever since. I wish I could grow a pair and ask her out without coming across as self-conscious; she's way out of my league.

This whole evening is rubbing me the wrong way.

I turn right at the top of the staircase, heading down a long hallway. A spindled banister is the only thing stopping me from falling to the first floor, and it gives me a good view of this *lame* party.

Suddenly, I'm grabbed by the hood of my sweatshirt and tugged along into the nearest bathroom by someone I can't see. The person's grip is weak, but I don't fight it. It isn't long before I am released and the bathroom door shuts.

I swiftly turn around, "What're you . . ." I'm shocked as I come face-to-face with Mae. "Oh, hey."

She chuckles before smiling, "Sorry if I startled you. I saw you headed upstairs and came to say hi. I'm happy to see that Simon passed along my invite."

"Yeah, me too," I say, sticking my hands into my hoodie pouch.

"Are you enjoying Nacht-Fest?"

"Want me to be honest?"

"Totally."

I'm about to drop the truth-bomb on her, but before I can, I see an excited look spread across her face. She's the host; of course, she wants positive feedback.

I hesitate, "It's been . . . great. Just kinda stressing over some tests I have tomorrow. I still don't know why Nacht-Fest is hosted on a school night. Why not a weekend?"

She shrugs, "I've wondered that a lot, but last year's host said it's just tradition."

"Dumb tradition, huh?"

She fixes her jet-black bangs out of her amber-colored eyes, "You look kinda *meh*. Is everything okay?"

It would be creepy if I told her I was upset over her kissing Jeremy, so I come up with another white lie, "Oh, yeah, I'm good. Like I said, just stressing over tomorrow."

"Oh, okay," she looks at me with an unsure expression. "Well, one more thing. . . I thought I should let you know Jakob's here. I didn't even invite him, but I guess he let himself in. I know that you two don't get along, so I thought it would be better to just tell you now."

My eyes go wide, "Please tell me you're kidding."

"I'm sorry. I didn't want him here, and you know I can't just *ask* him to leave. He'd cause a scene."

You look up dick in the dictionary, and a picture of Jakob Holmes is plastered all over it. He's the biggest guy at Lakeshore High; he's huge, he's ugly, and he's a total jerk.

I honestly have no idea why, but ever since elementary school, he's picked me as his main target. Many people don't even believe me when I name off some things he's done. He's broken bones, slashed the tires on my bike and on my parents' car, given me multiple concussions, and so much worse. He was the reason my dog had to be put down last year; he kicked her repeatedly to get a rise out of me, and I guess it was enough to cause internal bleeding. I tried telling Tommy, but Jakob held me at knife-point and said if I told anyone, that he would find a way into my house after curfew, and, well, the rest is self-explanatory.

I sigh, "Yeah, you should probably just stay away from him."

She looks guilty, "I'm really sorry. I know how horrible he is."

I place my hand on her shoulder, flashing her an artificial smile, "It's cool, I promise."

An abrupt knock at the door interrupts us, "Mae, you in there?"

She looks over at the bathroom entrance sheepishly before glancing over at me, "It'll look really bad if my friends see me in here with you."

My cheeks burn, "What do you mean?"

"It's a party, it might seem like something's going on, you know?"

I glance down at my shoes, her words chipping at my self-esteem, "Oh, gotcha."

"You don't think I'm embarrassed to be seen with you or anything, right?"

I meet her gaze, slightly shrugging, "Sure."

More knocking at the door, "Mae? Are you in there with some guy? Need a little privacy?"

Mae goes red in the face, "What? No. I'm on the phone with Jess. Meet me in the kitchen, I'll be there in a few, okay?"

"Whatever."

She gives me her attention, "I've gotta get going. Come down in a bit and I'll dance with you, alright?"

"Yeah. Alright."

She gives me an unexpected hug then quickly heads out the door, leaving me alone in the small but decorative bathroom. I stand there for a second before heading over to the mirror. My shoes slap against the domino floor tiles.

I halt in front of the mirror, studying my reflection and making sure I look decent. My eyes are an electric blue- identical to my mothers. My sandy blonde hair is shaggy but looks suitable. I know some guys try it to look cool but end up doing quite the opposite. For me, though, a shaggy hairstyle appears natural. Short hair doesn't look bad on me either, but I prefer to keep it longer in the winter. Since it's the beginning of February, I'd say I'm okay for just a bit longer.

I hate my glasses, but I can't see jack without them. I've tried contacts, but my eyes just can't do them. So, I do my best to deal with the black frames and clear lenses that are part of my face.

I take a step back, noting how there's a bit of mud on my lower left pant-leg. It isn't too noticeable, but I cringe knowing Mae probably saw the dirty mess.

I wipe some of the gunk off, and suddenly I hear a roar of chants boom out from around The Manor. At first, it's kinda hard to make out what everyone's saying, but after a moment or two of listening carefully, I'm able to make out what they're screaming: "Fight! Fight! Fight!"

I turn around, curiosity getting the better of me as I make my way to the door.

I wonder if anybody will get stabbed this time?

I exit the bathroom, approaching the wooden banister that serves as a wall. I look down upon the first floor; instantly my heart is racing like a drum.

Simon and Jakob are face-to-face with a crowd surrounding the two of them. Simon's screaming his head off at him, but I can't make out a single thing he's saying over the loud music and even louder chanting.

What the . . .?

Simon is a fit kid. He's tall, muscular, definitely has had his fair share of fights, but come on, Jakob is over six-foot-five and three hundred pounds. His sheer size is enough to be top dog around here.

I quickly step away from the banister and briskly shoot down the steps. I forcefully make my way over to the crowd, pushing my way through the mass of high school students.

I finally get to a position where I have a good view of Simon; the expression he and Jakob share remind of two rabid dogs preparing to rip out each other's throats.

"*Yo, Simon,*" I holler at him, hoping he can hear me.

He doesn't notice, and I don't blame him. The obnoxious level of noise bouncing off the walls of the mansion is enough to leave a ringing in your ears for a bit.

Simon and Jakob have fought in the past, but the most recent incident was back in middle school, and Jakob pounded him. Thing is, Simon has grown a lot since then, and after the whole thing with his dad, I wouldn't be surprised if he *at least* held his ground.

Before I can think any further, Simon throws a fist into Jakob's face. The piss-wad stumbles back before quickly retaliating. He charges at Simon and attempts to swing at him, but since Simon is ten times more agile, he dodges out of the way and counters by slamming his foot into the side of Jakob's knee.

He cries out while crumbling to the floor, and I'm not going to lie, watching everything play out makes me feel good on the inside.

Some kid from the crowd cheers, "Break his friggin' legs!" The crowd explodes.

Simon approaches Jakob and crushes his nose with the heel of his shoe. The oversized oaf screams, and excitement pours through me.

He deserves all of this.

Simon screams at Jakob, but again the crowd is too loud. I push my way through a few more people before being able to make my way over to him. He slams his foot down onto Jakob's chest.

The crowd roars again, and Jakob howls.

I quickly put my hand on Simon's shoulder, "Dude, what's going on?"

He looks over, nothing but untamable rage swimming in his eyes, "I'm going to kill him, Jay. I swear, I'm going to kill him."

The crowd simmers down. The immense fury on Simon's face makes the scene a lot less entertaining.

"Don't think you're so tough, Davis," Jakob says, blood streaming from his nostrils. "I'll stab ya, I'll stab ya really good."

"Shut it," Simon kicks him in the side. "Just shut it."

A lot of the people in the crowd disperse, and the song playing changes to something a lot more calm and melodic. More of an old-school hip-hop type of thing.

Simon looks down at the pudgy idiot, his teeth clenched, "You ever, and I mean *ever* call my girlfriend a cheap whore again, I *promise* it won't end pretty."

Jakob lets out a snide smile, "Why? It's true. Saw her last week with one of my buddies."

The new look on Simon's face is enough to get me to take a step back, and the next thing I know, he's kicking the crap out of Jakob's face. The result is a puddle of crimson soaking his buzzed blonde hair.

I want to step in and tell Simon to stop, but honestly, I enjoy watching this. See, I've never tried fighting back. I always thought it was pointless and that I'll just get even more hurt, but after witnessing Simon beat Jakob to a pulp, it makes me want to join in and get payback for all those years of torment. In the end, I stay out of it and watch Simon kick Jakob repeatedly until his eyes roll into the back of his head.

The people around us stare at him blankly, but before any words are spoken, Simon storms off. I chase after him, following him through the kitchen and out the back door, and once I tail him to the edge of the property, he finally stops.

"Hey, man, are you okay?" I ask, the frigid breeze making my teeth chatter.

He keeps his back turned, but I can tell he's sniffling.

"Dude . . ."

"You don't think Jules would ever cheat on me, do you?" he asks, his voice shaky.

"No, she would never do that. Come on, you've been dating her for four years. You know she wouldn't; don't let the words of that psycho ruin your night, and more importantly, your relationship."

"But why would he tell me he saw her with one of his buddies?"

"You know he likes to get in people's heads like that."

Simon pulls his phone out of his pocket and unlocks it, "I'm going to give her a call."

"Why?"

"To apologize for being such a jerk lately."

He taps a few things on the screen before putting the phone up to his ear, and after waiting a few seconds, he starts talking. I want to give him his privacy, so I turn around and head back inside.

Back in The Manor, everything's resumed to normal. Jakob's gone, but there's still a puddle of blood from where he was laying. A faster, more electronic type of song is playing, and everyone is either dancing or talking to each other.

I grab a red plastic cup of punch I know is undoubtedly spiked with alcohol and take a big swig. I'm about to take another when Mae attempts to startle me by popping out of nowhere and jabbing me in the hips with her fingers.

"Oh, hey," I greet, flashing her a little smile. "I was just about to come looking for you."

"Well, here I am," she smiles back, a red cup identical to mine in her hand. "Hey, is Simon okay? I saw you two head out back."

I shrug, "He's fine. Just kinda upset and worried, but he'll be alright."

"That's good to hear."

"Yeah."

"So," Mae starts, a smile still bright on her face. "How's Veronica?"

I tilt my head to the right; the name causing one of my eyebrows to raise.

"You know, Veronica Whitney?"

"Oh, her? Beats me, I haven't talked to her in like eight months."

She looks puzzled, "Wait, you two broke up?"

"We were never dating."

"What? She keeps going around saying how you gave her a promise ring and all that."

Her words are news to me, "We had a thing back last year, but we were never official. We stopped talking a while back, so I literally have no idea what you're talking about."

Mae's expression grows more and more bewildered, "That's so weird. So, you're telling me that she's been making all this up? You *are* single?"

"Yep. Single and ready to mingle."

She giggles, "That makes me happy."

"It does?"

The smile hasn't left her face, "Yeah. Hey, you busy tomorrow after school?"

"I'm never busy. Why?"

She twirls her hair with her finger, "Well, I'm kinda wondering if you'd like to–"

The front door to the mansion abruptly bursts open and in comes Jeremy Dorth - the guy who's allegedly responsible for making Nacht-Fest possible. He's drenched in sweat and panting like crazy.

"Cut the music! Cut the music!"

The song stops, and in its place is silence.

Jeremy quickly exhales, "The Saints screwed me over. You all need to get out of here before it's too late!"

Everyone, including me, stares at him with wide eyes.

He looks at all of us with a confused expression plastered all over his dreadful face, "What are you all waiting for? Go, get out of here, and hurry. Do you all want to *die*? They're coming up the hill, now!"

It's as if a play button is suddenly pressed, because the next thing I know, everyone in the mansion is rushing toward the back door like a herd of startled animals.

A deafening gunshot booms through the air, and my head instinctively snaps back. I see Jeremy crumbling to the floor with a bloody mist bursting from the back of his skull.

Screams echo off the walls of The Manor as five Saints storm the mansion and open fire on the crowd of teenagers.

Mae and I are at the front of the mass, approaching the back sliding-glass door. Stray bullets are shredding the walls and wooden floors all around me, and I feel one of the rounds graze my forearm. I blurt out a swear before sliding the door open and grabbing Mae by the arm. I pull her outside and run, the only way out of this sticky situation being to slide down the large hill.

"Where's Simon!" Mae asks, sprinting as fast as she can as I pull her along.

"He's already on his way back," I assume, blood running out of the wound in my arm. "Just follow me."

We get to the edge of the hilltop before swiftly getting to the ground. It's there when we begin our descent down the large, steep, and unforgiving hillside. All the while howls from an oncoming canine unit blare into the starry night sky, and I'm left wondering if I'll live through the night.

CHAPTER FIVE

A string of profanity springs from my lips as I fly down the hillside. I hit numerous objects on the way. Branches, bushes, rocks- they all bash into me as I stream the rest of the way down.

Eventually, my lungs deflate as my chest goes slamming into a solid oak tree, and I fight to take a breath while my vision goes wacky.

Mae crushes into my spine at full speed just before I get to inhale.

"I'm so, so sorry," she says, my lungs refusing to cooperate.

I collapse to my side, and after what feels like an eternity without a single breath of air. My lungs finally fill with life, and I spend the next few moments sucking in as much oxygen as I can.

"Are you okay?" she asks while quickly getting to her feet.

I gradually push my glasses up my nose, "I'm- I'm good."

She helps me to my feet, but I feel as if I'm about to fall over and pass out. She steadies me, and once my brain takes a step off the tilt-a-whirl, I'm able to regain my balance.

"You didn't hit your head, did you?"

"Maybe on a few branches. What about you?"

Mae pauses for a second before responding, "Maybe? I don't think so."

Suddenly, I hear rushed footsteps all around us. My blood freezes, and judging by the look on Mae's face, she feels the same way I do.

"Spread out and search for suspects," a Saint barks from somewhere inside the darkened, wooded area. "My hound went after some idiot wearing a black tank-top, jeans, and a black beanie. I want him rounded up, along with anyone else you find."

I go pale and my stomach knots up, hoping Simon got away. I grab Mae by the hand and quietly make my way through the small forest. The leafless branches sway ever so slightly in the breeze.

I believe the shortcut he and I used is just up ahead, and if he's anywhere, it's around there. I hope he's already made his way back to Brookhaven, but in case he hasn't, I keep a close eye out for him.

"Where are we going?" Mae whispers as I hurry her along through the inky black woods.

"Just follow me," I demand, she and I hop over a fallen tree. "You see those beams of light all around us?"

She moves her head around, studying the moving columns of light shooting through the shadowy trees, "Yeah."

"You might want to avoid those. Whatever happens, stay by me, and don't get spotted."

"Okay, I won't."

If it weren't for the bright moonlight slightly illuminating our path, I'm certain we would've already tripped or been detained, probably worse. Thankfully, I'm able to make out the path ahead of me.

After a few minutes of sprinting through the woods, we make it to the large and muddy slope Simon and I used to get down here. Most of the Saints have disappeared, but there's still one that's uncomfortably close to our location.

A sudden yelp gets me to look up, and my pupils dilate. At the top of the slope and near the wooden fence, I can make out Simon with a large canine latched onto his arm; its razor-sharp teeth glinting in the moonlight.

"Is that Simon?" Mae asks, her jaw dropped.

"C'mon, we have to get up there and help him."

I've never attempted to climb up the slope before; the last time we came to The Manor, we just used the road that led up to the mansion when we left and snuck back to our homes using the backstreets.

I jump up and grab some weeds sticking out of the side of the slope, but I'm interrupted by a bright light shining at the back of my head and a Saint harshly telling me to get down on the ground.

My stomach twists up, and my heart beats out of my chest. I slowly back away from the slope, my hands raised in the air.

"I said get on the ground," the soldier demands, his voice makes my stomach churn.

I swiftly turn around, the bright light from his flashlight blinding me, "Okay, okay."

I gradually lower to my knees, Mae does the same, and her eyes get misty with tears.

The Saint's flashlight is attached to the end of an M4 barrel that's pointed at us. My heart feels like it's about to burst out of my chest when I see his finger wrapped around its shiny black trigger.

"Please don't," Mae begs, her arms trembling in the air.

The soldier slowly approaches her, the gun's muzzle aimed at her forehead. He doesn't speak to her; instead, he uses the hand he had positioned under the rifle's barrel and unclips a walkie-talkie off his tactical vest and brings it up to his mouth.

"I've got two suspects on their knees, what're my orders?"

It goes quiet for a moment, and I wish it would've stayed that way, because the words that blare through the radio a second later make me puke in my mouth.

"No survivors."

"Copy that. Mitchell out."

He clips the radio back onto his vest before aiming the gun at me. The air stops. I can't even hear Simon getting mauled when the Saint mutters his notorious last words: "May God have mercy on your soul."

"No, no, wait—"

A big object bashes into the side of his face; it's a large jagged rock. He swears, stumbles back and drops his weapon.

Mae is running off into the woods without me. She's making as much noise as possible.

She's creating a distraction for me.

I dive into the nearest bush. The Saint is in too much of a daze to keep track of me or make out where I am. I watch him regroup his senses and grab his M4 up off the ground. He points the lighted barrel toward the direction Mae went before grunting and sprinting off after her.

Holy crap . . . my heart rate's slowly decelerating.

I want to cool down, but an abrupt scream from the top of the slope reminds me that Simon's being ripped apart by the military hound, and I'm the only one around who can intervene.

I hastily get up and out of the bush and rush over to the slope. Without thinking, I quickly leap up and grab a hold of a long and strong weed poking out from the side of the muddy incline. I hoist myself up and slowly make my way to him.

A prolonged minute of constant cries for help echo through my ears before I'm able to make it all the way up. The scene before me makes me sick to my stomach. The dog is on top of Simon and ripping deep into his forearm. It's trying to bite at his throat, but Simon is using his bloodied limb as a shield.

I kick the hound in the muzzle as hard as I can.

It yelps but doesn't retract the teeth from deep inside Simon's arm.

I kick it again, and again, and I don't stop until it gets irritated enough to release Simon and lunge at me. I dodge out of the way, but the dog is fast. He jumps on top of me and takes me down to the wet grass. It snaps and bites at my throat, but I'm able to keep it away.

From out of my peripheral vision, I can see Simon weakly getting to his feet and picking up a giant rock from up off the ground.

"Get this thing off of me," my grip on the dog's face loosens allowing its teeth to get closer and closer to my sweaty throat.

Simon does his best to hurry over. He bashes the back of the hound's skull with the rock just as its teeth touch my neck. It cries out before falling off of me. Simon continues smashing the dog's face in with the boulder.

I sit up. The animal is motionless. My eyes find Simon's, "Crazy night, huh?"

He forces a pained grin, "I would be dead if you had showed up a second later."

I let out a nervous chuckle, getting to my feet, "That's for sure."

"No kidding," he looks down at his forearm before becoming white as a sheet. "Crap . . ."

"What?"

He flashes me his arm, and I blanch. It's ripped apart, and I swear I can see bone. It's bad, the wound is oozing blood onto his sneakers like a leaky faucet.

"What're we going to do?" I ask, gawking at his nasty injury.

"We need to get to Julie's," he replies, gritting his teeth. "Oh, this hurts *so* bad."

I wipe the mud off my jeans, "Why her house?"

"Think about it. You told your parents you were sleeping over at my house. I told my mom I'd be sleeping over at *your* house. See what I'm getting at here?"

I nod, "Gotcha, but what about your arm? Dude, you're bleeding bad."

Simon makes his way over to the gap in the wooden fence that leads into our neighborhood, "Jules is smart, and you know she wants to be a nurse when she's older. She'll be a good help until we figure out a better plan."

I don't speak. Instead, I follow him over to the fence, hoping that Mae isn't on her way to the morgue.

We make our way back into Brookhaven, creeping through people's lawns and keeping to the shadows so the cameras on the lampposts don't pick us up. After a few minutes, we make it to Julie's yard. We spy a patrol of Saints searching the streets armed with fully automatic assault rifles, so we quickly hide behind a few of the trees.

Simon pulls his phone out of his pocket, and instantly an ear-piercing chirp of an alarm blasts out from an unknown source, signifying that Brookhaven Estates is now under lockdown.

Simon dials Julie's number.

"Hey, you up?" he greets, pain drowning his voice.

Standing close to the phone, I hear her drowsily reply. "Yeah, that siren was *super* loud. What's going on?"

"Something went wrong, and the Saints that were supposed to be paid off ended up storming The Manor and killing a bunch of kids. Jay and I got away, but they're hunting everyone down. This stupid dog tore apart my arm, and I'm bleeding pretty bad. You up for a little nursing?"

"You're kidding me. . . right?"

I butt in impatiently, "You can see bone. We need help, *ASAP.*"

"Okay, okay, I'll help. Only one problem."

"What?" Simon asks.

"My dad's up. I think he's heading out to patrol the neighborhood. He loves you guys, but if he sees you out there, you know what he'll have to do."

Simon pauses for a moment, his eyes swimming in thought, "We could wait 'till he leaves the house then sneak in. Your thoughts?"

"Yeah, that could work. There's a thing of gauze in the cupboard next to the dishwasher. Bring that up and *make sure* you're not noisy, okay? My mom's still sleeping."

"Got it. Is the window in the back unlocked?"

"It always is."

Simon sighs with relief, "Okay, good. We'll be up as soon as he leaves. I love you."

"Love you, too. You both be super careful, alright?"

I smirk, eyeing the blood dripping from where the stray bullet grazed my arm, "Aren't we always?"

"Har har," she says. "Good one."

She and Simon say goodbye before the two of us slide down to the damp ground behind two large trees in the yard. Eight Saints march by, and I feel like at any moment gunfire will wake our neighbors as Simon and I are riddled with bullets.

Eventually, the patrol passes, and Mr. Briggens, Julie's father, exits his house and walks off after them. He's also one of the good ones, but I know how loyal he is to our President.

If he catches us, I have a strong feeling that he'll do what he's been ordered to do.

Kill us.

Simon gets to his feet, stumbling over to the unlocked window at the back of the house. He's looking pale, which is jarring considering how tan he is naturally.

"C'mon," he mutters, "help me get this stupid thing open."

I walk toward him and help him pry the window open.

CHAPTER SIX

S imon is the first one to climb through the unlocked window, and as soon as I hear his feet plant quietly on the other side, I hoist myself up onto the edge. My arm stings like crazy from where the bullet nicked me. I want to yelp, but the fear of being caught keeps me quiet.

I land silently on the hardwood floor. Julie's large kitchen is lightless, and I'm about to step forward when a sudden creak from upstairs causes me to freeze.

Simon and I wait silently for what seems like an eternity before breathing normally again.

"You go get the gauze," he whispers softly. "I'll go wait next to the stairs and be a look-out, capiche?"

Without speaking, I creep past him to the dishwasher that's behind the island counter. I open the cupboard located to the right and listen as Simon sneaks over to the staircase in the front room. My hand wanders around the packed cabinet until I grab something that feels like gauze.

"Psst," I hiss at Simon while sneaking under the archway that connects the kitchen to the family room. "How're things looking?"

I can vaguely see his head turn toward me, "Good, I think. Did you find the stuff?"

I nod, although he probably can't see me, "Yeah. Let's go."

The two of us proceed cautiously up the creaky staircase. The second story is basic. There's a long yet narrow hallway at the top of the stairwell with doors spaced out on each side. Julie's door is the last one on the right. Her parents' room is at the end of the hall, making the trek difficult. Simon and I carefully inch down the hall, the blood from his arm dripping out onto the floor, creating a gory mess that trails down the hall as we silently tread. We wince at every creak and groan that squeals out from beneath the floorboards, and just when we're about to Julie's room, I think I can hear someone walking around downstairs.

Simon carefully grabs the knob and turns it, glancing over at me with a painful yet prideful look in his eyes.

The hinges swivel back and the door slowly breathes open, revealing Julie's small bedroom. She's sitting on top of her covers when we enter. Our sudden presence startles her.

"Shut the door," she mouths, stepping off her bed.

I do as I'm told, shutting the door before turning her lights on. The entire area brightens up. Julie gets a load of Simon's ripped arm and goes just about as pale as he is.

"Whoa, you weren't kidding when you said you could see bone," she stares unnervingly.

Simon walks over to her bed and plops down, the blood still consistently streaming from the wound. He looks like he's about to faint, and the thought of him dying from blood loss makes me jittery.

I turn to Julie, "What do we do? How're we going to stop the bleeding?"

She looks panicked, "Um, go through my closet and look for a belt. I'll cut off circulation to his arm."

I quickly move to her little messy closet. I dig my way through a pile of her clothes while Julie questions Simon about all the details of tonight's events.

After a minute of digging, I come across a brown leather belt with a large buckle. I take it to Julie.

"Will this work?" I ask.

She studies it for a second, "Wow, I haven't seen that thing since last Halloween."

"Julie."

"Sorry. It'll work. Did you bring the gauze like I asked?"

I pull the wrap out of my back pocket and hand it to her, "Yeah. Here."

She grabs the bandages and sets them down next to Simon before looping the belt around the top of his elbow and strapping it tight. After making sure it's secure, she grabs the gauze and wraps the wound.

"How are you going to hide this from your mom?" she asks Simon, tossing the gauze back. "If she sees this, she'll freak and report you. She already *hates* you."

"Exactly, she hates me," Simon mutters. "Hence the reason I'm *never* around her. I'm not worried about her seeing it, I'm more worried about what my teachers and school security will have to say."

The door behind me creaks open before I can speak. I don't turn around, but the look of shock on Simon's face is enough clarification to know we're screwed.

"Jason? Simon?" a deep and intimidating voice spills into the room. "What're you two doing here past curfew?"

My blood runs cold as I realize that Julie's father is standing only a few feet behind me. I slowly turn around. He's dressed in his military uniform and gripping a handgun. Judging by the look in his brown eyes, he's angry and apprehensive.

"What're you doing here?" Julie creaks, her voice shaky. "I thought you left."

"I saw these two sneaking in through the window."

"But how?" I didn't mean to speak, but the words just came out. "We saw you leave."

Mr. Briggens steps closer, grinding his teeth, "Do you think I'm stupid?"

I back up, "No, not at all."

He moves closer, "Then you shouldn't ask questions like that."

I try taking another step back, but I collapse onto Julie's bed. Her dad treads closer, and despite knowing him for as long as I can remember, he still looks as if he's about to put a bullet in my head.

"You two were at that stupid party, weren't you?"

I choke, not knowing how to reply, "Um . . ."

He slightly cocks his head to the side, "Come on, you wouldn't lie to me, *would you?*"

Simon gulps, "You're right, we were at the party. Some Saints crashed it and shot a bunch of high school students before siccing a bunch of dogs on the runaways. I got ripped up by one and thought your daughter could help me."

Mr. Briggens looks at me, "And what about you? Your arm's bloody there."

I try to look him in the eye, but fail, "A bullet nicked me while trying to get away."

He's silent for a while before exhaling, "I should radio you two in," he pauses. "You're lucky I have a soft spot for the both of you."

CHAPTER SEVEN

Mr. Briggens put me, Simon, and Julie in the back of his patrol car and quickly drove us to the nearest hospital. Since he's a Saint, nobody stopped him at any of the checkpoints.

There was a skeleton crew at the hospital, and the doctors were only on shift to make sure that no one died unnecessarily throughout the night. Luckily for us that also meant that there wasn't a wait to be checked in. The main doctor, Eddy Bay, wanted to report me and Simon upon learning how we were injured, but Mr. Briggens wasn't having any of it. He threatened to put one in between his eyes if he didn't keep his mouth shut and work on us.

The doctor patched me up and sent me home with Julie and her dad. Simon's injury was so bad he had to spend the night for surgery and stitches. We told the other doctors he was taking out the trash when a stray dog attacked him and tore into his arm which seemed to appease everyone.

After Mr. Briggens threatened Dr. Bay one last time about keeping his mouth shut, they told us that Simon would be ready for pick up tomorrow at five.

WITH HARDLY ANY SLEEP, SITTING THROUGH FOURTH period, Government Ed, is tough. I'm wishing that Simon was here to suffer Mr. Cook's bland lesson with me.

Mr. Cook is a complete idiot who thinks President Mills is God. He constantly tells us how he's our nation's savior, and how we need to worship him. Nothing annoys me more than his stupid class and his stupid, cocky, little attitude. All the other teachers are like him, which is why I can't wait to graduate.

"Now, can any of you *mindful* students tell me how Mills came into power?"

Some redhead in the front of the class raises her hand.

Mr. Cook points to her, "Yes, Ms. Collins?"

She straightens her posture, "Mills won in a landslide during the election in the year 2028, and then in his re-run in 2032. At the end of what was supposed to be his second term, there was a massive war between all the nations that broke out and he was put into a third term by government procedure, right?"

"That's only half of it, Ms. Collins," Mr. Cook states, now gazing around the classroom. "Can anyone finish the rest of the history behind our ruler?"

I roll my eyes, thankful to be in the back of the class.

"Anyone?"

No one responds

He strides over to the whiteboard and jots something down in red marker, "The United States defeated its enemies. We eliminated the inhabitants of Canada, Mexico, and many other opposing countries. This was all possible because Mills disbanded our old military and replaced them with the Saints. We were unstoppable, and after removing the other hostile countries, the rest surrendered. Can anyone tell me what happened next?"

Some kid who I don't care to know raises his hand before being called on, "He turned the US into a solitary country and told everyone who surrendered that we were done with trade deals, and how they were now working for the U.S. when it came to mining, farming, manufacturing, and other crap like that."

"Mr. Wyatt, I believe you're referring to The Incommunicado Act," Mr. Cook says, still jotting something down on the whiteboard. "The only time we communicated with other countries is when it was time for their yearly deposit of resources. No one was allowed in, no one was allowed out. Jason Pinder?"

I cock an eyebrow at the sound of my name, "Yes, sir?"

He stops writing and steps to the side, "Care to read this out loud for the class?"

"Can you ask someone else, sir?"

Mr. Cook gives me a funny look, "Why? You're capable of reading, aren't you?"

I stare at the paragraph he wrote long and hard; it looks like a mess of jumbled red.

My dyslexia acts up bad when I'm under pressure or a lot of stress, so it's impossible to make out. Usually, it only takes me a few moments to unjumble a word, or a minute for a paragraph, but with everything that happened last night, reading is not going to happen.

"Pass," I say. "Please ask someone else, sir."

"Okay, fine," Mr. Cook glares at me. "Since Mr. Pinder is obviously an illiterate, will you read what's up here on the board, Ms. Sheeran?"

A petite brunette who sits in front of me nods before reading what's on the board, and Mr. Cook turns around. I flip him off, my entire chest burning with agitation.

Screw you. Yes, why don't you keep telling us all about your lord and savior Joseph Mills, douchebag?

For the rest of class, I suffer through Mr. Cook's preaching about how Mills never left office, and how he has stayed in power for twenty years with no other person getting in the way.

In reality, people tried to overthrow him but were all killed off. Anyone under him in authority was killed, so he was free to do whatever he desired. The Saints were, and still are, corrupted killers who lust for power and authority. And since they hold such fear and rulership over the people of the US, they want to keep Mills in power, so they protect him and do whatever he says.

After class, I head down to the cafeteria for lunch and to find Julie. Tray of food in hand, I find her sitting at the table in the back of the spacious lunchroom. I drop next to her.

"Hey, what's up?" she greets, flashing me a half-hearted smile.

I shrug, still upset over being called an illiterate, "Nothing much. Kinda wishing that Mr. Cook was pushed in front of a moving train."

"Why?"

"Forget it."

I take a bite out of my sloppy joe.

"I know I say this every day," Julie starts. "But I seriously hate our school uniforms."

We're forced to wear a light blue polo with our nation's flag on the upper right corner with a pair of brown khakis to school every day. If we don't, we're expelled and are sometimes beaten by security for disobedience.

"What's the reason for hating them today?" I ask, clearly uninterested.

"So, you know how we got new uniforms at the beginning of the semester?"

"Yes?"

"Well, the ones they gave me a month ago are *way* too tight and these two guys keep on trying to grab my butt and won't stop saying *super* creepy things."

Hearing this makes me even angrier than I was a moment ago.

I drop my sloppy joe back down on my tray and look over at her.

"Who are they?"

She sighs, sounding uncomfortable, "Jakob and his freaky little friend Eli."

I grit my teeth, wanting nothing more than to go up to those two little idiots and pound their stupid, fat faces into a bloody pulp. I'd probably get my teeth knocked in, but they're harassing Julie while Simon isn't around to protect her. It irks me *far* more than being made fun of in class.

Julie fixes a stray strand of blonde hair from her face, "Don't worry. I heard what Simon did to Jakob last night. I'll just threaten to tell him if he touches me, again."

I'm about to agree with her idea, but Mae appears and suddenly takes a seat next to me. She abruptly places her lunch tray next to mine.

"Hey, Jason."

I look over at her, relief sweeping through my chest, "Mae? I haven't seen you all day. I thought something might've happened to you last night."

She shakes her head, "I've lived in Boston my whole life. I know all the backwoods, subdivisions, and streets like the back of my hand. That Saint was after me for a while, but he never caught me. Is Simon okay?"

I'm slow to reply, so Julie does it for me, "He lost a lot of blood, but he'll live. He's in the hospital right now. Jason and I are picking him up later today at five."

Mae looks over at her, "I'm glad he's okay. Did you hear about his beatdown on Jakob?"

Julie nods, "Uh-huh. I think most of the school has too."

Mae lets out a little sigh, bringing her attention back to me, "You know how Jeremy was shot last night?"

"Yeah, I saw the back of his head burst open . . . What about it?"

She seems shocked at how blunt I am, "Well, they found his entire family dead this morning. You know how he said the Saints screwed him over?"

"Yeah?"

"Well, I think he was the one who did the dirty work. I was

talking to Becca Channing, and she said he gave the Saints a bunch of counterfeits, and that's why Nacht-Fest was stormed last night and why his family was killed."

"Mae?"

"Yes?"

"I don't want to know about this."

"Why not?"

"Because if you tell me, I get pulled into it all. I'd rather not know why or how Jeremy screwed the Saints over. What happened last night was crappy. I'd rather forget it ever happened."

Her expression drops, "Oh, I'm sorry, I didn't know. I thought you'd like an explanation. I won't talk about it anymore," she pauses for a moment, seeming nervous. "Hey, would you like to get a bite to eat with me after school?"

I try to fight the sudden smile that makes its way on my face, "Just us two?"

"Well, yeah."

"Are you asking me out on a date?"

She chuckles, "I guess I am. So, what do you say?"

My smile grows even bigger, and my heart pounds, "Of course. I'll meet you at your locker after our final period and we'll go from there. Sound good?"

The smile on her face matches mine, "Yeah. Can't wait."

CHAPTER EIGHT

The rest of the school day seems to speed by, which is usually the opposite of what happens when something remotely exciting is taking place afterwards.

I'm sitting in science, my final period, finishing up the prep-list for Monday's test. It's so much easier to read now that I'm not under pressure. In fact, I'm reading through the papers on my desk with ease since I'm so calm and relaxed.

My mind keeps wandering toward Mae and her beautiful amber eyes, her contagious smile, and her heart-melting laugh. Like I mentioned before, I've had a thing for her since my freshman year, so the fact that she's suddenly so interested in me makes me feel euphoric, alive with sheer electricity.

The rhythmic bell finally releases us from school. I stand from my desk and grab my backpack from the floor next to me.

"Enjoy your weekend," my science teacher says as the bell stops ringing. "Make sure you prepare more for Monday's test. It counts as half your grade."

The class piles through the doors, eager to get to their separate destinations. Out in the hallway, I see Julie with the novel she's been reading tucked beneath her right arm.

"Hey," I call out after her. "Jules."

She stops and turns around as I walk over to her. Before I can even get a word out, she tells me I have to be back at my house by five because she and her mom will pick me up. I tell her I will be, then ask her for some last-minute advice for my little date with Mae.

"If I give you advice, you won't be yourself," she says as a crowd of students pass by. "Look, she likes you for you. So, be *you.*"

"Fair enough."

She places a hand on my shoulder, "I better hear about a kiss when I pick you up."

I chuckle, "We'll see."

She flashes me a smile, we exchange goodbyes, and then she turns around and walks off.

A few minutes later, I come face-to-face with Mae at her locker. She tells me she has to go get something from one of her classes and that she'll meet me out front. As I walk away, I think of all the things I could accomplish on this date. I know a lot of guys who get all jittery when it comes to being around someone they have feelings for. Thing is, I'm just not like that. Sure, I'm nervous, but I'm more excited to be around her than anything.

Maybe I'm just telling myself that.

I open the main doors to the high school and step outside. I watch my breath float in a misty mass into the cool February afternoon; there's a storm brewing. I push my glasses up and walk down the slick concrete steps. I can hear other students chatting amongst themselves as they head home.

I really hope Mae isn't vegan.

On the third to the final step, I feel a big pair of hands slam into my back, and I crash down the rest of the way. I let out a groan, and I hear someone laugh. It's the same cold, smug, prideful laugh I've heard a thousand times before.

Jakob Holmes. His right eye is swollen shut and his nose looks crooked.

"Hey, Pinder," he grins, flashing me his yellow teeth.

I slowly turn to my back and sit up, feeling a stinging sensation spring throughout my entire body, "What do you want?"

An explosion of white mist flies from his mouth, "Where's Davis? I have some unfinished business to settle with him."

"Unfinished?" I laugh, which probably isn't the best thing to do. "It looked pretty finished to me when he beat the absolute crap outta you last night, douche-face."

"Oh, don't be so *stupid*," he strides down the last few steps and towers over me like a skyscraper, a bloated skyscraper. "I was drunk and high off my rockers. I couldn't even see straight. If he and I fought right now, I'd bash his face in."

"Tough luck, pudgy," I shrug. "cause I'm not telling you where he is."

"I'm gonna give you three seconds to tell me, and believe you me, ya little prick, I'm not in the mood to screw around today," spit carries every single word with loaded anger and hatred, but it doesn't fill me with dread like usual. "Three . . . two . . . one . . ."

I stay silent.

"Fine, be that way," he grabs me by the collar of my shirt and drags me over to the right side of the school, my glasses slipping from my face. "You just *had* to play the heroic role, Pin-man. Hope you don't mind crapping your teeth out for the next month, you little *rat*."

He releases his grip on me once we make it to our secluded destination. Then, before I can even think about getting up, I feel his large and heavy foot slam down onto my frozen hand and fingers.

I yelp as he puts large amounts of pressure on it, "*Ah*, stop!"

"I gave you a chance to walk away from this," he remarks before removing his foot from my hand and ramming it into my mouth. "So, don't even try begging, you dumb rat."

My eyes go wide, pain soaring to life throughout my freezing face while my frigid lips feel warm as rosy red liquid spills from between them.

Jakob grabs me by the collar once more and lifts me up like a rag doll, smashing me against the side of the school. He then throws his balled-up fist into my nose and laughs as blood pours out my nostrils like a bursting dam.

"It looks like you're about to cry," he laughs hysterically. "Come on, Pinder, *cry*."

He wraps both meaty hands around my throat and pins me against the brick wall. He squeezes tighter and tighter, causing my vision to go black at the edges. I use my hands to slap and scratch at his, but he shows no signs of letting go.

My heart races out of control as my pinched windpipe burns. I should be used to this sensation after all these years, but I'm not.

"Stop," I hear a voice to my right demand. "Let him go."

Instantly, the fleshy hands around my neck retract, and I drop to the hard and frozen ground. A jolt of pain shoots up through my tailbone.

My lungs flutter to life and I sputter for air. Jakob turns his head to the source of interruption. To both of our surprise, Mae is standing a couple yards away.

"Piss off, Bernhard!" Jakob hisses.

Mae flinches at his sudden outburst, but she doesn't step away, "Leave him alone. He didn't do crap to you, okay?"

"Stay outta this," Jakob spits, obviously trying to intimidate her. "I'll pound you, slut, I will."

Mae takes a step back before taking a hesitant breath, "Just go away, okay? Look at him, there's blood all over his face, you've had your fun."

Jakob glances down at me and chuckles, "You think this is bad? Ah, man. I could do so much worse. In fact, why don't you watch me?"

Without warning, vicious strikes come raining down on me like bullets, and for a moment, I feel as if I'm about to black out.

This torment doesn't stop until I hear someone being smacked, and I carefully open my eyes to see a shocked Jakob rubbing his bright red cheek with his palm.

It takes my disoriented mind a prolonged moment to put two and two together. I'm shocked. Mae had just slapped him across his fat face.

Jakob swears at her before swiping his hand back and catching her on the nose out of retaliation. My veins burn with rage as she falls to the ground. Mae cries out and winces in sharp and sudden pain.

Fury burns through me like a fire, "You stupid fat *psycho!* What are you *doing?*"

Everything goes silent as Jakob looks down at me with loathing eyes, "I just hit her. What're *you* going to do about it?"

Before I can respond, he grabs me by the collar again and lifts me up into the air like I weigh nothing. I feel large amounts of adrenaline race through me as he snarls. *I'll be ripped apart if I don't think fast.*

Jakob brings his right hand back, and I do the only thing possible. I lurch my head to the rear then shoot my forehead into his face. Yowling, he liberates his grip on me.

I land on my feet, let out a nervous grunt, and then charge my knuckles into his already broken nose. He grits his teeth before clutching his face. I then slam my foot down onto his.

Mae calls my name. She quickly tells me she will go get school security. I try to nod, but instead I take a fist to my already bloodied and beaten face.

Stars explode into my vision as I stumble back into the side of the school. I try to regroup, but my attempts are cut short as Jakob knees me in the gut, knocking the wind out of me.

"You thought you could actually fight back?" he angrily growls like a dog. "You're going to be begging in a pool of your own blood when I'm done with you, Pinder."

He tries to swing at me, but the adrenaline flowing through me is persistent. I dodge out of the way, causing his knuckles to crack against the hard and unforgiving brick wall. He screams while rapidly shaking his injured hand, and I kick the small of his back.

He goes face-first into the solid wall, and I can't help letting out a laugh of pure satisfaction.

He stumbles around for a moment, notably dazed as he jams his hand into one of the front pockets of his school uniform, "You've really, *really* screwed yourself, Pinder."

My eyes focus on the object he retrieves from his pocket.

My heart races like a drum as he turns away from the brick wall and faces me. He uses his thumb to slide the little black switch on the handle of a switchblade. The blade springs from the handgrip.

I gawk at him, my stomach knotting up like crazy, "What're you-"

"I've been wanting to do this for a while," he smirks, waving the knife around. "You ready for this?"

I back up a few feet and put my hand out in front of me, "Calm down. Put the knife away and leave me alone, you crazy *freak*."

My entire body is shaking. I wasn't scared before this point, no matter what he *said*, I didn't feel intimidated. Now that he's slowly creeping up on me with a sharp blade in his hand, I can honestly say I'm utterly terrified.

He grabs me by the arm, swings me into a 180, and hurls me into the brick wall.

My mind blackens and doesn't return for what seems like forever.

My eyes finally open, and I find myself on the ground.

Jakob stands over me with a grin plastered over his fat, ugly mug, "Hey, buddy."

My bloodied face feels heavy and numb. I'm aching all over,

and I'm doing my best to hold back the tears that are begging to be released from my eyes.

Jakob waves the switchblade in front of my face before squatting down and pointing the tip toward my throat, "I'm gonna jab a hole in your neck and watch you bleed to death. Nobody will miss you, nobody will even *care*. You know that, right?"

The look in his eyes petrifies me as he readies his arm back to thrust his blade into my throat. I do the only thing I can think of; I let out one final scream for help.

I clamp my eyes shut and wait, looking back on everything I never did, everything I'd never be able to do in my life. It makes my heart sting and ache all at the same time.

This can't be it, can it?

Freezing cold rain falls from the sky, the trickles splash against my eyelids as I prepare to be shanked through the throat.

"Get on the ground!" orders an abrupt low-pitched voice.

My eyes flash open, and behind Jakob stands two Saints, my school's principal, and the beautiful girl with amber-colored eyes who just saved my life.

The two Saints have their handguns trained on Jakob, and the new look on my tormentor's pale and terrified face makes me feel euphoric.

My eyes meet his for all of a second, and I grin widely at seeing the gut-wrenching horror that swirls in his irises. Jakob gets to his feet and swears loudly, not once turning around to see the Saints.

"What did I just say?" the first soldier barks. "Get on the ground, now!"

Jakob slowly drops his switchblade, the world slowing in suspense as everyone waits for his next move. It takes a lengthy moment, but he finally steps to the side and gradually gets to his knees before putting his hands behind his head.

Acting like he had just disobeyed orders, the two Saints charge toward him and one of them tackles him to the ground before they both pull out their metal nightsticks and beat him bloody like a rabid dog.

I watch as every blow to Jakob's skull forces a bit of life out of him, and before he can black out, something unexpected happens. One of the Saints forces Jakob's arm out to the side and holds it in place while the other unsheathes his combat knife.

"You know, kid," the soldier pinning Jakob's arm says. "Carrying weapons is illegal and punishable by any means we believe necessary."

"What- what're you doing?" Jakob asks, struggling to get free but failing miserably.

The soldier with the knife gets on one knee and places the steel blade up to Jakob's right fleshy wrist, waiting for his next order.

"And judging by the looks of you," the first soldier begins, a look of pure satisfaction in his stormy grey eyes. "You're a really *rotten* apple," taking a deep breath and glancing over at his partner, he mutters. "Do it."

I watch with a sort of gratified horror as the soldier with the knife saws Jakob's right hand off. It only takes a few moments, and once they're done, they both get to their feet and drag the pudgy freak away. Jakob's screams echo throughout the wet and bitter-cold air.

CHAPTER NINE

Mae slowly approaches me after the Saints leave with Jakob. My entire face is still smeared in blood, both of my nostrils are still leaking red, my nose feels knocked out of place, and my left eye is swelling. That I still haven't let out any tears makes me feel less embarrassed to have Mae staring down at me.

"Here," she says sympathetically, handing me my glasses. "I saw these out front and thought you'd like to be able to see, you know?"

I take them from her and put them on, using my forearm to wipe away some blood that's streaming from my nose, "Thanks. Are you okay?"

"Am *I* okay?" she asks, trying to hide she's shaken up after witnessing the removal of Jakob's right hand. "I'm not the one who was pounded."

My head is spinning as I retain my balance, "Still. How's your nose? He hit you pretty hard."

She shrugs, "It hurts a bit, but I'll be okay."

I'm about to ask her if we can reschedule our date, but our principal comes up to me, rain drenching his suit coat, "Are you okay, Jason? Are you in need of medical attention?"

I shake my head despite wanting to nod, "No, I think I'm fine . . . Principal Smalls, what do you think will happen to Jakob?"

His face tightens, "I don't know, nor do I care. I've wanted to get rid of that student for as long as I can remember. And are you sure? You look really banged up. The school's nurse is still inside, and I'm sure she'd love to help you."

I glance at Mae, not wanting to appear wimpy, "I'm sure it's not as bad as it probably looks, I'll go get washed up, and then I'll be as good as new."

Looking unsure, Mr. Smalls replies, "Well, as long as you say you're okay. . . I will get the janitor to come out here and clean this . . ." he pauses, trying to come up with a word to describe the bloody scene before him. ". . . *Mess* up. Have a good weekend Jason, and you too, Ms. Bernhard."

He turns around and walks away, leaving me and Mae in the freezing rain storm. The two of us stand there for a minute, but Mae eventually breaks the silence.

"I get it if you just want to go home and get cleaned up," she says, a disappointed undertone to her voice. "We can always reschedule our little date for Monday after school, or something like that if you're up to it."

I look at the severed hand that lies on the asphalt to my right, trying to forget the events that had just happened, "I know you were really looking forward to going out, so was I, but do you think we could do Monday? I want to get cleaned up, take some painkillers, and calm down. Food isn't really on my mind right now."

Her gaze drops, and so do her shoulders, "Yeah, sounds like a plan."

A heavy thought barrels into me like a moving train before I can get the words out. *I could've just died.*

Those four words swim around in my mind, making my stomach knot up. My mortality and the guilt for letting Mae down causes me to back up against the side of the school. My heart pounds, and my eyes turn misty from behind my glasses.

Mae shoots me a confused look, "Hey, what's wrong?"

I try to hold the tears back, but her words open the floodgate, and tears stream down my already wet cheeks. No, I'm not bawling or anything like that, but it's impossible to hold back the buildup that's been begging to be released ever since I was kicked in the face.

Mae doesn't say another word, instead she embraces me. The way her arms wrap around my neck is enough to calm me down. My heart steadies, and my breathing slows.

"It's okay," she whispers in my ear, standing on her tippy toes. "You're okay."

I take a deep breath. In any other situation, this would've been the most embarrassing thing ever. But it almost feels natural to cry in front of her.

I don't feel judged. Not at all.

I chuckle, the tears still falling, "You probably think I'm a baby, huh?"

She looks up at me, wet strands of dark hair impeding her sight, "No, not even a little bit."

One minute, we're staring in each other's eyes as rain soaks the two of us, the next, our lips are locked together. I don't know how it happened, but it just did. I guess escaping from a patrol of Saints, being held at gunpoint, and witnessing the removal of a kid's hand is enough to get two people attached to one another.

I won't say my heart exploded with rainbows and sunshine or any crap like that. In reality, it's just a kiss, but that doesn't make this moment any less special. It feels right, and makes me feel, I dunno, warm, I guess. I do, however, feel bad that she kissed me with all this blood covering my face.

We part.

"Jason?"

"Yeah?"

"I like you, a lot."

My smile grows bigger, and I let out a slight chuckle, "I can tell."

Lightning rolls across the sky and is quickly followed by a booming crack of thunder. Mae flinches.

I grab her hand, "I know we've rescheduled, but that doesn't mean I can't make sure you don't get jumped by a ferocious gang of midget monkeys on your way home, right?"

She laughs, "Midget monkeys?"

"Yeah, you know, half midget, half monkey? Quite vicious, and I don't think I would forgive myself if you got hurt by one. So, I think I will walk you home, just to be safe."

She laughs more, "If you're being serious about walking me home . . ."

"I am."

"I live in Devenshire, in that case. I'm glad someone will protect me from those *horrible* midget monkeys. Are they abnormally hairy short guys with tails? Or what's the deal?"

"There's literally a whole documentary about sightings. It's ridiculous."

"We'll have to watch it together sometime."

"Definitely."

The two of us chuckle before walking off together, leaving behind the bloody scene I hope I can someday forget.

CHAPTER TEN

After walking Mae home, I head back to Brookhaven. I pass through my checkpoint, tell Tommy what had happened in the past hour, and stumble over to my house as the glacial rain continues to soak me.

I better not get pneumonia, I think as I open the front door to my house.

I clamber up the staircase and barge into my bedroom, shedding my bloody and wet clothes, leaving them on the floor before climbing into bed.

My swollen eye is throbbing in perfect rhythm with my heartbeat, and my entire body just aches. I reach over toward my nightstand and grab a bottle of pills. I unscrew the lid, spill three ibuprofen into my palm, and toss them into my mouth before grabbing a glass of water that's also placed on my nightstand. A big swig forces the meds down my dry throat.

I don't remember falling asleep, but I must've, because I suddenly wake with a start as my creaky bedroom door slowly inches open. My eyes dart over to my room's entrance, and I'm immediately relieved to see both my mom and dad walking in with comforting smiles on their faces.

"Hey, bud," my dad greets, approaching the foot of my bed and taking a seat.

"Oh, hey," I greet back, their faces and tones make me assume that they know what happened between me and Jakob earlier. "I'm guessing you two heard about the fight?"

My mom joins my dad sitting at the foot of my bed, "Your principal called us just a little bit ago. Are you okay? How bad are you hurt? He said you didn't want to see the nurse."

"Mom, I'm fine . . . just a bit lightheaded. Did he tell you what happened to Jakob?"

My dad stares at me with a serious gaze, "They cut his right hand off and dragged him away to who knows where."

His words bring a barely visible half smile to my face, "Yeah, you're right."

"The principal wants the three of us to meet him tomorrow morning at the school so you can tell him why everything happened the way it did," my mom states. "So just be ready, okay?"

"Is Mae going to be there?"

"Who's Mae?" my mom and dad both ask in unison.

"Didn't Principal Smalls bring her up? She's the girl who saved my life."

"Oh, is her last name Bernhard?" my mom questions.

"Yeah, that's her."

My dad shoots me a reassuring smile, "She'll be there tomorrow with us, or at least that's what they told us."

The watch strapped to my left wrist chirps before I can form words with my mouth. I pull my hand out from under the covers and check the time.

It's five, meaning Julie and her mom will be here any minute to pick me up.

"I've gotta head," I say, stepping out of bed and grabbing a grey hoodie, a white undershirt, and a pair of jeans from up off the floor.

"Huh? Where are you going?" my mom shifts into a more comfortable position.

"Simon's being released from the hospital."

"The hospital?"

"He was attacked by a, uh," I think for a moment, trying to remember the alibi we came up with for answering questions just like this, "a stray dog. This morning he went to take out the trash, and he was chewed up pretty bad."

She grows concerned, "How are you getting to the hospital? Do you need a ride?"

"Julie's picking me up," I tell her, slipping the fresh new pair of clothes on and finishing the look by sliding a white sneaker onto each foot.

My dad stands from my bed and gives me a hug, "Alright, just be back before curfew."

"Don't worry, I will be."

He ruffles my hair. Both he and my mom tell me they love me and I say it back. Then I head out my bedroom door and to the bathroom. There's dried blood all over my face that needs washing. I turn the sink faucet on and wash it all off before grabbing the towel from its rack and wiping myself dry.

There's a knock at my door.

I take one last look at myself in the mirror before heading out of the bathroom.

RAINDROPS SPLATTER AGAINST THE WINDSHIELD OF Mrs. Briggens' car as we continue down a busy street. Classical music is softly playing through the car speakers, and at the moment, Simon and Julie are hounding me for details about earlier.

"I've already heard rumors about you, Jason," Julie confirms, shooting me a concerned stare. "Please, just tell us what happened. I wanna make sure what people are telling me aren't true."

I groan, leaning up against the window, "And what are some of these so-called *rumors*?"

"You probably don't want to know, honestly."

My eyes narrow, "Jakob and I got into a little bit of a fight and it ended with him getting his right hand cut off and being dragged away by Saints. There. Happy now?"

Simon gawks at me, "Wait, you cut his hand off? So, the rumors are true?"

I cock an eyebrow at him, "Are you serious? Me? No, dude, the Saints did the dirty work."

"I really wouldn't consider it as 'dirty work,'" he says, putting his good arm around Julie. "He deserved it- and I'm not saying that because of what he did last night. I mean, look at everything that fat little freak has done to you and so many others. Especially Fifi. The Saints should've put a bullet in the back of his head."

Julie snuggles up to Simon, "Hey, mom?"

"Yeah?"

"Has Dad ever told you where they put low-life criminals?"

Mrs. Briggens looks at her daughter through the rear-view mirror, "No, and I don't think he ever will. I would assume that Jakob is rotting away somewhere awful at this very moment."

"Good," I say, staring out the window.

I recall how he referred to Julie as a cheap whore, how he harassed her, and how he called Mae a slut and said he would pound her. He killed Fifi, broke my collarbone, and put a knife up against my throat.

I hope you kill yourself, I think, watching the endless amounts of rainfall drench the streets.

"I have a few errands to run," Mrs. Briggens states, concentrating at the wheel. "So, would it be alright if I dropped you three off for some ice cream? I'll pay for it."

"That would be awesome," Simon smiles, looking over at me. "What do you think?"

"I'm down. Where are you dropping us off at?"

"The Sweet-Tooth," Mrs. Briggens replies. "I remember taking you guys there all the time after school when you were eleven."

A stream of nostalgia flows through me at the mention of The Sweet-Tooth. So many good memories were shared there, and just at the mention of it, I'm eager to return.

"Think Brandon is still the owner?" Julie asks.

"He has to be," Simon remarks. "It's a family-owned parlor, and we *all* know Brandon doesn't have a kid. The guy has never been a ladies' man, sadly."

We all chuckle.

CHAPTER ELEVEN

We make it to The Sweet-Tooth about fifteen minutes later. It looks identical to a 1950s diner, so it's way out of place compared to the rest of Boston, but that's why the three of us love it so much. It's the only place in this city where you can feel part of a different time. You can actually feel peace, not to mention that it doesn't feel like you're being watched.

The three of us are sitting at a booth which has a huge window serving as the back wall. Rain is swiftly waterfalling down the glass; it's kind of hypnotizing.

I recognize the store owner walking out from the kitchen and heading over to us with a huge grin plastered across his clean-shaven face.

"I haven't seen you three here in *forever*," Brandon Yancey claims, parking himself in front of our booth. "You've all grown. How are you?"

"We're doing great," Julie smiles.

"So, what brings you to the Sweet-Tooth?"

"Just taking a trip down memory lane," I say, pushing my glasses up my face.

Brandon studies me for a moment, "That's great, but, uh, what happened to your eye? That's quite the shiner you've got there."

"I got into a little fight, but I'm fine. How's business been?"

He shrugs, "Slow, but good. Only get around thirty people here per day, but I manage."

"That sucks. Are you going to have to shut the place down if business doesn't pick up?"

"No, I always figure a way to keep things going. Plus, the less I have customers, the less ingredients I have to buy. I have a process, it all works out at the end of the day."

"Well, that's good."

"It definitely is, trust me. So, I'm guessing you'd all like the usual?"

"Right you are," Simon says while using a crayon to doodle in some of the drawings that are a part of the kids' menu.

"Y'know, there's a free junior meal if you can color in all the animals without going outside the lines," Brandon winks, making Simon laugh.

We pass a few more jokes around before Brandon turns around and heads back to the kitchen to prepare our dessert, and for a moment, things are nothing but calm and peaceful.

I stare out the window to my left. It hasn't stopped thundering outside since the fight.

I love this weather so much, which is positive considering it always seems to rain a few times a week here in Boston. I love the way the droplets splash against the earthy smelling asphalt, the way it casts a dark gloom over the whole city, the scent of nature after the storm subsides.

"*Boo-yah*," Simon shouts, making my heart skip a beat. "Hey, Brandon, bring out that free junior meal, man, because *this* dude just colored in all of Farmer Baldwin's farm animals *without* going outside the lines."

"It was a joke," Brandon hollers from the kitchen. "Dude, you're seventeen."

"But last year I was a *junior* in high school. That count?"

"No."

"Crap."

A few minutes pass by before Brandon exits the kitchen. He's carrying a platter cluttered with bowls filled to the brim with ice cream. He approaches our booth and sets our stuff down in the center.

"Bon appétit," he says in his mediocre French accent.

"Thanks," I smile. "How much do you think we'll owe you when we're done?"

He winks at me, "Free of charge."

I'm about to express my gratitude, but a girly shriek from Simon stops me. He eyes the junior meal on the platter like it was a million bucks.

"You magnificent human being."

"Mmmhmm."

The sudden sound of the door opening stops Simon from opening his mouth.

"How may I help—" Brandon turns his head toward the entrance and turns whiter than a sheet. "No . . . you aren't supposed to be here."

I sit up straight in order to see who he's looking at, and my blood runs colder than ice. My eyes widen, my stomach knots up, and my heart pounds like a tribal drum.

Standing at the door is a man wearing a black leather trench coat. He dons black combat boots, black leather gloves, and to finish it all off, a gas mask- a *Reaper*.

The Reapers are a part of President Mills' private squad. They perform assassinations for him, serve as bodyguards, and do all his dirty work.

"Mr. Yancey," the man greets, his voice modulated to a deeper and more metallic tone.

Brandon backs away from our booth, "What do you want from me? I did everything you asked!"

"If that were the case, Yancey, I wouldn't be here," the Reaper states, his modified, raspy voice sending chills down my spine.

"They promised you wouldn't find me," Brandon babbles. "They promised that nothing would happen to me if I ripped the photos up, that I'd be safe!"

The Reaper begins slowly taking a few strides closer, "They lied."

I press my back up against the window, my head spinning.

What's going on? What's happening?

This all seems to play out too fast. Just a minute ago, we were messing around and having fun, but now there's a military assassin in our midst, and I'm left wondering what will happen next.

I watch as the Reaper pulls a handgun out from under his trench coat and trains it on Brandon, "I hope you are burnt *to a crisp* in Hell."

Brandon throws his hands up to shield his face, "Wait, wait. I'll tell you everything about them! I'll give you names, appearances, everything!"

The Reaper chuckles, which sounds horrifying because of his metallic tone, "Mills doesn't want information. He does, however, want you dead," he pauses for a moment, pointing the barrel of the gun at Brandon's stomach. "Now, where was I? Oh yeah."

I flinch as two shots are fired.

Brandon screams, and I watch with a dropped jaw as he stumbles back and eventually collapses to the floor. He cries out, grinding his teeth and clutching his penetrated gut. His once white apron is soaked in red, and as my mind tries to wrap itself around this situation, the Reaper approaches him.

"Lazarus *cannot* and *will not* rise," the killer declares, hovering over Brandon. "Doesn't matter what you, or anybody else does. We'll kill every last one of their informants, then, when the time is right, they will all be wiped from the face of the earth. You'll die knowing you failed. You should've just done what you were told and left the rest to me, instead you decided to work for a bunch of terrorists. For that, I don't pity you."

I watch with shaky shoulders as the Reaper bends over, grips the sides of Brandon's face with both hands, and violently jerks his head to the side. I cringe at the disturbing sound of his neck snapping, and I get the sudden urge to vomit.

The Reaper straightens, and after a horrific moment of eerie silence, he turns to our booth. He says nothing, instead he carefully parks himself in front of us.

"Lovely weather, huh?"

I can't help myself from trembling, "Yes, it's great."

He stares at me a moment, two small circular visors that are shaded dark as night shielding his eyes from my sight, "I love the rain," he pauses for a moment before placing his pistol onto the table. "Tell me, what is your name?"

I gawk, "It's, uh, Jason. Jason Pinder."

"I see. So, what brings you here, Jason? You know that dumb sonofa-slut lying on the floor over there?"

I glance over at Brandon's motionless, bloodied body, "No, sir."

He continues to stare at me, "Would you like to know why I killed him?"

I gulp, "I'm . . . I think I'm okay, thank you."

"He informed Lazarus of some very *private* information. I'm sure you know who Lazarus is, don't you?"

"I think everyone does, sir."

He goes quiet for a second, before grabbing his gun and sticking it back into his trench coat, "Yes, I suppose you're right. Well, I won't keep you three. Enjoy your evening, alright?"

Julie is burrowed into Simon's side, "We will, sir."

He looks over at her, "Indeed."

He turns around and exits the store, leaving behind a deceased man lying on the floor in a puddle of his own blood.

CHAPTER TWELVE

Thunder rattles the sky above as Simon, Julie, and I approach Brookhaven's checkpoint. The rain has seeped through my sneakers, my black eye is throbbing, my clothes are soaked, and I feel numb on the inside and out.

"This is messed up," Simon says, his nearly purple right hand clasped with Julie's. "I feel like we're being followed by that maniac."

I peek over my shoulder, my mind pushing unnecessary thoughts into my brain, "Don't worry, we're almost home, alright?"

Julie's teeth chatter, "I still can't believe Brandon was an informant for a terrorist group."

"I wouldn't consider Lazarus a terrorist group," I say, stuffing my freezing cold, wet hands into my front pockets. "This stays between us three, but I kinda support them."

Julie looks at me like I'm insane, "You kidding? They murder Saints, assassinate government officials, and need I mention that they are trying to take out our nation's leader?"

"Exactly," I start, our checkpoint less than fifteen feet away now. "Look, I know we never discuss politics, but I agree with Lazarus and what they're doing."

"But why?"

"I have my reasons."

Simon shrugs, "I'm with Jay, here."

Julie shakes her head, "You two better hope that the cameras didn't hear you say that."

We come to a stop in front of our checkpoint and are instantly greeted by Tommy.

"What're you guys doing out in weather like this?" he asks.

"We just came from an ice cream place," I remark, not wanting to bring up the whole incident. "How has your day been?"

"Pretty good. Still can't believe you saw that kid get his hand cut off."

"Trust me, I would go back in time just to see it all happen again."

"I wish I was there," he holds his hand out for my identification card. "Did you recognize the two Saints who apprehended him?"

I tug my wallet out of my back pocket and retrieve my card, "Of course not," I hand him the ID and watch him look over it carelessly. "You all wear the same uniform, are all around the same height, and all have the same body type. Sometimes I can't even tell that it's you when you come up and talk to me."

He hands my card back, "Fair point."

"I'm *freezing*," Julie chatters. "Can we please hurry this up so I can get home?"

Tommy glances over at her, "You think *you're* freezing? I've been out here since five this morning, with only two thirty-minute breaks."

"You're also wearing a military uniform," she protests, handing him her card. "I'm in leggings and a t-shirt."

He examines her card, "Sucks to suck, huh? Maybe you should've bundled up."

Simon chuckles, "He's gotta point."

Julie nudges him, "Shut up."

Tommy hands her, her ID, "I'm just messing with you, Briggens. Here. Tell your dad I said hi."

She slides it back into her wallet, "Thanks, and I will."

Simon's the last to get his identification checked, and once he's cleared, Tommy turns and gives his partner in the security booth a thumbs up. Simon and Julie say goodnight to Tommy and enter Brookhaven, and I'm about to do the same, but I'm pulled to the side.

"I need you to listen," Tommy says, his eyes locked on mine.

I'm thrown off guard, "Okay. What's up?"

"Things will change, but it will be fine, you hear me?"

"Are you feeling alright, man?"

He shudders a sigh, "Embrace being the puppet, and I promise, one day, you'll become the puppeteer. Don't be afraid."

"Are you high?" I question, raising an eyebrow.

He smiles and pats me on the shoulder, "I'll miss the old you."

"You're freaking me out, man."

"Goodnight, Jason."

I stare at him for a moment, but eventually say it back, "Goodnight, Tommy."

I slowly enter Brookhaven.

CHAPTER THIRTEEN

My well rested eyes open, seeing nothing but thunderous gloom through my rain painted window. I yawn, stretching my arms and legs.

I sit up and grab my glasses off the nightstand near my bed; the events from yesterday feeling like a bad dream.

Honestly, I don't even feel phased by the death of Brandon. It isn't settling in.

I get out of bed and slip on a pair of jeans, a gray undershirt, and a white zip-up jacket along with a white pair of sneakers. I head over to the bathroom, fix my messy blonde hair, brush my teeth, and eventually head downstairs.

My parents are both sitting at the kitchen table, a somber expression glued to the both of their faces. My heart speeds up as I take a seat. I really would rather not know what's going on, but my curiosity is setting in.

"Is everything all right?" I ask, grabbing an apple from the fruit basket in the center of the table. "You both look like you're about to cry."

My mom looks as if she's trying to find the right words, "Something happened last night."

"What?"

My dad slides over the morning paper, and after a moment of focusing on the jumbled mess of words, I make out the large and bold headline.

Five Saints Murdered in Lakeshore High Shootout

I lower my eyes to the sentences below the headline, trying my absolute best to make out every word, and after a good two minutes, I'm able to make out the first few paragraphs.

"Late last night, the silent alarm at Lakeshore high went off, and multiple Saints were sent to the site. Once on the premises, they spotted seven armed individuals attempting to leave the property. The suspects spotted the Saints and thus began the firefight that ended with multiple casualties on the military's side. The armed individuals were all able to escape. These are the names of the fallen: James Holk, Brett Clarke, Benjamin Fields, Logan Ellis, and Thomas Price."

My eyes widen with unbelief as I finish that last sentence.

Tommy is . . . dead?

I blink a few times, setting the paper down on the table fretfully.

None of this seems right. None of this seems *real*. I mean, just last night I was face-to-face with him. I was talking to him. He was *breathing*.

Now he's gone?

I look up at my parents, my jaw slightly slack. I want to speak, but I can't find the words that build their way up inside my mind.

My dad slowly takes a sip out of his coffee mug, "His wife is pregnant, and he has two little girls. Awful, just *awful*."

My eyes turn glassy as I stand from my chair, "I've gotta go."

"Where?" my mom asks.

"Simon's," I say, a burst of emotions coursing through me. "I just need some time to think."

"We need to do something first."

"What is it?"

My dad sets his mug down, "We have a meeting with your principal in twenty minutes, remember?"

"The school's a crime scene, don't you think it's canceled?" I ask, my stomach in knots.

"That's what I was thinking," my mom sighs. "But we were called a little bit ago and told to still come."

I attempt to speak through the lump in my throat, "We should get going, then."

CHAPTER FOURTEEN

I can't explain the feeling emanating from inside me as I put one foot in front of the other. It's like a concoction of emotions: sadness, anger, curiousness, confusion, and shock.

He's gone. I keep pounding the same words into my brain. *Denial won't change that.*

My dad drapes his arm over my shoulder as we walk toward our checkpoint.

I look over at him and our eyes meet. His are a warm light green that make him look a lot younger than he actually is. You can definitely tell I'm his son just by looking at our faces. I look exactly how he did when he was my age.

"So, do you have a thing for her?" he asks.

"For who?"

"That Mae girl."

I shrug, "Sure."

"Sure?" he echoes, cocking an eyebrow. "That really isn't an answer, now is it?"

"We were supposed to go on a date yesterday, but we had to reschedule until Monday because of everything that happened."

My mom glances over at me with an excited look in her eye, "You have a date?"

"Yeah, so?"

"Why didn't you tell us?"

"Didn't think it was that big of a deal."

"Well, it is. You will be eighteen this August."

"What does that have to do with anything?"

"Around this age, you date to find *the one*. Every date you go on has the potential to be the 'how we met' story you tell your kids in fifteen years."

I laugh out loud, "*The one*? Mom, I think you need to calm down, it's just a date."

"Whatever you say."

We keep walking and talking; the checkpoint nearing with every step we take. Once close enough, I can make out two Saints standing guard in front of the security arm. Usually only one Saint checks IDs, while the other mans the security booth, *weird*.

"That's odd," I point out. "What do you think's going on?"

"Nothing," my mother replies, scanning the sight for herself. "They're new to the area and probably want to get familiar with everyone. Tommy and Logan did that when they first got here, didn't they?"

The mention of Tommy's name makes me feel ill. Things will never be the same.

Not without him.

We halt in front of our checkpoint.

"Identification," the first Saint orders, not looking up once from the flooded asphalt. "And make it quick."

My dad pulls his ID out of his pocket and hands it to the tall burly soldier who just spoke. The rain is soaking all of us to the bone

He examines it for a moment before looking up at him, "Good morning, Michael."

"You too," my dad says.

He hands the ID back to my dad before fixing his gaze upon my mom and asking to see her proof of identification. She complies and hands over her card and watches him study it.

"Stacey Pinder," he mumbles before glancing up at her. "What a pretty name," he quickly turns over toward my father. "You, sir, are one *lucky* man."

The Saint then turns to me and puts his hand out, "Wow, you're a tall kid. ID?"

His voice is deep and intimidating, a hint of snark bellowing beneath his monotone.

"Here," I say, handing him the plastic card.

He inspects it carefully, letting out an unsettling grin while doing so, "Ah, the last person in the Pinder family. You're all on the list."

The way he says this unnerves me.

"Kid," he looks me directly in the eyes. "C'mere."

I hesitantly take a step forward, face-to-face with the man. Neither of us talk, and for a few moments, the only sound is from the thunderstorm overhead.

He leans into me, his lips centimeters from my ear.

"May God have mercy on their souls."

These words turn my entire body into pure lead, "What?"

I hear the loudest *pop!* imaginable erupt in my left eardrum, making my head reel to the side out of reflex. My mother stands with a look of fear branded across her face. Her bright yellow raincoat turns crimson with blood. A bullet just penetrated her chest.

The second Saint, who hasn't uttered a single word, points the smoking end of a pistol at my dad and squeezes the trigger. Another gunshot rings out, resulting in my father's loud and heart-wrenching cry. I watch as he collapses to the wet ground, a weak groan escaping his throat.

I back up, my eyes wide and arms trembling. I get about two feet back before the Saint with the handgun switches his gaze to me. There is no remorse in his eyes, just sick humor identical to his partner's.

"Leaving so soon?" he asks me, his voice even deeper and twice as intimidating.

I stop dead in my tracks and watch as the first Saint forces my dying father to his knees. He then faces him toward me and grins wildly. The second Saint slowly walks up to my dad, pointing the handgun to the back of his skull.

"Jason," my father mutters, blood and rain pouring down his frame. "Don't loo—"

The Saint shoots a mixture of lead and copper into the back of his head.

I feel my body jerk as my dad slumps downward, the rainwater around his now dead body turning into a scarlet pool. I don't even know how to react. I stand there, my eyes wide like 50 cent coins.

"No! Mi-Michael!" my mother howls while sobbing, clutching her chest. "You basta—"

Before she can finish speaking, the second Saint aims at her head and fires twice.

I clamp my eyes shut, not wanting to see the woman who gave birth to me take a bullet to the brain.

I feel empty as I hear her head hit the asphalt.

An extended moment passes, and I risk a peek. Both of my parents lie sprawled out on the rain-soaked road, pools of blood forming beneath the both of them. Directly in front of me, stand the two Saints.

The second one is aiming the barrel of the gun at me, a serious and stone-cold look on his face.

"No way," the scream of terror beams from the pit of my stomach. I hastily turn and run, desperately trying to get away. *This isn't happening.*

The familiar sound of the gunshot explodes a millisecond before the flesh around my right shoulder blade absorbs the searing bullet. I blurt out a swear as the right side of my body lurches forward, and I collapse. Before I come into contact with the flooded street, another scorching bullet hollows through me, this time striking my left hamstring.

My body slams harshly against the road, and hellish stinging springs through me like shock waves as I begin my struggle for life. I try getting up after a second, but it only causes the pain to tear deeper into my body.

Cruel laughter booms into my ears as loud footsteps approach me, "He actually tried running away? I wonder if the rest will do the same?"

I cry out, trying to crawl away. My attempts are cut short as a boot slams into my side, flinging me over onto my back. Rain pelts my face, and the two Saints tower over my prone body. One holds the pistol that just slaughtered my family and the other grips a metal baton tightly in his right hand.

"No, please," I beg, vomit making its way up my throat. "Don't do thi—"

I puke, the stomach acid burning my mouth.

The world around me then flashes white as I feel blunt force bash into my skull. A boot follows.

Everything around me becomes disoriented as a warm liquid pours from my nose. I don't even get a second to think before the next swing of the baton comes, and this time it smacks against my jaw, forcing a booming wet snap to explode in my ears.

For the next ten seconds, there's a non-stop downpour of metal on bone. Every single hit makes the world around me turn black and white.

When the torment finally stops, the only thing visible is darkness seeping through reality at the corners of my vision.

"Put him out of his misery, Matthew," one says.

A moment later, I hear a voice, but I wish I hadn't, "May God have mercy on your soul."

My ears erupt as he fires the gun, and I'm left to drown in an ocean of darkness.

CHAPTER FIFTEEN

I don't know how my eyes open, but somehow, they do. The atmosphere makes me instantly feel bewildered. I'm standing outside of the playground that belongs to my old middle school. It's as if everything's on pause; the trees sway violently, shielding the entire school-yard. They are frozen mid-action; the gloomy clouds overhead don't seem to move an inch, and there's not a single sound to be heard.

I glance down at my body, my eyes widening as I note that my clothes are soaked with red, in fact, there's so much blood covering me it's sliding down my arms and dripping from my fingertips.

Am I dead?

I gingerly reach my hand up to my chest in an attempt to find a heartbeat.

There is none.

I carefully take a step forward, entering through the small chain-link gate that serves as an entrance to the enclosed playground. I survey the area, and as soon as my eyes meet the play structure, I realize that this *isn't* a reality. It's a memory.

On top of the fort, I see a younger version of me being

intimidated by a younger version of Jakob. They, like everything else here, are frozen in place.

Younger me wears a cocky yet horrified expression, and younger Jakob dons a mask of hatred. I remember this day *so* vividly. I forgot to bring Jakob the money I *owed* him, and by forgot, I mean I spent everything I had on lunch before the incident, but I sure didn't admit that at the time.

What am I doing here?

I head over to the stairs that lead up the fort, climbing up to the two individuals. Being here brings back so many painful memories, memories I'd love nothing more than to forget.

The scene abruptly un-pauses, causing me to flinch back in shock. The trees sway again; the clouds seem to resume soaring through the sky, and the bitter cold wind zooms past my ears.

"C'mon," Jakob shouts, bringing a fist to the younger me's face. "I *know* you have it."

"What can I say?" younger me arrogantly mutters, swiftly rubbing his cheek to soothe the pain. "I left it at home."

I've always had a bit of a cocky and defiant side, and honestly, that's probably why I got pounded all the time. I restrain that part of me now, but back then, I kind of liked being that way.

It was my way of feeling in control and leveled.

"Don't lie," Jakob backs younger me up against the guardrail. "Either you give me the money I was promised, or I fling you over the play-fort."

"I don't have your money," younger me retorts, not backing down despite being *way* smaller. "So, why don't you do me a little favor and screw off."

Jakob gets up in young me's face, "You're such a *freak*, Pinder," he abruptly picks young me up by the collar and hauls me over the guardrail. "I hope this hurts really bad."

He drops me.

I wince when my young counterpart lands awkwardly, making an awful crunching noise I can hear from all the way up here.

Jakob laughs crudely as younger me howls in agony.

The memory re-pauses, and the scene before me gradually turns white. It goes so white that my eyes instinctively clamp shut. I don't open them for a moment, but once I do, I find myself in an entirely different setting.

This time, I'm standing at the back of my government ed. classroom, and the memory causes me to blanch. The entire room is frozen in chaos. Students are wide-eyed, Mr. Cook is panicked, and a kid I used to attend school with, Damian Brung, is standing on top of his desk, his face paused in a twisted rage.

This day messed me up. This was the day they killed Damian right before my eyes.

The memory snaps to life, leaving me to relive this horrible moment I've been trying to suppress from my mind for years.

"Mr. Brung, you get down from there this instant," Mr. Cook orders

"You're all brainwashed," Damian explodes, spit flying from his mouth. "Brainwashed by these government-controlled puppets."

"Please, just get down from your desk and control yourself," Mr. Cook pleads, stepping out from behind his desk. "Don't make me call in school security."

Younger me, a freshman, stares up at Damian in shock, "What are you doing?"

"Yeah, just *stop*." shouts a younger Simon.

"You two are delusional," Damian looks over at Mr. Cook, hysteria in his blue eyes. "You're a pig. You hear me? A friggin' pig."

Suddenly, the door to the room flies open, and in storms two soldiers who are a part of the school's security team. Their guns are drawn, and even though they wear ski masks that hide most of their facial features, I can see combativeness in both of their eyes.

"What's going on in here?" one asks.

Mr. Cook points over at Damian, "This student is *out* of control. He's speaking ill of our government and rebelling."

The two Saints train their guns on Damian, and without warning, they both fill the room with gunfire, and I watch as Damian flies from his desk, fresh bullet holes littered throughout his entire body.

As soon as he slams against the floor, the memory pauses and the scene before me goes dead silent.

Seeing him die causes a certain thought to slither to the front of my mind. At first, it's silent, but its volume gradually increases.

You're dead, too, just like him.

The thought hits me like a runaway train, and before I know it, I collapse on my knees.

You're dead, you're dead, you're dead, you're dead, you're dead!

I claw at my face in an attempt to wake up from this *nightmare*, but it doesn't work.

Another blinding white light forces my eyes to clamp shut, and I'm unable to open them for what seems like minutes. However, once they cooperate and part, I find myself in yet another memory.

I watch from the back of my bedroom as a fifteen-year-old Simon and I sit at the foot of my bed. This memory is paused like all the rest, but it only takes a second for it to resume.

"He's going to pay," Simon mutters, his head lowered.

"I don't know man," I hear myself say. "This doesn't seem like a good idea. You haven't been to your house for what? Over half a year? And you're telling me that you're gonna storm in there and beat him to a pulp?"

"Yeah, that's exactly what I'm going to do," he remarks, an ominous tone to his voice. "He'll never touch me or Claire ever again."

"But what if someone calls the Saints? Then what?"

Simon shrugs, "Who cares? Look, nothing you say will change my mind. I just need to know if I can stay at your place again, tonight?"

"Of course, you can. This is all just bizarre though. First, you disappear for six months without even saying goodbye, and now you're here and want to get revenge on your dad, and– look, I just need some time to process all of this."

"I know it's a lot to take in, but I need to know that you have my back."

"You know I do. Like I said, you can stay here for as long as you'd like."

"That means a lot."

"Don't mention it."

Simon heads for the door, glancing over at me, the younger me, "I'll be back in a bit, okay?"

"Stay safe."

"I will. Trust me."

He leaves the room, then the memory pauses.

This day changed Simon's life forever; little did he know they would drag his dad out of his house covered in bullet holes, that his sister would hate him, and that his step-mom would become chronically suicidal and blame him for it.

A sudden pounding abruptly emits from inside my body, and at first, it feels foreign. But after a moment, I realize that it's my heart beating.

What's going on?

I feel my chest; the beating, pulsing through my palm.

Without a second passing by, another bright white light blinds me, causing my eyes to shut. Something's off though. This light is the brightest out of the three.

My ears ring, and next?

Nothing but horrific pain.

CHAPTER SIXTEEN

The loudest, most agonizing scream I've ever heard shoots from my throat and out my mouth as my eyes spring open. My entire body feels like it absorbed Hell itself. My upper left leg burns and stings, my right shoulder blade feels like a dull knife was shoved into it and left there for days, my entire face feels wired to the bone, and it's as if acid fills my entire stomach.

"Help me!" I howl, letting out another scream.

I'm alive.

This isn't possible.

I hastily scan the area with my dry eyes. I'm in some type of infirmary bed surrounded by white walls, white tiled floor, and a ceiling with bright white lights built into it. I attempt to sit up, but my head spins like a cyclone, and I end up plummeting from the bed onto the icy cold floor. I weakly look up. There's a metal sink attached to a wall with a mirror hanging just above it.

An ongoing chorus of groans and screams escape my mouth as I try to get to my feet, and I stumble over to the sink, a million different thoughts popping up in the prolonged process.

How can I possibly be awake? How am I not still dead? I was shot, I was killed, I'm not supposed to be alive . . . What is this?

I thoroughly examine myself in the mirror, and I'm immediately spooked by the new changes that a second life has handed me. My skin is the color of fresh snow, a very visible scar is etched onto my bare upper right chest, and as I scan my eyes down my naked body, I make out another scar the same shape as the last engraved on my left thigh.

The biggest change of all, though, is that everything is clear despite not wearing any glasses.

Warm liquid streams from my tear-ducts, and I watch in absolute shock and ample horror as blood spills from my eyes.

I freak out, swiping the backs of my hands across my cheeks in hoping to make it stop somehow, but it doesn't. Blood dribbles from my neck down to the floor, creating a sickening patter.

The sudden sight makes the contents of my stomach rush up my throat, and the next thing I know, I'm puking all over the place. The fluid from my body is shaded dark red, just like my tears.

"Don't worry," a woman's voice says from behind me. "It's just a side effect."

I swivel toward the voice. A young lady dressed in tight blue jeans and a hoodie stands in the room's doorway. She looks young, maybe in her early twenties, and has long wavy brown hair.

"Who are you?" I ask, trying to keep from retching again.

She studies me with her brown eyes, "My name's Marcy, but others around here call me Bleach. I see you finally, um . . . got up. How are you feeling?"

"How do I feel? Are you kidding me?"

She shrugs, "Just asking. I know you're probably *super* confused, right now."

"What is this place? How did I get here? How am I—"

"Alive?"

I don't reply, the finished stream of blood sticking to my cheeks.

"It's a very long story, but to sum it up, you've been given a second chance at life."

I feel more liquid rush up my throat, but I quickly swallow, "Second chance?"

Bleach flashes me a sympathetic half smile, "Like I said, a *very* long story. I'll have more time to tell you about it later. 'Till then, just take it easy. Here, uh, you might want these."

She hands me some clothes, reminding me that I've been naked this whole conversation.

My face burns as I quickly grab the clothes out of her hands, "Thanks."

"Don't worry about it," she winks at me. "Now hurry and put on some boxers, you can finish getting dressed once I show you to your dorm."

"Dorm?"

"Well, yeah. C'mon, just go with the flow and ask questions later."

I stare at her blankly, my head spinning, my stomach churning, "But–"

"Put them on."

I take a moment, but I eventually comply, silently slipping on the pair of underwear.

CHAPTER SEVENTEEN

"Welp, here we are." Bleach leads me through a pair of double doors. "Welcome to the dormitory. C'mon, your room number is twenty-seven."

From where I stand there is a massive and wide corridor with a countless number of steel doors on each end that seem to go on forever.

As we walk down the well-lit hall, Bleach gives me little tidbits of information; my thoughts jammed all throughout my mind.

"Just to give you some closure," she starts, passing the endless dorm doors. "You're in a below-ground facility."

"It looks like a school," I mutter in a daze, walking at her side.

"Yeah, sorta."

"How can I see?"

"What?"

"I've worn glasses since I was eight and now I can suddenly see *perfectly*. How?"

She snorts, "You've just been brought back from the dead and that's the first question you ask? Look, I tell you what, survive tonight's initiation, and I promise that things will become a lot less foggy."

My stomach churns, "Survive?"

Bleach laughs, now elbowing me in the side, "Just screwin' with you. For real, though, if you make it through today without messing anything up, I'll be happy to answer a few things on your mind."

My brain is on autopilot, "Alright."

Bleach leads me to my dorm room which is around the halfway mark of the corridor. She turns the silver knob and softly nudges the door open, revealing a small and practically empty room, containing a bunk-bed and dresser.

She softly shoves me inside, "Welcome to your new abode, you'll be sleeping here for the next little while. Your roommate's name is Marcus Terrell, he'll be back soon. Oh, I almost forgot, you'll hear a bell in a couple of hours. Just head down to the gymnasium when it sounds off."

"Where's the gymnasium?"

"We passed it on the way here, remember? Look, just follow the crowd," she pauses for a moment before turning away. "Well, it's been fun chatting, but I gotta go. See ya tonight. Oh, and you might also want to clean that dried blood off your cheeks. Another thing, that side effect will trigger again, and when it does, don't panic. It's normal."

Normal?

I watch as she steps away and lets the door shut on its own, leaving me in a foreign environment with nothing but questions on my mind. Questions that need to be answered before I go completely crazy.

How did this happen? I ask myself while approaching the bottom bunk and carefully sitting down onto the uncomfortably firm mattress.

None of this seems real.

I pinch my bare forearm, causing a stinging sensation to spring through me.

Definitely not dreaming.

This is all so random and dizzying. Nothing feels real, but it all somehow is.

Maybe that whole "initiation" tonight will shed some light on all of this.

I lick the palms of my hands and wipe the dried blood from my face. My mind feels fried. I look down at the clothes under my left arm. There's a folded up black hoodie, dark blue jeans, white sneakers, and fingerless black gloves. After I finish getting dressed, I lie my head down onto the firm pillow and slowly close my eyes.

My thoughts drift to my death. One of the Saints spoke to the other before I was killed.

"Put him out of his misery, Matthew."

Matthew. . . I'll remember that name.

I've never felt this well rested before in my entire life, but I still manage to let myself slowly drift off to sleep, hoping deep down that when I wake up, I'll be in my own bed.

CHAPTER EIGHTEEN

The door abruptly shutting forces my eyes open. A massive kid stares at me from the front of the room. He looks around my age wearing the same attire as me, black hoodie, jeans, white sneakers, and all that.

"You're on my bunk," he spits, staring me down with murky brown eyes.

"What?" I ask, his anger throwing me off guard.

"Did I stutter?"

"Maybe."

He storms up to the bunk, lifting me up off the mattress and into the air, "You gonna be smart with me?"

I chuckle, "You have a problem with keeping your hands to yourself, don't you?"

He throws me down to the floor, the harsh impact sending jolts of pain down my back and knocking the wind out of me, "They just *had* to pair me up with someone like you. A friggin' retard who doesn't know when to shut his *fat* mouth."

I fight to take a breath, staring up at him, "I get that a lot."

"Better learn some manners, because I'll beat you into next week, freak."

I ignore his threat, trying to regroup my thoughts, "You must be Marcus."

He grunts in annoyance, "And you must be Jason. *Pleasure* to meet you. Now get off the floor, get up into your bed, and shut your mouth."

I glare at him, "Sure thing, *pal.*"

He plops down onto the lower bunk before proceeding to wipe the sweat from his brow. He looks as if he'll rip me apart if I say anything else, so I get up off the floor and climb to the top bunk.

Once I get all situated, and the pain in my back simmers down, I stare up at the ceiling, allowing my mind to wander all over the place. None of this seems real, but somehow, it all is. It's like my body is in denial; it won't face the facts.

They murdered my parents and me, I should be six feet under, but somehow, I'm not.

Matthew . . . Matthew.

I won't forget that name.

I sigh and turn over, facing the wall.

It's hard to process that just a little while ago, I was sneaking out past curfew with Simon and heading over to The Manor. Now I'm here, lying in an unfamiliar bed in an unfamiliar environment.

For the next bit, I zone in and out of consciousness. Whenever I'm awake, my thoughts overwhelm me with hundreds of questions. When I'm sleeping, I dream about my parents' death. The image of them being executed is branded onto my eyelids, never letting me escape the geysers of scarlet that poured from their penetrated skulls.

"Put him out of his misery, Matthew."

A sudden deafening alarm chirps throughout the entire room. I flinch and almost bang my head against the bed railing. The alarm lasts about twenty seconds before fading into nothing, leaving an eerie silence in the air.

The bed below me shifts around as Marcus rises to his feet, "C'mon, we have initiation to go to. I don't know what's going on, but I rather not anger these people, so you better not do anything to screw me over, or else I'll–"

"Yeah, I get it," I mutter before leaping down to the floor, "Let's go."

THE GYMNASIUM IS MASSIVE, RESEMBLING THE ONE AT Lakeshore High almost entirely. The differences are few but noticeable. Toward the front lies a podium, no bleachers, and placed toward the back is a large boxing ring with a metal cage suspended over it. Steel cables are used to keep it at its altitude.

Marcus and I stand near the front of the enormous crowd forming in the gym's dead-center. Bleach quickly gets behind the podium and addresses us all. She tells us that a man will be here soon to erase some questions we've had on our minds. After that, she steps aside and ignores those in the mass that demand answers immediately.

The tension seems to grow as the minutes fly by, at least twenty kids in the crowd are screaming at Bleach, begging for some answers. Just as the tension reaches its peak, the doors at the other side of the room swing open. We all turn our heads toward the interjection in unison, and instantly my jaw slides ajar with surprise.

No friggin' way.

"Welcome," Tommy steps into the gym and over toward the podium, a scowl glued to his face that's sprinkled with blood. "Sorry, I know I'm late. Just sorting out some . . . affairs."

He steps up behind the podium, grabbing a tissue from his pocket and ridding the scarlet speckles from his face.

I'm in Hell.

"Well," he starts, stuffing the tissue into his pocket and rolling up the sleeves on his black turtleneck. "Let me start this initiation off by saying one little thing: I *don't* tolerate disrespect. So, if you yell and scream at me like you did with Bleach, you'll regret it. Do I make myself clear?"

There's a wave of nods that surf their way through the crowd, so he continues.

"Some of you may have heard of me before. Name's Thomas Price. I won't go into any backstory; all you need to know is that I'm one of the leaders here."

"But where's *here*?" some kid in the large gathering blurts out.

Tommy snorts, which turns into a little chuckle, "You're all in an underground facility that belongs to Lazarus, an organization I'm sure you've all heard about in the news."

It goes silent as he finishes his sentence.

Lazarus, the terrorist group that's been causing mass chaos around the United States for the past few years. The group notorious for assassinating political figures, murdering and torturing Saints, and attempting to take out the President.

"The time is now yours to ask questions," Tommy states. "Just raise your hand, and I'll call on you one at a time, alright? You aren't little kids, so be patient."

Every single hand in the crowd, including my own, raises into the air faster than a bullet. Tommy's eyes go wide with what looks like excitement. After a moment, he points toward a brunette girl in the middle.

She lowers her hand before speaking, "How am I alive? I was shot in the head."

Tommy stares at the girl, an amused look on his face, "How are *any* of you alive? You all were brutally murdered one way or another, right? Look, you were all brought back from the grave. Now, please no more questions involving your deaths. We'll go into that a bit later."

The next hour, words are exchanged in a nonstop parade. Tommy points to every raised hand in the gymnasium, and near the end of the session I feel dumbstruck.

Apparently, Lazarus has chosen all of us to be part of their *Beta program.* Kids ages sixteen to nineteen will become a part of the organization and trained in an attempt to see if we'll make for stronger, faster, and more agile members who can contribute more to Lazarus' revolt against our nation.

As I piece this information together, my heart beats rapidly. Chills slide down my spine, I get goosebumps, not to mention the sudden urge to vomit.

This is utterly insane.

"We're outta time," Tommy says upon answering the last question. "Bleach will quickly run you guys through tomorrow's schedule and all the rules here. I will see you all around. Welcome to Lazarus."

With that, he steps away from the podium, walks across the gymnasium and out a pair of double doors. Throughout the gym, there are four sets of doors, each one leads into a different part of the facility. I know that one set leads to the dormitory, and another leads to the infirmary I woke up in. The rest remain uncharted.

Bleach approaches the podium and flashes us all a smile, "There's a schedule in each of your dorm rooms that will notify you all about tomorrow's list of events. The rules are printed on the back. With that being said, it's time to head back."

We all just stare at her, the information still settling uneasily in our guts. After a moment, one teen in the crowd walks toward the set of doors that leads to the dormitory. I assume that his roommate is the one to follow him, causing the others to mindlessly follow.

Marcus and I follow the long line streaming through the double doors, not muttering a word to each other. Once we get to our room, I pull open the heavy door and climb up on the top bunk, releasing a long exhale as my head touches the firm yet comfortable pillow.

I can't think straight. My mind is swirling, and I have a massive migraine.

"You forgetting something?" Marcus tosses a piece of paper up at me, it floats gently down onto my stomach. "It's the schedule. Look it over then hand it down to me."

I grab the piece of paper and sigh. Like usual, every sentence is a blob of ink, and I can't make out a single word.

They fixed my vision, but not my dyslexia.

I focus on the schedule, trying my best to make out the printed words.

Five minutes pass of hard concentration. Marcus yelling at me to hurry doesn't help. I'm finally able to make out the front page. As of tomorrow, we'll start a group of classes. None consists of *anything* academic.

I look over my assigned classes. My knotted thoughts keep threatening to explode inside my head like an aneurysm. All of this is crazy.

The Lazarus Guide:

1: The elevator is off limits (those that attempt to escape will be met with lethal force).

2: You must comply with all instructors in this institution, no questions asked.

3: Those who disobey orders will find their consequences to be quite harsh.

4: If you kill a fellow recruit (without being commanded to) you will be severely punished.

5: Lights out at 10:30.

Lazarus is looking out for your best interest. Follow all of these rules and you'll fit in just fine at this establishment ~ Bleach

"I'M DONE," I MUMBLE, MY VISION WHACKY AFTER reading so much.

"About time," Marcus reaches his hand up from the bottom bunk. "Gimme it."

I hand it to him, lying my head back down onto my pillow.

I'm dazed. The fact that I'll never see my family or friends again causes a slight numbing feeling to overtake me. The moment my eyes shut, I hear the words, "Put him out of his misery, Matthew."

CHAPTER NINETEEN

Warm water sputters from the shower head and onto my back. The events from earlier this morning still fresh in my memory.

After everyone woke up, Bleach led us all on a tour, and I got a good look at the entire facility. There are four sectors. A, Z, K, and T.

Sector A is one of the larger parts of the facility, and it's where the showers, cafeteria, bathrooms, and laundry are located.

Sector Z is the second largest part of the facility. It's where the infirmary, weapon cache, and instructor dorms are located.

Sector K is actually pretty small. It's just a long corridor where the classrooms, weight room, and the elevator with cherry red doors are located.

And finally, there's Sector T. It's the dormitory, nothing else to it.

I'll be heading over to Sector K after my shower for my first class, *firearms*.

How long do you really think you'll last in here? I mean, firearms? Combat? The art of torture? Stealth training? Gadget education? You've never even held a gun in your life, let alone used one to take away someone's life. You will die in here.

I let out a groan before resting my head up against the shower stall. There's a depressing vibe lingering throughout the area. The only audible sounds are the running water splashing against the tiled floor and the occasional sob from terrified individuals.

I glance down at the back of my pale hands, hoping deep down that the washed-out color won't be permanent. Upon examining my skin, I bring the tip of my index finger to the scar on my upper chest. The bullet that had caused it entered through my shoulder blade, so I'm assuming an identical scar is etched there as well. I remember there being a third shot before I died, the finishing blow that robbed me from life, but where did it make an impact?

I feel all over my face, it only makes sense that the scar would be somewhere around there. To my surprise, I'm not able to identify anything, so I slide my fingertips down lower, feeling around my neck.

Bingo.

Branded at the center of my throat, is another small scar. I don't know why, but finding it relieves a tiny fragment of stress in my chest.

Some time goes by before I turn the hot water off. I grab the white towel that hangs over the stall and take my time tying it around my waist before exiting the shower curtain.

About thirty guys with towels wrapped around their bodies wander around. They all have the same bewildered expression glued to their faces.

I make sure my towel is secure before walking over to the massive rectangular mirror that many others are loitering at. Below the mirror lies a long marble counter with a row of built in sinks. I fix my wet and messy hair when a sudden eruption in the room startles the crap out of me.

My eyes snap over to two guys toward the back, engaging in a fight. They're throwing punches and kicks. I avoid watching as the fight grows more violent, and instead focus on my pale face. My drenched dirty blonde bangs partially obstruct my sight, so I flip them to the side.

"No way. . ." I hear a voice from behind me mumble in awe. "Jason?"

My eyebrow raises at hearing my name. Simon's reflection is in the mirror standing right behind me. He looks as white as a vampire, same as everybody else.

"Simon?" I gawk. "Dude, what are you doing here?"

"I could ask you the same thing," he says.

"Well," I start, smoothing a hand through my wet hair. "I was killed, and so were my mom and dad, and the next thing I know, I'm here," I pause a moment, staring at the scar etched across his throat. "What happened to you?"

"What do you mean?"

"It looks like someone sliced your throat open."

"I don't really remember. I was sleeping when some noise woke me up, and the second my eyes opened, I felt something sharp slide across my throat. Then, I woke up on one of those infirmary beds in Sector Z."

"Two soldiers." I pause, the memory making my heart ache unlike yesterday. "Two soldiers shot my mom, then my dad, then they came after me."

"That's just . . . crazy. I'm sorry, Jay."

The two of us stay quiet for a moment.

"Dude, what's up with Tommy being in charge here?" I ask him, trying to expel the memory of being murdered from my mind. "He's a Saint. Well, at least he *was* before they killed him in that shooting at Lakeshore."

"Wait, Tommy was *killed*? When?"

"The night Brandon was executed."

Simon steps to my side. He looks into the mirror and messes with his hair, looking as if he wants to change the conversation.

"So, who's your roommate?" he eventually mumbles.

"Some douche named Marcus," I reply, my voice laced with bitterness. "He's a try-hard half-wit who thinks he's top dog. What about you? Who's your roommate? Is he cool?"

"Yeah, *she's* awesome."

"Whoa, you gotta girl?"

"Uh-huh. I think you might like her."

"Bet I will."

He pauses, "Lazarus . . . we were just talking about them the other night, and here we are now."

A sudden voice booms from the P.A. system, interrupting my thoughts.

"Attention all rookies. Classes will start in fifteen minutes. I repeat, fifteen minutes. Get out of the showers and get dressed into your uniforms, *ASAP*."

Simon exhales a long breath, "What's your first class?"

"Firearms. You?"

"Firearms."

I grin, and he does the same. We both head over to a large shelf near the back of the room that's full of cubbies where clean uniforms are stored. I grab a black hoodie and a pair of jeans that are my size before acquiring a pair of socks and my white sneakers.

Simon and I exit the showers. It's sort of like old times, walking to class and discussing a plan on how to survive this new reality. Sort of.

CHAPTER TWENTY

Simon and I choose seats at the back of the classroom. The room has no windows, the whole facility being underground and all. There's a long, wide table placed in the front with various firearms littered across its smooth, black surface.

Our instructor, Feline, stands at the front of the classroom with her arms folded. She wears the same uniform as the rest of us. There's something that's off about her, though. Her eyes. They are bright yellow, resembling those of a cat. I guess that's where her name comes from.

If I'm being honest, it kind of makes me feel uneasy.

Feline turns her back to us, picking something up from the table, "Who here is afraid of guns?"

Most of the students raise their hands.

She turns back around, a pistol gripped tightly in her right hand, "Understandable. They taught all of you to believe guns are despicable if used by the general population. Luckily, by the time you pass this class, you'll *love* these little things," she approaches one kid toward the front and places the gun on her desk. "What's your name?"

"Um," the girl strokes her auburn hair. "I'm Callie."

"Well, Callie, I want you to pick up that handgun, alright?"

The girl complies. She grabs the gun by its handgrip and lifts it from the desk trying not to point the muzzle at Feline.

"Good. Now tell me, how do you feel about the object in your hands?"

"It's kinda heavy."

"Does it spark any emotion?"

"It makes me feel anxious."

"Why?"

"It can hurt people."

Feline studies Callie for a moment before taking the gun from her hands, "Thank you for the cooperation."

For the next twenty minutes, she goes up to each individual student and has them hold the gun, asking them the same questions she asked Callie. Some feared the gun, but others actually felt empowered by it. I'm at the back of the class, so I go last.

Feline steps to my desk, staring at me before setting the pistol down, "Pick it up."

My heart accelerates as I grip the object by its handle and lift it from the wooden surface. It isn't as heavy as I expected it to be. It also seems to fit perfectly in my hands.

"Thoughts?" Feline asks.

"It's light, and it doesn't feel awkward to hold."

"Does it spark any emotion?"

"It makes me feel, I don't know, a little excited, to be honest."

"Hmm," she studies me thoroughly. "Why so?"

"I can't really explain it. Sorry."

Feline's parts her lips to speak, but the door suddenly opens.

I look over at the doorway.

No freaking way.

Standing in the doorway, is a girl with jet black hair, amber eyes, and skin just as white as mine. She's unmistakably Mae.

"Sorry I'm late," she says, looking tense. "I got a little lost."

"What's your name?" Feline asks, her arms folded.

"Mae Bernhard."

Feline slowly approaches her, and to my surprise, she slaps her across the face with her palm. Mae's head lurches to the side. Rubbing her cheek, she looks more embarrassed than before.

"Show up late again, and I'll snap a finger. Go take a seat."

Mae sheepishly nods before heading over to the desk on my left. She sits down, but doesn't acknowledge me in the slightest.

I want to say I'm shocked, but that would be a lie. If Simon's here, then why not her?

"Sorry about that interruption," Feline strides back to me. "I forgot to ask for your name."

"Oh, it's Jason. Jason Pinder," I reply, eyeing the gun still placed on my desk.

Out of the corner of my left eye, I see Mae's head whip toward me. Her eyes are wide, but not with fear. Her jaw drops, and the feeling emitting from her makes me think she's *excited*.

"Well, Jason, thanks for the cooperation," Feline takes the weapon off my desk and immediately sets it over next to Mae. "Pick up the gun."

I zone out as she's questioned about her feelings on the gun.

You've been murdered, brought back to life, been picked to be a part of a beta group of political anarchists, and to top it all off, your best friend and the smoking hot girl you have puppy eyes for is here.

I grin.

CHAPTER TWENTY-ONE

For the rest of firearms, Feline taught us every part to a basic 9mm handgun, and to tell the truth, I'm fascinated with it all. She told us all that tomorrow we'll be firing the same gun we held today. I didn't bring it up, but I'm curious where we'll be firing. If I remember correctly, there's no shooting range in the facility.

I guess I'll find out tomorrow morning.

I'm leaving the classroom with the rest of the recruits when someone runs up from behind and greets me with a tight embrace.

I turn around after she lets go and hug her right back, holding tight. The two of us don't speak for a moment. I take a step back, Mae smiles.

"I can't believe you're here too," she says. "I thought I was all alone."

"Why were you so late to class?" I ask, not knowing how to reply to her statement.

The smile drops from her face, "Can we talk about that out in the hall?"

A spark of uneasiness surges through my chest, but I ignore it,

"Sure, but only for a minute or two. I don't want you to be late to your second class."

The two of us head out into the large corridor of Sector K. A few other kids are talking to one another in hushed whispers.

"So, what happened?" I ask, raising an eyebrow.

"I was looking for a way out of here," she leans in closer, the dark fabric from our hoodies touching. "Promise you won't tell?"

I give her a strange look, "I'm not going to rat you out, but why would you do that?"

"Because, Jason. I don't know about you, but I'm not fit for all this. Me? In a terrorist group? Yeah, not gonna happen."

A sudden chuckle escapes my mouth. The way she said that was so cute.

"This isn't funny. I don't want to be caught up in all of this. Yes, I understand why they're trying to take out President Mills, but I'm not gonna join some uprising to overthrow him. That's *insane.*"

"Okay, fine, let's say you somehow find a way out of here," I say, "You're dead to the outside world, remember? It's not like you can go back to being normal. We're the opposite of normal, I mean, we were just brought back from the dead. Plus, if they catch you trying to escape, they'll kill you."

"But—"

"No buts. Face it, Mae, you won't make it out of here alive."

She looks surprised, "So you're okay with all this? Becoming a terrorist?"

"I never said that," I correct. "I just said that trying to leave this place isn't a good idea. Look, we better head to our next classes. Wanna meet up at lunch?"

She looks lost for words, "Guess so. See you then."

I watch her walk off. The disappointment in her eyes makes me feel guilty, but what was I supposed to say? Escaping, no matter how rational it may sound to her, is stupid. Giving her false hope will only get her killed for a *second* time.

My next class is combat. The classroom, if you can even call it that, has dark oak flooring and walls the color of ash. There is a large blue mat dead center of the room, and our instructor stands on top.

He oddly doesn't wear the Lazarus uniform. Instead, he dons jet black athletic shorts, has his knuckles wrapped, and wears no shirt.

"Listen up, grave walkers, I'm Lynch," he says. "I'm just gonna cut to the chase. Who're the two strongest kids, here?"

Circling the massive mat that takes up a good portion of the room, we all glance at one another, seeking the toughest-looking kids.

Why's that idiot gotta be here? I ask myself as my eyes find Marcus.

He's standing directly across from me, and the second his brown eyes meet mine, he scowls, mouthing the words, "Kill yourself."

I glare.

I can predict with confidence he'll be one kid who gets picked. I mean, people call me a big guy, but Marcus is bigger. He's *at least* six-foot-four, not to mention he looks like a gym rat.

About a minute goes by with nothing but silence before Lynch clears his throat. "You," he points to Marcus and then to another kid. "And you. Come over here."

The two of them do as they're told.

Lynch backs up off the mat and next to a few recruits, "Alright, this is how things will play out. You two will fight until one of you is incapable of going on. Any questions?"

"Wait, why?" the kid who was called up with Marcus questions.

"What's your name?"

"Bryan."

Lynch's gaze narrows, "I wanna see who my strongest student is. That clear enough for you, Bryan?"

"But this isn't—"

Marcus' fist stops the sentence from being finished. A sudden spark of excitement shoots through the crowd that walls off any chance for the two to escape.

"Wh—" Bryan looks stunned, trying to recover. "I wasn't ready, you jerk."

Marcus sneers, "You talk too much."

He throws another punch that connects to Bryan's nose, causing his head to snap upwards and to the side.

I look over at Lynch; he has a twistedly amused smile planted on his face.

"C'mon," Marcus laughs, tossing Bryan to the ground before proceeding to stomp on his ribs. "Is this all you've got?"

He gasps for air, his eyes wide, "Dude, *sto*—"

Marcus grabs Bryan's collar with one hand and beats him with the other. The scene is all too familiar. My mind flashes to all the times I've been in Bryan's position, getting beat to a pulp and feeling nothing but hopeless.

"You're so *weak*," Marcus says, letting go of his victim's shirt. "You haven't even thrown one punch."

The look on Bryan's face twists into a mask of hatred, "I'm going to hurt you *so* bad."

"That's kinda what I'm waiting for."

Bryan, who's still lying flat on his back, lets out a low-pitched growl before jumping to his feet and throwing a balled-up fist into Marcus' throat.

He gags while stumbling back, "See," he wheezes, which eventually turns into a chuckle. "Now was that so hard?"

Bryan glowers with a dark expression, "Screw you."

Marcus looks thrilled, regrouping, "C'mon. Throw another one."

Bryan lets out another low-pitched growl before rushing him. He throws his knuckles at Marcus' face, but to everyone's surprise, Marcus catches Bryan's fist mid-air and throws it away before kneeing him in the gut.

Bryan gasps for air, collapsing back down to the mat.

"I'm getting tired of this," Lynch snaps. "Just finish the fight."

"With pleasure," Marcus lets out a snarky grin, meeting eyes with his opposer. "Light's out, buddy."

He rams the heel of his foot into Bryan's face, causing him to go limp.

As much as I hate the guy, I would never want to go up against him. I mean, I can just imagine all the things he'd do to break me.

I better stop getting on his bad side.

Lynch walks back out onto the mat, eyeing the mass of recruits circling him, "Who wants to go next? I want to see if anyone can take this freak down."

Marcus takes visible pride from Lynch's words.

"What . . . no volunteers?" he sighs. "Guess I'll just have to pick one of you sorry saps."

My heart skips a beat as he scans each of us. He starts with the nearest kid to him, examining his body thoroughly before moving onto the girl beside him, repeating the same process.

You better not pick me.

After a few moments of suspense, he finally chooses Marcus' next victim.

"You." Lynch shoots anxiety into my veins. "I pick you."

He points his index finger in my direction, but a girl next to me steps forward.

She looks to be around five-foot-nine. Her hair is long and light blonde, and her emerald green eyes tensely glance around.

"What's your name?" Lynch asks.

"Chloe," the girl replies.

"Okay, Chloe, well you know what to do," he grabs Bryan by the feet and drags him off the mat. "Let me move him, then you two can start the fight."

Chloe doesn't look like she can keep still, she keeps tapping her foot and swaying her arms slowly back and forth, "Do I really have to? This isn't even a fair lineup."

"Think I care?" Lynch asks, hauling Bryan to the back of the room. "Put your big girl pants on, and suck it up, buttercup."

She doesn't argue anymore. Instead, she does as she's told and steps out in front of Marcus. I switch my gaze between the both of them. Their difference in height is almost comical.

She's inevitably about to get the crap beaten out of her.

Lynch walks back to his spot in the crowd that surrounds the mat, another amused smile planted on his face, "Okay, you two, you may begin."

"You gotta be kiddin' me with this," Marcus' laugh makes me want to knock his teeth out. "Her? You want me to fight her? Gimme a break."

Without warning, he grabs Chloe by the neck, lifts her up off the ground, and violently throws her down onto the mat.

She lands on her back, all the air forced from her lungs.

"Making me fight a stupid, little, dumb blonde?" Marcus bends over, grabs Chloe by the neck once more, and lifts her back up into the air. "You have to be screwing with me, right?"

He bashes his fist into her nose, making her cry out.

This whole scene makes my chest fill with fiery anger, but I'm powerless. I could go out and try to help and ultimately get my butt handed to me. Not to mention probably getting in trouble, but it isn't worth it. I don't even know who this girl is.

Chloe's legs flail around as Marcus wraps his other hand around her throat and chokes her. She struggles, but within a matter of seconds, she grows motionless.

After she's unconscious, Marcus throws her back down onto the ground.

Lynch walks onto the mat, staring down at Chloe's motionless body, "You're pretty rough, aren't you?"

Marcus doesn't respond, he stands there with a stupid look of pride stuck to his face.

"Well, clearly nobody's going to beat you, so I might as well do it myself."

"Wait, what?"

My eyes go broad and a little smile creeps its way onto my face as Lynch abruptly crashes his elbow into Marcus' chin, making him instantly crumple to the floor next to Chloe.

He gives none of us a chance to process this before abruptly straddling my roommate and beating him unconscious; the bandages wrapped around his knuckles turning red with blood.

Holy crap.

Lynch gradually gets to his feet and breathes. The rest of us stare at him blankly, all silent and refusing to utter a single word.

"I want all of you to find a partner," he says, grabbing Marcus by the legs and dragging him away from the mat. "Trust me, you're all going to look bloody after this class, but you better get used to it."

The crowd disperses and everybody finds themselves a partner for whatever Lynch has planned for us. I find a kid named Keagan. He's a tall but scrawny sixteen-year-old who looks like he wants to rip my throat out. I'm guessing he's just trying to look tough. He looks like a complete pansy.

Lynch drags Chloe off the mat before telling us all to line up across from our partners. We all do as we're told before he tells us all to engage in a fistfight.

This will be easy. I tell myself as Lynch counts down from three. *This kid looks like he's never been in any sort of fight before.*

"Go," Lynch barks.

I throw the first punch.

CHAPTER TWENTY-TWO

My knockout punch to Keagan's jaw forced a tooth from his mouth. I didn't even think I hit that hard. I bruised my knuckles. He got a good hit to my eye which made it blacken a little, and I got tired. Either it was a superb punch, or that kid never brushes his teeth. Lynch pulled me to the side afterward and poured a bunch of rubbing alcohol over the little gash on one of my knuckles, telling me I received a fight bite. He gave me some antibiotics and told me I'd be fine.

I'm in Sector A enjoying lunch in the large and spacious cafeteria. Simon and I alone occupy a table. We're both eating these square-shaped pizza slices. They taste kinda funny.

"How was your second class?" he asks.

I shrug, "It was . . . interesting."

"What do you mean?"

"They paired us up and had us beat our partners to a pulp."

"You won, though, right?"

"Well, yeah."

"Okay good. I couldn't be seen with a loser."

"Shut up."

He pauses for a second, "This is so bizarre."

"What do you mean?" I ask, taking a bite out of my lunch.

"We're practically enrolled in an underground high school."

"Yeah, you're right."

A girl's voice comes from my left, "Hey, do you two mind if I take a seat?"

I'm surprised as Simon invites Chloe to sit next to him, introducing her as his roommate.

"Roommate?" I ask. "This is her?"

Chloe sits down next to him with her lunch tray, "Yep, that would be me."

Her nose looks red, and there's slight bruising around her neck from where Marcus choked her. She looks to be in a lot of pain but is trying to hide it.

"Hey, I remember you," she says after a moment. "You were standing right next to me in combat."

I nod, wearing a sympathetic smile, "Uh-huh. Sorry you had to go up against Marcus."

"Marcus? Man, even his name sounds douchey," she rolls her eyes. "Well, I'm Chloe."

She balls her hand up into a fist and extends it out a little.

I answer by bumping her knuckles with my own.

"Jason," I say. "Nice to meet you."

"I'm gonna go out on a limb and assume you know Simon?"

"Since we were kids."

"That's cool," she picks her pizza up and takes a bite out of it. "You guys are lucky to have each other in a place like this."

Simon takes another swig of water, "No denying it."

"Hey," Mae's sudden appearance startles me. "Can I sit next to you?"

I glance over, "Yeah, sure," I scoot over, bringing my tray with me. "How was your class?"

"It was good, I guess," she sits down next to me before eyeing Chloe. "Who's she?"

"I'm Chloe," she reaches her fist out like she did with me, but Mae ignores it.

"I'm Mae."

Chloe lowers her hand, "Mae? That's a really pretty name."

She seems surprised by the compliment, "Oh, thank you."

"You're welco—"

Screams interrupt the entire cafeteria. I cringe.

Behind me, one recruit stands up on a table with a pocket knife up to his throat. His eyes are puffy, and I can see bloody tear-tracks on his flushed cheeks. I recognize him. It's Bryan, the kid who Marcus beat before Chloe.

"Get one of the instructors," he hisses, the knife trembling in his grip. "Do it, now!"

One of the girls at his table rushes out of the cafeteria.

"What are you doing?" a kid hollers from across the room.

"What do you think I'm doing, *you idiot?*" Bryan retorts.

"He must've snapped after this morning," Chloe says in a hushed tone. "Poor guy."

"Wait, what happened?" Mae asks, not taking her eyes off of Bryan.

I look at her, "He got his face pounded."

"C'mon," another random kid mockingly shouts. "If you're too scared to last in here, then just do it already. *Nobody's* gonna miss a loser like you."

The doors to the cafeteria burst open. Tommy and Feline quickly approach the end of Bryan's table. The looks on their faces are intimidating.

"What do you think you're doing?" Tommy asks, his teeth clenched. "What is this? Some publicity stunt?"

"Let me out of here," Bryan demands. "Let me out of here or else I swear I'll kill myself!"

"Oh, you might wanna hurry then," Feline chuckles. "Because if you don't, we'll have to do it for you."

Bryan lowers the knife from his throat, his eyes widening, "Wait, what?"

Tommy reaches into his back pocket, "You don't have the guts kid, I know that just by looking at your face. You think that if you threaten to commit suicide that we'll just let you go? I *don't* tolerate this kinda crap, and neither does Lazarus."

He pulls a handgun out of his back pocket and swiftly aims it up at Bryan's head.

"No, no," he throws his hands in front of his face to shield himself. "I'm *sorry—*"

Screams echo throughout the cafeteria as Tommy lowers the pistol to Bryan's kneecaps. My entire body flinches as two gunshots explode into the air. The screams reach a crescendo as Bryan collapses off the lunch table and to the floor in agony.

Tommy approaches the downed recruit and flies his black, steel-toed boot into his face repeatedly until he passes out, blood soaking his hair, mouth, and jeans.

Feline then grabs him by the feet and drags his limp body across the cafeteria and out the doors that lead to the infirmary, leaving the entire room in an eerie silence.

"Are you kidding me?" Tommy yells, spit flying from his mouth.

A few of the girls in the cafeteria sob.

"Do any of you understand what's going on out there, right now?" Tommy continues, pacing around the entire room. "We're under a *nasty* dictatorship. People are dying every day. You're all dead to the outside world. There's *no* going back to a normal life. We here at Lazarus have given every one of you a second chance, and you're all treating it like it's *nothing!*" he stops pacing and takes a deep breath. "You've all *seen* what our government does, so why are you trying so hard to get back out on the streets? They've killed you, they've killed your families, yet you all have the nerve to go back and continue this vicious cycle? How freaking *pathetic!*"

"Wait," a recruit speaks up, her voice a little squeak compared to Tommy's. "Our families are dead too?"

A wave of murmurs swim through the cafeteria, causing Tommy's expression to harden even more than it was, "Yes, each of your families were murdered. The Saints went on a mass killing spree, ordered by President Mills himself. They were purging certain areas in Boston. Now will you all shut up and stop crying? You're all going to be a part of Lazarus for crying out loud!"

The whole room goes quiet.

"Get back to your lunches," Tommy takes a few more deep breaths. "The next recruit who tries rebelling against us will be shot in the head. Mark my words." He exits the cafeteria, leaving the entire area speechless.

Chloe exchanges looks with all of us, "He's really pissed off, isn't he?"

Mae buries her face across the table-top. "This can't be happening."

I can hear her cry.

"Are you going to be okay?" I ask, still trying to process everything that just happened.

She looks up at me, blood streaming from her eyes. I recoil, but I soon remember that crying blood is one of those side effects, "I know I died, but I thought my family was still out there."

Simon swears under his breath, "You think they only killed the people in Boston? Or did they kill *everyone* related to us? Why purge only some of the population? What did we do?"

"I don't know, man," our eyes meet, and I can tell he's about to freak out. "Let's just hope the murders were based here. That's what Tommy said."

"Wait, am I the only one who saw my family get killed?" Chloe asks, the subject making her seem more vulnerable as the words come out of her mouth.

"No, I watched my parents get shot," I mumble. The familiar

stinging sensation of guilt and sadness in my chest is noticeably absent. I feel numb.

For a moment, we all listen to the hushed whispers that surround us.

"We need to get out of here," Mae brings up the subject of escape, again. "I won't believe it until I see it. I need to know if my family is dead."

"They are," I say.

"How do you know?" Her eyes are puffy and rosy tears are tracking down her cheeks.

"Like I just said, I saw my family get executed."

"Same," Chloe mutters.

Mae fixes her bangs out of her eyes, "What if it only happened to you guys? We've got to at least try finding out the absolute truth, right?"

"No," Chloe shakes her head. "Jason and I are right. They're all dead. I'm sorry."

"You know," Mae's voice reeks of frustration. "It's really starting to sound like the three of you love it here; like you want to become a member of this crazy group."

"Oh, shut up," Simon says. "Are you seriously *this* dense? Face it, princess, your rich father probably got offed in his sleep, same with your mother, and if you have any siblings, know they're most likely dead, too."

"Guys, stop it," Chloe demands, switching her gaze back and forth between Simon and Mae. "I know emotions are running high right now, but we all just need to cool off, okay?"

"Oh, look, the pretty blonde girl is trying to unite us all," Mae says bitterly. "You're probably just as stupid as you look."

Simon snorts, "Pretty funny coming from the most popular *slut* at Lakeshore High. I bet that you slept your way into the twelfth grade. Everyone knows you're just about as bright as a burnt-out lightbulb."

Chloe bursts out with laughter, and Mae just scowls.

"All of you need to stop," I say, grabbing their attention. "You guys are acting like a bunch of three-year-olds. I mean, seriously, do you three not realize where we are? None of us are going to stay alive if we keep acting *so* dumb."

Mae's expression falls, "You're right. I'm sorry, Chloe."

Chloe shrugs, also looking solemn, "No problem. Sorry for laughing."

The three of us look over at Simon, waiting for the last apology, but it doesn't come. Instead, he catches me completely off guard.

"Crap. Mae's right."

"Really?" Mae asks, beaming with excitement.

"Huh?" I gawk.

"I haven't seen Julie in here at all, and if she's still out there, she'll think I'm dead. I have to go find her and let her know that I'm still alive."

"That plan is absolutely stupid," exasperation dripping from my words.

"Your point?"

"My point?" I let out a humorless chuckle. "My point is, that this'll get you killed, again."

"Yeah, I'm with Jason. That idea's insane," Chloe remarks.

"Who cares if it's insane?" Mae argues. "Staying in this place is psychotic. I'm going with Simon."

Simon looks at me, "I'm leaving in the morning."

"In the morning? Are you crazy?"

"No, but I want you to come with me."

"I can't."

"What's stopping you?"

"First of all, I like *living*. Second of all, I need a legit reason to go. I have *nothing* out there. My parents are dead, and as far as the outside world is concerned, so am I."

"Again," Chloe butts in. "He's right. How do you think the

public will act when they see a dead person walking around town?"

"They can act however they want," he shrugs. "Bottom line is that I'm going to find her."

"Who's *her*?" Chloe asks. "Who's this Julie person?"

"His girlfriend," I say.

"This is all for a girl?" Chloe rolls her eyes. "You kiddin' me?"

Simon glances down, "*She* isn't the only reason I'm leaving."

"Well, then what's the other?"

The long chime of the bell rings out.

"Time for third period," he mutters instead.

The four of us exchange no more words. We stand from the table with our empty trays before putting them away with the rest of the recruits. Before leaving the cafeteria, I glance over at the table where Bryan was shot. There's still blood pooled on the floor, and a long streak of it leads out of the doors that Feline dragged him through.

Simon and Mae will end up just like him, but worse, if they try leaving in the morning.

CHAPTER TWENTY-THREE

For my third class, I have the art of torture. When I walk in, the whole class is tense; Tommy is our instructor. At the front of the room there's a man tied to a wooden chair with a sack over his head. Tommy explains that we have a special "guest" and that today we will witness a torture session.

He pulls the sack off, and to my surprise, it's a gagged and blindfolded Saint.

I watch Tommy beat, maim, and break the soldier all before the class ends.

For my fourth class, I have stealth-training. Our instructor teaches us how to sneak around making no noise, how to successfully and quietly take someone out, and how to jump and land alerting no one; which is actually fun. This class is my favorite so far.

My fifth and final class of the day is gadget education. I learn the most in this class. It was incredibly interesting.

Our instructor shows us a Ceeax. It's a light sphere-shaped metal contraption. There's a small button on top, and once you press it, you toss it into an area where there are security cameras. Not only does it disable the cameras, but it also erases the previous hour of footage. The downside would have to be the noise it gives off once activated. I can only describe it as an ear-splitting shriek, but it's far worse.

Toward the end of class, I get into a little fight with Marcus. He's being a snobby little freak as usual, so we exchange a few words. I get a little arrogant, and we end up getting physical. Our instructor calls Bleach in to escort me out since I *technically* started it. I think I will be beaten, or worse, but walking down the hall she tells me she's taking me to her room so we could talk and settle down.

"Here we are," Bleach stops in front of a metal door with her name stenciled onto it.

She opens it up and ushers me inside.

The room is *way* bigger than mine. A queen bed rests against the farthest wall on the left, and beside it lies a nightstand with an open newspaper sprawled across its dark, wooden surface.

She heads over to her bed and sits down before patting at the fabric next to her, "Shut the door then come take a seat."

I do as I'm told, shutting the heavy door before approaching her and sitting down; nausea sets in. What if she punishes me? I know she said we were just coming here to calm down, but this whole situation feels off.

"You're ballsy," she tells me, chuckling. "Getting into a fight with the toughest recruit. I don't know many people who would do that."

I glance down at my sneakers, "So I'm *not* in trouble, right? Like at all?"

She shakes her head, "Nah, you're good, just don't go looking for trouble or else I can't promise you'll be punishment free after."

"Thanks."

"No worries. Now, three questions. If I don't answer them, it means I'm not allowed to."

I raise an eyebrow, "Wait, seriously?"

"Yep. Best way to calm down is to get some closure. So, ask away."

"How am I alive? How was I resurrected? And that's just one question mashed together."

"Tommy was going to tell all of you tomorrow," she says. "but a serum code-named Rebirth resurrected you. The serum is filled with millions of nanobots that, once injected into the bloodstream of a dead host, will repair any internal injuries before jumpstarting the heart with pulses of electricity. After it resurrects the host, the nanobots loiter in the body until the heart is healthy. They also repair any fresh injuries that may occur shortly after resurrection. After all of that, they'll gather in your stomach and stimulate your nerves until you throw up."

I'm dumbstruck, "Whoa. So, what happens if the host is, I don't know, let's say decapitated? Would they still be fit for resurrection? Still tied in with the first question, I'm just curious."

"Sadly, no. A little while back, I went on an assignment with another member, and half his head was blown to pieces by a shotgun. I was able to escape with his body. Once in the clear, I injected him with Rebirth. The serum had no effect on him. Since then, Tommy and I have experimented on freshly dead Lazarus members, and they weren't able to be brought back."

"Are the nanobots still in me?" I ask, my craving for details growing.

"Have you thrown up since that first time in the infirmary room?"

"No."

"Then they're still in you. As I said, they won't leave until you're completely healthy."

"Can I ask one more thing about the serum before we move onto question two?"

"Go ahead."

"Can you revive *anyone* that's dead and still has their head intact?"

"As long as your brain and heart are still intact to your body, you can be resurrected. But here's the thing. Rebirth only works up to an hour after the host's death. The nanobots need a fresh body. An hour with no heart activity makes resurrection impossible. Rigor mortis, or any of the other death-related complications make Rebirth ineffective."

I want to ask so many more questions about Rebirth, but I move on.

"Did Lazarus pick their teen recruits randomly? Or were each of us specifically chosen?"

She smirks, "All the male instructors here, and at every other facility across the United States, were posed as Saints. They kept an eye on every teenager that used their checkpoints daily, finding potential recruits."

"Why were they looking for so long though? They stationed Tommy at my checkpoint for years."

"We had moles, and he was one. The original purpose wasn't to find teenage recruits, but last year Vice ordered that we find some for the Beta Group."

"Who's Vice?"

"He's our founder. He created Lazarus. He's the one who calls all the shots. We didn't know you and the others would die until the week it happened. The original plan wasn't to find freshly dead recruits. Things just fell into place in its own sick sort of way, I suppose."

I tap my foot against the ground, astonished, "Are there any problems I'm going to experience from being resurrected? Also, how long will my side-effects last?"

"The only side-effect caused by Rebirth would be the haemolacria. It's what causes you to cry blood. It typically only lasts a few months, but some members are still experiencing it to this day. As for the complications, there are a few *very* rare cases of members only living up to a year or two after being revived."

I can feel my stomach churn, "How *rare* are we talking?"

"Throughout the course of this all, only thirty people have died from it."

"*Thirty*?" I ask, shocked at the numbers. "That's like a quarter of the people here."

The door to her room opens, "Bleach, are you busy?" Tommy appears in the doorway, and he sees me, "Oh, Jason, what're you doing in here?"

"I promised to answer some questions he had on his mind. He's one curious kid," she slowly stands from her bed. "Is something wrong? Do you need me?"

"Sorta," he remarks. "I'm gonna need you to take care of our *little friend* we used for my class, today."

"Where is he?"

"My room. He's still tied up to the chair. There's a gun on my dresser if you need it. I'm going to be up top speaking to Randy if you need me."

Up top?

"Alright. I'll get right on it."

Tommy nods before looking over at me. He says nothing, but I can see his eyes soften. Maybe he's sorry that I'm in this whole situation. He turns around and leaves, shutting the door behind him.

"Hey, can you excuse me really quick?" Bleach asks, our eyes meeting.

"Yeah, sure."

"I'll only be a minute or two. Just wait here."

I watch her exit the room, fixing her pretty brown hair while doing so.

The door shuts as soon as she disappears.

So, what now?

I survey the room, and make it over to the nightstand next to me. I concentrate on the large headline at the top of the newspaper. It takes just a moment before it reads clear, "Obituaries."

The entire page is littered with pictures of families, and under them lie paragraphs upon paragraphs of inky black blobs.

Tommy wasn't lying when he said Mills ordered a purge on some of Boston's population.

I glance over at the door, making sure it's shut all the way before swiping the paper up with my hands. I search for the picture with me and my parents. I finally find it and feel the sudden urge to punch a wall until my knuckles bleed.

Matthew . . . I'll never forget who you are and what you've done to me and my family.

The picture the paper used was taken late last Autumn. We had our annual family picnic at this park, and it was practically empty, so we had it all to ourselves. It was such a beautiful day; the birds were singing, the sky was cloudless, and orange leaves fell from every tree. Most importantly we were together.

In the picture, my mom and dad were on either side of me. I had my arm wrapped around my mom while my right hand made bunny ears over my dad's head. Centered in the middle of us all, is my late dog Fifi.

It takes about a minute, but I'm able to make out the paragraph under our family photo.

"The Pinder Family came to an untimely death Feb. 25th, 2048. Their joint funeral will take place March. 3rd at the Boston Memorial Gardens at 4:30 P.M."

You've gotta be there. I say to myself. *You have to attend their funeral.*

The sudden sound of the doorknob makes my heart jump, and I hastily place the newspaper back where I found it. The creaking hinges break loose.

I lean back onto the bed just as Bleach enters. Blood is sprinkled all over her face.

"Sorry for the wait," she says, approaching the dresser on the other side of the room. "The gun jammed, and then some other stuff."

She says this in such a normal tone; it kind of freaks me out.

"So," she grabs a Kleenex from a tissue box that's placed on top of her dresser. "Where were we?"

I think back, "Um, I think we were talking about the complications."

Bleach wipes the fresh blood from her face, "Oh, that's right, the complications. I believe I answered that, though. Remember, I told you how thirty people have died prematurely after being injected with Rebirth?"

"Oh yeah . . ." I glance over at the paper for a quick second. "Hey, just an odd question, but what's the date today?"

She raises an eyebrow, "Why?"

I shrug, "Only curious. I'm sort of a freak when it comes to time, y'know?"

"It's February 27th," her tone exposes her suspicion.

"Thanks," I say, quickly changing the subject. "Hey, I know I've already asked you three questions, but you mind if I ask just *one* more?"

She approaches me and takes a seat by my side, "I guess *one* more couldn't hurt."

I mess around with my fingers, "Is anybody from the outside suspicious that all these teenagers have disappeared after being killed?"

"Nope, not at all. We replaced each of your bodies with a Brenix. It's a highly realistic robotic humanoid. It can mimic anybody's appearance and voice. Originally, they were used for military training, but one of our moles got his hands on a set of blueprints. So, now Lazarus gets to use them."

Robotic humanoids, resurrection serums, moles? No wonder the government hasn't been able to exterminate Lazarus. They're practically unstoppable. The thought terrifies me because I'm escaping in the morning with Simon and Mae to attend my own funeral.

CHAPTER TWENTY-FOUR

"*Psst*," I knock on Simon's door. "Simon, you in there?"

It takes a few moments, but the large, metal door opens, and he peeks his face out.

"Yeah?"

"Can I come in?"

He sighs, "Sure."

I can tell he's still upset with me from lunch.

The door opens wider allowing me to slip in. His room is identical to mine in every way.

Chloe sits on the bottom bunk and is staring down at her fingernails.

"Hey, Chloe," I greet, causing her to look up.

"Oh, hey Jason. What's up?"

"Nothing much. Just came to talk to Simon."

"Need me to leave?"

"Nah, you're good."

She flashes me a quick smile before bringing her attention back to her nails.

Honestly, Simon was right. Chloe is pretty cool. I wonder if I can convince her to come with us. She could be a reliable strength.

Problem is, she didn't seem too fond of the idea back in the cafeteria, and I can't blame her, because neither was I. I'm still not, but I don't feel like I have any other choice.

"Let me guess," Simon shuts the door, looking over at me. "You came to lecture me about going? You're going to say it's too dangerous and that I can . . .," he lets out an over dramatic gasp, "get hurt, right?"

"No, you d-bag," I say. "Quite the opposite, actually."

He looks thrown off, "What then?"

"I'm leaving with you in the morning."

Chloe's eyes raise from her nails once more, "Did someone slip you crazy pills too?"

Simon smiles, his eyes lighting up, "What changed your mind?"

"My parents' funeral is in four days, and I'm going," I reply. "I need to know the whole plan if I'm going."

"Plan?" Simon chuckles. "When have I ever had a plan? We're just going to casually walk into that elevator in Sector K and leave. Simple as that."

Chloe sighs, "You aren't that observant, are you? There are two guys that guard the elevator, in case you haven't realized. So, your idea will get you, Jason, and Mae all shot in the back of the head."

The grin washes off his face, "Well, I don't see you coming up with anything."

"That's because I'm not going, remember?"

I switch my gaze to her, "You should, though."

"Ha ha, very funny," she says. "I'm flattered and all, but I kinda like living and breathing, y'know?"

"Would you rather stay here?" Simon asks. "C'mon, we'll all—"

"You know what? Let's say I go," Chloe interrupts. "Then what? Tommy's right, we're dead to the outside. We can't go home, we can't get help, and we definitely can't live a normal life.

But let's say we escape and things are going well; you find your girlfriend and update her on everything, Jason goes to his folks' funeral, Mae checks to see if her parents are dead, which they definitely are, and I go with the flow. What happens next?"

Simon looks dumbstruck, "Well, I, uh. . ."

"We'll think of something," I reply for him. "Trust me, I want to stay here, too. It's just . . . I *have* to make it to their funeral."

Chloe looks at me with her hypnotizing dark green eyes, "Yeah, I get it, but haven't you read the rules? 'Anyone caught trying to escape *will* be met with lethal force.' Even if we escape, they'll still send someone after us. Trust me, Jason, it isn't a bright idea. Just stay."

I'm about to continue my attempt to convince her, but violent knocking on the door stops me dead in my tracks, "Open up! I know you're in there, Pinder!"

My heart drops. The voice belongs to Marcus. Chloe's eyes widen.

I can tell exactly why he's after me. He wants to get revenge for what happened back in our last class when we got into our little fight.

"Jason isn't here," Simon says, catching on that Chloe and I are hesitant.

"Bull," an unfamiliar voice says from the other side. "We saw him come in."

I swear under my breath, but then I remind myself that I'll never have to see Marcus after today since I'll be gone. Long gone.

I smile, my defiant and arrogant side overtaking my common sense, "You're right, meathead. First time in your life, I bet."

Chloe looks at me like I've gone insane, "What're you doing?"

"Get out here, *right now*," Marcus demands. "If you don't, then we're coming in and breaking both of your freaking legs, Pinder."

Simon glances over at me, "Who is this guy?"

"Marcus," I reply, my eyes narrowing.

Simon rolls his hoodie sleeves up, "He sounds *crazy*."

"He is," I confirm.

Chloe stands from the bed, also rolling up her sleeves, "I've got your back if things go south. Well, at least I'll *try* to have it."

I shoot her a slight nod, "Thanks."

Marcus reminds me of Jakob: the height, the intimidation, the attitude. He acts like such a top dog, and I absolutely *hate* that.

Simon approaches his door, mumbling something under his breath before grabbing the knob and twisting it. He swiftly opens the door. Some brown-haired pretty boy and Marcus are waiting, and they both wear looks that promise *pain*.

"*You*," he shoots fire out his eyes while storming in past Simon. Simon gets pushed out of the way by Pretty Boy.

Marcus stands face-to-face with me. His dumb snarling makes me laugh out loud.

"Come on, laugh some more, I dare you," he shoves me back, causing me to stumble around before regaining my balance.

I chuckle just to spite him. "Aww, does angry, little baby need a bottle?"

He grits his teeth, "You little . . ."

"You're just mad because you *know* you won't last in here. People like you never make it," I interrupt, waiting for him to explode.

"That's what you really think, huh?" he backs me up against a wall. "I'm not gonna last because I'm better than everyone? Wow, you're a pretty oblivious little punk."

I raise my left hand and flip him off, my eyes narrowed down to slits, "Bite me."

Chloe is standing by the bed, looking sick to her stomach. Simon and Pretty Boy are in each other's' faces, looking as if they're about to rip each other apart. The overall tension in the room feels like it's about to snap in half.

"I'm really going to *love* hurting you." Marcus sneers.

"Oh, I bet you are."

He's about to slam his knuckles into my face, but he's interrupted by the sound of an opening steel slide.

Chloe jumps onto his back, and I'm stunned.

"Get away from him!"

"Get offa me, you crazy bi-"

Chloe punches him in the throat. With her other hand, she desperately tries to lunge the sharp tip of the blade into the side of his skull. He stumbles around the room as Simon throws a punch into Pretty Boy's face, knocking his nose loose and sending him to the floor.

Marcus slams his head back into Chloe's face. She flies off his back and onto the carpet, the knife springing from her grip. I rush for it, but Marcus shoves me out of the way and wraps his dark hand around it before pointing the razor edge at me.

"You've really screwed up now."

I freeze. Chloe's on the ground unconscious, and Simon is too busy pounding Pretty Boy's face in to realize that I'm backed into a corner.

"What? You gonna stab me?" I ask, my teeth gnashed, undecided on the fight or flight response.

I flinch readying to be knifed as Marcus aims for my throat.

I stagger to the right when the door to the room swings open.

My eyes shoot to Tommy and Bleach standing in the doorway.

CHAPTER TWENTY-FIVE

"Dude, that was sweet," Simon says as he washes the blood from his hands. "I can't believe we won that fight."

I stare at myself through the mirror, "And we got off scot-free. Good thing Tommy took our side."

"Yeah, definitely," Chloe dabs her bloody lip with a wet paper towel. "It's a good thing they caught Marcus with the knife and not me."

The three of us are in the boys' showers cleaning ourselves up. It kind of caught me off guard when Chloe followed us in, but it doesn't feel awkward. It's not like anyone's showering in here, anyway.

The only word I can use to describe this past hour is *insane*.

They instructed us to get cleaned up before we head down to the cafeteria for dinner.

"What do you two think will happen to them?" I ask, turning away from the mirror with clean hands. After pulling guns on us, Bleach called in a few people to take Marcus and Pretty Boy - whose name happens to be Trevor - to the infirmary. We had heard nothing else.

Chloe shrugs, "Who knows. Hopefully, they'll get punished."

"Yeah, hopefully. The two of them deserve it," Simon says, checking out his now crooked nose in one of the other mirrors. "I wonder if they torture kids around here."

"I think they do," Chloe remarks.

I look at her with a raised eyebrow, "Why do you say that?"

"Rumor has it that that Bryan kid, who caused that scene at lunch today, was seen being taken back to his dorm room with all his fingernails missing. His eyes were completely swollen, and apparently, most of his face was black and blue."

"Wait, seriously?" Simon asks, turning away from the mirror.

It goes silent for an awkward moment before out of nowhere, Chloe says, "I'm coming with you guys in the morning."

"You are?" I ask, a little smile appearing on my face.

She nods, "I know what I said earlier, about how stupid the whole idea was. But honestly, I don't think I'll make it here without you two, so is it cool if I tag along?"

"Of course," Simon smirks. "Welcome aboard."

We take turns fist bumping each other before heading out of the showers. On the way, I stop Chloe and pull her to the side.

"Can I talk to you, really quick?"

"Sure. About what?"

I pause for a moment, trying to find the right words, "I just wanna say thanks for having my back in the dorm. It was pretty gnarly when you jumped on his back."

"Hey, no problem," she softly punches me in the shoulder. "I just hope that someday you can return the favor and have *my* back."

I shoot her a half smile, "No promises."

Simon peeks his head back into the showers, "You two coming, or what?"

We follow him out.

I have to fight the urge to tell them both that I have a really bad feeling about escaping. I know I want to go to the funeral, but is it worth risking my life over? I got a second chance. A re-run. I shouldn't be wasting it on this.

I try my best to push the feeling down as the three of us head to dinner.

CHAPTER TWENTY-SIX

Sitting at the table with Simon, Chloe, and Mae almost feels normal. We're all having some type of vegetable stir-fry, and as we discuss recent news with Mae, the uneasy feeling inside me doesn't subside.

This isn't a good idea.

"Is there anything else I need to know?" Mae asks, bobbing her knee up and down.

Simon shakes his head, "Nope. Now we just need to think of a plan on how to escape."

"Wait," Chloe interjects. "I thought of something."

"What is it?" I ask.

She hushes her tone, "We're going to need a gun."

Simon glances around, making sure nobody heard what was just said, "You *crazy?* If we get caught, the whole plan is off. Not to mention that we'll probably get shot in the back of the *freaking* skull."

"I'm with Simon, here," Mae agrees. "We can't jeopardize our escape."

"No, Chloe's right," I argue, also hushing my tone. "We need a gun. There are too many situations where we might need one."

"See, he gets it," Chloe says.

"Have you ever even fired a gun in your life?" Simon asks me, already knowing the answer.

"Well, no. But after today, I'm sure I have a basic idea on how."

"A basic idea doesn't save our lives in a dangerous situation. I agree that we need some sort of weapon, but a gun? No way, man."

"You wouldn't have to sneak it, if that's what you're worried about. Chloe or I could do it."

Chloe nods, "He's right."

"Fine, whatever. Just please don't get caught," Simon says.

"We promise." Chloe and I reassure in unison.

"I think we should all stick together, tonight," Mae suggests. "I mean, it'll give us more time to go over a plan and stuff."

"Good idea," Simon looks up at the large clock mounted to the wall on the other side of the cafeteria. "Okay, so right now it's seven-thirty. We'll all meet at Jason's room at lights out. Sound good?"

"Which one is Jason's room?" Mae asks.

"Eleventh door to the right," I reply before Simon can.

"I'm in," Chloe says.

"So am I," Mae follows.

I raise my index finger, "Ditto."

"Alright, so it's settled," Simon whispers. "Jason's room at ten-thirty."

"What about your roommate?" Mae looks over at me. "Will he be okay with this?"

"He's actually in the infirmary," I don't like it, but there's pride in my voice. Tommy wasn't lenient about the knife thing. "So, we don't have to worry about him."

CHAPTER TWENTY-SEVEN

Two guards stand side-by-side in front of the elevator at the back of Sector K, shielding it off completely. The two of them don the Lazarus uniform, including black morph masks that stick to their faces like a second skin.

"Think they'll be suspicious that we're going into a classroom so late?" I ask Chloe while we walk along the wide and lengthy corridor.

She shrugs, "No idea, just play it cool. If anyone asks, we forgot something in firearms and need to get it back, alright?"

"Alright."

The firearms classroom is toward the back of the sector. I try to remain calm as we approach it, but I can't stop my heart from rapidly accelerating, or the beads of sweat from forming on my forehead.

"What part of 'just play it cool' don't you understand?" Chloe asks under her breath.

"I'm *trying*."

I'm not nervous to pass the guards on the way in, it's the way out that scares me. What if they get skeptical and check us?

They'd find the gun, and I can picture them shooting us. Frankly, it probably wouldn't come to that, but *what if?*

We reach the end of the hallway.

"What're you two doing?" one of the guards question us as Chloe reaches for the doorknob to the last classroom on the left. "No one goes in there."

She meets their eyes, "I'm sorry, it's just that I forgot something in there."

"What is it?"

Chloe softly nudges me. I assume she wants me to make up something.

"It's her class schedule."

"Why isn't her schedule back in her dorm room?"

Chloe sounds hesitant, "Some of my friends are here, and I wanted to see if I could switch some classes around. I tried to ask Feline, but she said no. In all the disappointment, I left the schedule in the classroom."

The guard stares at us skeptically, "Be quick. I want you out of there in *exactly* one minute."

"Yes, sir. But are you sure you don't want to follow us in?"

I stare at Chloe with broad eyes.

What is she doing?

One of them growls, "No. Now get in and get out."

The two of us nod before quickly entering the classroom, and once the heavy door shuts itself behind us, I snap into action.

Chloe turns to me, looking panicked, "Where do you think they keep the guns?"

I look over at the table where all the firearms were placed this morning.

No guns in sight. None.

I swear under my breath, "I have no idea."

"Hold on, let me search over there, really quick."

"Hurry, we only have like thirty seconds."

She hurries over to a small desk placed in the left corner of the room, rapidly opening the drawers in search of any gun.

I wait ten seconds before hissing, "*Hurry.*"

"I'm trying, dude."

I finish counting to sixty, "We gotta split. We're going to get caught."

She looks up at me while sighing, "I found one."

My heart pounds, "Well come on, then."

The door opens.

My head swivels toward the entrance. The two elevator guards have their hands placed on the black, tactical gun holsters that are latched to their hips.

"It doesn't take a minute to find a piece of paper," one barks. "What's the holdup?"

Even though the lights in the room are switched off, I can vaguely see Chloe place something in her hoodie pouch.

"I can't find it anywhere," she says, walking out from behind the desk.

The other guard cocks his head to the side, "What are you doing behind your instructor's desk?"

Chloe chokes, "I, uh—"

"She thought Feline might've put it over there," I help, my right eye twitching.

"C'mere," the first one demands. "I'm checking the both of you."

My heart almost explodes, "What? Why?"

"Don't ask questions, kid."

Chloe and I hesitantly comply. *We've been caught.*

My face is burning red, and Chloe looks like she's about to puke her guts out onto the floor.

"Spread your arms and legs apart," the guard orders, approaching me first.

He pats me down, checks my front pockets, my back pockets,

then my hoodie pouch. After finding nothing, he checks my hood, failing to find anything at all.

"You're clear," he mutters, now side-stepping over to Chloe.

He pats her down at the sides, checks her front pockets, her back pockets, and he's about to check her hoodie pouch, but the walkie talkie attached to his uniform goes off.

"Copper? You there, man?" Tommy's voice blares through the radio.

The guard known as Copper stops checking Chloe, sighs, and detaches the walkie talkie from his body before bringing it up to his mouth and holding the button down, "I'm here. What do you need?"

"We're going to need some backup. Lynch just reported that two kids are getting violent in the gymnasium. Some dispute. Could you and Myth go break it up? The rest of us are busy."

"If Lynch was the one who reported it in, why isn't he the one stopping it?"

"Because there's another fight going down in the showers. I swear, this whole Beta thing is going downhill."

"Alright, Myth and I will go break it up. Over and out."

I watch Copper attach the walkie talkie back to his uniform.

He looks at Chloe for a moment before sighing, "I don't want to see you or him again, tonight. Either hit the weight room, or go back to your dorm rooms," he says, still seeming skeptical.

Chloe nods, taking a deep breath, "Yes, sir."

"Good. Now get out of here."

Chloe and I do as we're told, walking off and toward one room on the right.

"What are we doing?" I ask.

"Just follow me."

We park in front of the weight room, both watching as Copper and Myth leave the firearms classroom and lock the door behind them. They rush down the hall, passing us on their way to the gymnasium.

Chloe grabs my hand and opens the door to the room.

The inside is massive and filled with equipment. There's also about six other recruits in here, all lifting weights and socializing. Once the door closes behind us, I turn to Chloe with a puzzled look on my face.

"Why are we here?"

"I've got a little surprise. Don't worry."

She leads me toward the back of the room, and once no one is looking, she bends over and picks something up from behind a dumbbell rack.

A pocket knife.

"You stole another one?" I ask, glancing around the room to make sure that the coast is clear.

"Yep. It was back when I stole my first one. I took an extra just in case and hid it in here while nobody was looking."

"So, you've got the gun, right?"

"What do you think?"

"Give it to me. We can hide it in my pouch that way it won't look as obvious."

"Smart thinking."

She cautiously pulls the handgun out of her pouch and slides it into mine, making sure nobody is looking. She situates it so it looks more natural, and after a moment, steps away.

To kill time, she and I both stay in the workout room and lift dumbbells. For the first bit, we have a competition to see who could do the most reps. She does fifty before giving up, and I'm able to reach ninety-eight.

We spend time asking each other stupid questions, both demanding honest answers and all that crap.

Throughout our conversation, I learn that Chloe's seventeen, and her favorite colors are pink and white. Before Lazarus, she spent most of her time with some horrible people; she lived in Collingsworth. Everyone here in Boston calls it the bad part of town. And finally, the stupidest thing she's ever done was steal her dead father's wedding ring from her mom's jewelry box and sell it for money.

She tells me it was about a year ago when she cut ties with all the bad influences in her life to focus more on her grades and help out more at home. That was when she and her family got close.

The two of us leave the workout room when the mounted clock on the wall reads *10:25*.

CHAPTER TWENTY-EIGHT

I enter my dorm room with Chloe following right behind me.

I flip the lights on, then unexpectedly let out a startled scream as Simon and Mae jump out at me while shouting like maniacs.

"What the—" I breathe, clutching my chest with my left hand. "How long have you two been here?"

"About an hour," Mae attempts to stop laughing, but fails. "We heard footsteps, so we hit the lights and waited."

"Don't do that," I say bitterly. "I'm already jumpy. Stealing a gun can do that to a dude."

Simon cups his hands around his mouths, then shouts, "Buzzkill."

Chloe shuts the door, "Simon's right. It was just a joke."

"Yeah, whatever," I say, walking past everyone to the bunk bed. "Like I said, we stole the gun without too many problems."

"And a knife," Chloe adds as I grab the pistol out from my hoodie pouch and place it under the bottom bunk's mattress.

"Did anyone catch you guys?" Mae's tone turns more serious.

"Almost," I reply. "Don't worry about it, though, everything's fine."

She blanches, "Almost?"

"Yeah, *almost.*"

She sighs, "Alright. Well, what's the first order of business for tonight?"

Chloe speaks before I can, "Something isn't right."

"What do you mean?" Simon asks, raising an eyebrow.

"This all seems too simple," she says. "I mean, the only way out is through the elevator. So, what do we do? Just distract the two guards and leave? I feel like there's more to this facility than meets the eye. Like, what's up top? Wouldn't you almost assume that Lazarus would guard up there, too? I dunno, this is all just too *simple.*"

"You're right," he agrees, his eyes widening. "I mean, now that you mention it, it seems *way* too easy. Lazarus is America's most wanted terrorist group, so wouldn't you think that they would have more security than this?"

Mae looks sick to her stomach, "Ah, man. You two are totally right. They probably have hidden cameras everywhere, a bunch of guards up top."

"Calm down," I switch my gaze between the three of them. "You're all just paranoid. We're over thinking this, okay? We will think of a plan and execute it in the morning during breakfast. That way no students get in the way. And if there happens to be any complications, we'll deal with them then."

Chloe nods, but she seems sick to her stomach, "Maybe you're right. Let's come up with a plan and hope for the best. If we die- well, then I guess we die."

Her words make me feel a little sick. It's the same feeling I felt at dinner, and I know that this whole thing is stupid. Why am I even leaving? Why am I risking the possibility of throwing away my second chance at life?

I keep dwelling on the thought of death. Dying, the first time was so bizarre . . . painful. I mean, do I really wanna go through that again? This whole escape plot isn't worth it, at least not in my mind. Why do Simon and Mae want to leave so badly, anyway? Seriously, what kind of selfish idiots would want what happened to us to happen to so many others? We can *at least* try to help and stop this from happening again. We can join the revolt.

Maybe attending my own funeral isn't worth it.

"Jason?" Simon snaps his fingers in front of my face. "Dude, you okay?"

I blink rapidly, coming back to my senses, "Oh, yeah, I was just thinking."

"Did you hear a word of anything we just said?" Chloe asks me.

"No, I zoned."

Simon sighs, "Like you said earlier, this whole thing will go down during breakfast. We decided that you will distract the guards by saying Bleach sent you to tell them that there's some gas leak in the combat classroom that needs to be checked out immediately. You'll then follow them in and make sure we have *at least* fifteen seconds to call the elevator down. After that, you'll rush out and make a break for the rest of us. Then, once you're inside, I'll get us out of there."

"This seems way too simple." I state, tapping my foot against the floor.

"That's what I said," Chloe remarks.

Simon raises an eyebrow, "What's wrong with simple?"

"It shouldn't be this easy," I reply, glancing at everyone in the room. "I have a weird feeling about all this."

Chloe yawns, "Me too, but you know what? Screw it. I think I'm ready to hit the hay."

"Awe, you're going to sleep?" Mae asks.

"Yeah, what's wrong with that?"

"I mean, what's the point of staying here tonight if you're just gonna go to sleep?"

"Look, we already went over the plan. There's really nothing more to talk about. Also, aren't you the one that wanted us all to sleep in here?"

"Yeah, but . . ."

Chloe puts her finger up to Mae's lips and shushes her, "Goodnight."

She walks over to my bunk bed and comically collapses down onto the bottom mattress. Without looking, she grabs the gun from under the mattress by the handle and stuffs it underneath the pillow.

"Night, everybody. Hope you don't mind that I'm stealing your bed, Jason."

"That's actually where Marcus sleeps," I correct.

Chloe shoots her head up, looking at us with heavy eyes and a scrunched nose, "Ew," she slowly gets up off the bed and climbs to the top. "There, *now* I hope you don't mind."

"Kinda do," I mumble.

"Well, if she's going to bed, so am I," Mae sighs. "I'll take the bottom bunk. Goodnight."

"Wait, what about us?" I ask.

She shoots me and Simon a smug grin, "That floor looks comfy."

Simon glares at her, making her giggle. She then heads over to the bottom bunk, pulls the gun out from under the pillow, hands it up to Chloe, and then lies down.

Simon and I exchange looks before hitting the lights and finding somewhere on the floor that would be comfortable enough to sleep on. Simon is particular when it comes to where he sleeps, so it takes about three minutes before we're able to find the perfect spot.

By then, both girls are asleep and snoring.

"So," he starts, leaning his back up against the wall directly behind us. "You still have the hots for Mae?"

I chuckle, "Wouldn't you like to know."

"Don't be a d-bag."

"Oh, I will."

"What about Chloe? She's cute, right?"

I glance up at the top bunk, double checking to make sure she's actually asleep, "Way outta my league."

"Ah, c'mon that's not true. Well, I mean, it is, but there's still hope for you."

"Gee, thanks."

We both laugh quietly and momentarily go silent.

"Man," he puts his arms behind his head and uses them as a makeshift pillow. "Today was seriously whack."

"No kidding," I say, copying his arm-pillow idea. "Just to think, we only met back up this morning in the showers. You probably liked seeing my smokin' hot body, didn't you?"

"Oh yeah, *totally*," he laughs. "It distracted me from your ugly face."

"Hardy har har."

He looks over at me, taking a deep breath, "Can I ask you something?"

"Go for it."

"Okay, but you have to answer with nothing but the truth."

"Deal."

He looks hesitant at first, but eventually unties the knot in his tongue, "Do you think we will die?"

"Like, tomorrow?"

"Tomorrow, the next day, a year from now."

"We all die, eventually."

"That's not what I meant, Jay."

"Then what do you mean?"

"Do you think we will get killed, again? Murdered."

I think about the question long and hard, "The way I see it, it's like we all have cancer. We're *sick*, Simon. We're running out of time, but if we fight long and hard, then maybe we'll get less and less sick. The harder we fight, the more likely we are to get better, and once we're cured, well, hopefully we'll stay that way. The ones who fight stay alive."

Simon's expression hardens, "Let's be the ones who give everything, then."

"I'm with you there," I say. "Look, just don't choke and everything will be good. If I'm being open, I don't think we should leave, but I'm doing it for you and my parents."

"Thanks, man."

"No worries."

I situate my body and lie on the floor. Simon does the same.

"Night, dude," he says.

"Night."

I'm about to doze off when I hear muffled sobbing. My eyes reluctantly open, and I glance over at the source of the noise. Since my eyes have long adjusted to the dark, I'm able to make out Mae on the bottom bunk, her shoulders are shaking.

"You okay, Mae?" I ask sleepily. "What's wrong?"

Suddenly, the crying stops, and in its place lingers silence.

CHAPTER TWENTY-NINE

I'm running down the corridor of Sector K, wearing a staged mask of pure anxiety. The gun feels heavy in my hoodie pouch. I approach the two guards, Copper and Myth, and I feel like my legs are about to give out due to all the stress I'm under.

"Hey," I shout at the guards, picking up my pace. "We have an emergency!"

Copper exchanges looks with Myth before bringing his attention back to me, "What are you talking about, kid? And why aren't you with the rest of the recruits eating breakfast?"

I stop about a foot away from them, panting, "Bleach told me to tell you guys that there might be some sort of gas leak in the combat classroom, and that you need to go check it out *immediately*. She thinks it's one of the pipes that busted."

"A gas leak?" Myth asks with a suspicious tone. "Why didn't she radio us about this?"

I freeze. The fact that they have walkie-talkies spaced my mind. *Crap!*

Copper stares at me, "Wait, aren't you that kid from last night? The one who went into the firearms classroom with that blonde chick?"

"Look," I attempt to act more serious. "Bleach said this leak could potentially be toxic and that we would have to evacuate."

Myth chuckles while grabbing the walkie talkie from his hip, "Yeah, I think I'm going to radio this in before we look at this so called 'gas leak.'"

I panic, "We don't have time for this."

Myth holds the button on his radio down, "Hey, Bleach, this is Myth. You copy?"

It goes silent for a moment.

"This is Feline," a female voice pours through the walkie talkie. "Bleach is doing security in the cafeteria because of yesterday's incident. What's up?"

Myth sighs while holding the button down once more, "We gotta recruit over here who says Bleach told him to inform us that there's some sort of gas leak in the combat classroom."

"She doesn't have a radio on her, at the moment. I could send Lynch over to the cafeteria to go ask her if you'd like?"

"No. We'll quickly go check it out."

"Alright. Good luck."

Myth attaches the walkie talkie back to his hip before grunting, "Let's go."

The two of them walk toward the combat classroom, and I follow. The three of us enter, and once inside the room, Copper and Myth look around, still not seeming to take it all too seriously.

"Did she mention where the gas leak is coming from?" Copper asks. "Kid, I don't smell anything. If this is some kind of a joke-."

I shake my head, "Why would I screw with you two? Look, do you want me to ask her for more information? I don't like being in here, I'm getting lightheaded."

"Yes. Go," Myth demands, his voice low-pitched and scratchy.

I turn around and walk out of the room, a weight being lifted from my chest.

I did it.

Out in the corridor, Simon, Chloe, and Mae are all at the elevator, and I can tell that something's terribly wrong. Simon is swearing.

"What's going on?" I ask, my relief turning into anxiety.

Simon turns his body sideways, pointing at a small object that's placed where the elevator call button should be, "We can't open the friggin' doors without an ID card."

My heart drops into the pit of my stomach, "Wait . . . you're kidding me, right?"

He slams his fist against the solid steel doors, blurting out another swear, "Do any of those guards have an ID tag on them?"

"I don't know, but I'll go take a look. Stay here and keep quiet."

"Be careful," Mae says as I turn back around and head back into the classroom.

Inside the combat room, Copper and Myth are still looking around for the non-existent leak, and turn around when they see I have returned.

Myth tilts his head to the side, "That was . . . quick."

"She said it might come from the vent over there," I point to the only air vent in the room, ignoring their suspicion. "She wants you to find the source. Like I said, she thinks it's coming from a pipe."

They both grunt, and I swear that the two of them are grinning under their skin-tight masks.

They walk over to the vent and kneel. I notice an ID tag around each of their necks, dangling over their chests.

Their backs are turned to me, and I only have moments to act.

Then a particularly *dark* thought enters my mind.

Shoot them, then rip an ID tag from one of their necks.

I rapidly shake my head, but what other choice do I have? Any second now, they will catch on that the gas leak was a lie, and then I'll be in some *deep* crap.

I give the idea some more thought before reluctantly reaching into my pouch and pulling out the shiny black pistol. It feels heavier than before. Sweat beads up all over my forehead. I recall every part to the object: the muzzle, the safety, the hammer, all the basics.

I'm out of my mind.

I grit my teeth, set the gun off safety, then hesitantly aim. At first, I point the end of the barrel at the first guard's head, but my conscience eats away at me. I aim at his lower back.

This is absolutely insane.

I hold my breath, blink, blink some more.

My stomach is churning, my fingers are twitching, and I can't breathe properly.

"There's *nothing* here, kid—"

I squeeze the trigger, and the bullet hits its mark with a deafening blast. Copper howls in agony. Before Myth can react, I aim over at him and fire twice.

He screams out a swear, collapsing to the floor.

In a split second, I'm hovering over Copper and struggling to rip the ID tag from his neck. His grip on my right hand is tight and secure, so I use my left to aim the handgun down at his gut and fire two rounds, my hand lurching back as the weapon kicks.

He screams, reaching for the holster on his hip.

I rip the tag from his neck before he can draw his gun, sprint off toward the door, and flinch as a bullet slams into the wall two inches from my head, making my right ear ring like a church bell.

Debris from the wall flies into my face briefly blinding me as I hurl myself into the hallway, booking it toward the elevator like a runaway convict.

Simon, Chloe, and Mae stare at me with wide eyes.

"What just happened?" Chloe hisses.

I ignore her and sprint over to the elevator's scanner and hastily scan the ID, blocking out their chorus of words.

A loud beeping booms from the scanner before the cherry red, metal doors slowly slide open.

"Hurry, get in!" I demand, hastily entering the elevator.

The three of them do as they're told, and Simon quickly examines all the buttons in the interior. I can't read any of their stenciled in labels since the anxiety pumping through my veins is overwhelming to my dyslexia, so I have no choice but to leave the task at hand to him.

"There's a main lobby, is that where we should go?" he asks. sweating like a track star.

"I don't care," I practically scream. "Just get us out of here!"

He does as he's told, slamming his fingertips into one button.

A loud *ding* thunders out, signifying that the doors will shut momentarily.

I let out a heavy sigh, relief flooding my chest.

We did it. We actually did it.

Myth abruptly bursts out of the combat classroom and into the hallway. His hoodie is stained red, and even though he's wearing the mask, I can see the scowl he wears through the skin-tight fabric.

"I'm going to kill you!" he blurts, clutching his gut with the hand that's not holding a pistol. "I'm going to kill all of you, dumb grave walkers!"

The elevator doors shut.

"Jas—" Mae blurts out before an explosion of blood sprays my face.

My eardrums break into a chorus of rings, my vision becomes disoriented with red blotches, and my heart feels like it has just stopped.

What just happened?

I hear prolonged gasping coming from Chloe. Everything around me looks like a fuzzy stop-motion animation. Everything is so . . . strange.

Simon is fine, but the look on his pale face makes me nervous. Chloe also seems unharmed.

I look down.

Mae lies sprawled out on the elevator floor, the bullet hole in her head oozing blood.

"Mae!"

My voice seems distant.

Within the span of a second, everything stops. The ringing in my ears die down to a faint humming, my vision snaps back to normal, and my mind focuses.

I stare down at Mae in doubt, not knowing what to do.

"No *friggin'* way," Simon's eyes are broad.

I bring a hand up to my face and trail it down to my chin, noting the blood that covers most of my palm and every inch of all my fingers.

I drop next to her, every breath of mine shaky as I hold her in my arms.

Just a few days ago, we were at a party. We were kissing in that alley.

And now?

Now I'm holding her dead body, blood tracing down her face and onto my lap.

This can't be happening

"We need to concentrate," Chloe's voice sounds shaky just like mine. "Or else we'll end up just like her."

Simon shutters.

I can't keep my eyes off Mae.

"Jason," Chloe tries to get my attention. "You need to get up and be ready to run if you want to stay alive."

Fight to stay alive.

The elevator comes to a halt, and a moment later, the doors slide open with a *ding!*

I give Mae one last look before putting her down and getting to my feet, my sneakers soak in the puddle of blood she lies in.

I look ahead, suddenly stunned. It's a fancy hotel lobby packed with a bunch of people. Some sit on the couches near the front doors, some stand in front of a check-in counter waiting to be assigned to their rooms, and some are on their way out with luggage gripped in their hands.

The Lazarus facility is under some hotel?

"We need to get out of here," Chloe reminds us over the loud chattering that echoes around the lobby. "There could be Lazarus members up here, so we *need* to be quick."

I exit the elevator, my eyes wide.

The chaos from the lobby makes me go into overdrive. Everyone seems to talk over each other and this kid at the front desk keeps tapping the bell placed on the wooden surface, forcing it to chime.

Out of sheer panic, I aim my gun up at the ceiling, and fire three shots, making a wave of screams emit from the large crowd. Everyone gets down onto the ground, and some younger toddlers cry.

I don't speak. Instead, I rush through the lobby, Simon and Chloe following close behind me as I swiftly head through the revolving glass doors.

There is at least two feet of snow covering the ground. There's a countless number of snowflakes falling earthward.

"What now?" Chloe asks, hastily looking around for some means of escape.

I eye a silver four-door Sedan across the street. The snow-covered windshield signifying its lack of recent use.

"Any of you know how to hot-wire a car?" I ask, determined to escape the hotel with my brain intact.

Chloe sheepishly raises her hand, "I do."

"Let's go then."

The three of us run across the street to the car. Chloe tries the handle, and miraculously, it's unlocked.

We all get in. Chloe's in the driver's seat, Simon's in the back seat, and I'm riding shotgun.

Chloe begins hot-wiring the vehicle, and I lie my head back against the seat's headrest and exhale a long, shuddery breath.

I can't believe how much just happened in two minutes.

I'm an idiot. Why did I ever encourage this insane escape plot?

"*Yes,*" Chloe blurts in triumph after a few minutes, the sound of a car engine roaring to life. "Where to now?"

I wipe my blood sprinkled face, "Anywhere but here."

CHAPTER THIRTY

According to the digital clock installed into the dashboard, we have been driving for three hours; it's currently *10:17*. Mae's blood is dried to my face.

We haven't been apprehended yet, and we've managed to avoid the checkpoints, until now.

Chloe slows down a couple hundred yards from a checkpoint that guards Collingsworth, the violent ghetto where she used to live.

"Why are we heading into this hellhole?" Simon asks, letting out an unenthusiastic groan.

She looks up at him through the rear-view mirror, "There are a lot of vacant houses around here, It's our best bet. Plus, the car's almost out of gas, so unless you plan on freezing tonight-."

"Yeah, yeah. I get it."

Chloe turns right, pulling into an alleyway just outside the main entrance.

"Jason," Chloe looks over at me. "Think we need to wipe the car down?"

"No, why?"

"Our fingerprints are all over the dash, the steering wheel, and the doors."

"But we're dead. What're they going to do? Dig our non-existent bodies up and place them under arrest? I think we'll be fine."

"Guess you're right."

The three of us step out of the stolen car. All of our teeth start chattering simultaneously. It's still snowing, and according to one of the downtown electronic billboards, it's negative two degrees.

"It's *so* cold," Simon cups his hands over his mouth and begins breathing heavily in an attempt to warm them. "I hate winter."

"How are we going to get in?" I ask Chloe. "There's a checkpoint at every entrance, and we definitely can't use them."

"There's a little passage that I know of," she states before running off through the alley, using her right hand she motions for us to follow. "C'mon."

Simon and I exchange looks before chasing off after her. It takes everything we've got to keep up. We end up about a half mile from where we stopped. Gasping for air we approach an icy cold chain-link fence. My eyeballs feel like they're frozen in their sockets.

"You guys seriously need to work out," she says.

"So," Simon fights to speak. "Where's this way in of yours?"

Chloe points down at the bottom of the fence. There's a small gap capable of crawling through. Seeing it brings back bittersweet memories from the night of Nacht-fest. The gap is similar to the one we had to slither through a few nights ago to get to The Manor.

Beyond the chain-link fence is a collage of trashy homes, small town businesses, multiple alleyways, and a lot of patrolling Saints.

Typically, Saints only patrol neighborhoods when a criminal is on the loose, but that's not the case with Collingsworth. There's at least one murder here every other day. There are only three types of people that live here: ex-criminals who've somehow shown back up after being taken by soldiers, really poor families that can't afford anything other than this cesspit, or my *personal favorite*, gangsters. The Saints who patrol here are the most savage, most abusive, most revolting throughout all of Boston, and for good reasons.

"Are you sure this is a good idea?" I ask Chloe as she crawls through the small gap.

"Of course, I'm sure," she replies. "I even know a place where we can stay for tonight."

She finishes getting through, then gets to her feet.

My turn.

"I don't know," I say, getting down on my stomach and slowly inching through the gap. "This place is a total nightmare."

"Stop worrying."

Chloe helps me to my feet, and next up is Simon.

I ask Chloe, "Do you know anyone who could hook us up with some food?"

"I do, but it doesn't matter. We're dead to everyone, and the last thing I want to happen is for anyone to recognize us. I wasn't exactly the *greatest* person around here."

Half way through the gap Simon asks, "So what do we do about food, then?"

She begins to look hesitant, "I know this sounds bad, but I know how to get into most stores around here after hours. Tonight, we'll go and take whatever we need."

"We're going to steal food?" my numb fingers are the only things that aren't covered by my light-weight black gloves. I breathe over them. "That's kinda douchey."

"I'm with Jason," Simon agrees, getting to his feet.

"We already stole a car," Chloe remarks. "This is way less than that, we're taking food that we *need*. This is totally justified."

Simon brushes off the snow that sticks to his jeans, "I dunno."

Chloe sighs, "Do you have any better ideas?"

"Look," I interject, snowflakes covering my hair. "We can figure this out later. Let's just get to that place you were talking about, alright?"

"Alright," she says through chattering teeth. "It's just a few blocks away from here."

CHAPTER THIRTY-ONE

Chloe leads us to an old run-down apartment complex toward the back of Collingsworth. The lobby is filthy. When the guy at the check-in counter asks us if we want a room, Chloe says we're just staying with a friend for the night.

He doesn't say another word, just nods. He doesn't ask why there's blood sprinkled all over my clothes and face, or why there's a gun handle sticking out of my back pocket. He nods.

The elevator is out of order, so we take the stairs up to the fourth floor and Simon breaks down the door of a vacant room. The inside is even worse than the lobby. Cigarette butts and beer bottles litter the floor, the walls are covered in graffiti, and the kitchen is infested with rats.

Better than nothing, I guess.

I walk over to the living room and sit on an old raggedy blue couch. It reeks of smoke and other smells that burn my nostrils. The fact that almost every other room in this place is occupied is beyond me.

"Looks like there's a working shower," Chloe states. "You two mind if I get washed up?"

I shrug, "Go ahead."

Simon nods, "Yeah, you're good."

Chloe finally walks out from the bedroom after twenty minutes of silence. She's dressed in the clothes she was wearing earlier, and there's a somber look in her eyes.

"Only perk about this place is the hot water," she says.

Simon laughs, "That's true."

After a few hours of waiting and debating on our next move, we start to feel hunger pains eating away at our stomachs.

Chloe flips her bangs to the right, "Alright, so down to business; getting some dinner."

"More importantly," Simon adds. "*How* do we get dinner?"

"I'll take care of it," I say, standing up.

She raises an eyebrow, letting out a slight chuckle, "You? You've never even been to Collingsworth, so shouldn't I be the one to do it?"

"I need some time to think," I reply.

"But what if you don't find anything?"

"Don't worry about it, I will" I gradually walk over to the door before pulling my hood up and over my head. "I'll be back before curfew."

"Whoa, hold up, man," Simon stands from the couch, stretching. "Won't you need any help? It's dangerous out there."

"No, I'm good," I reply, reaching for the doorknob. "Like I said, I need time to think."

"But—"

I head out the door and shut it behind me before he can finish.

In hindsight, I should've washed the blood from my face before leaving, but hey, it's Collingsworth. Nobody's going to say anything. Not even the Saints.

They'll be too busy with the gang activity.

I head over to the stairs and begin my descent to the lobby, letting the thoughts of Mae haunt me. It's still hard to believe that she's gone, especially after everything we have been through together. It all seems too sudden, too abrupt, not right.

Is it my fault?

If I didn't encourage this stupid plot, then she and Simon would've probably chickened out, and in that case, we'd all be in our classes right now. Mae would still be breathing.

I'm gonna puke.

I enter the lobby, and the check-in clerk stares me down. I glance over at him, causing his eyes to shift down to the floor. I assume he's suspicious, and why wouldn't he be? I'm covered in blood, there's obviously a gun sticking out of my back pocket, and I probably look like I belong to one of the local gangs.

The dirty stare from the clerk burns into the back of my skull.

"What's your problem?" I mutter, stopping under the doorway and keeping my eyes on the sidewalk. "It's rude to stare, buddy."

He clears his throat.

I step outside, a bitter tone in my voice, "Whatever."

The blizzard has ceased, and the full moon shines between the clouds moving across the sky. It illuminates my path as I tread through this crummy town.

※

I DIG THROUGH A DUMPSTER BEHIND ONE OF Collingsworth's bigger grocery stores. The frigid air stings my nostrils. It's snowing again, and my fingers are dark purple.

The dumpster is filled with old expired food still in packages. I'm hoping to find something fresher I could bring back. Just a few days ago, I was eating ice cream at an old-fashioned diner, and now I'm checking garbage food for expiration dates.

How nice.

My digging ends when the sound of a knife being flipped open causes my heart to jump into my throat. I pull my hands out of the dumpster and throw them in the air, thinking it might be some psychopath who's out looking for a fresh victim. The Saints won't even care if they find my body. In their eyes, it's just one less person they have to worry about.

"I don't want any trouble," I eventually say through my chattering teeth.

"What're you doing back here? In my territory? Wow, you're one ballsy kid."

I take note of everything I could use as a weapon. Lying by my foot is an old beer bottle, there's the handgun in my back pocket, and I see an old paracord rope hanging out of the dumpster.

"What do you want?" I ask.

I feel the point of a blade softly rest up against the back of my hooded head, "Any money on you?"

I laugh humorlessly, "Think if there was, I'd be digging through a dumpster, piss-wad?"

"Fair point. Any weapons?"

I know he can see the handle of the gun sticking out from my pants, and since I don't have any plans on getting stabbed in the back of the neck tonight, I nod, "Yeah. A pistol."

"I take it back, you're not ballsy, you have a death wish."

"Look, is there a point to this conversation?"

"Yep. Give me your gun, your clothes, your shoes, everything."

I sigh, "Really, man?"

"Do you want me to screw you up, kid? I will make sure no one can recognize your frozen, dead body after I'm finished with you."

"You're going to be one of those guys?"

"Uh-huh. Now hand *everything* over. Start with the shoes."

I should've taken Chloe's knife with me. I don't want to shoot anyone.

I bend over to untie my shoe- my left one in particular, "You're the boss."

The beer bottle by my feet will have to be what I use. It's only an inch away from my hands, so I've got to find the perfect opportunity to use it.

There's a green metal door next to the dumpster, and directly above it is an attached light bulb emitting enough light so I can see the man's shadow cast out next to me. I watch it carefully while pretending to untie.

"What's taking you so long?" he asks, coming off jittery. "Curfew's in thirty minutes."

I watch his shadow look down at something.

I grip the bottle in my left hand and sneer, "It's cold, prick."

I spring up, swing my body around, and shatter the bottle across the guy's face. He blurts out a swear as he stumbles back and eventually collapses to the snow-covered ground, blood gushing out of his broken nose.

I hastily reach for the gun in my back pocket and pull it out, "How much money do you have on you? And don't lie to me."

His eyes widen with fear as I point the muzzle of the gun at his face, "Piss off, kid. I ain't giving you nothin.' I've got people to watch out for."

I flip the switch to my conscience off, so I don't choke, "How would you like it if I blew each of your kneecaps off and left you out here for the Saints to find?"

I wrap my finger around the trigger, making sure he's intimidated and feels I'm serious, which I'm definitely not.

"You crazy *freak*," he flinches, reaching into his coat pocket. "Here, take it and *go*."

He hands me about twenty dollars.

I keep my gun trained on him while reaching my free hand forward and snatching the cash from his frozen grip, "Good. Now, I'm going to turn around and leave. If you follow me, or tell anyone about *anything* that happened here—"

"I get it," the man interrupts, strands of black hair hanging out of his beanie.

I stare at him a moment before turning around and walking away. I head to the front entrance of the store. A sign hanging from the double doors reads "Open," I think.

I sigh, sticking the gun back into my pocket. Without

permission, my conscience comes back to life, making me feel like a horrible person for what I just did.

I've been murdered, resurrected, told that I was going to be a part of a terrorist organization, and witnessed my friend get blown away in front of me. I just can't think properly. My mind feels short circuited.

I throw my hood off, grab my hair with both fists, and tug out of frustration.

I'm a mess.

I take a deep breath, letting go of my hair.

None of this should be happening. I'm supposed to be dead, not alive and on the run from a group of killers.

Why did I even escape?

I sigh once more and enter the store.

CHAPTER THIRTY-TWO

I walk through the entrance of the apartment complex a few minutes before curfew. There's a plastic bag of groceries gripped in my right hand. I use my left to pull the bottom of my hoodie down and over the pistol handle that peeks out of my pocket.

The guy who was at the front desk is gone, and in his place, lies a piece of paper on top of his desk that probably reads, "Be back tomorrow," or some crap. This is just an assumption though, because all I see is a bunch of gibberish I'd rather not waste my time on.

Behind me, the entry door opens. Instinctively I turn my head to see who it is, and standing in the doorway is some tall guy who looks drunk. He stumbles inside, and after realizing that I'm looking at him, he gives me a little wave.

"Good evening," he slurs.

I begin the climb to the fourth floor. I feel like an awful person for robbing that dude.

What am I going to tell Simon and Chloe? That I bashed a beer bottle across some dude's face, pulled a gun on him, and told him to give me all his money?

Yeah, that's gonna suck.

I head down the hallway that leads to our room. I stand at the door and reluctantly knock a few times. After a moment the door opens.

"Where were you?" Chloe's pretty face comes into view. "I was getting worried. You should've just let me go, I know this place, you don't."

"Sorry, but hey, look," I hold the bag of groceries up. "I got us some food."

She gawks, her eyes widening, "Whoa, where did you get all of that?"

I chuckle, "I've got my ways," I reach into my pocket and pull out a couple bucks. "I also got some cash left over in case we need anything tomorrow."

She reaches her hand out for the money. I watch as she examines it. She's almost done when Simon makes his way behind her.

"There you are," he greets. "What's in the bag?"

"Food," I reply, lifting the bag over Chloe's head and giving it to Simon. "Put it on the coffee table."

"Aye-aye, cap'n," he turns away from the door.

"Twelve dollars," Chloe says before stuffing the cash in her pocket. "Only for emergencies, right?"

"Right."

She moves behind me as I enter the apartment, asking me how I got the money. I make up a lie and tell her that someone dropped their wallet, and I helped myself to the contents inside.

Sounds better than robbing a dude at gunpoint. Right?

The three of us gather around the couch and eat some candy bars I bought from the store. We talk about tomorrow's plan and decide to find a different place. Collingsworth is too dangerous and risky for us to stay.

"So where do we go next?" Simon asks.

Chloe shrugs, "We could always head to one of our houses and stay there."

I shake my head, "Too obvious. Those are probably the first places Lazarus would look. We need somewhere less predictable."

"Like where?" Simon asks.

"What about another hotel-type-place?" I suggest.

"That could work," Chloe agrees. "Or . . ."

"Or?" I raise an eyebrow.

She pauses for a moment, and it looks like she's debating whether or not to tell us her idea, "I'll tell you guys about it in the morning. I'm gonna hit the hay."

I sigh before gradually getting to my feet, "Me too. Question is, who's going to get the bed?"

Simon's eyes go wide and he chuckles, "Definitely not me, man. Who knows what's gone down on that mattress."

"Yeah, I'm staying on the couch." Chloe says.

I shrug, "Guess I'll take it. I mean, it looked fine to me."

We all take turns saying goodnight before heading in separate directions. I open the door to the bedroom and proceed taking off my clothes as I stumble over to the bed. I sigh as I plop down onto the comforter.

Why did you escape?

I lie my head down onto the limp pillow and stare up at the ceiling, trying to answer the question before feeling like I'm being watched. I gradually look up, gasp, and blink.

Mae stands at the foot of my bed, a hole pierced in between her eyes, her face smeared in fresh blood.

I hastily rub my eyes, and she's gone.

Wiping sweat away from my forehead I lie back down. My eyes fill with bloody red tears.

I need sleep, and I need it now, but I instead head over to the bathroom and wash my face of the blood that stains my pale face.

CHAPTER THIRTY-THREE

"Hey," I feel a hand shake me gently. "Hey, wake up."

My eyes slowly open, seeing Chloe standing by my bedside.

I let out a little yawn before lazily sitting up, "What's up?"

"C'mon, we're about to head back to the car," she pulls the blanket from my body. "There's some breakfast waiting for you on the coffee table."

"Wait, why are we going back to the car?"

She bends over and picks my clothes up from the floor, "Simon and I were talking last night, and we decided that we should scout out some other areas where we can stay like you suggested. Here, put these on."

She tosses me my clothes, and I put them on, "Any places in mind?"

"No, not really . . . well, not at the moment."

"Gotcha."

I get out of bed and head over to the living room where there's a bag of powdered doughnuts sitting on the coffee table. After I'm done scarfing them down, I look around.

There's no sign of Simon.

"Hey, where's Si?" I call out toward Chloe in the other room.

"Oh, he left a little bit ago."

"Where to?"

"He went to go find us a newspaper."

"A newspaper?"

"Yeah, to see if there's anything we need to know about."

"Good idea."

I sit down on the nasty old sofa and wait, recalling the horrible dreams I had about Mae last night. Every one of them were the same; she and I were in the elevator trying to escape, and the next thing I know, a gunshot goes off, and she's on the floor with her brain blown out of her skull.

It takes a while, but eventually the apartment door swiftly opens and in walks Simon who's gripping a newspaper in his right hand

"You guys should take a look at this," he pants, sweat dripping down his forehead.

"What is it?" I ask, wiping the sugary doughnut powder off my jeans, "Something bad?"

He rapidly nods his head, "Big time. We need to get out of here as soon as possible."

I'm about to concentrate on the headline in order to read it, but below the large, dark line of words, I see a black-and-white photo of Simon, Chloe, and me making our way through the hotel lobby. It's not too easy to see the gun gripped in my left hand, the blood splattered across my face, or the sheer panic in my eyes.

"We made the front page?" I ask, my eyes growing wide. "No friggin' way. . ."

"Wait," Chloe peeks her head out of the bedroom. "What's going on?"

"Every Saint in Boston is looking for the three of us. Luckily the picture isn't that clear, so you can't really see our faces." Simon replies, waving the newspaper around. "Hurry, come and check it out."

Chloe quickly hurries over to me and Simon. She grabs the paper from his hands and reads it out loud.

"Shooting at The Boston Inn leaves thousands wondering if the United States security force is still able to keep guns off the streets and people safe. Governor Andrew Hales says 'Absolutely!' He goes on to say that every Saint stationed stateside is hunting the three individuals that are responsible," she pauses for a moment. "Sources say they believe the bunch to be a part of Lazarus. If you happen to see anyone shown in the picture above, call the hotline number listed below."

"Shooting?" I ask. "I shot a few times up in the air, nobody even got hurt."

"Taken out of context to get more people to read it," Chloe mutters. "C'mon, we need to leave and find somewhere to lie low."

Simon grabs the fabric of his hoodie, "What about these? It's clear as day we're wearing hoodies in the picture, and we can't just take them off, we'll freeze."

"What we need are school uniforms," I say. "They would be the perfect look. Nobody would expect high school students to be a part of Lazarus."

"How are we going to get a hold of any uniforms?" Simon asks. "They only hand them out at the beginning of each semester."

Chloe glances around, "Well, I know *one* way we could get our hands on a few uniforms."

"How?" I ask.

She sighs, "You two won't like the idea, not one bit."

"Lay it on us."

"I know this group of gangsters who can get their hands on anything, drugs, knives, clothes, you name it. If I give them a call, they can have three uniforms for us within thirty minutes, if they're in a good mood."

I tap my foot against the floor, trying to figure out if I agree or disagree with this idea of hers. It seems like it would work, but dealing with gangsters? Sketchy.

Simon takes a deep breath, "Can you tell us for a fact that this will work?"

"Yeah, I'm pretty sure."

I switch my gaze back and forth between Simon and Chloe, "Let's do it, then."

After spending a few minutes figuring out a little plan, I find myself in the filthy lobby on the main floor, my shoes plodding against the dirty tile as I approach the front desk.

"Hey," I greet the sleazy man behind the check-in counter. "Mind if I use that phone?"

He sees me pointing at the stationary phone placed on his desk, "Get outta Collingsworth before I turn you in, kid."

I raise an eyebrow, "Is something wrong?"

I've washed the blood from my face and made sure that the gun in my back pocket isn't visible in the slightest.

The man glances down at the newspaper on his desk before staring up at me like he just won the lottery, "You walked into my establishment shortly after the Boston Inn shooting covered in blood with a gun in your pocket. I know you're a wanted man, so you and your two friends either need to get out of here or pay me some big cash to keep quiet."

I stare at him a moment. He caught on, and if he did, anyone can.

"You're gonna let me use that phone," I say, gritting my teeth.

"And what makes you so sure of that?"

I glare at him before slowly reaching my left hand around my back and grabbing the handle that's sticking out of my back pocket, "Oh, I don't know," I retract the pistol and swing. "Maybe this?"

Before he can react, I smash the handle of the gun into the bridge of his nose with a wince-worthy crunch, making him yelp before stumbling back.

I quickly vault the desk, knocking over numerous items.

"Wait, wait!" is all he's able to yell before my fist crashes into his gut.

His upper-torso lurches forward out of reflex, giving me the opportunity to bring my knee up to his chin. His head swings back, and I grab him by the neck with my right hand and shove him back against the wall behind his desk.

I raise the barrel of the gun up to his face.

I won't let him turn me in. I'd rather get captured by Lazarus than tortured by the Saints.

"Please don't hurt me. I didn't do anything wrong."

"Shut up!" I demand, all my walled-up anger clear in my voice.

"Okay, *okay*. I'm shutting up."

"I need you to do something for me, alright?"

He nods, not uttering a word.

"I need you to get out of here, find a Saint at a checkpoint, and tell him that the three Lazarus suspects from the news are here in this apartment complex."

He nods.

I can't help my chest burning with guilt.

Who am I becoming?

My grip loosens on his throat, letting him breathe easier. I then let go of his neck entirely before telling him again what he needs to do. He says he'll get right on it, then rushes away from me and out the front entrance, blood leaking out from his nose.

I sigh, clear my throat, then turn around while putting the gun away, "We're clear."

Simon and Chloe appear from the stairwell and approach me. Both seem jittery.

Chloe chuckles, "Wow . . . you sure got the job done. I could hear you yelling at that poor guy all the way from the stairs."

I walk out from behind the counter, guilt eating me alive, "I get it."

"Why'd he scream?" Simon asks, observing the surrounding scene.

"I pistol-whipped him," I reply. "Look, can we just get on with things? Saints will swarm through this building in less than fifteen minutes."

Chloe approaches the phone lying on the desk, picks it up, and dials in a number. Once done, she puts the phone's receiver up to her right ear and waits for a few moments.

"Hey," she greets, "It's Chloe."

It goes silent for a couple seconds.

"Long story. I'll tell you about it later."

More silence.

"I need three high school uniforms as soon as possible. Think you could do that?"

Even more silence, this time it takes a little longer than before.

"Thank you *so* much. I'll meet you there in twenty . . . Yep, see ya."

CHAPTER THIRTY-FOUR

"This is sketch," Simon says, his breath turning into mist every time he speaks. "You sure about all this?"

"Of course, I'm sure," Chloe sighs. "I used to meet up with these guys all the time."

"Even if it is shady, we have no other options," I interject. "We *need* these uniforms."

The three of us stand outside a deserted alleyway toward the back of Collingsworth. It's snowing again, and to be honest, this whole situation seems horribly wrong. I don't want to agree with Simon and make Chloe feel even more uncomfortable.

"They're not even here," Simon points out. "I mean, is anybody else having that alarm going off inside their heads? Or is it seriously just me?"

"Trust me," I walk forward, stepping foot inside the alley where Chloe's guys told us to meet them. "Alarms are definitely going off."

The three of us head to the middle of the alleyway and wait. We talk about the other possible places where we can stay after this, but each of our ideas don't sound as good as they did last night.

It takes fifteen minutes for the gangsters to show up, and I feel relief wash over me. Four guys wearing winter coats and covered in face tattoos and piercings enter the alley. One of them carries a small cardboard box filled with uniforms.

The biggest one out of the four steps forward, "So it really is you. Thought you and your family were all dead. It was in the papers."

"You thought wrong," Chloe's tone darkens. "I see you brought the uniforms."

He glances back, eyeing the guy who's carrying the box, "Yep. You bring the money?"

"Uh-huh."

The man steps closer, eyeing Simon and me as the snow crunches underneath his boots, "Who are these two jokers?"

"This here is Jason," Chloe points to me, "and the other is Simon."

The man studies us, "I'm Badger. I'm guessing you're friends with Chloe, here?"

Simon and I nod.

Badger switches his gaze back to Chloe, "Let me see the money, then we'll talk uniforms, 'kay?"

She reaches into her pocket and pulls out the leftover money, "This is all I've got."

Badger looks down at the money, "What? You kiddin' me? Twelve dollars won't buy you jack-squat around here, girly."

"C'mon, dude. You and I have been doing stuff like this for years. Can't you cut me just a little bit of slack? Just a *little*?"

The tension in the air rises.

Badger glares at her, "What do you think this is? A friggin' charity? I'm trying to make a living here. Do you know how much these stupid little uniforms cost? Fifty bucks. I have a wife and two kids that depend on me to put food on the table, and how am I supposed to do that when I give into little punks like you who're asking for a *massive* handout?"

Chloe backs up a few steps, obviously uncomfortable about the short distance between her and Badger, "Look, we're in a really tight situation. What will it take to get these uniforms?"

"Seventy-five dollars," he replies, his eyes narrowing even more.

"*Seventy-five?*" she blurts, her tone harsher. "You just told me you got these for fifty."

"Yes, but I gotta make a profit somehow, don't I?"

"You're so full of—"

"Hey, Badger," the guy carrying the box interjects. "Those three look like the guys from the paper this morning, don't they?"

He pauses for a moment, studying the three of us, "You're right," he says. "Hey, I've got an idea. I bet if I call that hotline number and say I have information on the three suspected Lazarus shooters, I can make a little money. Don't you think so, Zeke?"

The man with the box nods, a snide smile wide on his face, "Oh yeah. That sounds like an *amazing* idea."

"Better yet," Badger starts, stepping closer to the three of us. "I bet if I said I had them with me right now, they'd give me a *huge* amount of moola for my location."

Zeke chuckles, "Even better."

Simon takes a sudden step forward, nose-to-nose with Badger, "And what makes you think we will let you do that? Huh?"

Badger grins, "Oh, you'll see . . ." he whistles loudly. "Come on out, boys!"

Simon, Chloe, and I quickly turn around upon hearing heavy footsteps. Four more guys pop into the alley from behind us. Each carries a baseball bat.

I go wide-eyed, "Whoa, whoa, whoa. This *isn't* necessary."

"Oh, but I think it is," Badger snaps his fingers from behind me. "I want these three beaten to a *pulp!*"

I'm about to reach for the gun in my pocket, but one of the bat-wielding thugs swings his weapon into my skull, making me instantly crumple to the snow-covered asphalt.

My vision goes blurry, but that doesn't stop me from seeing Simon lunge toward the guy that hit me. He's about to make contact, but a boot flying into my face obstructs the view.

"You're going to make me some serious money, kid," Badger slams his foot down onto my face once more, laughing.

So, this is it, I think to myself as I feel a bat bash against my kneecap and a steel-toed boot ram into my jaw. *This is how my second life ends.*

My assault suddenly stops, and as I open my eyes, the world around me freezes.

Badger stands above me with a look of pain and confusion branded to his face. The bloody tip of a blade peeks out of his stomach.

Chloe must have used her pocket knife. But as Badger lets out a heavy groan and collapses down next to me, I realize that I'm wrong. It's a man donning a Lazarus uniform. He has a camo colored backpack strapped around his shoulders and wears a gas mask. It covers his whole face, and the circle-shaped visors that cover each one of his eyes are tinted black as midnight, masking his identity.

He looks down at me, then slowly shakes his head, "Jason Pinder."

The other thug who *was* beating me with the bat, stares at the figure in disbelief, "Who– who are you?"

The man in the gas mask chuckles. He suddenly aims the pistol in his right hand up at the thug and fires. The bullet penetrates his eye and goes all the way through his brain before exiting out the back of his skull.

I flinch as he crumbles backward, a mist of blood spraying into the air.

The figure glances around at the now fearful men who were previously beating Simon and Chloe. Every one of them gawks with wide eyes and dropped jaws.

"See you all in Hell . . ." he says almost inaudibly.

In a flash, gunshots echo through the air, and I watch as the figure sprays each thug with bullets. Their corpses drop to the ground.

"The name's Raphael," he eventually states, carefully sheathing the knife in his left hand through his belt-loop. "Vice has sent me to kill the three of you."

CHAPTER THIRTY-FIVE

Raphael points his gun down at my face, "I applaud you for escaping. People usually don't have the balls to do that."

I quickly throw my hands in front of the muzzle, shielding my face, "Wait, no, don't."

"You're scared to die, aren't you?"

"Please, there's gotta be some sort of arrangement that we can make, right?"

He glances over at Simon and Chloe. He motions to the dead thugs collapsed in pools of their own blood, "An arrangement?"

"*Yes*, an arrangement," I nod frantically, carefully reaching into my back pocket. "Please, anything but killing us."

Raphael tilts his head to the side, "I tell ya what, Jason, I'll kill you first and make it quick."

I wrap my fingertips around the handle of my gun, "Or . . ."

"Or?"

I pull the gun out of my pocket, aim it up at his face, then pull the trigger.

Click.

My eyes go wide . . . the gun is jammed. I don't know how; it won't fire.

I pull the trigger again, and again.

Nothing.

Raphael laughs before slamming his foot down onto my left hand, bending over, and ripping the pistol out of my hand, "Man, you're pathetic," he stops crushing my hand and tosses the gun into the snow behind him. "Now, where was I?"

He grabs me by the hood and hoists me up to my feet before shoving me up against a brick wall. He bashes his palm into my face before head-butting me and violently slamming the back of my head against the solid, unforgiving foundation.

I feel like I'm about to black out. Shockingly, Chloe rushes up from behind and jabs her knife into his shoulder, then into the side of his neck.

Blood squirts from his throat, and I watch with a slack jaw as he falls to the ground, gasping and clutching his neck with both hands.

"C'mon!" Chloe demands while rushing over to Zeke's dead body and picking up the box of uniforms. "We need to go *now!*"

I stare down at Raphael, almost in a trance. He's reaches into his pocket and pulls a syringe out, stabbing it into his gut. He then injects himself with whatever liquid is inside before taking one last gulp of air. Dead.

Simon grabs me by the arm and pulls me along with him and Chloe out of the alley. A few minutes later, we make it to our car. I feel sick to my stomach.

"Did all that really just happen?" I ask as Chloe begins hot wiring the car.

She's frantic, "Yes, now shut up, and let me concentrate."

I lean my head against the headrest and take a deep breath, my nose throbbing, my head pounding, my hands trembling, "Sorry."

She gets the car started, and we take off.

CHAPTER THIRTY-SIX

The days that led up to the funeral went by in a flash. Simon had led us to a nasty, old apartment complex, and we pulled the same stunt we used back in Collingsworth, telling the check-in clerk we were visiting a friend. The idiot bought it. The three of us picked a room on the top floor, making sure there weren't any cameras before breaking in.

Simon went out and bought as much food as he could with the rest of our cash so we wouldn't have to leave the room unless needed, and mostly, we hung out, talking about what *needed* to happen in order for us to keep safe.

Simon planned on finding Julie. Chloe didn't really go into anything, she told us she had some *unfinished* business she had to take care of. And I, of course, would attend my family's burial.

The morning of the funeral I let Simon and Chloe take the car. The Boston Memorial Gardens was only a few blocks away. We agreed that we'd meet back at the complex before it got dark, then went our separate ways.

Outside the black metal fence that surrounds the graveyard, the snow has stopped falling from the sky, and a brisk, cold breeze screams through the air.

I leap up onto the fence; my skin sticks to the frozen metal. I pull myself over. When I land, my almost numb feet jolt back to life.

I turn around and take note of my surroundings. Dark grave markers stick up out of the icy ground. Many are shaped like crosses, and the more I study them, the more I grow uneasy. Toward the back of the cemetery, I can make out two men planting charred crosses into the snowy earth.

They're the only other people in the entire cemetery.

That can't be it? Can it?

I expected a large gathering to celebrate my family's life, but this is quite the opposite.

Why isn't anyone else here?

"Hey," I call out while approaching the two men. "Is this the Pinder service?"

The man hammering a cross looks over at me, "There wasn't one."

"What?" I question. "Paper said it started at four-thirty."

"The paper said a lot of things," the other man dismissively says. "Those who are executed don't get a service; they get burned. We just plant markers. Sorry, pal. You family, or something?"

I glance down at the ground, feeling a knot form in my stomach, "I guess you could say that . . . If you two don't mind, I'm going to stay and watch."

The two men exchange looks, both seeming puzzled.

"I won't get in the way," I say before they can speak.

One of them says, "Alright, kid."

I watch them finish. With each marker piercing the ground, my heart bruises the inside my chest. I know they're already dead, but this really seals the deal. They're gone, it's official. I know it's stupid. My entire body wants to crumple into the snow and shut down.

"Hey, buddy," one of them looks over at me upon stomping on

the last bit of dirt. "You okay? Your eyes, they're turning red."

My bottom lip quivers uncontrollably, "Yeah, could I just have a moment?"

The two men leave, not saying a word. Once I know for sure they're gone, I let the bloody build-up in my eyes burst free.

"I'm sorry," I whisper softly, staring down at the two crosses that mark my parents' graves. "You didn't deserve this. You two should've been the ones to come back, not me."

I've seen people talk to their loved-ones like this in movies, and I would laugh and joke around about it, "I will avenge you, mother!" I'd blurt, forcing a wheezing laugh to burst out of Simon's mouth.

Yeah, those movies are stupid.

The blood from my eyes drip down onto the snow below me, and I silently tell my parents I love them, and how sorry I am that they were executed. The only way I'll be able to find closure is to avenge our deaths.

I will find you, Matthew. . . I swear I will find you and do what you did to them.

I can still see it whenever I close my eyes. I see the blood gushing out of my dad's skull and the bullet that penetrated my mom's face.

I shudder with my teeth clenched.

It's funny, really. We never know what we have until it's gone. I was always close to my parents, but I didn't say "I love you" as much as I should have. Now they're gone, and I'll never be able to tell them how amazing they were.

My shoulders drop, more blood spilling from my eyes.

"Wow," a sudden deep, metallic voice says from behind me. "This is kinda pathetic."

My heart free-falls into the pit of my stomach, and my bloody eyes go wide.

Raphael . . . he's still alive.

I step back from him, "I saw you die."

Raphael laughs coldly, "You were shot in the neck, weren't you?"

I pause, anger surging through me, "Well what are you waiting for, huh? Just kill me already! Why are you playing with me? Is this some sort of mind game?"

Raphael chuckles, then sighs, "Don't be so dramatic, Pinder."

Something snaps in me. Rage swells through my chest, adrenaline spikes inside my veins, and a scream bursts from my throat. I lunge at him.

We both go flying to the ground. He slams his knuckles into my face, and before the pain can register, I jab my elbow into his sternum. We go back and forth, each receiving devastating strikes.

"You *pendejo!*" he yells, slamming the palm of his hand into my nose.

I cry out before forcing my fist into his gut rapidly, *"Shut up!"*

He quickly reaches for his knife, and I try to stop him, but it's too late.

"Now will you stop?" he asks snidely, holding the razor-sharp blade up against my throat. "Don't think I won't do it. You're extremely arrogant, you know that? Just so you know, your life is in my hands, right now."

None of my blows even seem to have phased him.

"No matter what I do, you're just going to kill me," I say through gritted teeth. "So just get it over with."

"I'm not here to kill you, anymore," he says. "I came here because I wanted to talk."

"You're screwing with me."

"No killing, just talking. Alright?"

"Fine."

I get up off him. We stand face-to-face.

"Talk on," I mutter, preparing myself mentally for another fight.

He brushes the snow off the backside of his jeans, "Your

parents were murdered, and so were you. You guys were innocent, but that didn't stop the execution from happening."

"Where's this going?"

"Aren't you angry?"

I snort humorlessly, "What do you think?"

"What do I think?" he asks. "I think you're dead on the inside."

I glare, "Now *you're* the one being dramatic."

"You can get revenge. You can make sure that your parents' death doesn't go unavenged."

"Don't you think that's been my plan? I just need to find a place to start."

"You start by going back to Lazarus. From there, you find your path of vengeance."

I chuckle, still no traces of humor, "They'd kill me the second I stepped foot back in there."

"Probably," Raphael states bluntly. "But there is a *slight* chance that they'll forgive you and your friends. Trust me, Pinder, this is your best option."

"And what if I decline your little suggestion?"

"I'll kill you and dump your body somewhere where nobody will ever find it."

For the next few moments, we just stare at each other.

Sure, if I head back to Lazarus, I may get shot on sight; but there's the chance I can get my revenge. I can *find* Matthew.

It's a risk, and I will take it.

I hold my hand out, "Fine. You have a deal."

"Good."

I flinch as he abruptly jabs a needle into the side of my neck, and I collapse to the snowy ground.

CHAPTER THIRTY-SEVEN

My eyes spring open, and I can only see black. My breathing turns quick and heavy as I try to move but fail. I quickly conclude that I'm restrained to something, and I also realize that I'm seated in what I assume to be a cold metal chair.

"He's awake," an unfamiliar voice announces.

"Where am I?" I ask.

The black sack is pulled from my face and the sudden light from a dangling bulb blinds me. In front of me, I can make out three people: Tommy, Bleach, and some light-skinned Hispanic kid who seems to be around my age.

The room is small and dimly lit, and my assumption was correct. I *am* seated in a metal chair. Both my hands and feet are handcuffed to the arms and legs of the seat.

"You're back in Lazarus," Bleach replies, her tone lacking any pity it used to carry. "How do you feel?"

"Piss off," I mutter.

The teenager in the room examines me up and down, "I like him."

"Who're you?"

He chuckles, "That doesn't really matter, does it?"

I shake my hands around once more, making the cuffs rattle, "So, what now? You gonna kill me?"

Bleach's eyes narrow, "Why don't you take a closer look around."

I do as I'm told, gazing down. Positive and negative jumper cables are hooked up firmly to each arm of the chair. I'm in for a world of horrific pain. My chest floods with the bitter sting of anxiety.

I struggle even more, "C'mon, you don't need to do this. I came back didn't I?"

"Not on your own free will," Tommy reminds me. "You were forced," he turns over to the other guy. "Isn't that right, Raphael?"

The guy shrugs, "I gave him a choice. Either die or come back. He made his decision."

My face twists into a mask of rage, "Wait, *you're* Raphael?"

He doesn't reply.

"*You said* they would accept me back in," I abruptly shout, spit flying from my mouth.

"I said they *might*," he corrects.

Tommy parks himself in front of me, obstructing my view of everything else, "Why would you do this? Don't you think I would've taken care of you, here? Don't you trust me?"

"Trust?" I laugh. "You lied to me for *years*. You made me feel safe around you, but the whole time you were just slithering your way into my life and now look where we are!"

"I did what I had to do," he says, his expression growing somber. "Me looking out for you wasn't fake. You and Simon were like family. Do you know how much it hurt to put you two in this situation?"

"How much it hurt *you*?" I retort, gritting my teeth. "You're not the one who's being forced into this, the one who was resurrected back from the dead, and who left *everything* behind."

"You kidding me?" he asks. "I've sacrificed more for this organization than you could even *believe*. I left my pregnant wife, my two kids, my mom, my dad, *everyone*. At least you can be at peace with the fact that your family is dead, to know nothing else will happen to them. Emily is now a single mother who has to raise an entire family by herself because *I'm* gone," he pauses, breathing deeply. "All because of that snitch, Brandon Yancey."

"Brandon Yancey? You know him?"

He stares, "Rumors were starting, Jason. People were catching on that I was getting relaxed, that I wasn't checking ID's thoroughly, and that I didn't do much when I saw minor laws being broken. Saints at the other entrance were also taking bribes, letting kids go out past curfew for money. It wasn't good, and I suppose other people outside of Brookhaven weren't too happy with this. It didn't look good that our checkpoint cameras would 'go out' periodically," he pauses again, his teeth gnashed. "Word got back to higher authority about our little community, and a Reaper was sent out to find someone who could catch us in the act. They chose Yancey, and he got plenty of evidence. I caught on and sent Lazarus after him. We made him a better deal. If he'd get rid of the evidence and lie to the Reaper, we'd pay him. He accepted, but when the Reaper came back the next week, he pissed his pants and said *I* confiscated the evidence and *burnt* it."

"And then what?"

"Well, it gets *even* better . . . Apparently the Reaper had bugged his restaurant with mics and heard our little conversation with him. This led him to believe Brookhaven and some other key areas were important to Lazarus. They believed Yancey was a traitor and informant. They had him killed. They would come after me next, but I set up my own death before they could . . ." he stops, this time raising his voice. "Brookhaven wasn't even *supposed* to be on Mills' watch-list! We weren't *supposed* to be touched!"

I lower my head, a mix of emotions bursting through me. Poor stupid Brandon. Swiftly I focused back on the present, "Don't do this Tommy. Don't kill me- not before I pay the man that executed my family a visit. Just let me go, I won't run."

Tommy sighs before turning around and snapping his fingers, "Let's go you two."

The three of them leave, and in their place walks in two tall and muscular men in the Lazarus uniform. Each don a hockey mask, one blue, the other red.

"At least kill me yourself, you coward!" I shout, hoping he can hear me.

The man in the red hockey mask connects his knuckles with my cheek, "*Quiet!*"

I glare up at him defiantly, "Bite me."

"I said *quiet,*" he hits me once more, causing my head to snap to the side.

"Ready for a spark?" the guy in the blue mask asks, kneeling down beside a large car battery stationed near the front of the room. The other set of positive and negative cables are in his hands.

The man in the red mask nods, "Always."

My eyes widen when a sudden flow of voltage surges through my entire body. Instantly, I violently thrash around against my will. My brain feels as if it's bashing against both sides of my skull, and I feel my heart combusting.

After a moment, the jolting stops, leaving me to frantically gulp down air.

"How'd that feel?" blue mask guy asks. "You ready for more?"

I try to tell him no, but drool is the only thing leaving my mouth.

"What was that? You want me to attach the cables back up to the battery?"

Slurred gibberish and saliva spill from my lips.

"That's what I thought you said."

The voltage sparks through me once more, my body lurching as if I'm having the world's most violent seizure. I let out a scream, my body throbs with each pulse of electricity. I'm about to black out, but Mae abruptly appears by the door. A bloody hole decorates her pale forehead. I scream louder. She disappears, and slobber streams out of my mouth.

"Alright, alright, cut it," red mask says. "It's time to spice things up."

The surge stops, and I gasp for air before vomiting all over my clothes.

The two men laugh.

"*Kill me*," I'm finally able scream. "Just *do* it!"

The guy in the red mask snorts, "Where's the fun in that?" He turns to his buddy, "Hand me the vinegar."

Blue mask does as he's told, picking up a carton of vinegar from up off the floor. He walks over to his partner and places it in his hands.

"Good," he says. "Now lift his shirt up and over his head."

"Aye-aye, captain."

I watch in terror as the guy in the blue mask approaches me, grabbing the bottom of my blue polo and lifting it up and over my head, blinding me. My stomach drops as the chair is tipped back, and before I can get a good breath of air, they pour bitter liquid all over my covered face.

My eyes are scorching, my nostrils sting, and the skin around my mouth is on fire. I gag as the vinegar makes its way down my throat, my chair leans back farther, the blazing liquid rushing up my nose faster.

I struggle, but my restraints don't give in. It feels as if I'm drowning in a lake of fire, unable to swim to the surface. I panic and knot up on the inside. I struggle even harder; my eyes instinctively clamp shut. The stinging is overwhelmingly unbearable.

After a few moments, they stop. The chair straightens back onto all four legs, and they pull the shirt from my head. Like clockwork, I puke up mouthful after mouthful of vinegar, my throat smoldering.

I cannot open my eyes, so I leave them closed. I scream in agony.

"So, tell me," one man starts. His voice is smug. "That girl in the elevator, the one who was killed while trying to escape, you knew her personally, right?"

"Kiss my—"

A fist goes flying into my jaw, "I asked you a question!"

"*Yes*," I reply, the burning in my nostrils not easing. "I *knew* her."

"Did you hear about the rumors? People say that they resurrected her, again."

My shaky voice immediately softens, "Really?"

They both laugh, "Nope."

I stay silent.

One man wipes my eyes with a dry cloth, and my eyelids can part. The stinging is still too much to handle, so I keep them closed.

"Well, it's been fun," I hear the cocking of a gun and consider opening my eyes. "But we have orders to kill you."

I lean forward, my restraints partly holding me back, "Go ahead."

He presses the barrel of the gun up against my forehead, the cool metal sending a chill down my spine.

"Good luck," he says.

My eyes stay closed and I wait, but the door to the room swings open, and my burning eyes flash wide.

Tommy screams, "We need him alive."

The two men turn around, both looking bewildered.

"Weren't we ordered to execute him?" one asks.

"Yeah, you *were*, but we received a call."

"A call from who?"

"Vice . . . he wants to meet him."

CHAPTER THIRTY-EIGHT

Tommy wipes the sweat from his forehead, "We need to get him up to the rooftop. The two other escapees are already there."

For a moment, the two punishers just stare at each other in disbelief.

"What're you two just standing there for?" Tommy snaps. "Uncuff the kid!"

Blue mask uncuffs my hands and feet, and red mask hoists me up. But as soon as he lets go of me, I collapse to the cold floor, incapable of maintaining my balance.

"The kid was just amped," Tommy says, exasperated. "He can't walk on his own."

The two men quickly pull me up, letting me use their shoulders for balance. Tommy leads us out of the room, and I fade in and out of consciousness. Every time my eyes open, I'm being helped through a series of corridors, but every time my eyes are closed, I swim around in darkness. My mind cannot focus on anything but keeping my abnormal heart beat from stopping.

The inside of my skull still burns, my heart aches, and almost every muscle in my body feels sore and tingly.

This is hell.

"Hey, you okay?" I hear a voice ask. "Jason?"

My eyes jolt open, my vision is blurred, and in front of me I see my mother's electric blue eyes. She's cupping my face with both hands, staring into my matching eyes.

"M-mom?" I utter.

Abruptly, the image of her is replaced by Tommy's panic-stricken face, "Stay with me, Jason. I need you to keep your eyes open, okay?"

I look from side to side, my two torturers are balancing me upright, "I'm fine . . ."

"You sure?"

I try to say yes, but crumple earthward, my eyes rolling to the back of my skull before I smack against the tiled floor.

My mind swims in nothingness for what seems like an eternity, muffled voices flood the inside of my ears.

"What's his status?" Tommy's tone reeks of anxiety.

"Sir, I can't find a pulse."

"Look harder!"

"There's nowhere else to look."

"Move, you idiot!"

I feel a fist slam down onto my chest, forcing my eyes to open and my starved lungs to function. Kneeling on one side of me is Tommy, and on the other, the dude in the red mask.

Tommy sighs, "He's alive."

I don't speak, just stare at him in utter confusion.

What just happened?

As if reading my thoughts, he says, "I think your heart just stopped," he pulls something out of his pocket and holds it out before me. "That voltage screwed you up. Here, take this, alright? It'll make you feel better."

He's holding a small red pill.

"What does it do?"

"I heard Bleach told you all about Rebirth, right? How the

nanobots in the serum loiter around in your body until you're healthy so they can repair any injuries that may occur to you shortly after resurrection?"

"Uh-huh."

"You puke them out, yet?"

"No, I don't think so."

"This pill will enhance them, make them work faster and harder. They'll quickly repair any internal injuries you have and then some. Take it."

I toss the pill into my mouth, swallowing it with some effort. Then, Tommy helps me back up to my feet, and I get a good look at the guy in the blue mask. He lies sprawled out across the floor. His blood is splattered across the wall behind him like a morbid pointillism painting.

Tommy catches me staring, "He disobeyed orders."

The three of us continue down the hallway, and as my senses become less foggy. I'm able to recall where I am. This corridor belongs to sector K. There's the elevator stationed at the back of the hall. Seeing it triggers that disturbing flashback. I shudder, shaking my head rapidly to rid the memory from my mind.

Tommy grips the ID tag around his neck and presents it to the scanner. Instantly, the elevator doors slide open with a *ding* and Tommy, red mask, and myself enter.

"Listen up," Tommy presses a button, letting the doors close. "Raphael will escort you and your friends to a location where you will meet Vice. Now, I'm not going to lie to you, whenever he wants to meet with somebody, it's for one of two things."

"Which are?" I ask, gazing at the clean wall behind us.

"Either he needs something done by you, or he wants to kill you . . . himself."

My eyes narrow down at the floor, "Peachy."

"Any questions?"

"Just one."

"What is it?"

"Why is Raphael escorting us?"

"Raphael is in Vice's personal squad. He's one of the few people on this entire planet who knows where he is even stationed at."

"He looks my age," I say. "I thought we were the first batch of teenage recruits?"

"With the exception of Raphael," Tommy remarks. "Vice and that kid have some type of a father-son relationship."

"How'd that happen?"

"All I know is that Raphael was just a boy when he found him. The kid lived on the streets and crap. I don't know all the details, but he's untouchable now. He's even next in line for power if anything happens."

Ding!

The elevator doors part from each other, revealing the hotel's rooftop. I'm surprised to see a large jet-black military chopper with its blades rotating furiously. Its side-door is open, and on the inside sit Simon and Chloe; they're both unconscious. Someone has beaten them pretty bad.

"What's that!" I shout over the deafening noise.

"Your transport!" Tommy shouts back. "Hey, Jason?"

"What?"

"No hard feelings, right? I was just following orders!"

I stare at him, almost laughing. He thinks we're good after what just happened? He had his men torture me, ordered them to execute me, but as soon as there's a change of plans, he thinks we're suddenly good?

I walk off without saying another word to him. The helicopter's noise threatens to blow out my eardrums. I enter the side-door and I'm greeted with a gruesome sight. Blood is everywhere, splattered all over the windows, spilled all over the floor, and sprayed across all the seats where I will sit.

I gag, just as someone places a hand on my shoulder. Raphael is wearing a black headset, and in his hand is an identical one. I take it he wants me to put it on, so I comply.

"You hear me?" I watch his lips move, but his voice is pouring through the headset.

"Yeah, it's fuzzy, though."

"You'll live."

I glance around, "What happened, here?"

A grin makes its way onto his face, "Right when your little torture session started, Vice called saying he wanted to meet with you and your friends. He also said a helicopter filled with Saints was patrolling around Boston, and how some of our undercover moles were among them, awaiting orders. So good ol' Tommy-boy gave them a little call and let's just say things went off without a hitch."

"How many of your guys were with them?"

"Two."

"And they killed an entire transport of Saints?"

"Element of surprise, Pinder," he points toward Simon and Chloe. "Take a seat. I'll be with you in a moment, I've gotta go give our new pilot and copilot directions."

I take a seat next to Chloe. Her head is leaned back and resting against Simon's. The area around her right eye is black and purple, and there's also some dried blood trailing from each one of her nostrils.

Simon doesn't look too good either. His left cheek is littered with minor gashes and his lower lip is slightly busted and bleeding.

I sigh before leaning back in my seat. Raphael speaks with the two pilots. Their voices flow through the headset and into my ears so perfectly that it feels like they're living inside my head and barking orders to my brain.

The only thing that unsettles me about meeting with Vice is that I'll either die today as a somewhat innocent person or live on in a life filled to the brim with death. I'll be a pawn in a game of murderers by selling my soul to Lazarus.

Isn't that what you wanted though? I ask myself. *To help overthrow the government? To get revenge?*

"Your hands are twitching," Raphael's voice snaps me from my thoughts.

I look up from the floor, "I was just hooked up to a car battery."

He takes a seat next to me, patting my shoulder, "You have no idea how lucky you are, Jason, do you?"

"Oh, yeah," I begin. "I feel *oh so privileged* to meet the czar who's in charge of all this."

"Watch yourself, Pinder. Respect is key to living through this."

"What?"

"I already know what will happen to you."

"Really?"

"Yes, really."

I breathe in deeply, closing my eyes. I want to ask him what will happen, but I know I won't get an answer. So, what's the point?

The helicopter gradually ascends from the rooftop. The two pilots chat with each other, going over multiple safety protocols.

"Enjoy the ride, Pinder," Raphael's sinister tone bounces in my skull.

CHAPTER THIRTY-NINE

"Wake up," I feel a pair of hands shaking me. "We're landing."

My eyes open, and I sit up from leaning against Chloe. She and Simon are still out like a light, both snoring, blood still dried to their faces.

"How long have I been asleep?" I ask Raphael, who's sitting by my side.

"A few minutes." he replies. "Wake your friends up."

I gently shake Chloe until her eyes open full of puzzlement. She attempts to speak, but it's inaudible.

I point to my headset, slowly mouthing, "I can't hear you."

She seems to catch on.

I reach over her and rapidly tap on Simon's shoulder. He jolts awake, scanning his surroundings. Eventually, his line of sight is aimed toward me, and I'm able to tell him to hold on through various hand movements.

The helicopter descends onto another rooftop while a wave of unnerving suspense washes over me. At the moment you face your mortality it's not too bad, you don't have time to think. But there's no feeling worse than knowing you're being led to your potential execution.

I'm not ready to die, again.

The helicopter lands on the roof's helipad, the rotating blades slowing to a stop. I take my headset off, shooting Simon and Chloe a sympathetic smile as the engine shuts down.

"Hey." I say.

"What's going on?" Simon asks.

"Yeah, and where are we?" Chloe adds. More blood trails from her nose.

Raphael beats me to the reply, "You three are meeting with Vice."

Chloe scratches the back of her head, still dazed from previous events unknown to me, "Who?"

"Our leader," Raphael replies, now standing, "Come on you three, we've got to go get dressed."

"Get dressed?" Simon asks, feeling his busted lip with his tongue.

"You two sure ask a lot of questions," Raphael sighs. "Just follow me and go with the flow."

The three of us follow Raphael to the side-door. He gives a shout at the pilots, telling them to wait where they are and not to leave without us.

⁂

"WHY ARE WE DRESSED LIKE THIS?" CHLOE ASKS Raphael as the four of us slowly make our way down a long hallway, doors line the hall on either side.

I was too distracted on the helicopter to realize that the rooftop we landed on belongs to the biggest hotel franchise in all the nation, The Sweet Spider. This hotel is probably the fanciest one I've ever stepped foot into.

"Don't ask," he replies, fixing the blue tie that's looped around his collar. "Just know when you meet with people like Marshal, you don't wear just any clothes."

"Who's Marshal?" Simon questions.

No answer.

The three of us guys wear white button-up shirts, each with a different colored tie. We each also wear black slacks and shiny dark formal shoes. Chloe wears a black skirt and a white button-up shirt that isn't buttoned all the way up. Finishing her look is a pair of high heels she doesn't look comfortable in.

Raphael helped the three of us get cleaned up in one bathroom. He fixed our hair and washed the blood from Simon and Chloe's faces. *Mostly*, we look alright.

"Why is such a *powerful* person inside a public hotel?" I ask Raphael, walking alongside him while eyeing the numbers stenciled into all the room doors. "I mean, I would've guessed he'd be in a secret place, you know?"

He snorts, shaking his head, "You really think this is the place? Vice came to meet *us*, not the other way around. Only certain people know where he's located, me being one."

"Can you please tell us why we're meeting with this guy?" Simon asks, adjusting his tie.

"Jason knows," Raphael says. "You can ask him."

Simon and Chloe look at me, so I enlighten them, "Vice will decide if the three of us will live or die."

"What?" Chloe looks at me with enlarged eyes. "Are you *serious?*"

Raphael groans, "You three should be grateful. Before, they had decided you would be executed. At least you now have a slight chance of walking away with a pardon."

"What do you mean by a *slight* chance?" Simon asks.

"I will let you all in on a little, tiny secret," Raphael starts. "But you never heard it from me, got it?"

We all agree.

"Jason will be the one who decides if you three get out of here alive."

I blanch, "What is that supposed to mean?"

"Just do as you're told, and you will all be fine."

My legs tremble as we turn into the next hallway, and at the end of this new corridor lies a set of brown oak doors.

I ask Raphael if that's where we're meeting Vice, and he nods.

My heart beats violently as we eventually come to a halt in front of the doors. That it will somehow be me who picks our outcome makes me want to curl up into a ball and vomit all over my fancy new threads.

Raphael glances over at us, "Shall we?"

I feel liquid rush up my throat, but I quickly swallow, "Let's get this over with."

CHAPTER FORTY

It looks like a conference room; not at all what I expected. Centered in the middle lies a massive oval shaped table with fifteen people seated around it. Four seats remain vacant.

Out of all the people in the room, the lean man who sits at the head of the table sticks out the most. He's dressed in a black suit and tie . . . and wears a mask. It's a metallic morph mask, hiding his entire face and making it impossible to identify any facial features or even his hair color.

I presume this is the man who will change everything.

Vice. The Head of Lazarus.

"Ah, Jason Pinder," he says, his Boston accent prominent. "I've been eagerly awaiting your arrival. Come take a seat, all of you."

He sounds like a mobster.

Simon, Chloe, Raphael, and I approach the four empty seats and sit down, not uttering a single word. After a moment of uneasy silence, Vice continues to speak, this time in a heavily harsh and bitter tone that scratches my sensitive bones.

"I will address the massive elephant in the room, here. You shot two of *my* guards, escaped one of *my* facilities with a few of your friends, and fired a gun in *my* hotel lobby. Not to mention that little miss blondie thought it would be funny to stab my successor in the throat."

I say nothing, just stare at him.

"You know how lucky you all are?" he asks. "I kill people for far less, and I mean *far less*."

"We're all here though, and everyone's fine," Chloe says, twiddling her thumbs.

Simon nods, "Yeah, she's right."

Vice laughs, "I *love* how you two speak to me as if we're equals," he pauses. Then he screams, "We're not equals! You hear me? We're not!"

The three of us stare at him in shock.

It's clear that this man isn't patient, and the last thing I want him to do is to shoot the three of us because Simon and Chloe weren't showing him any respect.

"Look," he says in a calmer tone, now pointing at me. "I don't want to kill you. I don't want to kill any of you, but sometimes, I don't have a choice in the matter. I will ask each of you a question, and you are all going to answer honestly; don't screw with me. Jason, I will start with you first. Are you willing to be my . . . puppet?"

I stare blankly, not exactly sure what to say.

"Well?" he leans forward, expecting my response. "Are ya?"

"What do you mean?" I ask, my heart speeding up.

"It's simple, really," his voice is dangerous. "Are you willing to let me be your ventriloquist and shove my hand *deep* up inside you and control your *every* move?"

"I, uh . . .," my tongue is tied.

Vice abruptly stands, making me flinch ever so slightly, "See, here's the thing, Pinder," he reaches his hand into his back pocket. "I don't like it when I ask someone a simple question and they don't respond."

My blood runs cold as he pulls a pistol out from his slacks and aims the barrel directly at my face. His finger is curled around the trigger, and he shows no hesitance.

"Yes!" I blurt out, my heart lurching. "Yes, I'm willing to be your puppet! I *am* your puppet!"

"See, now was that so hard?" he asks, his voice now dropping. "Don't know if I believe you though."

He aims the gun lower and pulls the trigger, causing a muzzle flash. He pulls it again, and again, and again. Each bullet penetrates my chest, ripping through my ribcage and exiting through my back.

I slide out of the chair. My back slams against the floor. I gasp for air and clutch my shredded chest. It feels like I was impaled with a smoldering hot metal poker. I can feel warm liquid rushing up my throat. I'm gurgling on my blood and it spews out from between my lips.

"I told you not to screw with me!" Vice shouts. His voice echoes in my ears, "I asked you one question, one friggin' simple question, and you hesitate to answer!"

Chloe screaming my name drowns out everything else and slips into white noise. Darkness seeps into the corners of my vision. I can't think. I can't speak. I'm about to fade away when everything stops. The screaming of my name vanishes, the blackness evaporates into nothing, and I'm left with a faint electronic humming, pounding inside my eardrums.

My eyes bulge as a wave of agony surges through each wound and then all the pain simultaneously stops. I cough up the blood pooled in my mouth, and to my great relief, I'm able to breathe perfectly.

I look down at my chest, shocked at the lack of pain.

What's happening?

I remember the pill Tommy gave me. He told me it would enhance the nanobots inside my body temporarily. Never would I have guessed that it would magnify their abilities *this* much.

I burst into a fit of uncontrollable laughter, catching everybody in the room off guard, including myself. Simon and Chloe stare down at me with horror leaking from their eyes.

I've already been resurrected, defying human nature, but with this . . .? I took four bullets to the chest and here I am, still alive and laughing like a rabid hyena.

I'm a freak.

Blood flows down my cheeks like wild streams straying from a river. My bloody tears blend with the crimson spewing out of my mouth and the blood drenching my white shirt. I must be one hellish sight to everyone else in the room.

Vice chuckles, "Man, you're a *mess*!" he drops the gun down onto the table. "I suppose it makes sense you still have those nanobots inside you. Who gave you the enhancement pill though?"

I wheeze out my answer, my side aches as maniacal sounds escape my throat along with the blood. I'm laughing hard, and I can't stop.

"I *love* this," Vice eventually says, now sitting back down in his seat. "One of you, get that *freak* back in his chair. Be mindful of the blood though. You don't know where this kid's been."

The guy who was sitting to my far left stands from the table and approaches me. He grabs me by the arms and lifts me from up off the ground, forcing me back into my seat.

Vice looks over at the two people sitting to his right. He's silent for a moment before muttering, "Bring in our little guest. It's time to see if these three will be put down or not."

They nod and walk toward the brown oak doors. Once they're gone and shut the doors, Simon turns to me, a look of concern plastered to his face.

"How did you survive that?"

I'm giggling. I attempt to talk, but I'm unable to. I can't control my actions and it makes me giggle even harder.

"*Ah, man,*" Vice says. "Pinder, my man, you are a riot. A *friggin'* riot."

"What's wrong with him?" Chloe asks, her eyes wide. "What did you do?"

"Me? I didn't do a thing," he replies. "It's the pill he took. The side effects are quite *nasty*."

"What pill?" Simon breaks our gaze and stares at the masked man.

Vice looks as if he's about to answer, but the doors to the conference room swiftly open. We all turn, and my laughing instantly ceases.

Vice's two members stand in the doorway. Clutched between them stands Jakob Holmes.

CHAPTER FORTY-ONE

"What is he doing here?" I grit my teeth, blood still uncontrollably spilling from my eyes. "The Saints took him, he's supposed to be rotting away somewhere."

"Pinder?" Jakob's face is black and blue from what I assume to be recent beatings. His right hand is still missing, and the middle finger on his left is absent.

Vice drags a chair over to the corner of the room, "Bring him here."

"You said you were letting me go," Jakob mutters, struggling helplessly. "You pricks said you wouldn't do anything else to me as long as I cooperated!"

"Oh, I'm not going to do a *thing* to you," Vice says. "It's Jason who'll be doing it all for me, you pudgy little worm."

"What?" I look away at Jakob and stare at Vice.

He slowly strolls back over to the table as they place Jakob in a chair, "You have a choice here. Either you prove your loyalty this instant, or you and your friends die."

"Prove my loyalty? How?" I ask, getting revenge on Jakob fuels my adrenaline.

Vice slides his gun across the table. It slightly spins and comes to a stop in front of me, "Kill Jakob. That's all I ask. You do this, and we'll discuss your new positions here at Lazarus. Do we have a deal?"

I stare down at the gun, "That's all? Kill the kid that made my life feel like hell?"

"Exactly. Follow that simple order and I will pardon you for all your wrongdoings."

I grab the gun and get to my feet, turning toward the now zip-tied Jakob. He's defenseless.

Jakob still taunts me.

Cocky little filth-bag, doesn't he know what type of situation he's in?

I narrow my eyes, "You're one stupid piss-face, you know that?"

"You're not man enough to shoot me," he jeers defiantly. "You're going to choke and screw it all up like you *always* do."

"Oh, you think so, huh?"

"I know so."

"I don't know why you're so sure. It's either I kill you, or my two friends and I get capped. Think I want to die, piss-wad?"

He smirks, "I sure hope so."

I aim the gun down at his foot, "You first."

I pull the trigger, watching the bullet go through his shoe, which makes him scream. I then fire again, this time shooting a round into his kneecap.

He howls once more, tears forming in his wide eyes.

I turn away and use my free hand to tug at my hair, conflicted. I mean, am I really going to kill him?

You have to.

I groan, tugging at my hair even harder.

Just get it over with.

I'm prepared to blow his brains out, but there's a part of me that's fighting. *I don't want to kill anyone, I honestly don't, because if I do, my life will change forever.*

But it already has, hasn't it?

If I don't do this, my friends and I will die right here and now.

"What are you waiting for, Jason?" Vice asks, his voice pierces my brain. "Shoot him."

I breathe while letting go of my hair, turning back around, "Yes, sir."

I aim the end of the barrel at Jakob's face, my finger wrapped around the trigger.

"You won't," he mutters, wincing. "You don't have the balls."

I squeeze but not enough. I want to put a bullet in his head, but I can't. I'm too scared of the guilt . . . of the change. What would my parents think?

Nothing, because they're dead, and Jakob is the only thing standing in your way of revenge.

He's tied up, and if I shoot him, it will be in nothing but cold blood.

I look over at Vice, my teeth grinding, "I can't."

He tilts his head to the side, "Well, that's unfortunate, now isn't it?" he grabs another pistol from his slacks and aims it over at Simon. "Guess we'll start with him, then blondie, and after the two of them are on the ground, dead, I'll make sure Mr. Holmes is the one who takes you out."

His words are the ultimate insult. *Me? Killed by Jakob?*

Jakob laughs, still wincing in pain, "It's okay, Pinder, I'll make sure you die quickly."

I bring my attention back over to him, overwhelmed by rage, "Shut up!"

He leans forward before spitting on me, "Just wait until they let me go. I'll break you."

I bare my teeth.

"Five," Vice counts down. "Four."

They will execute Simon and Chloe if I don't do this.

"Three."

Just do it

"Two."

I tremble, and Jakob throws insults.

"One."

I let out a raging scream before squeezing the trigger five times in a row.

CHAPTER FORTY-TWO

The gun slips from my grip, and it lands with a metallic thud on the white carpet.

I slowly turn to Vice, asking, "Was that to your liking, sir?"

He claps, his gloved hands dully smacking against each other, "Indeed it was."

Jakob's face is masked in red. His lifeless body slumps in the chair. He eerily twitches his hands and feet.

I killed him.

"Well, a deal's a deal, kid," Vice sits back down. "Come, take a seat and we'll talk about you and your friends' future."

I walk with wobbly legs back to my chair. Vice continues speaking, this time with a calmer and more business-like tone.

"Since you're mine, I will not execute you. Same with your friends. Instead, I'll reward you three with another chance here at Lazarus. You will go back to my training facility and you will continue your training with my instructors. Any questions before I go on?"

Simon raises his hand.

"Yes, Mr. Davis?"

"What if I don't want to go back?"

My heart lurches into the pit of my stomach the second I hear those words. What he just said is going to get him killed, making what I did *pointless*.

Vice stares at him for a moment, "And why wouldn't you?"

"There's stuff I need to know about first."

"Like?"

"My sister is at a college in Washington D.C. Is she dead like everyone else?"

"You had your throat slit in your sleep, correct?"

"I think so."

"It was. Listen, they pushed your sister off the roof of her dormitory that same night. They wanted no one related to those who were killed left alive. Also, your father's been dead for two years. Your mother met the same fate as you."

Simon blinks a few times, taking sharp inhales, his face turning pale, "You're lying."

"There would be no point for me to lie to you, Mr. Davis," Vice says, pausing. "I'm sorry for your loss."

I know the only death that saddens Simon is Claire's. They were close, inseparable, best friends. He couldn't give a crap for his dad's death, or his suicidal step-mom's. It was only ever Claire that he considered family even if she hadn't felt the same the past few years. She was the reason he wanted to escape.

I wait a moment before speaking, "So . . . where do we go from here?"

"I like that you are a man who wants to get right down to business, Pinder," Vice says. "I want - sorry - I *need* you three to do something very important for me."

"Like what?" Chloe asks.

"I need one of you to win Fight-Night."

I raise an eyebrow, "Fight-Night?"

Vice leans back in his chair, clasping his hands together, "It's a little event your facility is putting on in three months. It's where the best of the best of your division will battle it out to see who's the top recruit, and as of right now, you three will compete in my name.”

“What happens if we lose?” Chloe asks.

“Punishments. . . Harsh punishments. Like I said, you’re competing in *my* name; some of my top dogs and I place bets, and I don’t like to lose. There *are* a few perks if you win though- besides becoming official members.”

“Such as?” I question.

“Usually, yours truly assigns members to their squad, but if one of you wins, I’ll let the three of you pick your squads after completing my task.” he looks over at Raphael. “I need you to escort these three back to their facility.”

“Yes, sir,” Raphael gradually stands from his seat. “C’mon, you three”

Chloe and I do as we’re told, but Simon remains seated, bloody tears trickling down his pale cheeks.

I carefully grab his hand and help him up. I put my arm around him to steady his gait. The three of us follow Raphael out of the conference room.

I take one last look at Jakob. Blood drips from his corpse onto the floor. I swallow the metallic flavor in my mouth and turn away.

Suddenly, Vice stops us. “Wait, hold on.”

We all slightly turn our heads back to see him.

“I expect no more mischief, Mr. Pinder?”

I nod my head.

“Mr. Davis?”

Simon nods his head.

“Ms. Frye?”

Chloe nods her head.

“Alright, then. Hopefully, we’ll meet again here in three months. Good luck, you three.”

We exit the room.

Raphael leads us back to the bathroom we used earlier. I clean the blood from my face and hands while Raphael lectures us on how lucky we are.

I feel anaesthetized. It's as if everything warm in my body has been frozen over. I don't know if it's a coping mechanism, but I hate it. I *want* to feel horrible for killing Jakob, but I can't. The guilt I experienced the moment after I shot him faded. In fact, it was *so* minor I fear for my psychological state of mind. But the anxiety is quickly passing.

"You're clean enough, Jason," Raphael says. "Let's go."

"Hey," Chloe interjects. "Can he and I actually have a quick moment?"

He sighs, "Why?"

"I promise that we'll meet you and Simon up on the rooftop here in a minute."

Raphael grunts, "We'll wait outside the bathroom. I don't want any funny business. Come on, Davis."

The two of them leave, and when she senses it's clear, Chloe turns to me.

"Is everything okay?" I ask, sticking both hands into the pockets of my black slacks.

"I guess I just wanna say thanks," she says, glancing down at the tiled floor. "You saved our lives back there. I know what you did was hard, but remember that you had *no* other options, okay? What happened back there wasn't your fault at all. They forced you."

"Jakob didn't deserve to live, but thanks for the words."

"Anytime."

For a moment, we stare at each other. She surprises me by grabbing my tie, pulls me in, and kisses me.

Her lips are soft and warm.

After we part, she smiles at me, and without saying another word, we leave.

CHAPTER FORTY-THREE

The months leading up to Fight-Night were quite . . . eventful. We were treated differently the moment we stepped back into the facility. Some acted as if we were royalty for meeting with Vice. Others acted as if we were traitors to Lazarus for escaping, which I guess we kind of were.

Bleach had me bunk with Simon instead of Marcus for obvious reasons. After the incident in Chloe and Simon's room, he's wanted to twist my neck. I kept my same class schedule, so the two of us still had some classes together. It didn't bode well for either of us since we couldn't keep our hands to ourselves. He may be bigger, but the two of us were still bloodied to a pulp every time we were paired up with each other in combat.

As time went on, I got a little better at my classes. And despite Feline hating me when I first came back, I quickly became her favorite student. As a little reward for being the teacher's pet, she taught me extra after class hours. I'm fifteen lessons ahead of everyone else in firearms, making me proficient at shooting every gun available.

Meanwhile, in combat, I was learning a bunch of new dirty techniques. After a few days of me being back, Lynch mixed our fighting with weapon use. Not only were we beating the *absolute* crap out of one another with our fists, but we also had dull knives we used to slash our way to victory. At first, I worried that one of us would get killed, but Lynch washed away *some* of my doubts when he told us we couldn't thrust. We still got gashed up, but at least none of us were being gutted. The fighting and workouts added pounds of muscle to my frame.

They also required us to receive haircuts. Simon and I went with a shorter style while Chloe went with a pixie cut that I prefer more than her long hair.

The three of us are closer than ever. We watch each other's backs; we eat every meal together, work out every night, and spend every free second together.

For once in a long time, everything seems *normal*. Waking up in an underground facility is exciting, eating the same food every day never gets boring, and classes are exhilarating.

My relationship with Tommy is returning to normal. I still hold a few bitter feelings toward him for what he did, but what can I say? The guy's hard to hate. One day after my classes, he took me back up to the rooftop, and we sat on the ledge of the hotel for hours just talking. It was great being able to have that cool-down time with him. We were just two guys talking about guy stuff. For a bit, it felt like nothing had ever happened. I was that kid that passed through his checkpoint every day, nothing was awkward to talk about, just like how things used to be. I told him how much I missed Mae, and how I felt responsible for her death because I went along with the stupid escape plan. He helped me cope. That had to be one of the best evenings I'd spent in Lazarus.

I threw up the nanobots. It made me feel anxious, because it meant the next time I was shot, stabbed, or beaten that I wouldn't be able to survive like I did when Vice unloaded those rounds into my chest. Bleach assured me it wouldn't be a problem.

They had assigned Lynch to be my mentor a few weeks ago,

and ever since then, he's been meeting with me in the combat classroom after classes to give me a few pointers.

Fight-Night starts in twenty minutes, so now is my last chance to train with him.

"How do you escape when someone mounts you?" he quizzes, dodging one of my oncoming fists.

"Simple," I start. "Thrust your hips, this will make them stagger, giving you plenty of opportunities to escape."

"Good," Lynch attempts to kick at my forehead, but I quickly duck. "What're the most sensitive parts to someone's head?"

"The temples, eyes, and jaw," I reply, connecting my fist with his sternum.

We go back and forth until I've answered each one of his questions.

I feel *so* amped for tonight. I become an official member if Chloe, Simon, or myself wins. Becoming a member means everything. I'll get to help rid the United States of its tyrant, and I'll be able to act revenge on the man who tore my life apart. I'll find Matthew.

"Here," Lynch walks over to the back of the room, picking something up from off the floor. "Put these on."

He hands me a pair of black gym shorts. On top of the shorts lies a pair of fingerless black gloves. There's something hard underneath the knuckles.

"Brass?" I ask.

"Nothing in the rules forbid it, and trust me, other contestants will have their dirty tricks."

After shedding my hoodie and undershirt and tossing them to the floor, I take the clothes from his hands. After putting on the new clothes, I slither a glove over each hand, situating the brass knuckles into the correct positions.

"Jason," Lynch grabs my attention. "You've worked *way* too hard to lose. There's a lot riding on tonight, but I know you can do it. You and some other kid are tonight's first fighters. There are two groups: A and B, ten kids in each. You win a fight, you advance up the chain; you get to the top, and you become your group's champion. If that happens, you'll go up against the other group's victor and you two will battle it out. I've gotta warn you, though, Marcus is in group B and you're in group A. The probability of him being his group's champion is high. That means to be the victor, you'll have to beat him."

"I've never been able to beat Marcus," I remind Lynch.

"Doesn't matter. I think tonight'll be different."

"No, you don't understand. It's not like he's a skilled fighter, but his fists are like freaking boulders. A few hits to the face and I'm out."

"I know, kid, I've seen you two fight. Look, *when* you and him have to battle it out, spring around like a rabbit. Don't let him get his hands on you. You're faster, more agile, use that to your advantage."

"Thanks for the advice."

"No problem. Any questions before we get out there?"

"Nope."

"Let's go, then. You have a competition to win."

We leave the combat classroom. Most of the lights in the corridor are switched off, leaving a surreal vibe in the air.

The two of us take a right and stop in front of the double doors that lead into the gymnasium. I can hear music blasting and people cheering. Tommy had told me earlier that a bunch of members from other facilities were attending Fight-Night including Vice's private squad. Combine all that with the recruits that are already stationed here, and there is a full house.

"How is nobody hearing this from up in the lobby?" I ask

"Vice owns the hotel, so it's closed for the evening," Lynch replies.

"Well, what are we waiting for? Let's get in there."

"We have to wait till you're introduced."

As if on cue, Tommy's voice emits through the p.a. speakers, "Welcome, ladies and gentlemen, to Lazarus' Fight-Night."

The crowd from beyond the doors roars with excitement, causing a spike of adrenaline to jolt through my veins.

I will win. Nothing will stop me from becoming a member. Nothing will stop me from getting my revenge.

"So, this is how things work: There are two teams- A and B. Each group will fight their own team members, and eventually a recruit from each side will become a champion. These two champions will go up against each other, and whoever comes out victorious, wins."

More cheering booms out.

"Tonight, our first fight will start off with Team A. Please bring your attention over to the pair of doors to my far left," Tommy pauses for a moment. "Weighing in at two hundred and ten pounds, please welcome Jason Pinder!"

The crowd erupts, and Lynch looks at me, "Let's do this."

The two of us enter the gymnasium. The scene before me feels like something straight out of a bad movie. Strobe lights hang from the ceiling, large speakers pump music, and a massive cheering crowd is flocked around the caged boxing ring centered in the middle of the room. Tommy is standing in the middle of the ring, nodding at me. I shoot him a little nod back before approaching the caged arena. Lynch and I head through a chain-link gate and climb up and over the ropes. I shake hands with Tommy while the crowd's thunderous noise rattles my bones and forces my heart to beat faster, causing my adrenaline to pump faster.

Tommy shields the top of the mic with his hand, "You've got this, bud."

"Thanks."

He points over at the pair of doors opposite to the ones I left. Tommy un-cups the mic and puts it back up to his mouth,

"Through these doors, weighing in at two hundred and fifteen pounds, please welcome Mac Johnson!"

The crowd's voices surge like a tsunami as the doors on the other side of the gym open. In walks a kid with messy brown hair; he's easily just as muscular as I am but is shorter- maybe five foot ten.

"This will be easy, Jason," Lynch tells me. "Don't let me down."

"I won't," I say.

Following Mac is a man I've never seen before. He wears all black and I assume that it's his trainer. The two of them make their way up and over the ropes, and after both shake hands with Tommy, we're separated to opposite sides of the ring with our trainers.

"Alright, mentors," Tommy says, his voice echoing throughout the gymnasium. "Now is your last chance to talk to your recruits. I want you two out of here within twenty seconds."

Lynch turns "Remember everything I've taught you, and you'll come out on top."

I watch him step out of the ring along with Mac's mentor. Once they're gone, and the guard locks the gate, Tommy speaks once more, "Before we start, I must state our one and only rule: no killing. The match will end once someone is beaten unconscious. We clear, gentlemen?"

Mac and I nod. Tommy climbs out of the ring and waits by the locked gate. A second later, the colorful strobe lights are replaced with a bright spotlight that shines down from above the caged arena.

"You two may begin," Tommy says, his announcement triggers the crowd's roar.

Without hesitating, Mac rushes toward me, but I side-step out of the way. He crashes into the ropes, giving me the opportunity to turn him around and quickly knee him in the gut as hard as I can.

He grunts, and I knee him again.

Mac soon recovers from his daze and swings a fist at me, but I duck out of the way and counter by throwing a few fists of my own. Each one connects, and he staggers back.

He emits a *stupid* war-cry before charging me again, and this time, he gets lucky and tackles me to the floor. From on top of me, he pounds his fists into my face. Before he can cause too much damage, I thrust my hips as hard as I can. He loses balance, giving me the chance to hit him square in the jaw. The impact is so hard, that he goes flying off of me and onto his back.

I quickly get into a better position, and lunge. The roles swiftly become reversed. Now on top, I plant him face-first against the ground.

I don't waste my time punching. Instead, I grab his head with both hands and rapidly slam his face against the floor until blood gushes out of his nose. It creates a small pool of rosy-red snot and sap.

He struggles violently, but I don't stop, more and more blood pools out from his shattered nose. As he grows more dazed, I take my left hand and bash my brass knuckles into the back of his skull until he grows motionless.

The crowd goes insane. I let go of him.

CHAPTER FORTY-FOUR

The adrenaline surges through me as the crowd screams my name. I feel as if I finished a race, euphoria overtaking my emotions.

Tommy climbs back over the ropes and stands by my side, raising my left hand high into the air. The crowd somehow gets even louder and my ears feel like they will burst.

"Jason will participate in Team A's next fight," Tommy shouts. "Which will occur after Team B's first match that will start here, momentarily."

He cups the mic with his hand before turning "Great job, Jason. You can go take a seat with the rest of your team. They're right outside the cage sitting on the black bench."

I nod before turning around and climbing out of the ring. I approach the cage's gate and watch as a Lazarus member unlocks and opens it for me.

I step out and am instantly greeted by Lynch.

"Amazing performance," he says, taking me by the shoulder and leading me over to my team's bench. "You keep this up, and there's no doubt you'll come out as the champion."

I take a seat, but he doesn't, "Aren't you gonna sit down?"

"Can't. I have to stay in the crowd. I'll see you after your next fight, though. Good luck, kid."

"Thanks."

Lynch walks into the crowd, a look of pure pride on his face. I'm glad he's my mentor. *I would've lost if it weren't for him.* He's made me ruthless, a violent animal that refuses to be put down.

"Hey, you did a good job out there," a soft voice penetrates the noise.

Chloe sits next to me. She's wearing a black sports bra, black fingerless gloves, and women's athletic shorts.

"Thanks, man. So, you're on Team A, too?" I ask.

"Yessir," she replies, holding her knuckles out. "Fist bump?"

"Fist bump," I echo, bumping her fist with my own. "Isn't this all really cool?"

"What? Fight-Night?"

"Yeah."

She shrugs, "I haven't fought anybody, yet. But yeah, it's alright, I guess."

"Has Bleach still been pissy?" I ask.

"She's been *great* these last few days," Chloe replies. "She's *actually* been training me."

"It's about time."

Tommy's voice pours through the overhead speakers, "Our next fight will comprise of two members from Team B. Please bring your attention to my left," he pauses before pointing over to Sector K's double doors. "First off, weighing in at two hundred and forty-two pounds, please welcome Marcus Terrell!"

Everyone in the enormous crowd, except me and Chloe, cheers as Marcus enters the gymnasium. Following behind him is our stealth-training instructor, Hornet. The two of them make their way over to the caged ring. I feel my eyes narrow.

"This matchup will be sick," Chloe says.

"Who's he fighting?" My eyes are glued to Marcus as he and

Hornet climb over the ring's ropes and approach Tommy to shake his hand.

"Oh, you'll see," she rests her arm on my shoulder. "It's going to be awesome."

Tommy points to the doors opposite to Sector K, "And over here, weighing in at two hundred and five pounds, please welcome Simon Davis!"

The entire crowd roars with excitement as Simon enters the gymnasium. Feline follows him. Tommy sorts Simon and Marcus into separate corners and gives them a short amount of time to speak with their instructors.

"Who do you put your money on?" Chloe asks, a grin on her face.

"That's a hard one," I say, tilting my head to the side. "Your thoughts?"

Chloe bites down on her bottom lip, "Marcus? No, Simon. Ugh, I don't know."

I watch Feline and Hornet exit the caged ring before Tommy climbs over the ropes and waits by the gate. Once the guard locks it, Tommy speaks.

"You two may begin."

Marcus lunges at Simon, who jumps out of the way and counters by throwing his fist into Marcus' jaw. He stumbles back, but before I blink, he's back in Simon's face, swinging his knuckles into his upper chest. The two of them go back and forth, throwing numerous punches and kicks at each other.

I closely study Marcus' every move: how he dodges, how he strikes, how he maneuvers. I don't plan on losing tonight, and if that means I have to fight him, then so be it. Lynch is right. I'm faster and more agile. I have more skill than Marcus, so what's stopping me from winning Fight-Night? Nothing. All my worries are pointless.

The din rises to a crescendo as Marcus swiftly connects his foot with Simon's groin, making him cry out in agonizing pain. I wince as he crumples to his knees, and then his puke covers the arena floor.

"That *had* to hurt," Chloe mutters as the crowd roars.

Marcus howls with laughter while kicking Simon to his back. He then stomps on Simon's chest over, and over again. Simon is clearly unconscious, but he doesn't stop. Finally, Tommy and the gate guard step in and pull him away so he doesn't kill him.

I've gotta beat Marcus.

Tommy raises Marcus' hand into the air, a slight frown on his face, "Marcus is Team B's winner."

The crowd applauses.

"Team A is up next, but before that can happen, we will need a little intermission to clean the inside of this place. Remain where you are."

Tommy turns his mic off and walks out of the ring. Two gorgeous brunette women carrying cleaning equipment pass him.

Chloe watches the girls while they dispose of Simon's fluids, "What do you think's gonna happen to Simon?"

I watch the gate guard drag my best friend's motionless body away from the caged arena. My teeth gnash, "They'll probably take him down to the infirmary."

"So, who do you want your next opponent to be?"

"Someone weak."

"Y'know, if you keep this up, you'll eventually have to fight me."

"Yeah, I know."

"Don't hold back, okay? I know we're tight, but-"

"I fight you all the time in combat. Do I go easy on you then?"

She shrugs, "I dunno. Do you?"

I shake my head, "No. Not usually."

"Usually?" she groans, nudging me in the side. "Please, just for tonight? Don't hold back."

"I don't get why this is such a big deal."

"I'm sorry, but Jason, I know for a fact you can come out as champion, so you better not go easy on me because you don't wanna hurt my *precious* little feelings, alright? I won't be able to beat half the guys on our team, and I don't know about you, but I rather not face Vice's *harsh* punishments if we lose."

"You kidding me? You have a better chance than I do. People undermine you because you're a girl."

"Still."

Tommy makes his way back into the ring. He waits a moment before speaking, making sure that everyone acknowledges his presence.

"For our next fight, we'll welcome back Jason Pinder!"

The crowd erupts as I stand from the bench and make my way over to the caged arena. Upon entering and shaking hands with Tommy, he readies to announce my next opponent.

"For our next fighter, weighing in at one hundred and forty-five pounds, please welcome Chloe Frye!"

What a coincidence.

Cheers boom throughout the entire gymnasium as Chloe makes her way into the ring. After she climbs over the ropes and shakes Tommy's hand, the two of us are put into separate corners. Our instructors climb into the rings.

I won't lie when I say I'm kind of nervous to fight her. I'm not the only one who's been surpassing my instructor's expectations: Chloe's one of the top fighters in combat. She's extremely flexible and fights dirtier than I do, not to mention that she's been able to beat everybody, except Marcus, at least once. I guess it's like I'm fighting the girl version of myself.

Weird analogy.

"Alright, this will be easy," Lynch says. "I've seen you demolish her before."

"True, but it's been a few days," I say.

"Don't worry about that. Just get this round over with and win."

I take a deep breath.

Both instructors leave before Tommy steps out of the ring. He waits for the guard to lock the gate, then instructs, "You two may begin."

Instead of lunging at one another, we take a quick moment to approach each other and engage in a fist bump. After that, we back up to our original positions.

That's when the real fun starts.

Chloe sprints at me, but rather than throwing a fist she unexpectedly slides to the floor, using her momentum to smoothly skid between my legs.

Before I even know what's going on, she makes her way up my back like a frenzied spider. Using one hand to pound my face she uses the other to keep herself latched to my back.

I throw my fist up at her face, my knuckles connecting with her eye. She doesn't seem *too* phased by this.

She won't expect this.

I leap up into the air, but instead of landing on my feet, I let myself slam down onto my back, crushing her.

She gasps, hammering her palm into my nose, but I don't budge. I let my weight starve her lungs of air. I assume she knows that she won't get out of this by attacking my face. In an attempt to make me move, she violently jabs my Adam's apple.

I let out a yelp, clutching my throat with both hands. She's able to escape and get to her feet, leaving me on the floor. Just as her foot is in route to my face, I grab it and twist, forcing her entire body to spin to the floor with a loud thud.

I hastily get up, hurrying over to her collapsed body and grabbing her by the throat. I lift her up into the air, and she fights to breathe.

I slam my balled-up fist into her temple repeatedly. The audience grows louder each time my knuckles make contact. I think she's blacking out and she suddenly booms her foot into my gut, forcing me to let go. Chloe fights to stay on her feet. Her unsteadiness gives me the opportunity to charge at her. Just before

I can wrap my body around hers, she fiercely swipes her palm into the side of my nose. The strike is so hard that I can hear a crack echo out into the electrified air.

I stumble back. Blood leaks down my face and onto the floor.

She doesn't even wait before rushing me. When I think she is about to tackle me, she sweeps my feet right out from under me.

I slam against the floor, my vision stinging black and white as my head crashes into the solid arena floor.

I blurt out a swear before attempting to get back up, but my attempts are futile. Chloe rams her fist into my face. I collapse back into my previous position, groaning.

She continues to beat me in front of the hundreds of spectators. The thought of losing twists my insides and gives me a burst of energy. I grab her by the hair and force her to the ground next to me, causing the crowd to go insane. I quickly get to my feet. My head feels like it will burst.

After a moment of dissipating daze, I'm finally able to see Chloe trying to stand up. She's rubbing her head with her free hand and the blood streams down her face confirming the brass knuckles did their job.

I rush her, crash my foot into her face, knocking her out so she doesn't get even more injured.

I'm the winner of round two.

CHAPTER FORTY-FIVE

Chloe wasn't out for too long after I K.O.'d her. The second Tommy got back into the ring, her eyes shot open.

Tommy announces that I will participate in the next round and that Team B's second group of fighters will be out momentarily.

Chloe and I exit the cage and head back to our seats. There are no hard feelings between us. An on-side medic cleans her up and gives her pain killers. We congratulate each other and talk like nothing ever happened.

Marcus and I continue winning each of our Team's matches, beating our opponents with little effort. Honestly, no one tops Chloe. She was the only one who got even close to taking me out of the competition. Everyone else seems lazy and slow compared to her, making it somewhat effortless for me to come out as Team A's champion.

As I had hoped, Marcus is Team B's champion.

It's time to face off. We stand face-to-face. Tommy is the only thing keeping us from tearing each other apart. The crowd is going berserk, chanting and cheering with such a noise that the ring in my ears feels like it will never go away.

"For the final round of Fight-Night, we will spice things up,"

Tommy says, causing the audience to grow so loud that the arena vibrates. "So instead of these two beating each other unconscious, they'll be fighting . . . *to the death!*"

My blood feels like electricity and I feel the buzz in my toes.

To the death?

The drum in my chest pounds as I catch a smile making its way onto Marcus' face. He glares with a promise of pain lurking in his pupils.

I mouth an insult.

After letting the crowd come down an octave, Tommy reaches into his back pocket and pulls out two razor-sharp knives, handing one to each of us.

Marcus flips his open, and I repeat the action.

Part of me wants to concede, but I'm *so* close to becoming a member. Marcus is the only person standing in the way of my revenge. If he wins, I die, and I can't let that happen. I only wish that Tommy would've given me a heads up. On the upside, I guess I really won't have to hold back. One little jab to his throat and I win Fight-Night. However, one little jab to *my* throat, and *Marcus* wins.

The world will be a better place without him.

"Alright, gentlemen," Tommy climbs out of the ring, approaching the locked gate. "You two may begin."

Instantly, the two of us swing our blades.

CHAPTER FORTY-SIX

NOW, HERE I AM IN THIS MESS.

Wait...

Seeing Marcus' silver blade planted deep inside my body oddly doesn't trigger any pain, which makes me wonder if I'm dreaming, but as he rips the knife out, my burning nerves assure me I'm not.

"That feel good?" Marcus laughs like a hyena before stabbing his weapon back in.

A grunt escapes my throat, the pain still not registering normally. He rips the agonizingly sharp blade out of my hip for a second time, laughing more. He needs to be put down.

Despite the pain, I swing my knife at him. The serrated steel slices through the skin around his upper-chest, causing him to howl and for the mass to explode with excitement. My legs feel like jelly as I step back. I stare at him for a quick moment, trying my best to control my erratic breathing.

Everything is moving slowly, and the open wound in my hip is sending jolts of agonizing pain throughout my entire abdomen like an unquenchable fire.

What are you doing? My inner thoughts scream, *you gotta kill him. Kill him, now!*

I snap out of my stupor, and the cheering crowd surges the adrenaline back into my bloodied body as I force my feet to move. I charge at Marcus before lunging toward him with nothing but murder on my mind.

I thrust my blade into his rib cage, rip it out, and shove it back in violently. The audience seems to lose their minds as I tackle him to the ring floor, rapidly throwing my right fist into his bloody face.

It's strange, really. The world around me goes from slow to fast and back again. It never seems to go at a normal pace.

Am I losing too much blood? Could it be the adrenaline?

No, can't be.

This nagging feeling is familiar yet foreign and it's as I crack Marcus' nose with my knuckles when the recognition comes flooding in.

Dying, I'm dying, again; but how? Being stabbed twice wouldn't kill me, would it?

The sick smile on Marcus' face yanks me from my thoughts, and before I react, I feel an explosion at the back of my skull. My vision is soaked in inky black. As I swim through the murkiness to find the light, I discover that I am pinned beneath the weight of Trevor. Marcus' little friend is pelting my face in with fists like sledgehammers.

I should've expected Marcus to cheat, but how did Trevor even get in here? The door to the cage was locked before the match even started. Was I set up for betraying Lazarus? Is this whole thing a cheap setup for my execution? Did Vice lie?

"Marcus *doesn't* lose," Trevor spits through clenched teeth, his blows making my vision tinge different colors; green, purple, and eventually black, again.

So, this is where you die. I think to myself. *Inside a caged arena surrounded by hundreds of people, being beaten to death by some pretty-boy punk.*

I close my eyes; my face is numb from the constant strikes. I have two options. Either I fight back with everything I've got and kill these two pieces of filth or give up and let everything fade to black.

The answer is obvious. I've gotta kill them.

I open my eyes just as Trevor lets out a blood-curdling scream that sends a chill down my spine. My eyes shoot up above his head, and I can't stop a sinister grin from appearing on my face.

Simon is standing directly behind Trevor. He holds the knife that's planted deep inside Trevor's shoulder.

Marcus, with blood streaming out of his wound, quickly tackles Simon to the floor, leaving me to deal with a screaming Trevor. I thrust my hips as hard as I can, making him buckle off my torso and slam into the ground.

My heart explodes as I hastily get to my feet, blood dribbling out of the wound in my hip. I take a swift breath to take in my surroundings. Marcus is on top of Simon and giving him a few nasty blows to the jaw, Trevor is writhing around on the floor in pain, and the gate to the arena is wide open. Tommy and the guard are shaking their heads, blinking rapidly. Tommy has some sort of knife stuck in his shoulder.

My knife is lying next to Simon's hand, its blade dripping with Trevor's vital fluid. I rush over to it, hopping over Trevor. The knife feels heavier than before, and the blood shimmering on its steel blade makes its way down to my fingers.

Without thinking, I shove Marcus off of Simon, and the two of us fall on the floor. I throw my fist into his already broken nose, causing him to let out a grunt that grows into a scream. In retaliation, he swings his forehead into mine, forcing more stars to explode throughout my line of sight.

"I'm going to kill you!" he screams, bashing his forehead into mine once more.

I thrust my blade into his side, and he cries out. I rip it out, then shove it back in with twice the force, gritting my teeth, screaming with rage. The air swirls around and makes my eyeballs sting.

A sudden piercing pain enters my thigh, forcing a guttural cry to escape my mouth. Marcus rapidly stabs his knife into me. I didn't even think he still had it.

"I hate you, I hate you, I hate you!" he cries, rapidly knifing my upper leg.

The only thing keeping me from blacking out is the adrenaline surging through my veins, which I happily use to my advantage as I jab my blade through his skin, past his rib cage, and deep into his chest. He yowls, but still rips the knife out of my thigh and shoves it into my side.

My vision glitters black at the corners, but nothing can stop me from killing him. I aim at his throat, but Trevor slams into my back.

I skid across the floor, coming to a stop near the ropes.

Trevor backs up and then barrels toward me like a bull. Simon rams into his side at full speed, forcing both to the ground.

I immediately get to my feet, leaving the two of them to battle it out on the arena floor.

Marcus is attempting to stand, but failing.

I eye my knife and bend over to get it. Gripping the slippery blade in my palm, I charge the kneeling Marcus. I crash into him head-on, this time the impact is so powerful that I hear something crack inside his broken body. Once we hit the ground, I quickly position my blade above his Adam's apple, and jab it into his throat.

He gurgles.

The crowd screams out, but it's just a buzz. I stare into Marcus' wide, brown eyes. He's struggling, but I make sure he can't move. He tries speaking, but his attempts only spray blood across my face and chest.

"See you in Hell," I whisper, my eyes never leaving his.

His eyes remain wide, but they focus on something I can't see.

Blood spills from his mouth and Marcus takes one final breath as his eyes close.

I've won Fight-Night.

If I survive.

I recall all the wounds littered throughout my body. My heart races and I lose strength as my fingers feel like they have fallen asleep.

"Jason!" Simon shouts. "Get him off of me!"

Trevor straddles Simon and is throwing undaunting punches at him. I try to get off of Marcus, but it's as if my entire body is suddenly purged of all adrenaline.

I collapse to my side, the pain instantly overwhelming me. I try getting up once more, but I'm physically unable to. Instead of fighting off my best friend's enemy, I slide my knife over toward him in a sloppy fashion.

Simon grabs the knife, and I blackout.

CHAPTER FORTY-SEVEN

My eyes slowly open.

Simon and Chloe greet me along with a slight ache permeating my every cell.

"You're finally awake," a breath of relief slips from Simon's mouth. "How do you feel?"

I glance around the room. I'm in the infirmary lying down on a bed.

My eyes make their way toward the door, and I'm shocked to see Raphael standing there. He isn't wearing his mask, and his messy black hair partially covers his eyes.

I try to sit up, but my aching body threatens to split apart, so I carefully lie back down, "How long have I been out?"

Raphael steps forward, "A few hours. That was quite the fight."

I look over at Simon, "How did it end? Is Trevor still alive?"

He shakes his head, "After you blacked out, Tommy came in and shot him. He looked like he was about to shoot me too, but I guess he had second thoughts."

"He shot him?" an achy eyebrow attempts to rise.

I guess I *wasn't* set up by Lazarus. The realization spreads relief through my chest.

Simon chuckles, "Well, wouldn't you if you were him?"

"I feel like I'm missing something."

"Wait, you know how he got in there, right?" Simon asks.

"No, how?"

"Trevor and I were in here getting examined. You see that T.V. over there?" Simon points over to a small black monitor hanging from the ceiling.

"Yeah, what about it?"

"All the fights were being broadcast over it, so we got a good look at your winning streak. Well, once you and Marcus swung at each other, Trevor bolted out of the room. I followed him, and the two of us sprinted into the gymnasium. He bull-rushed that gate guard, stole his key after knocking him into a daze, and entered the cage."

"What about Tommy?" I ask.

"Get this. Trevor *stabbed* him."

"Stabbed him? How? He didn't have a knife, did he?"

"I don't know how he got away with it, but that little punk somehow got his hands on a scalpel. Probably stole it when the chick checking us out had her back turned. But yeah, dude stabbed Tommy in the shoulder and ran. He didn't even take the scalpel with him, just left it in Tommy and jumped into the ring."

Chloe nods, "Then Simon hopped into the ring, grabbed the knife you dropped, and shoved it into Trevor's shoulder"

"Yeah, I know," I say before giving Simon a gratifying nod, "You saved my life, man."

"I wouldn't let him beat you to death. Not a chance in hell," he says.

"Well, I owe you,"

"Don't you always?"

"Whatever."

Raphael clears his throat, stepping forward, "Vice called."

My heart painfully skips a beat at the mention of his name, "What did he say?"

He's silent for a moment before letting out a little grin, "He wants you three at one of his private facilities come morning. Don't know exactly what he wants, but it'll be good."

I look down at my bare torso, it's all bandaged up and bloody, "Promise?"

"Guaranteed. Unless you screw something up tonight, it'll be great."

"How am I even supposed to make it out of here when all I can feel are my insides grinding into mash?"

"I'm glad you asked that," Raphael grabs the walkie-talkie clipped to the belt that loops through his jeans, then puts it up to his mouth before pressing a button down. "Bring her in."

A few moments go by before the door to the infirmary opens, and in walks a woman wearing nursing scrubs. She is seething fear and looks like she is on the verge of tears. Bleach holds a gun up against the back of her head with her finger on the trigger.

"Who's she?" I ask.

Bleach smiles at me, "Someone who will fix you up."

"Please, I did nothing wrong," the woman cries, her voice trembling. "I have a family—"

"Shut it," Bleach demands. "The next time you speak without being spoken to, I'll open the back of your head with a bullet, got it?"

The woman silently trembles.

Bleach looks over at Simon and Chloe, "I need you two to leave. Jason's about to undergo surgery, and the last thing I need is for you two to screw things up."

Saying goodbye, they quickly exit the infirmary.

Raphael doesn't say a word, instead he backs up against the wall and crosses his arms over his chest. Bleach doesn't tell him to leave.

"This is the person who needs help?" the woman asks, her arms quivering at her side.

Bleach glares, "What did I say about speaking without my permission?"

The nurse's eyes shut, "I'm sorry, I'm sorry. I was just wondering."

Bleach rolls her eyes, lowering the gun from the back of her head, "Yes, this is him. He's been stabbed multiple times. We've bandaged up all the wounds and were planning on stitching him up, but we think there's internal bleeding."

The woman slowly approaches me, "Your hunch was correct, he has internal bleeding. You see how most of his abdomen is dark purple? That's ecchymosis."

"Okay, cool, I don't care," Bleach says. "Can you fix him up?"

She nods, "Yes, but I'll need access to some surgical tools."

"All the tools you could need are to your right."

I turn my head, seeing a small surgical cart littered with a bunch of sharp objects, "How bad will this hurt, exactly?"

The woman ignores my question and looks over at Bleach, "Do you have anything I could sedate him with?"

She nods, "Look at the cart, there should be thiopental."

The nurse examines the cart before picking up a white syringe. She then brings her attention back to me, injecting a vein in my forearm with the sharp needle. It takes a few moments, but eventually, the room darkens.

***

SOMEHOW, MY EYES MANAGE TO OPEN. I'M NOT IN THE infirmary. Instead, I'm standing in the middle of an old cluttered attic. Junk is piled everywhere. Rats scurry all over the dirty, aged floor.

What is this place?

Suddenly, a loud crash of thunder makes me turn to the only window in the room. It's open, and its white curtains are flailing.

I push through the wind that is supplying the musty room

with oxygen. Gazing out the opening, I see all of Boston, but something's terribly wrong. Through the light fog blanketing the city, I see blood flowing through the streets, and noosed people hang from trees and buildings.

I back away from the window. I try to erase the images that have just been forced into my skull. This has to be a lucid dream, or, more fittingly, a nightmare.

I inspect the attic's viscera. A full-body mirror hangs in the back of the room. I don't know why, but I feel drawn to it.

I take a few long steps eventually parking myself in front of the old glass. I feel my eyebrows raise in response to what I see.

A boy stands before me. He has deep blue eyes, messy hair that comes to a rest below his eyebrows, black-rimmed glasses, and he wears the Lakeshore High uniform.

I tilt my head to the side, and so does he. I let out a little wave, and so does he.

Everything I do, he mimics.

It takes a moment to clear the confusion and see the kid in the mirror is me.

A me who no longer exists.

I place my hand up against the mirror, and so does he. Our palms match up against each other's through the glass. It's so hard to fathom. He was me a few months ago. He has this determined look in his eyes, stands tall, looks *so* hopeful and ready.

"What am I becoming?" the boy in the mirror speaks. "Look at you, look at what you've done."

I remove my hand from the mirror, and narrow my eyes, "I've done what I've had to do."

"You *had* to rob that man from behind the store in Collingsworth? You *had* to beat that desk clerk? You *had* to shoot those two guards while escaping? You *had* to kill Jakob? You *had* to kill Marcus?"

"Jakob and Marcus had it coming. It was either them or me." I respond to me.

"Doesn't matter," he states bluntly. "You're a killer, a thief, and a *real* prick. You're everything you've always hated. How ironic is that?"

"I would be dead if I hadn't done everything I did."

"They're training you to become an assassin, a manipulator, an anarchist."

"So? People like me, like Simon, like Chloe are dying every-single-day because of President Mills and his government. I grew up surrounded by death, by corruption. So yeah, I'll become a terrorist, an anarchist, a killer, anything. Because sometimes, a person needs to step up and become what they fear to save others, even if that person is *us*."

The figure in the mirror shakes his head, "What if you get us killed? Riddled with bullets."

I shrug, "Well, at least we tried. Besides, you aren't here, anymore."

The mirror suddenly shatters, and everything goes black.

※

My eyes slowly open, welcoming the infirmary back into my sight. I feel so much better. I don't feel any traces of pain. What a massive relief.

I gradually sit up. Bleach is sitting at the foot of my infirmary bed and looking at me from behind concerned eyes.

For a moment, neither of us speak.

"Who was that woman you brought in?" I ask, scratching the back of my head.

"Best surgeon in all of Boston," she replies. "Vice wanted none of our doctors to touch you, so instead he had us kidnap the best of the best. She do a good job?"

"Nothing hurts, so I would say yes."

"She slipped you some aburaek, that's why you don't feel any pain."

"Aburaek?"

"Yeah, it's this pill the military uses on wounded soldiers. It numbs any physical pain for a few hours."

"So," I pause for a second. "Did you kill her?"

"Who? The surgeon?"

I nod.

"No, of course not. We blindfolded her, threw her in a trunk, and took her back to her home. We don't kill innocent people unless it's needed. We're the good guys, remember?"

The good guys? I guess that's one way to put it.

I glance down at my patched-up torso, "Do you have any clothes I could put on?"

"Yeah," Bleach stands from the bed and heads over to a counter on the other side of the room. "Lynch came by to drop these off. He also told me to tell you to get feeling better."

She turns around, my folded Lazarus uniform tucked beneath her right arm. She hands it over without a word.

Once I finish getting dressed, I glance over at her, "Is it okay if I go?"

"Sure. Raphael wanted you to meet him back at your dorm, so make sure you head over there before doing anything else."

"Don't worry, I'll go there right away," I get up off the bed and stumble over to the door, walking doesn't quite feel natural yet. I park myself in front of the door. "Mind if I ask you something really quick?"

"Go for it."

"You seem to have taken quite the interest in me. I mean, you've told me some stuff most of the recruits here don't even know about," I pause. "Why?"

She chuckles, "Why not? You're different from the rest, I can tell."

I gradually open the door and step out, "Have a good night, Marcy."

CHAPTER FORTY-EIGHT

Simon, Chloe, and Raphael are standing in the corner of my dorm room, sharing a conversation together

Once they notice me, Raphael turns his head, "How you feelin'?"

I shrug, "A lot better, I'll say that."

He approaches me with a cheap-looking cell phone in his hand, "Vice wishes to speak to you. Be mindful of your words."

He places the phone in my hand, then tells me to dial a long number I have to repeat inside my head so I won't forget it. After I dial the receiver I pull it up to my ear and listen carefully.

Eventually someone picks up.

"Hello, Jason," the voice is deep and intimidating. The Boston accent detectable.

"Sir," I greet.

"I saw the fight. You made me very excited for your future. How are you feeling? Did the doctor I send do any good?"

"She did a fine job."

"Excellent. If not, I would've gutted her like a fish," he laughs. "I'm only kidding."

"Raphael said you wanted to speak with me?"

"I wanted to inform you I have an assignment lined up for you and your two friends."

"What kind of assignment, sir?"

"Y'know, Pinder, not all questions need answering. I mean, where's the fun in spoiling all the surprises?"

"You have a point, sir."

"Don't I always? Look, I have to go, but I'll see you and your friends bright and early tomorrow morning."

"Sounds good, sir. Have a good night."

The next thing I know, Raphael is ripping the phone out of my hand and chucking it to the ground.

"What're you doing?" I ask, taken aback.

"Phones are too easy to track."

I watch as he stomps the phone to smithereens, not leaving any parts intact.

"What did he want?" Simon asks me.

"He says he has an assignment for the three of us."

"What kind of assignment?" Chloe turns to Raphael. "Do you know?"

"Of course, I do. We have to be over there before nine-thirty, so I'll probably wake you guys up around eight. You should all think about going to bed."

"Don't have to tell me twice," Simon mumbles while stumbling to the bottom bunk and collapsing. "Man, my ribs are killing me."

"I bet. That Marcus kid stomped you pretty good." Raphael says.

"It feels like my chest is on fire."

"If it still hurts as much in the morning, tell me. He might've broken your ribs."

"What happens if he did?"

"I'll give you some meds, that's all."

Simon nods before getting situated into a *comfy* position, pulling his blanket up and over his body, "Alright."

Raphael opens the door to leave, "I'm out of here. See you all in the morning and remember what I said about getting some sleep. You're gonna need it."

He exits, shutting the door behind him.

Chloe asks, "Mind if I crash here?"

"I don't mind. Is something wrong with your room?"

"My roommate sucks. All she talks about are guys and she *reeks*. I don't even think she showers."

"Say no more," I tell her. "Here, you can take the top bunk. I'll just sleep on the floor."

"No, I don't want to kick you out of your bed."

"No, it's fine. I really don't care."

"You just got out of surgery. I'm not taking your bed."

"Say whatever you want, I'm sleeping on the floor."

She rolls her eyes, "You're so stubborn."

I walk past her and head over to a corner in the room, "It's a blessing, really."

"Well, thanks."

"Anytime," I say, sliding down the wall until my butt touches the floor. "Goodnight, talk to you in the morning."

"Goodnight."

I pull my hood up and over my head and use it as padding against the wall. Silence fills the room, and just as I'm nodding off, the door to my room slowly creaks open. My eyes fly open. Raphael is standing there. He's wearing the respirator gas mask he wore back in the alley where we first met.

I'm about to speak, but he shakes his head.

I raise an eyebrow.

"C'mere," he demands quietly, his voice raspy and modified.

I carefully get to my feet, creeping over to him, "What're you doing?"

He glances over at the sleeping Simon and Chloe, "We're going out on a little run."

"A run?"

"Just follow me."

I do as he says and step outside with him. My eyes clamp shut due to the excessive light coming from the fixtures above me.

Once Raphael closes the door quietly, I question him with my expression.

"I want to take you out," he says.

I tilt my head suspiciously, "I *kind of* like chicks, man."

"What? No, not on a date" he retorts. "I mean, like out of the facility. You up for a little fun?"

"I guess. Where we headin'?"

"You'll see. Trust me, you're gonna enjoy this."

"I just got out of surgery."

"So? Like I said, *trust* me."

The two of us stroll down the hall, making our way over to the double doors that lead into the gymnasium. I'm amused to see that the caged ring is still set up in the center. The entire place is vacant- minus us two, and there's an eerie vibe that lingers in the air which makes me feel sort of uncomfortable.

Just a few hours ago, Marcus and I were slashing each other up with sharp, serrated knives as a crowd of killers cheered us on.

I wonder what they did with Marcus' body, or Trevor's, or even Mae's. There isn't a morgue in this place as far as I'm aware. Did Lazarus burn them?

"Won't I get in trouble for leaving?" I ask as the two of us stride past the ring.

"No," he replies, pride audible in his tone. "I control everybody here. When Vice isn't around, think of me as the puppet master, and everyone else as the cheap marionettes."

I picture Tommy, Bleach, and the rest of the instructors with strings attached to each of their limbs, dancing wildly at Raphael's command.

Chills make their way down my spine.

We make it out of the gymnasium and into Sector K. At the back of the large and wide corridor, there are two members standing guard at the elevator. They tense up when they see us. Well, when they see Raphael.

"How are you, sir?" one of them asks, and I instinctively know it isn't Copper or Myth.

Raphael shrugs, "Can't complain."

"That's good," the man says, his posture revealing he's uneasy. "Sir, if you don't mind me asking, why is this recruit with you?"

"That's none of your concern," Raphael replies. "And he isn't just a *recruit* anymore."

"You're right, sir. I apologize."

"I need you to open the elevator for me, I forgot my card."

"Yes, sir."

I watch the man turn toward the ID scanner and let it approve his card. A high-pitched *beep beep* rings out, and the heavy doors part ways, I tense up. Mae stands in my way. There's blood running down her face, her eyes wide and filled with terror.

I shudder, shaking my head rapidly to rid my mind of her. She vanishes.

The two guards step aside, letting me and Raphael enter the elevator. He soon presses a button, letting the cherry red doors gradually reunite.

"Ready to have some fun?"

I nod, the sudden motion of the elevator rising makes my stomach churn, "I guess."

He reaches into his pocket and pulls out a bandana, "Here, tie this around your mouth."

I take it from him, carefully studying the colors. It's predominantly black with silver streaks.

"What's it for?" I ask, doing as I'm told and tying the fabric around my mouth.

"It's a disguise."

"Why do I need a disguise?"

"Why do you think? It's keeping you from being recognized. If a security camera gets a good look at your face, you can expect to see wanted posters all over Boston with your picture on it by morning."

"Good point."

The elevator halts to a stop, causing a loud *ding* to screech out. The doors swiftly open, and I'm excited to see the rooftop come into view.

"What are we doing up here?" I ask as the two of us exit.

Raphael looks at me, "Just enjoy, and don't ask questions."

"Yes, sir."

He stops dead in his tracks.

"What is it?"

He shakes his head, "Don't call me that."

"What? Sir?"

"Yeah."

"Why?"

"I'm tired of it, man. Tonight, just for tonight, treat me how you treat Davis."

I pause for a quick moment, pulling my hood over my head, "Got it."

It's raining pretty bad. Summer seems to have forgotten how to act. The snow is melted from the last time I was out, but the warmth is missing from the season.

Raphael leads me to an exhaust vent. A black backpack and a sniper rifle lean up against it, and he bends over and grabs the gear. After slinging the rifle over his shoulder, he kneels down. He unzips the backpack, revealing a shiny, black handgun.

"Take it," he says, handing the gun over.

I examine the pistol, noting how pristine it looks, "What type of run is this?"

"One that won't suck."

We both chuckle.

"Here," he reaches into the backpack once more, pulling out a tiny bottle of pills. "That aburaek they gave you is gonna wear off soon, and trust me, you don't want it to wear off."

Raphael tosses me the bottle, so I unscrew the cap, "How many am I supposed to take?"

"Two."

"Thanks, man."

I tilt the bottle and let two purple pills fall into my palm; my other hand slides the bandana down and tosses the aburaek into my mouth. The taste is chalky and my gag reflex kicks in. I wish I had water.

"Those suckers taste like cardboard," I say, pulling my bandana back up.

"Don't taste all too good, but hey, at least they stop the pain, right?"

"Right."

I toss the bottle over to him, and he stuffs it back into the backpack. He then pulls out an object that's foreign to me. It's black and could easily be mistaken for a gun, but the hook attached to the barrel prevents me from thinking it's a pistol.

"What is that?" I wonder in awe.

"It's an E-772, but I guess you could call it a grapple gun."

"Wait, seriously?"

He nods while standing up, "There's another one in there. Think you can follow my lead?"

I shrug, "Probably. Hold on, though, how does it work?"

"That's for me to know and for you to find out."

Without warning, Raphael turns and runs, abruptly jumping off the edge of the rooftop. The muscles in my body tense as he plummets out of view. A loud sound mimicking a gunshot blasts out before I can call out for him.

Instantly, Raphael shoots up toward another large building that's across from the one that I'm currently anchored to. His metallic screams of joy echo throughout the rainy night sky as he zips up toward the opposite building's rooftop. I'm speechless.

He doesn't expect me to do that, does he?

I sigh. There really isn't a choice in the matter. I rummage through the backpack until I find the second grapple gun. It feels so perfect in my hands, just like any gun would. I examine the trigger, assuming that's how I shoot the line.

From the rooftop edge I look down at the city below. It's after curfew. No street lamps are powered on and only a few Saints patrol the empty streets, making sure nobody is out sneaking about. Hopefully, they don't check if people are flying between buildings.

I double-check my bandana, confirming it's snug before taking a deep breath.

I've never been afraid of heights, but the fear of falling is a reality.

Here you go. Don't mess this up.

I swan dive off the roof, letting gravity take control of me as I gracefully soar through the freezing, wet air. After what feels like an eternity of free-falling, my eyes are directed up. The building Raphael is on looks so tall, and I can't help imagining it being a gruesome giant preparing to stomp me down to the earth's core.

I hastily aim the end of the grapple gun up at the building's roof and concentrate. I only have one shot at this, so if I miss, I'm road kill.

I quickly glance down, my eyes widening as I realize that I'm only a good hundred feet from the street below. I look back up, and putting all my faith into my aim, I squeeze the trigger. The hook at the end of the barrel screams upward, and I anxiously wait for contact.

A second goes by with nothing, and the ground and I get closer, and closer.

Crap! Crap! Crap! My heart sinks into the pit of my stomach.

Thirty feet.

Nothing.

Twenty feet.

Nothing.

Ten feet.

Still nothing.

I'm about to splat against the rain-flooded street, but instead my body jerks violently. It only takes me a second to realize that I'm swiftly zipping up toward the building, and I let my body relax, somewhat.

Rain pelts against my face as my speed picks up, and I am suddenly aware of the next problem. How am I going to land going this fast? I will reach the end of the gun's rope, and then what? I'm going so fast that I'm guessing the law of inertia will take over and I'll go springing to my doom.

The rooftop grows closer, and closer, forcing my mind into overdrive. If I don't think of a plan this instant, I will die. I analyze the angle I'm approaching the building from, and an idea pops into my mind.

I will use the inertia to my advantage.

I abruptly reach the end of my line, and the hook detaches from the roof's surface. As I had hoped, I fly past the roof's edge. Raphael stares up at me as I fly over his head. I fight against the wind and jerk my upper body downward, forcing a dive bomb onto the roof. The impact is sharp and painful, but oddly it all quickly fades.

I'm sure it's the aburaek inside me going to work.

"Yo, Jason!" Raphael calls, his anxiety detectable through his voice modulator. "You okay, man?"

I give him a little thumbs up, groaning, "Yeah, I'm good."

He quickly appears at my side, crouching down, "Luckily you're on a hefty dose of aburaek. Without it you probably wouldn't even be able to move."

I sit up, something feeling off in my hip, "I think I ripped a stitch or two."

"Be glad it isn't worse," he says. "I'm surprised you didn't snap your neck."

"How d'you do it? You stuck your landing."

"You can control your speed by holding the trigger down. Probably should've told you that."

"Yeah . . . that would've been nice."

He gets up, helping me to my feet, "We've got to get over to your old neighborhood."

"What, why?"

I sense that he is smiling beneath the mask.

"I will help you get your revenge."

CHAPTER FORTY-NINE

"Revenge." A loud thunder clasp echoes Raphael's words. A chill shivers down my spine and a surge of adrenaline rushes through my veins.

"Are you serious?"

Raphael nods, "Remember back in the cemetery? I told you that you could get revenge if you came back to Lazarus. So, that's why we're here, to kill those involved in your murder."

My eyes widen, not with fear, but with excitement, "You're kidding."

"Why do you think I brought this bad boy?" he asks, pointing to the sniper rifle slung over his shoulder. "I want to help you."

I grin under my bandana, "Where do we start?"

"Just follow me."

FOR THE NEXT HOUR, RAPHAEL LEADS ME ROOFTOP TO rooftop until we get closer to the housing districts. We can stop using the grapple guns and just jump the ten-foot gaps in between the smaller buildings. We sneak past Saints, checkpoints, patrol vehicles, anything and everything.

Eventually, we get to a flat-roofed building right outside my old checkpoint. Laying on my stomach, I place the rifle firmly against my shoulder, my cheek rests up against the butt. Peering through the scope, I stalk the two Saints who tore my family apart. One stands tall in front of the checkpoint's security arm, and the other is manning the booth.

"How're you feeling?" Raphael asks, disturbing the surreal silence in the air.

"Peachy," I reply, euphoric yet pissed off. "Just peachy."

Seeing them makes my blood boil like the molten lava inside an erupting volcano.

"Go ahead and kill them," he says, his voice normal with his mask now off.

I suck in a deep breath of air, steadying my aim. The Saint in front of the security arm is the one who beat me with a baton. He's the one who turned my father to face me before he was shot in the back of the head. He's the one who, despite all the pain and misery he was causing, laughed.

I rest my crosshair slightly above his gut, let out my breath, then squeeze the trigger. Thanks to the silencer screwed onto the barrel, the shot is silent and the bullet goes screaming into the air.

The Saint's body is abruptly obscured by a cloud of bloody mist the moment of impact, and before his body can hit the asphalt, my crosshair rests on the other Saint, Matthew. He looks startled, but I pull the trigger before he can react. The bullet whistles through the air, shattering the glass to the booth and penetrating the man's shoulder. From all the way over here, I can hear him howling in pain.

I quickly get to my feet, making Raphael raise an eyebrow and tilt his head.

"What're you doing? They're not dead."

I look at him, rain streaming down my body, "I don't want them dead. Not yet."

"Huh?"

I toss him the rifle, and before he can ask another question, I leap off the roof. A jolt of pain shoots up my ankles as I contact the street below. Raphael jumps down after me, but I don't wait. Instead, I sprint over to the checkpoint, stumbling around on the flooded asphalt.

"Put your mask on," I call out, not stopping to turn around.

I skid to a halt at the security arm. The Saint who beat me with the baton lies at my feet, blood oozing from the hole punctured through his chest. I take a moment and stare at him, remembering all the sick things he's done . . . to me, to my mom, to my dad, probably to many others too. He's wallowing around on the flooded street, clutching his wound with both hands while calling out for help. Help he *will* not get.

I pull the pistol out of my back pocket and aim it down at his face, "Lights out, prick."

A flash of fiery smoke escapes the barrel as I pull the trigger.

I look over at Matthew. His defiant expression tells me he's ready for more, and I *will* give him more.

I rush into the booth, violently shoving him into the back wall. He grunts and swings his fist at my face, but I quickly dodge out of the way and counter by ramming my head into his nose. He swears, and I beat his face until he collapses to the floor, his entire body limp.

An excited feeling washes over me.

"What exactly do you have planned?" Raphael asks, standing behind me.

I glance back at him, dark exhilaration beaming from my eyes, "I think it's time to send a message. What do you think?"

"What kind of message?"

I glance down at Saint Matthew, "You'll see."

CHAPTER FIFTY

"*Wakey-wakey*," Raphael taunts, harshly slapping Matthew across the face.

His eyes flash open, and once he's aware of his surroundings, his hard breathing quickens.

We tie Matthew to a chair inside my old garage, and it's a prolonged moment before he mutters, "If you want information, you've got the wrong guy."

"Good thing we aren't asking for information then," I say, taking a hammer from Raphael.

He doesn't reply, and his wide eyes start rapidly darting around the garage.

I lean forward, pulling the ski mask from his face to reveal his neatly trimmed black hair, brown eyes, and pale skin. He's the man who pulled the trigger on my parents, on me. He tore my life apart, crippling it to nothing but bloody ruins.

"Do you know who I am?" I ask, my chest burning with rage.

He glares at me, "No, but I can sure take a guess and say you're no friend of mine."

I gnash my teeth, "Does the last name *Pinder* ring a bell?"

Matthew smirks at the mention of my last name, and I can tell that it's to rile me up even more than I already am, "Pinder? Yeah, they were on Mills' hit list."

Smiling?

This man murdered my entire family, and at the mention of their names, smiles?

The rage that boils up inside me reaches the brim, and I abruptly swing the hammer in my hands down on his kneecap.

His screams echo the sound of his bone shattering.

"I'll ask you a little something, okay?" I mutter, parts of my body twitching.

He spits on me, his face growing paler and paler from the loss of blood, "I don't negotiate with terrorists."

His saliva trails down my forehead. I use the back of my hand to wipe it off, "We're going to do things that way, huh?" I hand the hammer to Raphael. "Well, let's start this off by showing you exactly who I am."

I lower the bandana from my face, revealing my identity.

Matthew stares, bewilderment written in his expression, "It's *you* . . . but how? I shot—"

I use my thumb and jam it into the wound in his shoulder. He winces at first, but after applying even more pressure, he screams.

I stop, "Where do you live?"

He looks at me, his eyes misty, "You're one *crazy* freak if you think I'd tell you that."

I don't reply, grabbing the pistol out of my back pocket and aiming it down at his foot. I pull the trigger and the bullet goes slamming through his boot and into his foot.

He hollers at the top of his lungs, stomping his foot against the cement.

My gaze is cold, "Ready to tell me your address?"

He stares up at me, his eyes wide, *"Piss off!"*

I exchange looks with Raphael, "Do it."

He nods, unsheathing a knife from his belt and slowly walking behind the restrained Saint. He then places one hand on the man's shoulder, positioning the knife above his left eye.

"Go ahead!" the man blares, his gaze rapidly moving left to right. "I ain't tellin' you!"

I step away as Raphael steals the sight away from his left eye.

I walk to the door that leads into my house, "Find out the address, I'm going to go look for something."

CHAPTER FIFTY-ONE

Walking through my house is bittersweet. Most of it is empty. It was probably cleared out by the government after my family was executed. The only rooms that still have stuff in them are my parents' bedroom and my own.

I walk into my room and flip on the lights, a feeling of homesickness springing through me. The air smells familiar. My bed is unmade and clothes are scattered across the floor.

I kneel at the foot of my bed. Simon used to tag the side of buildings. In order to prevent getting caught, he hid the cans of spray paint beneath my bed. Nobody would search there.

I grab two cans, one black, the other red.

The idea in my head is budding, and I know that the aftermath will be chaotic.

Before I head downstairs, something catches my eye. My parents' bedroom door is wide open. I don't want to go in there, but curiosity leashes me, and I approach the doorway.

Seeing their belongings make my legs tremble. The family picture my mother kept in a small frame sharply comes into focus. It lies on her nightstand, and it's identical to the one in the obituaries. My parents, my old dog, Fifi, and me positioned in front of a grove of trees with fiery leaves on their branches.

I pick it up, closely examining my parents' faces. I try memorizing every-single-detail, because I forget what they looked like more and more every day.

How happy I look. I'm smiling. My eyes are bright and blue. I look at peace.

I set the portrait down, taking a deep breath.

"Why did you two have to leave me," I mutter, gritting my teeth. "I miss you guys so much."

I think of all the things I should've done with them. Remember all the times I should've said I loved them to their faces.

I walk over to my dad's little desk he occasionally used for work. He told me countless times that if anything were to happen to him or my mother, to check his bottom drawer. Honestly, I don't want to know what's in there. It'll probably make my heart break, not to mention that it will just further seal their deaths as a reality. I fight against my curiosity and turn away from his desk. The sweet memories of my dad flood my mind, and I swear I can feel him standing right next to me with his hand on my shoulder.

I imagine him saying, "I love you, bud."

"Yo, Jason," Raphael calls from downstairs.

I clear my throat, "What's up?"

"You coming?"

"Yeah, I'll be there in a sec."

I grip the cans of spray paint and exit the lonely fog, feeling my mom and dad follow me out.

The garage is a total bloody mess. Matthew lies motionless in the chair he's tied to, the knife still in his left eye, blood pooled on the floor all around him. His hands twitch violently.

"Is he dead?" I ask, my voice low but shaky.

"No, not yet. I thought you'd like to do the honors," Raphael says, blood splattered all over his mask.

I step forward, setting the cans of spray paint down, pulling the pistol out of my pants, switching off the safety, and pointing it at Matthew's face. I could pull the trigger right now and watch the bullet pierce his skull and rip a bloody path into his brain, but something is preventing me from squeezing the trigger.

"What are you waiting for?" Raphael asks. "Put a bullet in him."

"Did you ever find out his address?"

"Yeah, he lives over in Devenshire. Exact address is 2240 Astronomer Lane."

My heart blisters with guilt. That's the subdivision where Mae lived. I remember walking her home that rainy day so many months ago.

What would she think of me now?

I turn to Raphael, "Promise me."

"Promise you what?"

"That we're going to take out Mills and make his government collapse."

He stares at me a moment, but a sudden scream causes the two of us to jolt. The Saint struggles violently. blood trailing down his cheek from his eye, his jaw is crooked.

He's howling.

"I promise. You just gotta give them hell," Raphael says.

I exhale, "Lazarus has been around for a long time, so why is Mills still in charge?"

"Assassinating the president and overthrowing the entire government isn't easy. Luckily though, plans are coming into place, and it'll soon be our time to bring everything back to how it was."

I nod and pull the bandana that's around my neck up and over my mouth.

Matthew is still screaming bloody murder, his entire body spazzing out.

"Shut up!" I demand, violently swiping him across the face with my palm.

His head jerks to the side, but his grunting and howling doesn't stop.

I grip the handle to the knife that's stuck in his eye, reminding myself what he did to my parents. He shot each of them in the head before coming after me and sending a bullet through my throat.

His screams reach a pitch reserved for screeching opera singers as I yank the blade from his eye-socket.

"I bet you wish you were dead like I was!" I shout, thrusting my knife into his thigh. "Huh? Does that sound good to you right about now?"

He bellows.

"Y'know what? I'm not just going to kill you. I'm going to get even."

"What do you mean?" Raphael interjects.

I turn toward him, "You have any Rebirth on you?"

"Yeah, but we will only use it if one of us bites the dust."

"I don't care about that. Give it to me."

He hesitates, but ultimately reaches into his back pocket and pulls out a white syringe. He then tosses it and as soon as I catch it, my other hand points the barrel of my gun at his chest.

"No! No!" Matthew blurts.

"You will regret ever screwing with me."

"You sonofa—!"

I squeeze the trigger seven times, each bullet ripping through him like paper, blood spraying from his chest, his eye bulging to the size of a fifty-cent coin.

I inject him with Rebirth.

"What're you doing?" Raphael asks, standing by my side.

"Pissing on everything he loves," I mutter, gritting my teeth. "Untie him, leave him here, and meet me over at the Brookhaven checkpoint in fifteen minutes," I point over to a can of gasoline at the back of my garage. "See that? Yeah, bring it with you."

"What do you have planned?"

"Meet me at the checkpoint in fifteen minutes," I say, trying to brush the thought of Mae away. "Like I said, bring the gasoline."

CHAPTER FIFTY-TWO

I step back to admire my work. The rain continues to fall from the sky. I used some old rope I found in my garage and strung up the Saint I shot earlier. He's hanging upside down from a building. I feel accomplished.

I used one can of spray paint, and on the wall behind the hanging ornament wrote *Lazarus* in bold black letters. Using the other can, I tagged a symbol beneath the wording. It was a crudely painted scowl with two creature-like eyes slanted in a rage.

I wonder what my seventh-grade art teacher would've thought?

"That's quite the piece of work you've got there," Raphael's metallic voice comments from a couple yards behind me. "That will get a lot of people's panties in a twist."

I look over at him, "Did you do everything I asked?"

"Uh-huh. You still haven't told me what you want to do with the gasoline though."

"Remember, you asked him where he lived?"

He lets out a little laugh, "We're going to burn his place to the ground, aren't we?"

"Indeed, we are," I turn around to face him. "Let's go."

We take a little while to get there. Standing on the Saint's front porch; the house is quiet. Raphael hands me the canister of gasoline.

"He has a young daughter, at least that's what he told me," Raphael taps his shoe against the concrete. "What do we do about her?"

"Nothing," I reply, tilting the canister and letting the liquid pour out onto a brown welcome mat that's placed in front of the door. "If she gets out, she gets out. She isn't my concern."

Raphael steps back as drops of flammable liquid splash onto his shoes, "Whoa man, careful. I don't wanna combust when we light this puppy on fire, okay?"

I side-step, pouring gasoline all over the walls and door, "Don't worry, we'll be fine."

I spend the next five minutes thoroughly dousing the house, and once the canister is empty, I toss it into one of the larger puddles I made.

I look at the large house, reminding myself that there's another human being in there, but I shove the feeling down.

It could've even been a bluff.

Doesn't matter, though, Matthew deserves everything I'm throwing at him. The Rebirth serum is coursing through his veins at this moment, and when his heart is jump started, he'll start his re-run. The re-run I *gave* him. Come morning everything Raphael and I have done tonight will be all over the news, in the paper, talked about all around the entire nation as another *terrorist act* committed by Lazarus.

The Saint that destroyed my life will go squealing about me, telling everybody I'm still alive. Brookhaven's checkpoint has multiple security cameras monitoring the area, so the entire assassination will be seen, as will the whole act of me tying the other Saint upside down and tagging the wall.

They will show the footage on every news network, people will talk, and Lazarus will get recognition.

I know that this whole thing is reckless, and that I'm out of control, but my only purpose right now is revenge, and that's what I will get no matter the cost.

"You got any matches?" I ask Raphael, stepping away from the front porch.

"Never leave home without 'em," he says, pulling a packet of matches out from his pocket and tossing them. "I'm guessing you want to do the honors?"

"Of course," I strike the match on the packet, "You ready for this?"

"Do it."

I cast the burning match into the puddle of gasoline, and an abrupt chorus of flames flash up, causing us to jump back. A collage of flames rises, clinging to the Saint's house and licking up its features.

"C'mon, we need to go," Raphael says, stepping down to the front lawn. "Saints will surround this place any minute."

His words spark an idea, forcing a smile beneath my bandana. I turn and run, motioning Raphael to follow me. He quickly catches up, and the two of us dive behind a bush in front of the house two doors down from the burning foundation.

"What're we doing?" he asks, quietly panting.

"We're gonna send one last message," I reply, pulling my handgun out of my pocket. "Think we can take on an entire patrol of Saints?"

"Possibly, but what's the point?"

"Could you imagine the headlines? Saints murdered, house set on fire, person back from the dead. Come on, it would be great."

"It would certainly stir the pot."

"Is that a bad thing?"

"Not at all."

"What do you say, then?"

He's about to reply, but the sudden sound of a loud siren shooting through the air interrupts him. It belongs to a patrol car.

Car tires skid to a halt.

I risk a peek, and survival mode is forced into my brain. There are eight Saints, and probably more on the way. They're all out of the vehicle and examining the burning building, hands firmly placed on their weapon holsters, looking confused.

"You have a knife?" I ask quietly.

Raphael nods, unclipping a blade from his belt and handing it over, "You sure about this, Pinder? These are trained killers. They're bigger, they're stronger—"

"How am I going to get better if I don't throw myself in these types of situations?"

"Guess you've gotta point. Just remember, it's your funeral."

"Ironic," I chuckle, gripping a knife in one hand, a handgun in the other.

"Lead the way, then."

I jump out from behind the bush, my stomach a knot of nerves as I sprint toward the flaming house. I bring myself to a sudden halt about ten feet away from the Saints and shout at the top of my lungs.

"Hey!" startled they turn to look at me, "Yeah, over here!"

"He has a gun!" one of them shouts, reaching for his pistol.

I aim at him and squeeze the trigger twice. I don't wait for the impact before sprinting toward another Saint. Before anyone can react, I leap onto the soldier and thrust my knife into him numerous times before we go slamming into the flooded asphalt.

Instantly, gunshots fill the air, and I'm relieved to see another Saint collapse to the street with blood spraying from the hole inside his head.

Raphael's joined in.

The Saint beneath me howls, using his free fist to bash my nose. I don't have time to mess around, so I take my pistol, shove the barrel up against his temple, and fire.

His head lurches to the side, his blood mists my bandana.

Raphael crashes his palm into a soldier's face. I aim my gun over at a Saint who is about to fire at him. I pull the trigger and watch the bullet zoom through his body before jumping to my feet and engaging another man. This one has his baton out and swings at me. It hits my chest, and I feel something crack inside me. I don't scream, instead I bring my gun up to his face and fire.

He crumples to the ground, and I quickly turn around. Raphael rapidly thrusts a knife into another Saint's body, using his free hand, which holds his gun, to shoot the Saint charging at him from the right.

I feel a hand grab my shoulder, and before I can react, a booming impact goes crashing into the side of my face. I fall to the flooded street. Another Saint with a baton is in front of me. He winds up to swing again, but I aim my gun up at his head and fire. The Saint drops to the ground, a scarlet vapor raining down on top of me.

I hear a scream. Raphael is fighting one-on-one with the last soldier. He is smashing the Saint's head against the patrol car's window until he goes limp. After the Saint collapses to the street, Raphael aims his gun down and fires twice at his body, making sure he's dead before letting out some heavy profanity.

I rub the side of my face where I was struck with the baton, "This hurts like *hell*."

He takes his mask off, letting his shoulders relax, "You okay? Did you get hit?"

"A few times with those stupid nightsticks, but other than that, I'm good. You?"

"Yeah, I'm fine. We caught them completely off guard, so consider yourself lucky that you weren't shot," he pauses, glancing over at the house on fire. "C'mon, we gotta split before more get here, okay?"

I take a deep breath. That guilty sensation regurgitates and overflows my stomach. I didn't expect this feeling one bit, but here it is. I can't help but think about the parents, wives, and kids that will receive a visit tomorrow from a soldier saying that their loved one was murdered by Lazarus.

I mutter a swear under my breath, looking down at the multiple blood-immersed bodies that lie sprawled out across the asphalt.

More sirens disturb the bitter cold midnight air, causing Raphael to sprint off in the opposite direction of the burning house.

I stare at the flames. *An innocent kid could be in there.*

"What're are you waiting for?" Raphael shouts at me, already down the street. "We may have gotten lucky with this patrol, but they're just going to send more and more."

Save whoever is in there. His daughter isn't a Saint. She's innocent.

This guilt is going to kill me.

I have to make sure the house is clear or else I'm no better than the Saint who murdered me and my family.

"Meet me back at the facility," I shout back at him.

"Are you *insane?*"

"Just meet me there, okay?"

"You have a death wish, Pinder. You're going to die without me!"

"I need to do something. I won't be too far behind, just go!"

"You're an *idiot!*"

He sprints out of sight. I rush up the lawn, and barge in through the burning door.

CHAPTER FIFTY-THREE

The walls, the carpet, the furniture, anything and everything is lit up in flames.

I'm thankful for the bandana around my mouth, because without it, I wouldn't be able to breathe.

"Anybody home?" I call out, the dark smoke causing scarlet tears to stream from my eyes.

There's no reply, so I keep moving. Fire engulfs the house, and If I don't get whoever's in here out soon, then we're both going to die.

My chest and face ache from the recent fight with the Saints. It's too hard to concentrate on the pain when I know that someone else is trapped in here because of me.

I rush through the kitchen. A burning corridor lies beyond with multiple doors on each side. The door knobs glow red, so I barge into the room using my shoulder. Inside is some sort of office, but it's vacant and drowning in flames.

I charge through the next room, and still there's no sign of life.

Crap! Where are you?

I check every door on the right side of the hallway, and almost every door on the left. There's only one room left on the first floor, and I'll asphyxiate from all the smoke if I don't get out of here soon.

I use all the adrenaline in my veins to shove through. On the inside, a little girl sits on a bed sobbing. My entrance gets her attention, and she cries out, telling me I'm not her dad and to get away.

Ignoring her wishes, I rush toward her.

"Come on, we need to go!" I shout over the inferno, grabbing her with one arm and slinging her over my shoulder.

"Stop it!" she cries, punching me as hard as she can, coughing and hacking. "Go away!"

I ignore her protests. Her life is all that matters at this point.

I quickly sprint out of the room, using one hand to keep her balanced over my shoulder, and the other to navigate.

Sirens are still screeching through the night, and a few sound like they're coming from right outside the house. As soon as my foot touches the kitchen floor, I realize the front door is a poor choice as an exit.

"Hey, sweetie," I say sweetly, hoping the young girl will cooperate. "Is there another way out of your house besides the front door?"

"Put me down!" she demands, still punching and kicking me. "Put me down now!"

I choose to ignore her suggestion and instead rush out of the flame-engulfed kitchen. I scan the area with my eyes. The entire structure looks as if it's about to crumble on top of me. The front door is gone from the entrance, and I can see that outside numerous Saints are on the scene, approaching the house with their guns drawn.

I blurt out a swear, gritting my teeth. My only way out of here is through the front entrance, meaning I will have to shoot my way to safety.

My free hand grabs my pistol. I remind myself that I only have six shots left.

I'm gonna die in here. I should've listened to Raphael.

"Stop struggling!" I yell, tightening my grip on the little girl; she coughs and hacks more.

She doesn't listen, just keeps kicking and punching, "No, Stop! Put me down!"

I rush out the front door, and as soon as I break free from the house, my lungs fill with fresh air.

I aim my gun up and fire a bullet into one of the Saints' head. He collapses to the ground, and I unload the rest of my rounds on the other soldiers. Each bullet slides through one of their skulls, causing them to drop like dominoes. Only two left, and they're charging at me with batons skillfully gripped in their hands.

I throw my gun to the floor and toss the little girl down onto the lawn. As fast as I can, I take my knife out and engage one of the Saints.

He swings his nightstick at me, and it connects with my sternum.

I cry out before thrusting my blade into his gut. He screams, dropping the baton and clutching his wound.

"You're dead!" the other soldier hisses, flinging his metal nightstick at me.

I dodge out of the way, counter by kneeing him in the groin. While he squawks, I grab the gun from inside his holster and aim at his face. Quickly I pull the trigger.

He collapses to the ground while blood sprays from his broken body.

"No, no, wait," the other Saint begs, still clutching his stomach. "Don't do this."

I fire at his body three times, each bullet hitting him in the chest. He falls to the ground, crying out in pain.

I aim the gun down at him, but before I can finish his pathetic existence, I hear helicopter blades rotating furiously. A news chopper is flying toward my position.

The government is in charge of all the news stations, so it

makes sense they want to capture this on film. It helps fuel their propaganda that our only cause it to promote fear and create chaos, which is and isn't true.

They're the bad guys.

My eyes search for the little girl, and I am frightened when I find her missing. Then something moves in my peripheral vision. She is running down the street as fast as she can.

I call out after her, feeling responsible for her well-being.

She runs even faster when she hears my voice. I sprint after her. She will get hurt wandering the streets like this past curfew. I need to save her. I need to save me from myself. This is all *my* fault, and if she dies, I'll be the monster they say I am.

"Wait, kid, sto—!"

A scorching pain hollows through my chest, and unexpectedly the little girl collapses to the ground.

My hands twitch. I force my eyes down and notice the bullet hole in the fabric around my chest, and it's squirting red.

I was just shot, and the bullet went through me and hit the girl in the back of the head. If it weren't for the aburaek, I'd be on my knees, gasping for air, clutching my chest and crying out.

My shock turns into sheer rage. I turn around without thinking and sprint after the Saint who just shot me and the little girl. The Saint is lying on the sidewalk outside the burning house. He is the one I didn't put down. He uses the hand that's not clutching his wounds to hold his gun.

He fires again, and the bullet zooms through my left shoulder, making one side of my body lurch back, but I continue sprinting toward him. The spotlight from the news chopper encourages my rage.

I lunge on top of the soldier, take my knife and fiercely drag it through his flesh, ending his life. A primal and involuntary cry escapes my body, I pound my fist into the cement beneath me. My head clouded with hate and sadness.

The spotlight directly above me illuminates the area as I continue to pound my knuckles into the ground until they bleed.

The voyeuristic helicopter watches, enraging me further. I gradually stand up and give the pilot the finger. The chopper still continues to watch me without action, the smoke from the burning building doesn't faze the oglers inside

"Get out of here!" I scream, gnashing my teeth from beneath my bandana. "Piss off!"

I can't stop the blood-tears from streaming. Blood oozes from out of the wound in my shoulder and out the wound in my chest. None of the physical wounds affect me. All I can focus on is the pain I'm feeling on the inside. I've killed multiple people tonight, tortured someone, set a house on fire, got a little girl shot in the back of the head. It's all *my* fault.

No, actually, it's all *his* fault.

Joseph Mills is the one who caused all this. He's the one who ordered the purge on so many lives including my own.

He's the monster.

It's right there on the front lawn, covered in blood with a soldier's corpse at my feet, where I swear to myself once more to do whatever it takes to rid America of its tyrant, to act out vengeance for all those who can't do it for themselves.

I take a deep breath, then take off running, cutting through people's backyards and hopping fences. I'm sprinting to avoid the chasing spotlight.

I get around three miles from Brookhaven Estates when I faint from blood loss.

CHAPTER FIFTY-FOUR

My eyes eventually open, and I'm surprised to find myself back inside the infirmary at Lazarus. Raphael hunches over me, examining my body. His eyes hold a quizzical look.

"Are you crazy?" he asks, backing away from me. "Utterly crazy?"

I blink, feeling excruciating pain stretch throughout my entire body, "What time is it?"

"It's eight in the morning," he replies, setting his mask down on one of the other operating tables. "You said you would be right behind me."

"I'm sorry."

He grabs a T.V. remote from off the surgical cart placed next to me, switching the television on. It hangs from the ceiling in front of me, and it's turned onto the news.

There's an enlarged picture of a hooded, masked me plastered across the screen from last night. I'm flipping the camera off, the skin above my bandana is smeared with blood. I also carry a knife and stand over a dead soldier.

A female reporter is talking, and she sounds horrified, "The video we're about to show is highly graphic and contains strong language, viewer discretion is advised."

The image of me disappears, and in its place is footage from last night. I'm shown getting shot, and as the bullet passes through me and hits the little girl in the back of the head, I feel an echoed sting of pain and rage. The image of me turns and charges at the Saint who shot me. I am shown slitting his throat and pounding my knuckles into the ground.

I look insane.

The footage finally shows cracked me standing up and flipping the camera off again.

A full screen school-picture image pops back onto the screen.

"A trusted source has informed us that the person on screen is Jason Pinder, a Senior at Lakeshore High who was recently executed by our nation's military for undisclosed reasons. This begs the question. How is he committing absolute carnage if he's deceased? We have no clue, but in the footage captured by a checkpoint security camera, he's shown tying a dead Saint upside down from a building."

They show the image of the man with the spray painted "Lazarus" across a brick wall.

"We believe this either means he has ties or even is a part of the terrorist organization who committed their first attack back in 2039," the reporter stops and shuffles a few papers. They prompt her to read a screen we can't see behind the camera and she begins again. "This just in, President Mills has commented on recent events. He says, and I quote, 'Last night's events were heinous, and I plan on punishing all those involved to the fullest extent.' Close quote. He made no direct comment on Jason Pinder. This is Brenda Howard, and you're watching BCN. We'll be right back."

Raphael switches the television off, "This is what you get for injecting that Saint with Rebirth. He's obviously the one who informed them on who you are."

I groan, resting my head back down against my pillow, "I just wanted to get even."

He chuckles humorlessly, "Even? Now his daughter is dead and I'm sure he thinks it's all your fault. You made everything way too complicated. You should've just left him to die. I'm stupid for going along with your every move last night. This is on me."

"I'm sorry for getting caught," I say, even though I already knew last night would play out the way it did.

"That's not even why I'm mad. I'm mad because you brought the only man who saw your face back to life, and now you're all over the news."

I sigh, forcing the subject change, "Where's Simon and Chloe?"

"Getting ready to leave. We would've left sooner, but a few doctors had to perform more surgery on you."

"More surgery? Why?"

"Why do you think, Pinder? You were shot twice, beaten with nightsticks, and your stitches ripped. You weren't in the best shape when I found you."

"How *did* you find me?"

"I was halfway back to the facility when I heard a bunch of gunshots and saw a news chopper flying overhead. I went sprinting back, but you weren't at the house. There was just a bunch of Saints patrolling the area. I searched around and eventually found you blacked out at the bottom of a ditch."

I go silent for a second, "Am I going to function properly, today?"

"Yes, but you will have to be on a hefty dose of aburaek for the next little while. I gave you a few pills a bit ago, so the pain will leave any minute."

I sit up. The agonizing tremors jolt through me, "I'm going to go talk to Simon and Chloe."

"Okay but here, take these first," Raphael walks over to the other side of the room and picks up a fresh Lazarus uniform from up off the counter. "We're leaving in fifteen, so be ready to go."

"I will." I grab the uniform from him and slip it on. "Thank you."

I hop off the operating table, the familiar companion of pain shoots up my body as I land on my feet. Raphael and I say goodbye, and I walk out the door.

CHAPTER FIFTY-FIVE

"Dude, what happened to you last night?" Simon questions as I enter my dorm room.

He and Chloe are dressed in the Lazarus uniform, and both have their eyes glued on me. I want to tell them everything about last night, but I don't want to be judged. Judgement is horrifying. It's panic inducing, and I don't want to receive it from them. What would they think if they found out about the killing spree I went on last night? How would they feel knowing I got a little girl killed? All in the name of spite? These two remind me that there's something good in this world; they remind me that love, laughter, and happiness all still exist although I don't feel the same. I need them to understand me, not judge me. I need them on my side, not against it.

"I was with Raphael," I reply, hiding both hands in my hoodie pouch.

Chloe raises an eyebrow, "You sure you weren't out and about murdering Saints?"

Our eyes lock, but it doesn't take long before I stare down at my shoes. I can't bear the scrutiny, "Maybe."

"Raphael told us everything," Simon says. "You killed a little girl, man?"

I shake my head, "No. Is that the crap he's been spewing at you? The Saints killed her, not me. You know I wouldn't do that, please just stop."

Chloe shrugs, "Hey, kudos to you. Killing a bunch of Saints isn't *exactly* a bad thing. We also heard that you burnt down a house and tied a soldier upside down from a building. That's kinda cool."

"No, it isn't," Simon disagrees. "Killing people isn't *cool.*"

Chloe rolls her eyes, "Says the guy who stabbed Trevor and tried to kill him."

"It's completely different when there's a purpose. Plus, I'm not saying that what he did was wrong, I'm just saying it isn't cool, and I'm sure he agrees."

"Yeah, whatever. You're a part of an organization that assassinates government officials and creates chaos to get rid of the dictatorship. Don't act like this isn't all part of the plan."

A few uncomfortable minutes go by before sound reenters the room. The door opens behind me and Raphael stands in the doorway. Emotion absent from his face. His brown eyes are trained on me, uninterested and irritated.

He's still royally pissed off.

"It's time to go."

He leads the three of us through the facility and over to the elevator, up to the lobby, and out to a parked black Cadillac. The four of us get in the car. Simon, Chloe, and I are in the back. Raphael rides shotgun next to some man in the driver's seat. He's wearing a tuxedo, a black fedora, and a pair of dark sunglasses.

"Confirmation code, sir?" the man asks, his hands firmly placed on the wheel.

"Darkest night," Raphael replies, putting his seatbelt on.

The man steps on the gas, and we move forward. The three of

us in the back strap our seatbelts in, all falling into resolved silence.

"Vice isn't pleased about last night, sir." the driver tells Raphael.

He chuckles, "I'm well aware, thank you. In fact, I received a phone call from him this morning," he looks back at me. "He *definitely* ain't happy."

I guess it really doesn't matter if Vice is agitated. If he wanted me dead, Raphael would've just finished me off in that ditch hours ago.

A sudden hand on my knee interrupts my thoughts. Chloe shoots me a sympathetic smile and rubs my knee with her palm.

"Yeah?" I whisper.

She leans in closer, "You okay?"

I take a quick look around the car; Simon is passed out already, Raphael is examining the handgun in his lap, and the driver is focused on the road.

"I'm good."

"No, you're not."

I glance over at her, "So? What's your point?"

"We're partners. Aren't you going to tell me what's bothering you?"

"Look, I just have a lot on my mind, and I'm really tired. Don't worry about me."

She frowns, "Oh, okay. Sorry."

Raphael glances back at us, "We're gonna gas up."

We pull into a gas station near an old rundown suburban neighborhood toward the edge of town. The whole area fell victim to a mass riot a few years back and lies mostly in ruins. The government didn't clear the aftermath. Something about remembrance of our mistakes and all that.

The riot ended with everyone involved being executed one by one on live tv.

We park in front of one of the gas pumps, and I open my door.

"Where are you going?" the driver questions.

"Bathroom," I reply, stepping out of the Cadillac. "Is that a problem, or something?"

Raphael sighs, "Just hurry up."

"I've gotta go too," Chloe chimes in.

"I swear I'm babysitting a bunch of four-year-olds," he mutters. "Hurry."

CHAPTER FIFTY-SIX

I walk into one of the family bathrooms, and Chloe follows me in before I can shut the door and lock it. She stares at me a moment before talking.

"Stop being closed off and talk to me, alright?"

"Why do you even care?"

"Because."

"Because why?"

She sighs, looking frustrated, "Because we're a team."

I turn away from her, feeling frustrated myself. Why can't she understand that I don't want to talk about it? Why can't she leave me alone?

"Remember back in the weight room when I told you I stole my dad's wedding ring from my mom's jewelry box?"

"Yeah, why?"

"I told my mom I hadn't seen it when she asked me where it was, and it was like my dad got into that car accident all over again. She was so sad. It made me feel *so* guilty, and you wanna know what I spent all that money I got from the ring on?"

"What?"

"Drugs to sell for even *more* money."

I don't speak.

"I felt so horrible," she continues. "I seriously hated myself for the longest time and felt the most gut-wrenching guilt. I recognize that feeling; it's all over you, Jason."

Angry rosy-red tears begin to trickle from my eyes.

"Just rant, okay?" she says.

I turn around, the sight of my bloody face causes her to recoil a little, "I got a little girl killed last night, and not only that, but I've killed Jakob, Marcus, Mae—"

"Whoa, you didn't kill Mae, alright?" she interrupts, placing a hand on my shoulder. "She died, but that isn't your fault. She's the one who wanted to escape, and all you did was try to help. I know it sucks, but let go, or else you'll turn into one of those emo kids you see on T.V. You know, the ones that wear eyeliner and black lipstick that can't stop moaning about their . . . *'paaaaain.'*"

I chuckle, "Kinda reminds me of Simon when he was fourteen."

"Look. You're part of Lazarus now. Mae clearly wasn't meant for any of this. Just let it go and focus on our new main goal."

"And what's that?"

"Starting an uprising."

"You sure are optimistic."

She abruptly wraps her arms around me and squeezes tight, sending a comforting thunderbolt throughout my body, "I promise, it all leaves eventually . . . the guilt."

She leans in, but before she can kiss me, there's a loud banging at the door that startles the both of us.

"Could you please hurry up?" a man asks from outside.

"Yeah, just one moment," Chloe replies, taking a deep breath.

I step over to the sink and wash the blood from my face. I can see Chloe smiling at me through the reflection in the mirror. I smile back.

The two of us exit the bathroom, receiving odd stares from people as we pass them.

Our feet pad against beige tiles as we make our way toward the entrance when someone calls out, "Hey, how are you two doing, today?"

We stop, and slowly turn around. A Saint. He's at least three inches taller than me, is solid muscle, and giving me an amused look.

My muscles tense, "We're doing good, sir. How about yourself?"

He lets out a little grin, but it seems snide, "I'm doing fine, kid," tilting his head to the side. "Y'know, you kinda remind me of someone."

My heart skips a beat. Obviously, he knows who I am, he's probably seen my face all over the news and wants to slide a bullet into my brain.

Run! No, no that's stupid. Just stay calm.

"Oh, yeah?" I flash him a smile. "And who would that be?"

He chuckles, "My nephew Jordan. He's about your age," he pats me on the arm. "Well, I'll let you two enjoy the rest of your morning. Have a nice day."

I hold my hand out for him to shake. He reaches out and grabs hold, jerking me closer, and he puts his lips up to my ear.

"Tell Raphael that Jenkins says hi."

He's a mole for Lazarus.

I let go of his hand and my breath. With a quick smirk I answer, "Will do."

He winks, "Thanks."

When Chloe and I get back to the car, I pass along the message from Jenkins, making Raphael snort. He then tells me they went on a mission a few months ago, and how it was "Pretty legit."

"Sir," the driver turns to him. "You ready to get going?"

He nods, "Yes, let's get moving."

"Yes, sir."

We pull out of the parking lot and continue into the ruined part of town, approaching a bunch of the larger buildings and structures near the trashy outskirts.

CHAPTER FIFTY-SEVEN

"We're here," the driver says less than twenty minutes later, parking the black Cadillac in front of a vacant warehouse. Every window and door appears boarded up.

"What? This place?" Simon asks.

Raphael sighs, "C'mon, get out and follow me. Also, pay no attention to the stupid douches who guard the first floor. They're just a bunch of mercenaries that Vice uses because they're disposable. If they try to scare you, don't be afraid to get dirty."

The three of us in the backseat nudge each other in agreement before exiting the vehicle. We follow Raphael up the brown lawn that leads to the warehouse's entrance. The structure looks like someone built it way before my time. I mean, it totally stands out compared to the stuff all around it.

I was sort of expecting some high-tech base with armed guards and everything.

"How do we get into this place, anyway?" Chloe asks, placing her hands on her hips and planting herself next to me. We all examine the boarded-up door.

"It's simple, just watch," Raphael remarks.

Raphael's knuckles contact the door and knock in a rhythm, almost like some sort of song. It's upbeat and amuses me.

"Prescott?" a raspy voice asks from behind the door.

"Lazarus," Raphael replies firmly.

"Welcome back, Sir. Gimme a sec."

Simon glances over at me, "What does Prescott mean?"

I shrug, "No idea."

"It's another way of saying *password*," Raphael answers, his eyes trained on the door. "Now shut up and don't say a word, especially when we get inside."

We do as we're told and stand at attention, looking straight forward. It takes another minute before something happens. I find myself in awe when the door somehow retracts into the floor beneath it, giving us access into the building.

A man donning the Lazarus uniform stands in the doorway, his face completely obscured by a black morph mask.

"Vice is expecting your arrival, folks. Don't disappoint him," he mumbles, side-stepping out of the way and letting us enter.

The inside looks like it belongs to a crack dealer. The walls are tagged with graffiti, beer bottles and cigarettes litter the floor, and everything reeks of pot. The bitter smell assaults my nostrils at first, but after a second, I get used to it. The aroma is exactly why I've never done drugs in my life. It's disgusting.

"These are the kids Vice is taking in?" scoffs a woman in the back. "They look pathetic."

I gaze over at her, she's wearing the uniform and dons a Lazarus issued respirator that only covers the bottom part of her face. She's tall, and definitely strong from the look of it. Her hair is dyed stormy grey, and she has a scar that runs from her eyebrow down to her lower cheek.

"Shut your *filthy* mouth!" Raphael shouts. His outburst makes me flinch. "And don't you *dare* question Vice, or I promise to have you thrown into T-Avenue."

The woman's feet shift, and she doesn't say another word.

"What's T-Avenue?" Chloe whispers.

Raphael glances over at her, "It's where we torture people."

Just as I'm about to respond, a strong hand grips my shoulder. My muscles flex and I slowly turn my head to see another person donning the Lazarus uniform. He doesn't wear a mask, but I wish he did. Half his face is grotesquely scarred, so much that I can make out his teeth behind a translucent layer of flesh that covers his cheek.

"You're Jason Pinder?" his breath smells like rotten tuna.

I stare at him in the eyes defiantly, "Yeah, what's it to you?"

The scarred man chuckles, "Watch your tone, kid. You have no idea what some people in here might do to you. We're just the upper-level guards, once you get down to the actual facility, you're going to have a lot more to worry about."

I brush his hand off my shoulder, "Do I look like the type of guy who gives a crap about what you have to say?"

The man growls, "Careful, or else I'll have to teach you some respect."

"Piss off."

Raphael leads me, Simon, and Chloe to the end of a large, trashy corridor. A man sits on a bar chair and directly behind him are a pair of blood red elevator doors that I assume will take us down to the main facility.

"Prescott?" The man asks before puffing on his cigar.

"Simmons," Raphael replies, sounding impatient.

The man groans before getting to his feet, and he positions an identification card beneath the elevator's scanner. A loud *beep beep* screeches out, and the solid steel doors part ways.

The man steps out of the way and lets the four of us enter. Raphael presses a button that's labeled *1*, and the doors shut along with a loud *ding!*

"Time to shut up and focus," Raphael mutters. "Those idiots up there are nothing compared to what lies below. The members down in the facility don't screw around, and trust me, if you talk back or *look at them funny* they will mess you up."

If they're anything like Vice, then I'll really be sure to not screw around.

The elevator halts after about a minute, and my heart falters as the loud *ding* announces our arrival. The doors slide open.

I am surprised to see a large white room. White walls, white marble floors, white ceiling, and white lighting adorns the palatial chamber. Such a stark contrast to the cesspit above.

What surprises me most, are the thirteen Lazarus members spaced out behind Vice who's holding a wooden baseball bat in his hands.

"Nice to see you all again," he greets, his voice dripping in poison. "Please, come in."

The four of us step out, letting the elevator doors close behind us.

"I was informed about last night's events, Pinder," he says bitterly. "I'm none too pleased."

I keep my defiant stare stapled to my face, standing at attention, "Sorry, sir. It won't happen again."

He grunts, "And how can I truly believe it *won't* happen, again?"

I take a deep breath through my nose, "I don't know, sir"

Vice looks back at the other members, "What do you guys think? Will he ever screw up again and have his face all over the news like he did this morning?" he brings his gaze back over to me. "Because honestly, I'm not sure whether I should bash his head in with this bat, or congratulate him for sending such a vehement message."

I shudder at the thought of being beaten to death with a bat, "I'm truly sorry, sir."

He nods, standing as tall as me, "Oh, I know you are, and if you aren't, you're about to be."

"What do you mea—"

My head rocks to the side as the bat goes crashing into my

skull. Everything simultaneously turns black and white, and I fall to the floor. My ears are ringing, and the next thing I know, I feel blunt force bash into my nose.

Blood spills out of my nostrils, staining my clothes, puddling up on the marble tile next to my face.

I cry out in pain.

Vice continues swinging the bat into my body, "You-stupid-piece-of-crap! Do you have any idea of what you've done? You dumb bastard!"

I feel like I'm about to black out from all the pain, but he has two members pull me up and balance me on my feet. My vision is blurry, but definitely not as bad as it was a moment ago.

"The next time you do anything stupid, I will put a bullet in your head, you hear me?"

I drool and spit blood, allowing my head to fall forward, "Ye-yes, sir."

He turns back to another member, "Bring out some Rebirth and enhancement pills."

I automatically think he will kill me and bring me back to life. One member jabs me in the wrist with a syringe.

"Why'd you give me that?" I mumble, my legs wobbly, my skull reverberating. "I'm still alive."

Vice grabs my chin with his gloved hand and forces me to look at him, "If you use Rebirth on a host who's still alive, it will act as a regenerator."

The man who injected me forces two pills into my mouth.

I choke them down.

"You're in bad shape," Vice continues. "You were stabbed several times last night during Fight-Night, you were shot through the chest and shoulder, and you were just beaten with a bat. You will need to heal up if you're going to do the assignment I have lined up for you."

I feel better internally, and my broken nose slowly shifts back into place just as I say, "Thank you for giving me another chance, sir."

He nods before dropping the bat, looking over at Simon and Chloe, "Frye, Davis."

The two of them stand at attention.

"You will receive some special training. I will put you through a program called Rewired."

"What's that?" Simon questions.

"Don't worry about it," Vice turns to another pair of members. "Take these two to Rewired and tell Dr. Genovese and Dr. Moore that it's time to start a session," he finally turns his gaze back to me. "You will follow me down to my office."

CHAPTER FIFTY-EIGHT

I follow Vice into a large conference room. As soon as I enter, he shuts the door and locks it, making me uneasy.

"That man you killed last night . . ."

"Which one?"

He snorts, "The one you tied to a chair, tortured, and eventually shot seven times before injecting him with Rebirth."

"What about him, sir?"

He sighs, "I was recently sent footage from one of the security cameras from the hotel your facility is under. They saw the man you murdered heading up to the eighteenth floor, meeting up with three Reapers, and traveling up to the roof where a chopper was waiting. We have identified the helicopter as President Mills' private transport."

"What would the President want with that nobody?"

"I have no idea. That's what I was going to ask you."

"He was the soldier who killed me and my family, so I got even. As far as I'm aware, he wasn't anyone important. How could he be? He was in charge of guarding a checkpoint."

Vice stands still for a moment before nodding, "Hopefully we'll find out more. Look, I want you to go get washed up and into a fresh uniform before the mission briefing. My personal assistant, Amber Scott, will escort you to the showers."

"Understood, sir."

He unlocks the door but holds the knob. He hesitates to open it, "That Rebirth I gave you wasn't a strong dose, so you should be puking them up by tonight."

I silently acknowledge his remark.

"Also, I need you to guarantee something for me."

"What?"

"That there won't be any more mishaps or problems with you."

"I promise that there won't be."

"Good, because I like your style, kid."

He opens the door for me.

CHAPTER FIFTY-NINE

"Hello there, Mr. Pinder," a shapely blonde woman greets me. "I was told to take you down to the showers?"

I study the woman. She looks like she's in her early twenties, has blue eyes, wears a suit coat and a white button-up shirt with heels, and has a welcoming smile glued to her face. I'm not fooled.

"You're Amber, right?" I ask, not caring that my face or clothes are still covered in blood.

"Uh-huh," she remarks, putting her hand out for me to shake. "Amber Scott."

I reach my hand out, "Lovely name."

"Thank you, sir."

"Just being honest."

Did she just call me sir? I kinda like that.

"If you will follow me this way," she starts, slowly walking down the corridor. "The showers are only a short little walk away. This is one of the main Lazarus facilities, and it is *much* bigger than any of our other establishments."

I set off after her, not slowing my pace until I'm walking by her side, "So, how did you end up in an organization hellbent on assassinating the President?"

She chuckles, "It's a long story."

"What do you mean?"

"I'm in hiding. Someone framed me for . . . oh, I really shouldn't be telling you this, sir. My apologies."

"You're fine."

She glances at me, "If you don't mind me asking, are you okay? I know Vice can be a bit rough; are you in need of medical attention?"

I shake my head, "No, I'm fine."

"Oh," she says, sounding sedate. "Well, let me know if that changes."

Suddenly a sickening scream pierces the hall. Simon's howl is unmistakable, and my head instinctively turns to find him. I finally see the door where I think the sound is coming from, and next to it is a plaque that reads, "Rewired." Strangely, I'm feeling calm; so, reading the sign wasn't hard. I resist the urge to interrupt his *training*.

"Is that where my friends are?" I ask, forcing myself to move on.

She nods, "Yeah. The subjects that make it out of there are never the same again, it's so strange. They kill on command, they-sorry, I probably shouldn't be telling you this either, sir."

I don't respond, the thoughts of Simon and Chloe being altered make my head spin.

"Are you okay?" she asks. "You don't look too well. Are you sure you aren't in need of medical attention?"

"I'll be fine. I just want to get cleaned up. How much further?"

"At the end of this corridor," she replies, sounding concerned. "Are you sure you're okay?"

"Yes," I lie, walking faster. "Let's just go."

I'm not in pain. I feel alert yet placid. It must be because of the nanobots.

Amber and I approach a door on the right side of the hallway.

"Well, here we are. Enjoy your shower. We already took the

liberty of placing a fresh uniform on the counter in there. Take as long as you need."

"Thanks, Amber."

"Yep, anytime."

Simon and Chloe will turn into emotionless assassins, and I will take a shower.

CHAPTER SIXTY

As the warm water from the showerhead rinses the blood off my body, I reflect on exactly how I got here. Breaking curfew to attend Nacht-Fest was the craziest thing I've ever done. Simon getting ripped apart by that military canine was also insane, and not to mention my fight with Jakob the next day.

I suddenly remember the Sweet-Tooth and witnessing the murder of Brandon Yancey. It dislodges the memory of his role in having the inhabitants of Brookhaven Estates and so many other subdivisions assassinated.

Everything washes over me.

I hate thinking of the past, but somehow, I can never stop myself from doing exactly that.

"How could you just let me die like that?" someone asks from outside my shower stall, disturbing the peaceful silence in the air. "In an elevator with a bullet in between my eyes?"

My heart races. *Mae?*

Your mind's playing tricks on you. Just like all the other times.

"What? Not even going to say hello?" she mutters.

"You *aren't* real!" I exclaim, my voice reverberating through the bathroom.

Everything goes eerily quiet, and after a few moments, she speaks again, "Well, why don't you open the curtain and find out?"

I hold my breath as the thought of Mae truly being alive rolls around my skull. It isn't impossible, far from it actually. She could've been resurrected again, and that possibility terrifies me. I don't know why, but something about the idea gives me the chills.

No, this is just another sick hallucination. Compliments to my mind.

I slowly turn the shower off. The only sound is each drop of water sliding off my body and splashing against the tiles.

I reach for the shower curtains. I count down from three. I jerk them to the side.

Mae stands directly in front of me. Startled I stumble backwards. I almost fall but the shower wall holds me up. She's wearing black skinny jeans and a white t-shirt. Her shiny black bangs slightly obscure her eyes, and her skin tone is bleached.

I want to faint, but I regroup, "Why are you doing this?"

She shrugs, a cutting smile slowly creeping across her face, "Doing what?"

I blink rapidly, trying to keep my breathing in check, "You aren't real."

"You've changed a lot," Mae says, turning around and heading toward the large mirror in the room. "Grown a few inches, got a haircut, gained *a lot* of muscle, became a murderer."

"What do you want from me?" I ask, stepping out of the shower. "You're dead, you hear me? *Dead!*"

She turns around and grabs my hand, pulling me over to the mirror. She positions me in front, and steps behind me.

"Look at yourself, look how strong and *handsome* you've become."

I study myself in the mirror. I'm not the same kid that snuck out to see Mae at Nacht-Fest; different. Scars litter my body from recent events and each one reminds me of all the hell I've been through.

Mae wraps her arms underneath my shoulders and places both of her pale hands over my chest, "So much trauma for such a fragile little mind to handle, huh?"

"Why are you doing this?"

"Don't you miss me, Jason?" she tightens her grip around me. "I bet you feel oh so bad for getting me shot in the face, don't you?"

I rapidly shake my head, my arms trembling at my side, "I'm sorry. . ."

"No, you aren't," she snarls, her grip around my chest turning violent. "Look down at the counter. There's a handgun. Grab it, put it up to your head, and blow your pathetic brains out."

I stare down at the counter. Neatly arranged on the surface is my Lazarus uniform, a combat knife with a black handle and a blade as dark as night, and finally, the pistol.

"You killed me," Mae says, softly planting her face into my bare back, her tone returning to soft and delicate. "I wasn't ready. I had so much to live for. Why'd you kill me, Jason?"

I grit my teeth, bloody tears streaming down my face, "I didn't mean to."

She kisses my shoulder blade, the one they shot me through, "Pick up the gun, Jason. You don't deserve life."

"Get the hell out of my *head!*"

I clamp my eyes shut before backing up, feeling absolutely nothing behind me, and when I open them, she's gone, and I'm left all alone.

My breath is heavy, and I have to focus on slowing it and my heart down. I stare at myself in the mirror, frantic, mentally hysterical. I wipe my cheeks with the back of my hands, throwing on an undershirt and hoodie before sliding on a set of boxers and a pair of jeans. I put on a pair of fresh socks and slip on the same pair of white sneakers I've been wearing for all these months.

They aren't completely white. I can still see some spatter on them. I guess there are some things you never can wash away. After tying my shoelaces, I grab the knife and pistol off of the counter and put them away. The knife finds its home through my belt loop and the gun in my back pocket.

I'm fixing my hair in the mirror when the door to the showers open and in storms one guy who's supposed to be guarding the upper level of the facility.

"Quick, you need to hurry!" he shouts, his eyes signaling danger.

I give him my full attention, "Why? What's wrong?"

"That girl, the one with the blonde hair who walked in with you, was just found out in the hallway with her throat slit. You need to come now."

Bile builds up in my throat, "You're kidding—"

"I'm not! Hurry, come now!"

CHAPTER SIXTY-ONE

I follow the guard down the hallway, my stomach churning, my mind swirling.

As we make our way to wherever, I hope that he's mistaken. Not Chloe. If she's *actually* dead, I don't know if I'll be able to go on living like this. She's the one that keeps me calm, keeps me focused, and . . .

We reach the end of the hallway and enter a pair of double doors.

Something isn't right. Inside a small foyer on either side is another pair of doors that lead to other unknown parts of the facility.

The doors shut behind me, and I turn around to see two more upper-level guards have joined our party. One of them is the woman who Raphael chewed out, and the other is the man who has half his face disfigured.

The man who led me here lets a malicious smile spread across his face, "I'd like you to meet Sasha and Dwayne."

They both have crowbars gripped tightly in their hands.

"I told you I would have to teach you some respect, didn't I?"

Dwayne asks, the teeth on the right side of his mouth showing through the light sheet of skin that covers his cheek.

I reach for my pistol, but Sasha is too fast and swings the crowbar into the side of my face.

Vacancy occupies my sight, but when it returns, I'm lying on the ground. Sasha hovers over me with the sharp blade-like weapon aimed just above my gut.

I'm so freaking tired of pain.

"I wouldn't move if I were you," she mutters.

I glare at her and slowly move my left hand up and flip her off.

Bad decision.

Dwayne slams his boot down onto my hand.

"You're a disrespectful little freak, y'know that?" he puts more pressure on my hand, but since I'm on enhanced Rebirth, it doesn't hurt that much.

"It's a blessing, like having a face," I say. "Also, I'm not too sure Vice would approve of this."

"To hell with Vice!" he blurts. "Plus, he'll never even know what happened to you. In case you weren't aware, there aren't any security cameras in the foyers."

I glance around the room, "Well, what's stopping me from telling him?"

Dwayne chuckles before handing his buddy the crowbar, pulling out a handgun from his pocket, and aiming it down at my face, "Oh, I don't know . . . killing you?"

I shoot him a bored expression, "You're really letting your panties get into *this* big of a twist over a little pissing match with some kid you don't even know?"

"Nobody disrespects me, boy," he chambers a round into his gun.

"Seems to me like Raphael and Vice disrespect you all the time."

He grits his teeth, waits a second, then shoots me in the back of the hand he was previously stepping on. I don't scream; I don't wallow around in pain, and I don't call out for any help.

Instead, I chuckle, the ruptured skin knitting itself back together right before their eyes.

Dwayne tilts his head to the side and raises an eyebrow, "What the . . ."

Sasha backs up, "He's on Rebirth!"

I swiftly reach into my back pocket, grabbing the handle to my pistol as the three of them panic.

"Shoot him in the head!" the third guard orders.

Dwayne moves his trigger finger, but I put a bullet in his neck before he can squeeze. He drops his gun, clutching at his gored throat. He gargles and hacks up a mouthful of blood before falling to the floor motionless.

The third guard moves for the door, but I shoot him in the back of the head before he can reach the knob, slowly getting to my feet as he collapses backward.

"Please, please no!" Sasha begs, putting her hands in the air.

I twitch my trigger finger, but the door abruptly swings open before I can pull it.

Raphael has his gun drawn. Sasha sobs telling him I just killed the two others in cold blood and that she was next.

I chortle at this nonsense and tell him my side.

Without a word, Raphael points his gun over to Sasha and paints the wall behind her in blood. The discharge of the gun startles me. I wasn't expecting him to react so fast.

"You okay?" he asks, his face covered with his mask. "The mercenaries here have always been a liability."

"I'm aware."

He unclips his walkie talkie from his belt and holds down the button on its side, "Marshal, I need you here, now. I'm in foyer D with Pinder. We've got a little mess to clean up."

CHAPTER SIXTY-TWO

When Vice found out a few of his upper-level guards jumped me, he was furious. So furious that he sent two members up to the main level and had the rest of the mercenaries slaughtered in a grotesque fashion.

He always had a problem with them, and this was the "final straw," in his own words.

After everything is taken care of and the new guards, who are actual members, are ordered to protect the main level, Vice and Raphael take me to their ginormous cafeteria to get some food. We chat for a while, like business associates having small talk. Finally, Vice asks if I would accompany him to retrieve Simon and Chloe from Rewired since they have been there for over eight hours.

I happily say yes, and the two of us stroll down the hallway.

"They will never be the same, will they?" I ask, walking at his side.

"Yes and no," he replies.

"So, what happens to who they were?"

"You'll see for yourself soon enough."

We stop in front of a large, grey metal door with a plaque mounted on the wall next to it labeled "Rewired."

From inside, I hear screams of agony, but they're not coming from Simon or Chloe.

"Right on time," Vice says under his breath, a flame of devilry emitting from him.

I flinch as a large and burly Lazarus member is thrown up against a long, rectangular window next to the Rewired door. His face is bloody, and the horrified expression he wears fills me with panic.

"No! No! Sir, you gotta get me outta here! How could you order them to—?"

I watch in shock as a dark and shadowy figure appears behind the man and jabs the blade of a scalpel through the back of his throat. The lights in the room are flickering, making the figure impossible to distinguish.

The sudden sound of the silver doorknob rattling, followed by rapid banging on the door causes me to reflexively take a step back.

"How could you do this to us? We're going to die in here!"

My ears drown with the sound of horrific screaming. Meanwhile, the figure at the window begins bashing the palm of its hand up against the glass, forcing it to crack. It continues to do this until the window shatters. I take another large step back.

The figure steps through the broken window, shards of glass crunching beneath *his* shoes as he steps into the corridor with us. He dons a bloody Lazarus uniform and wears a tight-fitting mask. I haven't seen these before; half of it is black, the other white.

Vice clasps his hands together behind his back, "*Bravo*, Mr. Davis. You've made me very proud."

My throat closes up.

Simon?

The mask he wears is so tight that I can make out the snarl he wears under it. He looks like a demon, ready to kill anyone on command. He looks nothing like Simon.

"Simon?" I whine, feeling at a loss for words. "Is that you, man? You okay?"

He looks over at me before cocking his head to the side, "Okay? I've never felt better."

His menacing tone sends a chill down my spine. Realizing the implications of such a transformation, I work on regaining my posture and keep my indomitable stare fixed, "Good to hear."

My eyes dart over Simon's head as I hear glass grinding beneath someone else's feet. I look with both awe and confusion as a woman steps over the broken window. She's wearing a blood-drenched Lazarus uniform and a mask identical to Simon's; half black, half white. She holds a serrated blade covered in fresh blood.

Vice chuckles with pride, his hands still clasped behind his back, "You're quite the mess, Ms. Frye."

I stare at the alleged Chloe, trying my best to hold my composure. I can't believe how much the two of them have changed in the course of just *eight* hours.

"Come on, you three," Vice commands. "It's time for your briefing."

CHAPTER SIXTY-THREE

Vice leads the three of us down a wide corridor, but before we can reach the end, I stop.

"Sir?"

Vice pauses, causing Simon and Chloe to stop, "Yes?"

"Before we begin briefing, I'm going to go use the bathroom, would that be fine?"

He sighs impatiently, "Hurry," he turns to Chloe, then points over at me with his black gloved finger. "Assist Mr. Pinder and make sure he makes it there and back with no problems. I want no one else here jumping him."

"Yes, sir," she says, turning around and heading toward me. "Come on."

I follow her, and I am not too enthused with the whole idea of her being my new babysitter. I know that Vice is concerned for my well-being after the prior incident, but Chloe could be just as dangerous.

We walk for over three minutes before she suddenly stops, "Good, they're out of sight."

"Huh?" I slow my pace a little before running into her. "What do you mean?"

Chloe turns around. I'm shocked to hear her sniffling, and to see her shoulders trembling.

I try to comfort her, but in all honesty, I have no idea what to say.

She takes her mask off, revealing her blackened eyes.

She wraps both arms around my neck tightly, burying her face in my hoodie, "I'm sorry, I just—" she sobs, her crying making it almost impossible for her to speak. "I can't believe that all just happened."

I hold her tight, "What do you mean?"

"They tied me and Simon to chairs and . . ." she takes a breath. "And . . ." another breath, deeper this time. "It doesn't matter."

"Yes, it does," I say, concern sweeping through me. "What did they do to you two?"

She unburies her face from my hoodie, looking up at me with tears trickling down her flushed cheeks. They're clear, not bloody. "They beat us to a pulp with night-sticks, showed us security tapes of . . . of our families being murdered, then duct-taped headphones over our ears and played all these audio recordings of a woman repeating the same twelve numbers over and over again until we couldn't take it anymore," she exhales before planting her face back into clothes again. "Those numbers were some sort of mind hypnosis procedure. They planted some type of computer chip in each of our heads, and at any given time, they can trigger the device and the numbers will play."

"What happens if you hear the numbers?" I ask, softly scratching her back as she continues to hold on to me with both arms.

"I don't know exactly how it works, but it'll snap us into a state of mind where we'll kill anyone on command by Vice. All he has to do is give us a target."

This bit of information astonishes me, "Did he tell you and Simon to kill those two back in the room?"

She sniffles, "Yeah, but they weren't members; they were some mercenaries from the upper level. Toward the end of our session, Vice sent in a few of them and told us to murder them all. The effects the hypnosis have on our brains only lasts for a few minutes, and I'm not even mad at myself for killing them. I heard what they did to you, so it doesn't bother me . . . it's that they showed me my family dying."

"That's insane," I say under my breath, pulling gently away. I stare into her beautiful, emerald green eyes. "You're feeling better now, though, right?"

"My head's pounding, but other than that, I guess so."

"You're one of the strongest people I know."

"You really think so?"

"I know so," I smile. "Hey, can I tell you something?"

She quickly wipes her nose with her hoodie sleeve, "You always can."

I stumble to find the words, "I just wanted you to know, well actually, now probably isn't the best time."

"No, just tell me. It's okay."

I sigh, tapping my foot, "I have feelings for you. Just thought you should know that."

She laughs before sniffling once more, "Well duh. That's been obvious for months."

"What?"

"Come on lover-boy, let's go."

"No, let's head back."

"I thought you had to use the bathroom?"

"It was just an excuse to think for a minute, but I'm good now."

She flashes me a little grin before turning around and striding back down the corridor. I follow with a little more energy in each step. My body electrified with Rebirth coursing through my veins.

CHAPTER SIXTY-FOUR

Chloe and I enter Vice's huge office. Simon and Raphael are seated around the large, oak table placed in the center of the spacious area. At the head of the table, the sharply dressed man in the metallic mask taps his gloved fingers against the wooden surface.

"Take a seat, you two," he demands, charismatically. "We have a *lot* to talk about."

Chloe and I do as we're told, sitting next to each other in identical office chairs that surround the table. It takes a moment for Vice to speak. Finally, his voice demands everyone's attention.

"I'm glad to see that my newest three recruits are trained to my liking," he looks over at Simon and stops tapping on the table's surface for a second. "How're you feeling, Davis?"

Simon sighs, sounding weary, "I'm doing just *dandy*, sir. They beat my face in with a baton, one of those freaks broke my ring finger, and I have a headache, but hey, I'm doing just great."

He isn't wearing his mask, and his expression is dark and hardened. His black hair has returned to a shaggy style, same as mine. The way his heavy bangs cover his eyes give him an ominous look and make me feel uneasy.

"Just be glad it worked," Vice looks over at Chloe, leaning back in his chair. "How about you, Frye?"

Chloe shrugs, "I'm doing good. My face hurts, but other than that, I'm okay. I might head to the infirmary after briefing to get my jaw checked out."

"Wise decision," he turns to me, and even through the mask he wears, I can tell that he holds pride in me. "And you. How are you feeling?"

"I'm just perfect."

He dips his head before bringing his attention to the large screen that's mounted on the wall behind him. The screen flashes multiple images of a man who is tall and built. He's clean shaven with a military buzz cut, has dark brown eyes, and a long scar that starts at his ear and ends at the corner of his lips.

"This is Mason Wolfe, also known as Rabbit. He will be executed tomorrow morning at dawn," our leader informs us. "This man is Lazarus' highest priority. He works for us as a mole. He was undercover as one of Mills' Reapers. They compromised him, but right before he was discovered, he uncovered information we *need*. So that's why I'm sending the four of you to save him from his . . . untimely demise."

"Sounds easy enough," Chloe says.

"Actually no, not at all," Vice remarks. "Mason is being held at a military base in the outskirts of Boston. The execution will be broadcast on live T.V., and since Mason is a part of Lazarus, the base is being heavily guarded by Saints and Reapers. Normally, we would have some of our moles get him out of there, but none of them are stationed there, and none of them can get permission to be on base at the time of the execution," he pauses a moment before continuing. "That's why I've had three Saints, who will work on the base during the killing, abducted and offed. Simon, Jason, and Raphael; you three will be using their uniforms and extracting Wolfe."

Chloe interrupts by raising her hand halfway into the air, "And what about me?"

"Since females aren't permitted to be in the military, we decided to put you as the driver of the getaway van. You will drive those three as close as you can to the base and park the vehicle, but keep it running. Mills' won't let Wolfe go without a fight, so I would urge you all to prepare for a lot of complications."

I raise my hand, "Let's say things get a little *too* complicated and Wolfe bites the dust, then what, sir?"

"When you first contact him, I want you three to gather the information he has right away. That way, if he does die, we still have the classified info."

"Understood."

Vice takes turns eyeing us for acknowledgement, "I have codenamed this mission *Operation Full-Moon*. At approximately *five-forty-five* a.m., you four will head out," he looks over at Chloe. "Frye, you know what you need to do."

"Yes, sir."

He grabs a remote off the table and clicks a button, replacing the images on the screen with an aerial view of the military base. "You see the large warehouse in the center of everything? That's where Wolfe is being held. You three will make your way there, kill Wolfe's executioners, destroy any cameras in the area, and retrieve the information. After all that is accomplished, you will attempt to get Wolfe out of there and back to the van safely. Make sure you have the classified information memorized. Any questions?"

None of us speak.

"Good. Raphael will take you to where you four will be sleeping. Get some rest, you've all had a long day, and heaven knows you need it. See you all tomorrow morning. Dismissed"

CHAPTER SIXTY-FIVE

Raphael leads Simon, Chloe, and me to the dormitory. There are three rooms available, but we all just end up picking one to bunk in. With only one mattress in the room, the four of us play Rock, Paper, Scissors to see who gets it.

Chloe wins. She hops into the warm and cozy bed while Simon, Raphael, and I lean up against one wall and slide down to the carpet.

"Listen," Raphael says, shifting into a more comfortable position. "I have this little thing I always do before going on missions with new people. Ready to hear it?"

Chloe shrugs. "Sure. Go for it."

Raphael turns to Simon and me waiting for our approval. We both nod.

"So, I don't like going on missions with members I hardly know," he states, smoothing his hand through his hair. "It's kind of a pet peeve, and since I'm trusting you three with my life, would you all mind talking for a bit? Not in a serious way, just be yourselves."

All of us agree.

"Well, for starters," he says. "I'm eighteen."

"I turn eighteen in October, so I have some months to go," Simon remarks.

"I'm seventeen," Chloe fiddles with her hair, but not in a nervous way. "but I'll be eighteen in August."

"Yeah, me too," I say, surprised that she shares the same birth month as me.

She turns to me, "Wait, you were born in August?"

I nod, "Yeah, August 14th, you?"

"August 17th."

"That's awesome."

Raphael flips the knife in his hand, "You guys mind if I go deep for a sec?"

"No, man, go ahead," Simon insists.

"My dad was a drug lord. He had been one long before Mills came into office. When the Saints patrolled the streets and laws got strict, he moved me and my family to Collingsworth so he could run his operation more smoothly with a smaller chance of being caught," he breaks for a minute allowing the silence to swallow the moment. "Growing up was rough . . . my father would, uh, *bring* his work home with him, and by work, I mean he would bring those who screwed him over to our house and kept them tied up in our basement for days before making them *disappear*," I watch him stop and chuckle for a moment. "I still remember what he would tell me and my older brother, 'Deez pendejos ain't noffin' but scum, and if you two go out d'ere and start snitchin' on me, you'll meet your God in Heaven, you hear?' Now that I look back on it, it's kinda funny, but when I was eight, it scared the crap outta me."

"Wait," I interrupt his story. "So, how did you end up here? Y'know, being Vice's successor and all."

"When I was eleven, I walked in through my front door after school. I saw my mom, my dad, and my brother all duct-taped to our couch, and in front of them were these two tall guys who both had shotguns. One of them looked over at me and told me I was just in time before putting the barrel of the gun up against my father's kneecap and blowing it to pieces. His scream, ah man, his scream is still pounding through my skull, I swear. He deserved it, but still, man."

"What happened to them?" Chloe asks. "Your family."

Raphael stares up at the ceiling, "Well, after shredding his knee cap, he did the same thing to his face. Then, without giving me any time to process what had just happened, the two of them unloaded on my mom." He stops a second and grits his teeth out of what looks to be anger. "I just stood there while this happened. It was her birthday, and I was just *standing* in the doorway holding a cool rock I found for her present."

Emotion fills the room, and it makes my stomach knot up, "What happened to your brother?"

He shakes his head, "I don't talk about that."

All of us go silent as an awkward vibe lingers in the air. I try to think of something to say.

"Today at the bank," Chloe starts. "Some old lady told me to check her balance, so I pushed her over."

We all stare at her, and a moment later, I laugh.

Simon joins in with me, "What? Where did that even come from?"

She shrugs, "It got depressing."

A few other jokes get thrown around, and I'm relieved to see Raphael back to himself and cracking off a little grin.

"Well, what about you?" he asks Simon, "What's your story?"

Simon's face goes from happy and gleeful to kind of dazed, "I don't really like talking about my past, if you don't mind. Jason and I grew up together, and he's one of the few people who know."

"No fair," Chloe groans. "You can't just leave us hanging."

"I'm not trying to leave you hanging," Simon retorts, his tone getting defensive. "I just don't want to talk about it, okay?"

"Yeah, guys," I start, deciding to back Simon up on this one. "Let's leave it alone."

"Tomorrow morning, it will be us three having your back," Raphael says. "If you can trust us to do that, then you can trust us with your past. And not that it matters, but it sounds like it will be juicy."

Simon sighs before gradually getting to his feet. He stands there for a second before he takes his shirt off and turns around, revealing a large tattoo he got when he was fifteen that covers much of his upper back.

"Nice ink," Chloe says. "When did you get it?"

"My father used to beat me and my older sister every single day," he talks almost inaudibly, completely ignoring Chloe's question. "He would usually come home drunk after a long day at his crappy job and go after us two. It started when I was eight. He would beat me until I blacked out, and then go for my sister, who was almost eleven," he stops, looking as if he's mentally preparing to finish the story. "One night when I was fourteen, he broke my nose for the ninth time, and I snapped. I ran away and slept behind this gym I had been spending most of my days in. No one even looked for me."

"Not even Jason?" Chloe asks with a raised eyebrow.

Guilt burns through my chest, "His mom told me he was away with his uncle who lived in Chicago. I didn't know."

Simon brushes the both of us off and continues, "After a few months, I showed up at Jason's house and told him where I had been and what I had been doing. Then, I told him I would hurt my dad bad, and that's exactly what I did. I still remember storming in through my front door. Man, I loved the shocked look on his face when he saw me rush toward him on the couch. I grabbed him by the collar of his shirt and threw him to the floor."

"Wait," Raphael interrupts, "How big was your old man?"

"At that time, we were the same height. He was skinny, not a lot of muscle, but there was just something about him that was so intimidating."

"Okay, okay, keep going. Finish the story."

"I remember my step-mom coming into the room and screaming. She tried stopping me, but I shoved her away and kept beating him. After more of this, she had the nerve to pull a kitchen knife on me. Can you believe that? Years and years of being abused, but as soon as I try to put a stop to it, she pulls a knife on *me*. She threatens to use it if I don't stop and get out, but I didn't care what she said at that moment. All that was on my mind was hurting the man who had hurt me for all those years," he pauses again, clears his throat, then finishes the story. "I backhanded my mom as hard as I could. In fact, I did it so hard that she flew to the floor. She hit her head and must've blacked out because she wasn't moving, but I didn't care. I just went back to beating my dad. I kept swinging, and stomping, and battering until I heard my sister screaming at me to stop. She was so sweet that she even felt compassion for him. Of course, her telling me to stop did nothing, so she got out her phone and called the emergency hotline. There was so much anger and hatred in me that I couldn't control myself."

Simon's back is turned to us, but I can tell that he's choked up. "I cussed her out and screamed at her, and . . . well, while she distracted me, my dad got a hold of that knife my mom was using and jabbed it into my leg. I fell to the floor, he got on top of me, beat my face in, and I was about to black out when my front door burst open and in came Tommy and his partner. He worked my neighborhood's checkpoint."

Raphael looks excited, "Tommy was your checkpoint's Saint? You serious?"

"Tommy has known me and Jay since we were nine, so he was protective over us. In fact, he must've been pretty pissed off over what he was seeing, because without muttering a *single* word, he shot my dad four times in the back. After Tommy cuffed and dragged that screaming sorry excuse of a father out the door, his partner, Logan, asked my sister and me questions, and that was the end of that."

Chloe and Raphael looked shocked.

"Whoa, whoa, wait," Raphael blurts, looking thirsty for more information. "What happened to your dad? And what about your tattoo? Dude, keep going."

"I never saw him again, but according to Vice, he was in prison and was killed two years ago. And as for this tattoo, I got it on the one-year anniversary of my dad being taken. He left a lot of nasty scars on my back, so I covered them up. Plus, my girlfriend thought the design was hot."

"Speaking of girlfriends," Chloe starts while yawning. "Where was she during all of this? Were you even dating at that point?"

"Her and I have been a thing since I was thirteen. But during that whole period of my life, me running away and not telling anyone, being gone for so long, and fighting my dad, we were taking a break. We didn't start things back up until about a month after everything went down. She knows about almost everything that happened, but she's probably with another guy by now. I'm dead to everyone outside of Lazarus, and that includes her," he grabs his shirt and puts it back on, turning around and facing Raphael. "I tried seeing her when Chloe, Jay, and I escaped, but you had other plans for me."

Raphael grows uncomfortable, "I'm sorry, man. I was under strict orders to hunt you three down. I didn't know."

Simon stares at him for a moment before sitting back down on the floor, "Yeah, I get it."

After a moment, Chloe goes on about her past. It's unnerving, but we all listen with open ears. It doesn't take long before we all go quiet and sleep finds our eyes.

CHAPTER SIXTY-SIX

"Jason," *my father mutters, blood and rain pouring down his frame. "Don't loo—"*

A mixture of lead and copper is shot into the back of his head.

"No! Mi-Michael!" my mother howls while sobbing, clutching her chest. "You basta—"

Before she can finish speaking, a bullet gets lodged into her skull.

My eyes shoot open, and I'm lying on the floor, staring up at the ceiling. It's dead quiet, and as I glance around, I see that Simon, Chloe, and Raphael are all still sound asleep.

My chest heaves, my inhales sharp, my exhales unsteady.

The image of their bullet-ridden bodies stay branded behind my eyelids.

"Oh, mom," I whimper, blood spilling from my eyes and staining the floor beneath me. "Why did you and dad have to leave me?"

My words make Simon stir, and eventually, his eyes open. At first, he lies there on the floor next to me, then he turns with a sleepy expression on his face.

"You okay, man?"

I pause, blood continuing to flow from my eyes, "How do I stop?"

"Stop what?"

"Stop caring."

He yawns, now sitting up a tad, "About what?"

"People that are gone."

"Like who?"

"My parents."

"Your parents were one of a kind, Jay. Never stop missing them."

"What about Mae? It's all my fault she's dead, and she won't stop screwing with my *head*."

"Mae? Are you really going to keep blaming yourself for that? Please, Jason, please tell me how her death is your fault in the slightest? Because I can't wrap my head around it at all."

I let out a shuddering sigh, "If I would've just killed those two guards, she wouldn't have been shot. I just can't seem to move on, man, and It's killing me."

"Do you want me to be completely honest with you, dude?"

"Yeah, of course."

"Mae's death was her own fault, and you're being too emotional. We wouldn't have even *dreamt* of escaping if it wasn't for her. She's the one who pushed and pushed and pushed. *She's* the reason why, not you. If anything, I have more to do with it. I agreed to leave, which put the whole thing in motion. Jason, you *need* to drop it. Also, killing people for no *reason* isn't okay. I'm glad you didn't murder those two guards."

I use my hoodie sleeve to wipe the blood from my face, "I want to drop it, but it keeps coming back, and I don't know what to do. Should I just—"

Out of nowhere, my mind suddenly plays Mae's death rapidly over and over in my head, causing my heart to accelerate faster than ever. I uncontrollably cry out while bringing both hands to my eyes to cover them.

"What's wrong?" Simon asks, his tone drenched in concern.

Mae's death stops, but instead my mind replays Jakob's demise. The way I shoot him in the skull five times makes my body shake and tremble. I cry out again, begging the memories to stop out loud. Raphael and Chloe wake up in a startle.

"Pinder?" Raphael calls out in a daze. "You okay?"

Marcus' death replaces Jakob's, making my heart sting and sink into the pit of my stomach. The guilt and pain is overwhelming, and it doesn't stop. I feel as if I'm about to die, as if my body is being crushed into nothing but dust.

Dread. Nothing but dread.

For the next few moments, all the people I've ever killed enter my head, reminding me exactly how I offed them. I leave my three partners trying to figure out what's happening.

I feel someone kneel close.

"Jason," Chloe touches my shoulder, "Are you okay?"

I uncover my eyes and reel back. Instead of Chloe, I see Matthew. My mind goes into overdrive, and I swing my fist into his face. His entire head shoots to the right, and he collapses to his side. I blink. Suddenly my killer disappears, and in his place lies Chloe on the floor, her nose spilling out a vast amount of blood.

Everything unexpectedly stops. The memories, the guilt, everything vanishes. My heart slows, and so does my quick breathing.

Everyone in the room is silent.

"I'm. . ." I start, my cheeks burning. "I'm sorry."

I quickly get to my feet, pull my hood over my head, and leave the dorm room.

CHAPTER SIXTY-SEVEN

I stare at my reflection in the mirror alone in the shower room. There's smeared blood all around my puffy, red eyes, and I use water from the sink's faucet to wash it all off.

I feel embarrassed and stupid, but I'm worried that what just happened will happen again. It felt like a panic attack, but so much worse. I feel terrible about punching Chloe in the face. I saw Matthew, and with everything going on, I reacted with no thought.

Way to go, pal. I think to myself, still studying my reflection. *You hit the only girl that cares about you. Good job.*

I'm about to keep beating myself up when the door to the showers opens. Chloe enters. Her nose has stopped bleeding, but she looks in pain.

"Mind if I join you?" she asks, a sympathetic smile on her face.

I pull my attention back over to the mirror, too embarrassed to maintain eye contact, "No, of course not."

She stands close enough that the molecules between our arms are buzzing. She looks at my reflection, "First of all, you pack a *hard* punch."

"I'm so sorry about that—"

"No, don't be. All I want to know is what happened back in the room."

I take a deep breath before shrugging, "I honestly have no idea. Out of nowhere, my mind just replayed all these things, and it sent me off the deep end, I guess. I didn't mean to punch you, but for some reason you looked like a Saint."

"Me? A Saint?" she asks, but after I don't reply, she turns. "Hey, I'm right here. Stop looking in the mirror and face me."

I reluctantly turn toward her and look into her pretty emerald green eyes, "I don't know why I saw you like that, I just did, and I'm *really* sorry for punching you."

She smiles, "Don't worry about—"

I don't let her finish before embracing her, "Thanks for always having my back, and thanks for always forgiving me for being so stupid."

She tightens her grip, making me feel warm on the inside, "You're not stupid, Jason."

I lean in, pressing my lips against hers. She wraps her arms around my neck, and neither of us part until the door to the showers opens.

"Vice says it's go time," Raphael says. "Come on."

I nod, "Alright, just lead the way."

SIMON, CHLOE, RAPHAEL, AND I STAND BEFORE VICE ON the upper level of the main facility. Raphael, Simon and I hold a uniform with some equipment, including a handgun, a combat knife, an identification card, a walkie-talkie, two hand grenades, and an empty black holster to strap onto our uniform.

"Alright, gentlemen," Vice says, clasping his hands behind his back. "You have five minutes to be geared up and ready to go," he looks over at Chloe, who's standing to my right. "Ms. Frye, did my assistant help you memorize the route you'll be taking?"

She nods, "Yes, she did."

"Do you feel confident in driving the van?"

"Yes, sir."

"Good," he looks back over at us guys. "Get dressed."

I set my uniform and equipment down on the ground before slipping my shoes off, unbuttoning my jeans and sliding them down and off my legs, taking my fingerless black gloves off and tossing them to the floor, and finally shedding my hoodie and shirt and tossing them to the floor. Afterwards, I bend over and grab the grey camo pants from my uniform stash and slip them on. They're nice and snug and make me feel warm.

"Hey, these pants aren't half-bad," I remark, buttoning them up.

Simon, who's also buttoning up his camo pants, laughs, "You can say that again."

I chuckle while bending over and grabbing a black skin-tight, long-sleeved shirt and putting it on over my bare torso, "You two nervous?"

"You three," Chloe, who's still to the right of me, corrects.

Raphael snorts, also putting on the skin-tight shirt, "You're literally just driving a van."

"I'll have to remember that when you're sprinting for your life *back* to said van."

Raphael laughs, "Piss off, Frye."

I grab the tactical vest from my pile and slip my arms through it, buckling it together, "How much more time do we got?"

Amber is standing by the entrance to the facility. She answers, "Three minutes, sir."

I glance over at her, forgetting she was there in the first place, "Thanks."

"No problem, sir."

I bend over once more and grab a pair of black socks. A pair of shiny black combat boots fit snuggly on my feet. I slip on a pair of black combat gloves.

Finally, I take the ski mask that lies by my feet and slip it on over my face, taking a deep breath. Once it's secured, it obstructs most of my facial features.

I quickly put my equipment together. I grab the black holster and loop it through my camo pants, then I grab my pistol and stick it in, making sure it's snug. The tactical vest contains a pouch I use to put my hand grenades in. There's a little black sheathe I use for my combat knife, and last, I attach a walkie-talkie to a black loop. I stick my identification card into a pocket.

Vice walks back into the main area just as we finish up, "I'm glad to see that you're all geared up and ready to go. I want you three to study the ID cards on the way to the base. They set those radios you all have on the same channel, meaning you'll only be in contact with each other. I gave Ms. Frye one. So, remember to give her constant updates."

We all give an affirming nod.

"Now remember, we'd like Wolfe alive, but as long as one of you retrieves the information he's holding, we understand if he comes back K.I.A."

"Understood," the four of us say in unison.

"Any last-minute questions?" Vice asks, his hands still clasped behind his back.

Simon raises a finger in the air, "Why aren't you linked up to our talkies?"

Vice clears his throat, "Because if something happens and they get a hold of one of your guys' radios, they can track the signal back to me."

"Sir," Amber says. "It's time for their departure."

"Acknowledged," bringing his attention back over to the four of us. "It's time to initiate *Operation Full-Moon*."

CHAPTER SIXTY-EIGHT

As heavy metal music blares throughout the moving van, I thoroughly study my identification card. I'm posing as a Saint named Michael Gigante. He is, I mean, *was* twenty-seven. We share the same height and weight, which I find genius. We almost look identical based on the card's picture.

The van we're in only has two seats, and they're both up front. The large empty area behind them is where, Simon, Raphael, and I sit. We've been driving for over an hour, and Chloe has been telling us that we'll arrive shortly.

"Your girlfriend has quite an exquisite taste in music, Pinder," Raphael says over the loud guitar riff and screaming vocals. "I'm actually kind've impressed."

"Girlfriend, huh?" Chloe shouts over the song. "I kinda like that."

Simon and Raphael exchange looks, both letting their jaws drop. I can't tell if it's in a mocking way or not, but once they laugh, I realize that it is.

I flip them off, trying hard not to grin but failing, "Piss off."

Despite the jokes, the air is thick with anxiety. It's unspoken, but we all know there's a chance we could all die this morning. I don't even know why I'm doing this.

Actually, that's a lie. I'm doing this because of the promise I made two nights ago on that front lawn while soaked in blood. I will remove America of its tyrant.

This is just one of the many steps.

I'm surprised as the music suddenly stops. The van slows down rapidly, so I keep as quiet as I can.

"Okay, this is where you guys get out," Chloe says, putting the vehicle in park. "Remember to keep me updated, alright?"

Simon nods, "Don't worry, we will."

Raphael opens the double doors at the back of the van, and steps out, "Keep the van running, Frye, and don't get spooked and leave without us."

"I won't."

Simon and I step out. I'm just about to slam the double doors shut when Chloe tells me to hold on.

"What's up?" I ask, my heart pounding and stomach churning.

I could die today.

She looks hesitant, "I just wanted to tell you to be safe. Get in and get out, okay?"

I flash her an artificial smile, "Yep."

"Also," she fumbles with her walkie a little. "I want you to know I care about you a *bunch*, and . . . you *better* not die."

Her words make my smile turn genuine, "I care about you a bunch, too," I swing the doors, but before they close, I look over at her one last time, "Oh, and I won't *try* to die."

They shut.

I turn around, facing Raphael, "So, where to now?"

He points over to the massive military base to my right, "Gee, I wonder."

I punch his shoulder, rolling my eyes while walking past him, "Let's go."

We walk toward our target, remaining in silence.

To enter, we have to pass through a military checkpoint. We approach the large security booth, and the closer we get the more anxiety runs through me.

"Remember to keep cool," Raphael is using a deeper tone than usual. "One slip up, and the three of us die."

"Got it," Simon says, his tone also deeper to match that of a Saint's. "We slip up, we die," exhaling a deep breath. "Okay."

"We're not dying," I say, also with the deeper tone trend. "No slip-ups."

The military entrance is set up with a tall and wide security booth placed a few feet to the side of a formidable solid steel gate. Four Saints holding leashes attached to vicious canines are stationed in front of the gate. Inside the booth, there's an armed Saint. He'll be the one asking for identification.

From sniper towers behind the fifty-foot wall, six soldiers have us in their crosshairs as we halt in front of the booth. The canines growl and snarl. I feel at any moment their leashes could snap and they'll be eating us alive.

The heavily overcast sky threatens to drench us at any moment. The air is smoky, and everybody, especially the dogs, seem on edge and paranoid. When the Saint in the booth asks me for my ID, my nerves could snap.

I reach into my pocket and pull out my card, handing it to the man, "Here."

He studies it for a moment before handing it back, "You're clear, Gigante."

I take the card and put it back into my pocket, not muttering a single word as I side-step to the right, giving Simon room to receive his security clearance.

As he's giving his ID to the man, I can't help staring at the sadistic and blood-thirsty hounds in front of me. They're Belgian Malinois. My Government Ed class covered their uses. They're entirely different from the canines that most patrols use; this breed is strictly used for the Reaper battalion's unit, or for guarding *Code 12* areas.

Code 12 is a location where President Mills is present.

Why is that little rat here?

Simon puts his hand on my shoulder, leaning in closer to my ear, "Take it easy. You look like you're about to pass out."

I blink rapidly, snapping myself out of it before leaning into his ear, "Mills is here."

He tilts his head to the right out of shock, "You screwing with me?"

I shake my head slowly, "No. Stay focused."

The Saint in the booth clears Raphael before pressing one button in front of him. The ground trembles, and I watch as the solid steel gate before me retracts into the earth, revealing the inside of the base.

The four Saints guarding the gate step aside, taking their dogs with them. The three of us step forward and enter the base. The gate raises back to its normal position as soon as we're a safe distance away.

"*Crap,*" Raphael mutters under his breath.

I glance over at him as the three of us continue walking, "What? What is it?"

"That's the only entrance, and it looks like the only way to open it is from the outside."

"Why is that bad?" Simon asks, keeping his voice lowered.

"Because, that means we're trapped here," he mutters. "They'll only open the gate if necessary. And if we're trying to escape with a traitor, I'm confident in saying they won't let us out."

"Look, we'll figure this all out. We have one objective," I remind the two of them. "Get Wolfe *in* and *out.*"

Out may be a problem.

CHAPTER SIXTY-NINE

The inside of the base is intimidating. Every few yards, there's a different building, each for a different purpose. Saints are everywhere, each one armed and dangerous.

I walk in the military uniform expecting the fight ahead, horrified to the point where I feel like puking.

"You see that huge warehouse right over there?" Raphael asks us. "That's where Wolfe is. We need to get in there, and we need to do it now. It's almost time for the execution."

I stare at the warehouse that's two hundred yards from us, sighing, "Let's do this."

The closer we get to the building, the more complicated everything becomes. They guard every visible entrance, and there's not a single window.

I nudge Simon as we get closer to the warehouse, "I don't see a way in, do you, man?"

He shakes his head, "Not that I can see," he looks over at Raphael. "Any possible entryways mapped out?"

"Just follow my lead," he says.

We approach the Saints who stand guard at one of the main entrances.

Raphael speaks to them, "We need to see the traitor. It's a last-minute prep for his execution."

The Saint being spoken to stays standing at attention while the other steps forward. He towers over all three of us. That's impressive since Raphael and I are above six feet tall.

"I will need a clearance code," he says, his voice low and raspy.

Raphael smirks, now chuckling, "I don't think you heard me. I *said* that I *need* to see the traitor. Trust me, I have no patience whatsoever, today. *Don't* test me."

The Saint glares at him before shoving him back, "No *code*, no *admittance*. Now get the hell outta here before things get nasty."

"You threatening a fellow soldier?"

"I don't think you understand my authority, here. I've been ordered not to let anyone in without the clearance code, and anyone who tries is considered to be the enemy. So, as I said before, *get outta here.*"

Raphael takes a step back, leaning into me so he can whisper in my ear, "Get in, get the info, and get out. I'll be okay."

I turn to him with a concerned expression, "What?"

Without warning, Raphael throws himself at the Saint and takes him to the ground. The initial scene catches me off guard, but when the rest of the Saints guarding the doors tackle Raphael and begin beating him with their fists, I lose myself for a moment. I watch as they stomp and kick him. It takes just a moment before everything comes back and I remember what I'm here for.

Quickly grabbing Simon by the arm, the two of us hastily enter the warehouse.

The inside is massive and lacking any furniture, shelves, or anything. Four Saints are gathered around a blindfolded man who's . . . nailed to a wooden chair. My jaw drops. They have hammered his hands to the chair's armrests with foot long spike-nails going through each of them.

One of the Saints turn toward us, "This is a highly restricted area, and is off limits. What's your business, here?"

My hand slowly makes its way to my holster, "Vice told us to come and check up on our little friend, here."

"Vice? Who the—"

My handgun is out before he finishes, and I blow a hole in the guy's face. I swiftly rob the rest of the Saints' of their lives, blasting each of their skulls wide open with a few bullets.

"Why'd you do that?" Simon blurts. "Everyone outside probably heard that!"

I walk toward Wolfe, "I wouldn't worry about it. They're too busy with Raphael."

Wolfe shakes uncontrollably, "Who's there? Who . . . who are you?"

He looks broken. He's only wearing a pair of grey boxers, and I can't even count how many lacerations cover his torso, thighs, and face. My stomach almost forces up my breakfast when I notice that his feet have also been nailed to the floor with large, *rusty* nails.

"*M-mom!*" he cries out, whimpering. "Is that you?"

"I'm not your mom, Wolfe," I swallow. "I'm here to get you out of here."

His shaking grows more violent, *"I'm sorry, mama! Please don't hit me again!"*

Simon slides over to my side, "This guy has lost his mind."

I swear under my breath while unclipping my walkie-talkie from my vest. Simon stops me before I report our status.

"What if they still have Raphael? They'll be able to hear everything you say."

I shake my head, "Knowing him, he's probably gotten away by now."

He sighs, "No, Jason, that's not a good idea."

I hold the button on the talkie down, ignoring him, "It's Jason. You copy, Chloe?"

I release the button, and Simon groans.

"Yeah, I copy. Get me up to date," she demands, her voice blaring through the radio.

"So, Wolfe's lost it. He's talking nonsense and acting like he belongs inside an insane asylum. I don't think we can get anything outta him."

She takes a moment to respond, "*Crap*. Well, what now?"

"I don't know. Give me a minute and I'll get back to you."

I clip the walkie-talkie back to my vest, stepping up to Wolfe and harshly slapping him across the face, "Listen to me, Mason. Vice has sent me and a few others to come and rescue you. Do you understand?"

He grows still, looking like he woke from a dream, "Y-yes. Yes, I understand."

I raise an eyebrow, surprised that the slap to his face worked, "Okay, good. Would you like me to take off your blindfold?"

"Yes, please."

I reach over and untie the cloth before pulling it from his face, and I reel back a few feet. One of his eyes are missing, and the other looks damaged.

"What? What is it?" he asks, sounding disoriented and confused. "And why can't I see anything? I thought you took the blindfold off?"

"I did," I tell him, trying my best to regain my posture. "They took one of your eyes out and jacked the other one up bad."

"Way to be blunt," Simon says.

Wolfe goes silent, and the next thing I know he's shaking again. It grows so violent that it unnerves me. He screams nonsense, talking about how his father was supposed to be coming home for dinner, but didn't.

"You with me, Wolfe?" I ask him with a discouraged tone.

"He slit his wrists right down the middle, mama! That's why he didn't show!"

I repeat a slap across the face, but he doesn't stop. He keeps going on about his father committing suicide.

I stop and think for a second, knowing this man is the solution for stopping whatever Mills has planned.

I'm about to give up, but that's when I see the hammer. I presume they used it to nail his hands and feet down. The sight of it gives me an idea, but it's morbid.

I bend over, picking the hammer up and taking a deep breath, "Please work."

"What are you doing?" Simon asks.

I look apologetically at Simon.

I slam the hammer down on the nail in his right hand, forcing it to go deeper. This makes Wolfe howl in agony. He snaps back out of it.

"*Please!*" he screams, tears streaming out of the only eye he has. "*Please stop!*"

I drop the tool, guilt springing through me like a river, "I thought we lost you, again."

"I'm- I'm sorry," he cries. "My mind keeps going blank, I don't know what's happening. You said that Vice sent you?"

"That would be correct," I say. "He said before they captured you, you uncovered a plan Mills has that would tear America apart. Can you recite what it is?"

Wolfe sniffles, "It's a biochemical weapon. He calls it *The God Code*, and once it's activated, it'll cover the entire Nation in this gas that will kill anybody who inhales it. He wants to rid our country of civilians."

He laughs like a madman.

Simon swears, "Did we lose him?"

I'm about to speak, but Wolfe suddenly stops. He exhales a long breath before leaning his head back.

"Lazarus can't stop this," Wolf sighs. "We can't win."

"You don't know that," I say, his words casting all hope out of me.

"Let me guess. You snuck in here, right?"

"Yeah, why?"

He goes quiet for a second before muttering, "You will die, kid. You and everyone else that came to help rescue me."

"And why do you say that?" Simon asks.

"Because . . . there's only one way out of this hellhole. If you attempt to *rescue* me, they'll shoot you on sight. Let's say you somehow get past the snipers and get the gate open, then what? Those dogs out there will tear you limb from limb."

My heart drops into the pit of my stomach.

He's right.

"But . . .," he quickly spits out. "There is *one* way you all can leave this place alive."

"How?" Simon asks.

Wolfe goes quiet again, after a prolonged minute he says, "You leave me here. There's no way you got in here without a military uniform, so I know you're both wearing one. Look, if you leave me, you two have a better chance of getting out of this place without getting lit up like a Christmas tree."

"If we were to leave you," I swallow, showing no emotion in my voice. "You'd have to give us more details on The God Code. Think you could do that?"

"Mills has plans to kill every citizen in the nation by December 24th. The weapon is located somewhere in Seattle. He's only told three people of its location. Vincent Murdock, Finn DeLuca, and Dennis Ingerman. Remember those names. Each of them knows exactly where it is."

A sudden loud banging on the door stops my heart, "It's showtime, boys!"

"You've gotta kill me," Wolfe abruptly mutters, gritting his teeth. "Shoot me in the head then fall to the floor and act dead."

My eyes go wide, "Why?"

"Do it, kid," he orders. "Do it or else we're all going to die."

There's more banging on the door, "I just got radioed! They told me the camera isn't rolling! Hurry in there!" an angry voice from outside hollers.

My heart pounds as I quickly aim my gun up at Wolfe's head, "Rest easy."

"Thank you."

I pull the trigger, then collapse to the blood-smeared cement floor with Simon. I fall into a position which allows me to face the two entrances of the warehouse- the large bay doors and the regular metal one.

I don't completely shut my eyelids, leaving a sliver of space for me to see out of.

The metal door directly ahead of me bursts open, and in walks the big guy Raphael took to the ground earlier.

He's pissed off.

"Why did a gun just go off?" he stops upon seeing the massacre in front of him. "I've got seven deceased- including Wolfe!"

Like clockwork, three more Saints enter the room. They all look bewildered and enraged, approaching the dead bodies.

"What happened?" one questions, his gun drawn and at the ready. "We were right outside. How did we not hear *any* of this?"

The large Saint stops dead in his tracks, "Those two soldiers were with that one guy who tried getting in without the clearance code. While we were beating on him, they must've snuck in," he pauses, his eyes bulging with fury. "That means there's three traitors dressed as Saints walking around the base, and we let one of them go."

At least Raphael's not dead.

One of the Saints lets his aim drop, "So you're telling me we just let a traitor walk off with a couple of bruises and a broken bone or two?"

"It was probably a distraction so his two partners could come in here and do this. C'mon, we've gotta check the bodies, then we'll call it in. Those three aren't leaving this base alive."

That's what you think, douchebag.

The four Saints search some of the dead bodies, and the big

guy looks over at Wolfe, "I guarantee these traitors are part of Lazarus. I bet they killed him so he wouldn't talk, the bastards."

He messes with my arms and legs, almost as if he's searching for something. Then, to my horror, he puts his fingers up to my throat to check for a pulse.

I grip my gun.

"Call in a medic, this guy isn't dea—"

I fire a round into his body, and he screams. I quickly bring the gun to his head and shoot throwing his lifeless body off of me. The three remaining Saints aim their weapons down on me, but Simon quickly leaps up and slashes one of their throats with his combat knife. This gives me an opportunity to fatally shoot another Saint, leaving the last one to throw his hands in the air.

"I surrender!" he blurts, dropping his weapon.

I hastily get to my feet and train my gun on him, "Get on the ground."

He drops his head, but without warning, defies my orders and swiftly unclips his walkie-talkie bringing it to his mouth before pressing the button, "Put the base on lockdown! Three Lazarus members are dressed as Saints and just killed—"

I fire a round into his stomach, and another one into his shoulder. He falls to the floor, dropping his radio and crying out in pain.

"You stupid little puppet!" I bellow, now aiming my gun at his head.

He coughs up blood before smiling up at me, "I hope they kill you slow . . ."

I pull the trigger, and the moment it makes impact, a roaring noise goes booming through the morning air.

It's a siren.

CHAPTER SEVENTY

An overwhelming sensation of dread springs through me as the siren booms its wailing rhythm into my eardrums, threatening to blow them.

Simon and I exchange looks, and we don't even have to speak to know what each other are thinking.

This is the end.

I briskly unclip the walkie-talkie from my vest, holding the button down, "Chloe, Raphael, do you copy?"

I release the button and wait, holding the talkie up to my ear to hear better.

"I'm here," Chloe's voice blares through the radio. "What's going on? Why is there a siren going off?"

I'm about to reply, but Raphael beats me to it, "You guys must've gotten caught!"

He has to scream in order for any of us to hear him.

I hold the button down, "We got the information from Wolfe, but he's dead. Long story short, we got into a big scruff with a few Saints and one of them just called it in!"

Raphael swears, "Well, at least you've got the info! Where are you two at!"

"We're still in the warehouse," I shout into the radio, holding the button down. "You?"

"I'm behind the latrine. We need to meet somewhere and find a way out of this place before we're hunted down and killed."

"Don't move, we'll meet you there."

"Copy that."

I clip the walkie-talkie back to my vest, looking over at Simon, "Let's move."

The two of us leave the carnage in the warehouse. On the outside, things are in a chaotic jumble of activity. Saints are running around, all following separate orders given to them. My heart beats out of my chest as three of them storm the warehouse that's now fifteen feet behind us.

I hope and beg they don't stop us, but life isn't fair.

"Hey! You two!" someone calls out from behind me. "Don't move!"

My heart freezes, and I yell, *"Run!"*

Simon and I sprint off as fast as we can. My stomach churns as bullets hit the surrounding dirt. Debris bounces up into the air, creating a dirty mist. We cut around all the small buildings that litter the base's interior. My brain keeps barking at me to make it over to the latrine.

Simon swears repeatedly, The Saints still hot on our trail, "Where to? Where to?"

"I don't know!"

After sprinting further, we finally lose them after turning a tight corner and crouching low between two buildings. We stop and catch our breath. The siren has just become white noise, my lungs are on fire, and my legs feel like lead.

Everything feels hopeless. I turn my gaze and fuzzily the latrine appears just twenty feet away.

A smile creeps onto my face, and I nudge Simon to get him to look at the building, "It's right there."

He looks up at the sky, "Thank you!"

I tug at my radio and unclip it, holding the button down, "We're in front of the latrine, Raphael. Come on."

I release the button. Nothing comes back but silence.

I hold it down once more, "Raph, do you copy?"

Simon pats me on the back, "He probably can't hear us. He said he was in the back."

I nod, and the two of us jog around the building. I'm stopped in my tracks when I am confronted with a sight that jars me to my core.

Raphael's on his knees with his hands behind his head, unmasked. Three Saints stand behind him with their guns trained to the back of his skull. My blood runs icy cold when I see the person standing next to him with a walkie-talkie up to his mouth.

"Cut the siren!" he barks into it, flashing me a snide smile. "Clearance code *7701*!"

Instantly, the deafening noise that has bellowed through the air these past five minutes suddenly stops, leaving a sinister silence to linger in its place.

The man who murdered my family stands tall, proud, and pale. A shiny black eyepatch covers his right eye. "Hey there, Jason," he says. "Remember me?"

I glare at him before pulling the mask from my face and letting it drop to the ground, "How could I forget? You killed me and I killed you."

He grins while letting out a little laugh, "After our last little run in, you know, where you had your friend over here jab a knife through my eye, kill me, somehow bring me back life, and murder my *seven-year-old* daughter, I was given a little promotion. Well, actually, *little* is an understatement. The president gave me leadership over a battalion of Saints whose main purpose is to *exterminate* Lazarus."

I burst out in laughter, "You think you can take out Lazarus? Three of us, just *three*, took out how many of your guys? Not to mention we infiltrated this base and no one even noticed until that one soldier called it in."

Matthew stares at me with amusement. He isn't wearing a military uniform. Instead, he dons a black leather trench coat, grey camo pants, black combat boots, and a black turtleneck. His look gives him this menacing vibe, but I don't let it intimidate me.

"You realize we have security cameras all over the warehouse, right? I watched you kill Wolfe after getting all the information you could out of him. I mean, how else did I know it was you? How else did I know where to find Raphael, that is his name, right? Look, I've been watching you, studying you. The only reason the siren didn't go off earlier is because I wanted to see what all you'd do. Finally, after Wolfe and many others were killed by your hand, I allowed it to be set off. You may think you're clever, kid, but you're not."

I swallow hard, "You're lying. You're just saying *that!*"

He waits a moment to speak, "Who's this Chloe person you guys spoke to on the radio?"

My eyes fill with dread, "Don't you dare do anyth—"

"Shut your mouth, Pinder!" he abruptly explodes, making me flinch. "You think you have us figured out? Well, guess what! You don't! I own you, now! You're mine!" he stops and calms himself for a second or two. "You're done with . . . And no, I will not kill you. I'm *not* done with you *or* your little friend . . . but him," he points to Simon. "He's useless. So, I'm going to make a little example out of him to show you what happens to *terrorists*," he turns to the three Saints behind him. "Bring that kid to his knees."

I watch in horror as two of the Saints march up to Simon and kick his legs out from under him. They then force him to his knees before pressing the barrels of their guns up against the back of his skull.

"Get offa me!"

I throw a punch at one, but I hear a pistol being chambered.

My murderer aims his weapon at my face.

"Don't do it," he says. "Put your hands behind your head."

I hesitate, but after a moment, I do as I'm told, "What's your name? Your full name."

He stares at me with his one good eye, "Matthew White. The man who loved putting a bullet into *each* of your parents' heads."

I let out a soft chuckle, "I promise you, Matthew, I *promise you-*."

"You promise me what?"

"I promise you I'll be the one who puts you down for the *last* time."

Matthew blatantly ignores my threat. He walks up to Simon, and he asks one of the Saints for a knife. He puts the serrated steel up to my best friend's throat and meets his stare.

"You've been found guilty of treason," he declares, a sick smile wide on his face. "Any last words before I take your life away?"

Simon, whose eyes are expansive and misty with tears, looks over at me, "No matter what happens, make sure he *rots* in Hell."

Blood streams from my eyes, and my body trembles, keeping me from speaking.

None of this is real.

Matthew's eye is large with excitement, "May God have mercy on your soul."

I clamp my eyes shut as he slashes Simon's throat, leaving the sound of him gurgling to echo in my ears. I remember all the memories we've shared the last thirteen years, both good and bad. I can't help falling to my knees and sobbing like a child.

Matthew looks over at me, "Judging by your actions, I'm guessing he was pretty close to you. Good."

I glance at Simon. He's collapsed face-first into the dirt with blood pooling all around his face. Burning rage seethes through me. I grab the combat knife out of its sheath on my vest.

"*I'm going to kill you!*" I scream, lunging at the nearest Saint, leaping onto him, and thrusting my blade into the side of his skull before plummeting to the ground as his body falls under my own.

The Saint behind Raphael aims his rifle over at me. Raphael seizes the chance to engage him.

I quickly get off the dead Saint beneath me and tackle the other one a foot away, slashing and jabbing his body until he goes limp. I charge at Matthew, but a scorching flame bursts through my shoulder blade, stopping me.

I cry out in pain and collapse on my side.

"Do you ever learn?" Matthew blurts, firing another round into my body, this time my hip.

I scream out with both mental and physical anguish.

He's about to shoot me again, but Raphael tackles him. I watch the two roll, throwing swift and heavy punches at each other. I get to my feet, mania and wrath pushing me toward my enemy.

I throw my foot into Matthew's face. His head reels back and smacks against the ground. I put my knife up against this throat and use my other hand to take the gun away from him.

Raphael gets to his feet, "Just kill him. We're dead men, so let's take him with us."

I shake my head, "No. We're not dead men. I'm getting us out of here."

"How?"

I put more pressure on the knife against Matthew's throat. Blood trickles from the edge of the blade, "Listen here. You're going to call off all your snipers up in those towers, have security open up the gate, and let us *walk* out of here, *you son of a slut.*"

He chuckles humorlessly, a bloody grin on his face, "Aren't you going to kill me?"

I ignore him, digging the knife deeper into his throat, "Do as you're told."

He flashes me a nasty smile, "Grab the radio out of my pocket, hold the button down, and put it up to my mouth."

I do so, making sure my knife keeps him down.

I hold the button on the radio.

"Calling off all snipers- clearance code *8703!*" he barks, a smile still present on his face. "Also, open the gate, clearance code *1125!* Two Saints will march outta here, let them pass."

I release the button, and simultaneously, hear the gate opening from the other side of the military base, "I'll make sure you *suffer*."

I get off of him, chuck his radio as far as I can, and aim the pistol I took from him down at his stomach, then squeeze the trigger three times. He howls while clutching his now bloodied gut, crimson red tears forming in his one good eye.

"Have fun bleeding out," I say before throwing the pistol as far as I can.

"I won't stop until you're dead," he mutters, blood drooling from his lips.

I heave out a deep sigh before hurrying over to Simon. His fingers twitch as the pool of blood he's collapsed in grows larger.

My lower lip trembles, and that's when I remember Rebirth.

I can *save* him.

"Do you have any Rebirth on you?" I ask Raphael as Matthew gurgles in pain.

He slowly shakes his head, "No."

My heart pangs, "Well, we can make it back to the facility in time, right?"

He again shakes his head, "It's over an hour away, Pinder. It won't work."

Matthew laughs, specks of blood flying from his lips, "He's *dead*, Jason!"

Raphael kicks him in the jaw, the loud snapping of his breaking bone shoots out into the air.

My eyes bleed more, my hands tremble, "There *has* to be another way."

"There isn't . . . I'm sorry."

I reluctantly stand, lifting Simon's body up with me.

I'm not going to leave your body to rot in this Hellhole.

We walk away.

"You two won't get far!" Matthew slurs, his jaw broken, his clothes soaked in blood. "I promise you!"

I shoot him a venomous glare, "Have fun with your daughter."

"Mills was here earlier," he continues. "We had a meeting! About you! Ever since your appearance on the news, he's wanted you captured! And whatever Mills wants, he gets! You hear me?"

We just keep walking.

"As soon as you leave this base, I'll have my men hunt you down! Then, I'll torture you and your partner until I find out every single-detail about Lazarus and then kill you all! Mark my words, Jason!"

I want to put a bullet in his head, but that would be too quick. He needs to feel what I've felt . . . agony.

We make our way over to the one and only entrance; the gate lowered into the earth. The guards and their hounds move to the side, and the snipers up in their large towers just stare at us, their sights still on both of our heads.

As we walk out of the base, the canines snarl and growl at us like we're walking prey.

The Saint manning the security booth looks at the both of us with a befuddled expression on his face. Why would his captain tell him to let us leave, and to have the snipers stand down? We are easy targets as we walk out of the compound carrying Simon's lifeless body.

After we're out of sight, the two of us begin laboriously sprinting back to the van, Simon's body still twitching in my arms.

Every step I take, my body threatens to break. My hip and shoulder blade are on fire and won't stop throbbing, my head is pounding like a tribal drum, and my heart is aching at the loss of my best friend.

We eventually make it back to the van. Raphael opens the back doors.

Chloe turns her head, lowering the volume of her music, "Are you three okay?" She stops the moment she sees Simon. "No . . . no, no, no . . . Simon?"

At the mention of his name, my eyes bleed more, and I don't respond. I climb into the back of the van and place Simon's body on the floor. Blood spills from my wounds as I sit back and try to find a position that won't make it too difficult to breathe.

Chloe cries, "He really isn't dead . . . *is* he?"

More blood pours from my eyes, "Get us out of here before we're hunted down."

"Hunted down?" Chloe asks, her lower lip trembling. "What happened in there?"

Raphael shuts the van doors before looking over at her, "Just drive, Frye."

Chloe stares blankly before tilting her head forward in response. She forces her attention back to the steering wheel and puts the van into drive before pressing her foot down onto the gas pedal.

CHAPTER SEVENTY-ONE

We've been driving for over twenty minutes. When I have enough strength, I periodically look up at Chloe through the rearview mirror. She's silently crying, and I want to comfort her, but truth is, I can't even stop *myself* from crying.

"He knew the risks of taking this mission," Raphael breathes, breaking the long streak of silence that's lingered in the van. "He died in the name of Lazarus."

I sniffle.

"How did it happen?" Chloe asks, her voice shaky. "How did he . . . die?"

"Executed on his knees by some new guy who's in charge of exterminating us."

His words make me cry even harder.

Chloe abruptly swears, catching me and Raphael off guard. "This isn't good."

"What?" Raphael asks. "What is it?"

"There's three patrol cars ganging up on us," she replies, stepping on the gas hard.

Raphael swears, "Are you joking?"

"No," she retorts. "I'm *not* joking!"

"How much ammo do you have left?" Raphael asks me, panic in his voice.

I don't respond. I am still unable to answer with Simon's motionless body at my feet.

This is all my fault . . . I think to myself. *If I would've left Matthew dead back in my garage, none of this would've happened.*

"How much ammo do you have left?" he repeats, yelling now. "Hello? Pinder? You there?"

I lower my head, covering my face with my palms.

"*Stop,*" he shouts. "I know you're hurting, but we will be captured if you don't step up and help!"

I let out a shuddering sigh before pulling the gun out of my holster and checking how many rounds I have left, "Three. It won't help."

Raphael grabs me by my vest and hoists me to my feet, "Make every shot count."

I stand there in a daze as he quickly unlatches the double doors. They go flying open, and wind blasts into the van.

Chloe was right, there are patrol cars, and they're definitely gaining on us.

Raphael turns to me, the brisk wind forcing him to shout, "These people killed Simon. They're the ones under White's command. Send them to *Hell.*"

His words snap me out of my funk, and a fiery rage and a burst of adrenaline fill up my *lust* for revenge.

I will kill every last one.

I aim up and over at the driver whose vehicle is at the front of the convoy, hold my breath, considering that the wind will affect my accuracy, adjust, and fire.

The bullet bursts through the windshield and penetrates the driver's head, making a cloud of bloody mist spray out and stain the windows. I watch with no remorse as the vehicle loses control and rams into the side of a building.

One down, two to go. . . for you, Simon.

The next vehicle speeds up, growing closer and closer. I aim at the driver and get ready to blast him full of lead. His passenger door swings open and a Saint with a submachine gun leans out and sprays the van with bullets.

"Get down!" Raphael blurts, dropping backward.

I follow his lead, dropping backward, "What do we do?"

Multiple bullets fly into the van- three hit the back of Chloe's seat, two hit the van's dash, and another one hits the windshield, causing it to spiderweb.

"Take care of him!" Chloe demands, speeding up.

While on my back, I aim over at the vehicle's gunner and concentrate, making sure I'll hit him before firing. The bullet zooms into his shoulder. His body lurches to the side, causing him to fly out of the patrol car. He goes slamming into the vehicle behind him, making the third driver in the convoy lose control and crash into oncoming traffic.

"Nice one!" Raphael cheers.

The last vehicle, the one I shot a passenger out of, speeds up. Passing our van and gaining some distance on us.

"What's he *doing*?" Chloe shouts back to us.

Raphael gets to his feet and quickly shuts the double doors, looking over at the cracked windshield that's almost impossible to see out of, "I have no idea. Do you think he's retreating?"

"I don't know, it's hard to see and . . ." she stops, her tone now becoming frantic. "Shi—!"

We crash into an indistinguishable object. The next thing I know, I'm flying through the windshield, and nothing but darkness.

CHAPTER SEVENTY-TWO

I wake in a daze. I'm lying down on a very uncomfortable bed, hooked up to an I.V.

As light finds its way into my eyes, I realize I'm in a . . . prison cell.

"So, the infamous Jason Pinder finally awakes from his coma," the voice causes my blood to boil instantly. "Took four months, but hey, at least you're awake. Doctors were thinking you'd never open your eyes, again."

I grit my teeth, and if it weren't because they handcuff my right arm to the bed, I'd be at his throat, "Where am I?"

"Salem Penitentiary, home to the worst of the worst."

I sigh, which turns into humorless laughter, "So, let me guess, time for countless torture sessions and interrogations. Am I right?"

Matthew White shakes his head, "As I said, you've been in a coma for four months. We've already gotten everything we need outta your two friends," he chuckles. "Let me tell you, it took a *long* time for the both of them to break, but it eventually happened. We now know about everything: the countless facilities, Rebirth, Vice, whose real name is Marshal Simmons, *everything.*"

I stare up at the ceiling feeling like a complete and utter failure.

"Don't worry though," he says. "You won't have to watch the fall of Lazarus."

"And why do you say that?"

"Because you and your partners will be executed here, soon."

I go silent, listening to the persistent chatter coming from the other prisoners. Some are screaming for help, others are laughing hysterically, and some are banging against the metal doors that are keeping them detained.

White stands from his chair, heading over to my cell door before taking a key out of his pocket and unlocking it, "This is Hell, Jason," he says, opening it up, stepping out, and locking it again. "Embrace it."

He walks off, leaving me cuffed to my prison bed.

I stare down at the orange jumpsuit I'm in before letting out a little chuckle.

Embrace it, huh?

A sinister grin flashes across my face.

I'll embrace it alright.

I close my eyes, plotting my escape, and more importantly, my revenge.

ACKNOWLEDGMENTS

Oh, where to start? There are so many people I want to thank, but I think I'll start off with my amazing mother, Shandy. She has supported me every-single-step of the way through this whole process! Not only is she the one who taught me everything I know, she's the best mom I could ever ask for. I love you, Mom.

Next, I'd like to thank my phenomenal editor, Stacey. Without her, Revolt would still be in a messy file on Google Docs without any further plans of publication. She has turned my novel into what it is, made my characters real, made my story come to life, and so much more. I wouldn't be sitting at my desk right now writing this acknowledgment if it wasn't for you, Stacey, and for that, you're the best ever!

I would like to thank my dad, John. Okay, not even gonna lie, without you, I'd probably be getting angry emails from fans telling me that I talked about certain guns the wrong way. And even though you think gasmasks are lame, I still love you dearly. You're seriously the coolest dad ever, and I thank the band Garbage for my existence (maybe too risqué, but who cares, right?).

I would like to especially thank my amazing, supportive grandparents. I love you guys.

Alright, alright, here's some shoutouts to some of the other people who made Revolt into what it is today.

To start off, I'm going to thank my best friend, Teagan. Dude, you're the Simon to my Jason, and without you, I would never have started writing. Thank you for suffering through my absolutely treacherous horror stories when we were twelve. Ugh, it still makes me cringe thinking about them. Love you, man.

To my girlfriend, Ashley. Even though you hate reading fiction (WHO HATES READING FICTION!?!), you've always had a soft spot for my writing. Thank you so much for your support that has gotten me through so much, and I love you, Goofball.

To one of my greatest supporters, Ashley G. Dude, your support for Revolt has been the best ever! Your suggestions, tears, and overall love for Jason has been such a huge motivation to me and my writing. Thanks for everything. I miss drawing religious sheep with you in class.

To my awesome friend, Ashley R (yes, I know a lot of Ashleys, I get it). Thank you for always being so optimistic about my book. Your input has helped me so much, and I can't wait for you to see how far this book has come.

To my phenomenal friend, Liv. Thank you so much for all your support, stressful hours helping me promote my book, and just being there for me! I wouldn't have such an awesome trailer if it wasn't for you, and I couldn't ask for a better bestie!

Shoutout to those who drew the COOLEST fanart for me: Liv, Courtney, Garion, and Madelyn. Fanart is literally like chocolate milk for my soul, and you four delivered!

I'd also like to thank Asher, Claire, Logan, Liv, Matthew, and Isaac for helping me promote Revolt by making the trailer and bringing it to life. You guys are the best, and I mean that.

Lastly, thank you reader! I love your guys' feedback and reviews- it really makes being an author much easier, knowing what you like and don't like impacts so much. Again, thank you greatly for all of your support, and I hope you enjoy the next instalment in The Revolt trilogy (Mutiny) which will be coming this fall! Make sure to follow me on social media to receive updates, trailers, cover reveals, and so much more! Love you guys.

ABOUT BENJAMIN VOGT

Benjamin Vogt fell in love with writing at the age of 12. Now, a seasoned 16-year-old author, his first book in the *Revolt Trilogy* is poised to break out. When not writing, the Idaho native can be found river rafting, camping, rubbing his cat's belly, enjoying a good nap, or sharing spicy memes with the boys.

facebook.com/AuthorBenjaminVogt

instagram.com/author_benjamin_vogt